From Darkness Into The Light

By: Nina Chrisnik

Copyright © 2025

By: Nina Chrisnik

All rights reserved.

No part of this publication may be reproduced in any form, or by any means, electronic or mechanical, including photocopying, recording, or any information browsing, storage, or retrieval system, without permission in writing from Nina Chrisnik Author.

Prologue

Everyone in the emergency room that night was upset as they watched the clock waiting for news on the ten-year-old girl's father. Her mother sat still in the corner praying, while Gus, her father's best friend and partner paced. Occasionally he offered the girl a reassuring smile. She could tell things were bad because the smile he offered did not reach his normally comforting blue eyes. He had been with her father when Officer Ryan McKay, was shot and knew that her life was probably about to change. After what seemed like a lifetime but was only several hours the doctors finally came out to speak with them. Her mother rose, tear-stained and weak as the doctors gave the news that her father had passed. To the girl everything was in slow motion as her mother collapsed into Gus' arms, screaming and crying for it not to be true. The girl sat still, with tears silently streaming from her face as she watched the scene unfold not fully understanding what was transpiring. How could her father be gone? He was young and strong. Suddenly in front of her was a young nurse who was holding a brown teddy bear dressed in a shirt with the hospital's logo on it. As she handed it to the young girl, she expressed what a hero her father had been. The girl knew she was right. Not just because he was a police officer who died in the line of duty, but because he was her hero. There was no telling how long they remained in the waiting room.

It seemed like hours, especially when her mother went back to see her father. Gus waited with the young girl while her mother said her goodbyes. Eventually, the nurse who had given the teddy bear to the girl came out and asked that they take care of her mother. Gus rose to go alone, but the young girl knew it was she who had to go. Even though she was scared to see her father, she knew she was going to have to be strong for her mother. It is what her father would have wanted. When they went back, her father was lying on a gurney, blood surrounded the sheets, but his face looked peaceful. Her mother had thrown herself over his body and was crying harder than she had ever seen anyone cry. Gus put his arm on her shoulder and whispered it was time to go. The girl squeezed her bear tighter as she watched her mother refuse to leave. It was she who was going to have to get through to her mother. "Lo siento Mami, necessito salir. Por favor. Estoy cansado." She was tired. It was late and all of this was scary. The night was supposed to be about celebrating her birthday, instead, they were in the hospital saying goodbye to her father. Gus whispered something to her mother, and she lifted her face. Her eyes were bloodshot and there was so much dark makeup around her eyes, the girl thought she looked like a raccoon. Slowly she kissed her father's lips and said "Te quiero me amor. Hasta que nos encontremos de nuevo." The girl knew her mother loved her father, but in that moment, she questioned if her mother would see her father again. Gus walked her away practically holding her up as they left the hospital. Before leaving the room, the girl took one last look at her father. She thought about hugging him, but it was not him and she was scared. From the door, she blew him a kiss and told him she loved him. She wanted to believe what her mother had said about seeing him again was true. It was just at that moment she was not so sure. She had been raised with faith and knew that was what she had been taught, but she was living a real-life nightmare and wasn't sure of anything. Leaving the hospital and the ride home was a blur. No one said anything. No one cried. It was simply silent as Gus drove them home.

At one point she must have fallen asleep because the next thing she remembered was Gus carrying her up the apartment building steps while she clutched the bear. He tucked her in bed and kissed her forehead before closing her bedroom door. Her exhaustion could not drown out the sound of her mother sobbing uncontrollably in the next room. There was nothing she could do for her. Even at a young age, she understood the love her parents shared. They were made for each other and balanced the other. Her father's calm nature evened out her mother's passionate side. Romance movies were written about the love that her parents shared. Eventually, her mother cried herself to sleep and so did she. In her sleep, her father came to her. He was dressed in full uniform. Just as handsome as ever.

"Don't be scared, baby girl. I know that this is confusing and hard, but I'm here and always will be, even if you can't see me. Mom and Gus will take good care of you. I'll be watching from afar. When you need me, all you have to do is look to the stars. You'll know where I am. I'm with the angels now, baby girl. The only thing that I'll regret is not being there to help you grow. You are my life, my pride, and my joy. I love you."

When she reached for him, he was gone. As she awoke, she knew he had been there because she could still feel his presence. Immediately, she got out of bed to look at the stars from her bedroom window. There was a bright star that seemed to be smiling at her. At that moment, she knew her father was right; she would always be able to find him. That thought gave her great comfort.

Chapter One

The early morning light from the window shines on a young nurse in her small, scarcely decorated efficiency in Brooklyn. The bright light awakens her as her head pounds from a hard night of partying at a local neighborhood bar. After opening one eye and then another, she sits up and realizes she is not alone. Instantly, she put her head into her hands, only a little surprised to find a man in her bed. The man next to her was well-built and completely naked. She knew because he was only halfway covered with the bedding. As she examined him further, it was clear he took good care of himself as his arms looked strong, and his naked stomach had a six-pack. With appreciation, she thought to herself that even drunk, at least she had good taste. He was clearly an attractive man in the all-American, clean-cut way. Even if he was attractive, she had no idea who he was. She had a pretty good idea of what had happened between them as this was not the first time she woke up with someone who she should remember. Through her pounding head, she quietly said to herself, "Oh, Lena, what did you do now? Who is this?" She tried to recall the night to avoid the embarrassing conversation she was inevitably going to have. To add to her misery, the last thing she remembered was going to the bar after work and having several tequila shots to dull the pain of the ER that evening. As an ER nurse, she was trained to know not all patients can be saved. They do their best, but sometimes God has another plan. Logically, she knew that, but when that patient was a young officer who was killed in the line of duty, and there was a young child involved, all that training went out the window. After her own father's death, there was no way that couldn't be a trigger for her. No amount of therapy could change that, but tequila often did. The problem with tequila was she also often landed herself in the situation she currently was in with an unknown naked man in her bed.

She must have met him after she had already had several shots of tequila because she had absolutely no recollection of him. In fact, she did not even remember him being in the bar at all. Tequila and hot sex only temporarily gave her comfort. It was great in the heat of the moment, but the next morning was always filled with regret. No matter how drunk she was, she always practiced safe sex, as evidenced by the three condom wrappers on the floor next to her bed. Not only was she relieved to see them, but she also was a bit impressed. Unless they used them for water balloons, she knew she had a good time. As she got out of bed, the focus was getting him out of her apartment without realizing that she didn't know who he was. It was a lofty goal but one that she had perfected. In no way was she an alcoholic. Truthfully, she rarely drank except when triggered by something traumatic. Although only twenty-five, she was a bit of a loner. There were very few people that she allowed into her life. Lena was friendly enough with her co-workers, but the only person who was her true confidant was Gus, her late father's best friend. Experiences had made her hard and not trusting of many people. That did not mean that she was unempathetic or uncaring. It was just difficult to open the door to the possibility of getting hurt.

There was no way she would be able to do anything without coffee. Quietly, Lena slipped out of her futon bed and put on a silk robe to cover her petite frame. With the kitchen only a couple of feet away from her bed and not ready to wake up the man in her bed, she walked across the hardwood floors as silently as she could. As she waited for the coffee to brew, she thought about the best way to get rid of the man without him knowing she had no idea who he was. If she had gone back to his place, she could have easily slipped out, but it was much harder with him at her apartment. She made a mental note of that to herself. The next time this happened, and unfortunately, she knew there would be a next time because sex was the best source of comfort for her, she should make a point of going home with the man. It is so much easier, and the bonus is that the stranger would not know where she lived. After the coffee was ready, she knew she was going to have to face the awkward moment of asking the guy to leave. She would tell him that although she had a great time, she needed to get ready for work even though she was not scheduled to work.

On her days off, she usually took care of household items. On that day, her only plan was to get rid of him and nurse her hangover. As she placed a cup of coffee on the wooden end table next to the bed, he awoke from the aroma and wished her good morning. He had such a cheesy smile as he looked at her that she could not look him in the eye. Instead, Lena turned her back to him and headed to the bathroom to shower. More than anything she wanted him to take the hint and leave as she went to the bathroom.

Mirrors never lie, and what she saw was a mess. Lena was a beautiful woman. She had long, dark, curly hair that cascaded around the upper part of her body when worn long. Her olive complexion showed her Spanish roots, but her light eyes also let her Irish descent come through. By all accounts, she was a vision. Her looks were something she knew how to use to get what she wanted from men. The previous night, she had not bothered to take her make-up off. Her large blue eyes were surrounded by the remembrance of her mascara and eyeliner. Looking closer in the mirror, she could also see that her lips were swollen from obviously a night of hard passion. As she removed her robe, she also could see love bites on her now tender breasts. If she were honest with herself, she knew that she was probably the aggressor. Even though this was not the person she wanted to be, she didn't know how to stop herself when she reached a certain level of pain. For years, Lena went to therapy to cope with a painful past.

However, nothing at all has changed her need for sexual connection as a coping mechanism. It was something she had accepted a long time ago, and since she had no desire for a relationship, one-night stands were inevitable. The church she was raised in had told her that was wrong, and truth be told, Lena knew it was not how her father would want her to behave. That made her sad and a bit ashamed. She thought to herself that she couldn't change what already happened and too much reflection was never a good thing. For Lena, it was not the part of having sex with a stranger that was upsetting her; it was more that she didn't remember anything that happened. A shower would make her feel better. After all, she could shower to wash off the night's activities, and it would be as if it never happened. Initially, while washing her hair, her pounding head caused her to wonder when she would learn that tequila shots only provided temporary relief. The next day she always felt like crap. To her surprise, when she stepped out of the shower, the man was in the bathroom. Now that they both were awake, she could see the ocean blue of his eyes. Silently, she thought about how someone could get lost in those eyes. When he was lying in bed, she could see his chiseled muscles, but standing there in front of her, she could get a full view of the definition, and she had to admit she liked what she saw. He was wearing only his boxer shorts, and for a moment, she wondered how what was under them would make her feel. He was making it clear that he had no desire to leave as he moved closer to her. In such a tight space, there was no escape without touching. At the hospital where she worked, she was completely competent and able to think quickly on her feet to do what was best for her patients. In this scenario, she was at a loss and had no one to blame but herself. It occurred to her that she was completely naked, and she quickly wrapped a towel around herself instinctually. Lena could tell from his expression that he was disappointed she chose to cover herself. Even she wondered why, as it was pretty clear he was already very familiar with every aspect of her body. Instead of making a comment, the man stood in silent appreciation and smiling. It was obvious that he was a nice man. If he was a dick, he would have had his coffee and taken off, that is, if he even bothered to stay the night. This guy was standing in her bathroom, trying to wish her good morning with a kiss. Oh no, she thought to herself, "What if he was the relationship type?" After watching her mother fall to pieces when her father died, Lena truly believed that love breaks people, and there was no way she would ever allow herself to get hurt like that. When you have a one-night stand, that is usually the message. She had no idea why this guy that she had bedded the night before was looking at her with such admiration. She wondered if the sex was that good, and if it was, she really wished she had remembered it. It was unavoidable with the enclosed space; he was going to kiss her, and she would have to allow contact. Before their mouths connected, he expressed to Lena what a great time he had. There was no way for her to honestly answer, so instead, she kissed him. It was a gentle kiss at first because it was clear he was trying to say good morning or thank you. Lena really didn't know. What she did know was how soft his lips were and how the kiss was making the lower region of her body feel, and she deepened it. He could tell what she wanted and tried to let her know that he could not stay long because he had to get to work. That was fine with her. Lena had no intention of spending the day with him, but some hot morning sex could be just what the nurse ordered for her hangover. It occurred to her that the longer he stayed, the more likely he was to realize she had no idea who he was. As his lips found that very sensitive spot on her neck, that was a chance she was prepared to take. Through his boxers, she could feel his desire. The feeling of his hard cock was enough for her to lose the towel and lead him back to her bed. She needed to feel him inside of her, and it was clear as he scrambled for the condom, he felt the same way. She must have shown him the condom drawer because he went right there. What impressed her more was that her electronic boyfriend shares space with the condoms, and he didn't comment. It could have been that they did the whole bit the night before. That she will never know. What she was excited to know was how he would feel inside of her. The wait was over. The condom was on, and she pushed him to the bed. Lena may not know his name, but the one thing Lena did know was that he really knew what to do with his mouth and hands. Quickly, she straddled him, prepared to take charge. His cock was the perfect size for her, and that feeling of penetration was like no other. At first, she moved slow to allow her body to adjust to his girth. Clearly, her body remembered what she didn't, and her desire made her quicken the pace. This was pure, unadulterated sex at its finest. Within minutes, her body collapsed on his naked chest, completely satisfied. He was so good, she might consider another night, but that would require remembering his name, which she knew was going to be a problem. As if she didn't already know the fact that she couldn't remember his name was a reminder that no matter how hot the sex, she isn't the relationship kind.

In the afterglow, he pulled Lena close as she pretended to be sleepy so that she could avoid conversation. Even though he mentioned he had to leave for work, she was counting down the minutes until he left, praying that he wouldn't find out her secret. Suddenly, her thoughts were interrupted as she heard the sound of an alarm off his phone. Quietly, she thought to herself that she had done it. He would leave and be none the wiser that the night before was a blank. With a grunt of disappointment and one last kiss, the man got up to get dressed. As he was dressing, Lena made the fatal error of asking him what he did for a living. When she did, the man's face went pale, and she instantly knew she had made a mistake. Quietly, she wondered how she could have made such an amateur mistake. Of course, they would have discussed their jobs. The thought made her want to pull the covers over her head and hide, but she couldn't. He was staring at her wounded and determined to find out more information, which is why it wasn't a surprise to her when he asked, "How much of last night do you remember?" He paused for a minute, waiting for a response, but when there was none, he continued, "We spent the better part of last night talking about the fact that I'm a personal trainer."

Lena's first thought was that it explained physique. There was no mistake that he was in good shape. Even though she tried to play it cool, she knew she made a blunder. To cover she pretended that she was testing him to see if he had been honest. Silently she prayed that was believable enough, however the look on his face confirmed that he didn't.

With an arch of his head, he asked the big question, "Do you even know my name?" That was the one thing she was hoping to avoid, and here it was, staring her in the face. Even though she knew he would press, she still tried to lie, "Baby, how could you even ask with that?" He lifted an eyebrow to motivate her to continue by giving her the name. She had two ways to play this. The first was to take a Hail Mary and come up with a name, and the second was to come clean and apologize. A big part of her wanted to just hide. He seemed like a really nice guy if you remove the fact that he went home with a very drunk girl and had sex with her. Given the fact that she had no recollection of him even being at the bar told her that she must have had a lot to drink before they met, so he probably hadn't realized how drunk she was. She may do stupid things drunk, but she was also able to hide how drunk she was to strangers. As much as she wanted to blame someone else, she knew in her heart that this was more than likely her own doing and decided to confess. "You're right. There are some details from last night that are a bit fuzzy." His response was unexpected, as he seemed angry. With a snide voice, he asked, "Is this something you do often?" Even though it was something that happened more frequently than Lena wanted to admit, his words stung, and Lena struck back as she thought to herself, how dare he, "Is it something you do often? I mean, taking a woman who is obviously drunk home to fuck?"

She could tell by his face that she took it too far. He was clearly hurt, and she instantly regretted saying it, especially as he seemed apologetic, "I didn't realize you were that drunk. Maybe I should have, but to be honest, with the way you came on to me last night, I'm not sure I would have been able to stop myself." The man raised an eyebrow. "But what about just now?" For that, she was embarrassed. Lena wasn't able to say that she regretted it, but she was embarrassed that she got caught. She owned her sexuality and shrugged as she said, "I guess I just wanted to see what I missed out on."

That lightened the mood as he smiled. "Honestly, you wound me, girl. Every guy wants to think that he's unforgettable in bed. In case you're wondering, my name is Trey." Out of instinct, she smiled and said, "Lena." As he looked at her as if to say he knew, she continued, "Look, I may not remember what happened, but I do know enough to know that all of this is on me. I was in a bad way last night, and I went looking for trouble. You were just the unlucky victim."

Cracking a smile that made his blue eyes glisten with laughter, Trey responded, "I wouldn't say that I was unlucky. Not that you are asking, but I work at Jumbo. If you ever go looking for trouble again, come by. I'd ask for your number, but given this conversation, I don't think that you would take my call. All this aside, I had a great time and would like to see you again sometime."

That was the confirmation she needed; he really was a nice guy. In a different universe, maybe this could turn into something. It just wasn't going to happen on this one. She had already wounded his pride enough and wasn't going to do so further by agreeing with him. Instead, she kissed his cheek and said, "That sounds like a great offer."

After the door closed, Lena leaned against it and thought to herself, "Why? Oh, why do I do this to myself?" She knew why but had hoped that one day she would stop.

For the first time that morning, she was glad that she was home and collapsed in her bed. Her apartment wasn't much, but it was hers and about all she could afford on her nursing salary with her large student loan debt. The decor was simple, with not much covering the white walls. Only two photographs were displayed. One of her and her father at a father-daughter dance when she was eight years old. He was dressed in full uniform, while she wore a pink, frilly dress that made her feel like a princess. It was one of her favorite childhood memories as she remembered dancing with her father and how proud she was of him. The second one was of Gus. It was Gus who helped raise her after her father passed, and she was forever grateful for him. In the picture, he too was dressed in full uniform and was receiving a commendation after 9/11. He was all she still had in this world. If anything, ever happened to him, she would have no one. After the night she had she decided that she could spend some time with Gus as he always made her feel secure and decided to call him to see if he was free for lunch. It had been a couple of days since they last spoke and even longer since they had seen each other. Since they both worked shift work, it was hard to get their schedules to sync.

Chapter Two

In a large penthouse on Park Avenue, Justin and Anne were having breakfast served by their long-time housekeeper, Ms. Warner. The penthouse structure was elegant, with large rooms and plenty of sunlight. They had done their best to make their luxurious apartment feel less elegant and more like a home lived in by a family. Anne had made sure there were plenty of items to show who they were as a couple. Everywhere one looked, there was a framed picture of the various points of their life as a couple. Little trinkets that they had purchased in college, on their honeymoon, and some of their vacations were prominently displayed. There was a large dining room with a table that would seat twelve easily, yet they always ate their meals together at a kitchen table made for four. It was Anne who insisted that there was no need for them to be separated by formality. They were a family and shouldn't allow any amount of money in their bank account to alter who they were inside. Anne was a beautiful woman with soulful brown eyes and long blond hair. Her beauty was secondary to her heart, which radiated kindness. She never spoke ill of anyone, and there wasn't anyone in need that Anne could turn her back on. After graduating college, Anne began a career as an advocate, mainly for children in need. Her father was a minister. As such, Anne spent her summers off from school working on missions. On her last mission before graduating, Justin went with her. It was against his father's wishes, but Anne was always so rejuvenated after coming back from a mission that Justin needed to see for himself what it was about. The mission was to build houses for the impoverished in Belize. At first, Anne and Justin worked side by side, but it became clear that Justin wasn't a handyman, so the church put him on supply duty. His job was to make sure the people building the houses had everything they needed. Often, during the mission, Justin would look at Anne in amazement. Whether she was handling the tools or interacting with the natives, she was a force. Even though English was spoken most times during their trip, through Anne's many missions in Africa and South America, she was fluent in Spanish and French. It didn't matter the age of the person she was speaking to, Anne always made everyone feel that she was one of them. Instinctively, she could sense how people were feeling and did her best to put them at ease. Anne's life was very different than that of Justin, who had grown up in a life of privilege. For show, Justin's family was involved in many charitable causes, however, that mainly entailed writing a check. There was no way his mother would break a nail by building a house, while his father was motivated purely by money.

Even though their differences were vast, the amount of admiration they had for one another was clear. Justin thrived on the love of his wife. When Justin looked at her, he could see the person he wanted to be. Anne saved Justin from himself. In his youth, Justin was a wild, rebellious teenager. Now, he was a well-respected attorney. Even though Justin primarily worked at his father's law firm, with Anne's encouragement, he would often take on cases pro bono. Initially, that angered his father, but when he saw the tax advantages, he relented, stipulating that Justin was not to let it get in the way of their paying clients. Justin always believed Anne was the best part of him, even if he did not understand what it was that made her love him. If asked that question, Anne would have answered that he, too, had a pure heart. Justin always encouraged Anne to pursue her dreams. Many times, she would get emotional about a family or troubled teen she was working with. First, he would listen to her before he would help her look for a solution. She couldn't have asked for a better partner to share her life with.

It took Justin no time to ask Anne to marry him. He knew the moment he met her she was the one for him. As soon as he finished law school, they married. For Justin, marrying Anne was the easy part, starting a family was a different story. It took Anne many years to coerce him to agree to have a baby. Although he never lacked material items, his family had not been a traditional family. Growing up, Justin had wealth and breeding, but there was no warmth in his house. Still, Anne was confident Justin would make a great father. Even if Justin wasn't convinced, having a baby was something Anne really wanted, and Justin was never able to refuse her desires.

As they ate their pancake breakfast in the kitchen under the skylight, they appeared to be untouchable because they had it all. Even several months pregnant, Anne was the most beautiful woman Justin ever laid eyes on.

"Feel this." Anne placed Justin's hand over her pregnant belly.

Justin could not contain his excitement as he felt the baby move. "I think we have a ballet dancer or a soccer player." While laughing and bending down, Justin told the bump that he could not wait to meet him or her. "It won't be long now."

Anne caressed Justin's firm back, feeling him tense up against her. "What's wrong?"

"Nothing. For the first time in my life, everything is perfectly in place."

"So why the worry lines?"

"You know how much I love you and this precious gift you have given me, but."

Anne finished his sentence, "You're worried."

Justin wasn't as optimistic of a person as Anne was. In the back of his mind, he believed when things were too perfect, there was more of a chance for things to go wrong. Even though he tried to fight it, there was a nagging voice in the back of Justin's head telling him something bad would happen. Anne knew Justin well enough to know that Justin struggled with childhood demons and wished that she had always been there to take them away. Since she wasn't, it was her job now to put his mind at ease. They were in for a lifetime of happiness. As she leaned over to kiss Justin, she could feel him relax.

"If you keep this up, I'm going to be late for my meeting with Dad and Luke." Justin didn't totally break from her kiss. He could feel her smile.

"And that's a bad thing?"

"Not for me, but I don't think they'll be very happy. You know I love you, right?" Justin finally broke their precious contact.

"If you love me, then stay."

Justin pulled her up into his arms to kiss her. She deepened it again, trying to convince him to stay. Even though she didn't understand why, there was a reason on that day that she didn't want to let Justin go. While Anne was trying to ease his mind, she, too, had an unnatural fear in her own head that it was not going to be a good day. Although Anne was passing her thoughts up to hormones from the pregnancy, she still felt an urgency to show Justin just how much he meant to her. It was a feeling she had since they were making love the previous night. Even in a crazy world, they could always close their penthouse door and have it be only them.

"Come home early tonight," Anne whispered, but Justin's look told her that was not going to be possible. They were working on a big case. Although Anne was not privy to all of the details, she knew that he would be working extra hours to have everything completely resolved before the baby arrived.

"I promise to come home as early as I can however, don't wait for me to have dinner."

Anne was disappointed but understood. She knew that Justin had to prioritize work, so that it wouldn't be an issue when the baby was born. With one final kiss on the cheek, Anne said, "Remember, I love you always."

"And I you. I have to go, though." Justin opened the door and headed into the open elevator. As the elevator doors closed, Anne whispered, "Always and forever."

Chapter Three

It was a beautiful, warm spring morning in New York as Lena got on the busy subway to meet Gus for lunch. Gus had been her father's partner on the police force. Having gone through the academy together, they were as close as brothers. As long as Lena could remember, Gus was a part of her life. He was the best man at her parent's wedding and was at the hospital with them the night her father was killed in the line of duty. After her father passed, he was the one person that she could count on since Lena's mother completely fell apart. Often, Lena believed that the night her father was killed was the night she lost both of her parents. She was lucky that Gus was always there for her. He married once, but it ended in divorce. Since they never had children, Lena was the light of his life. Whenever Lena was shaken up or did something stupid, Gus grounded her. His warm smile and sparkling blue eyes always made her feel as though everything would be okay. After what happened that morning, Lena was feeling bad about herself and needed his reassurance.

The subway was unusually crowded for the middle of the afternoon on a workday. There was one open seat next to an old woman talking to someone who wasn't there. Instead of taking the seat, she decided to stand. Standing was better because she was too occupied with her own thoughts to have a conversation with a random stranger. Not that the New York City subway system was a great place to meet friends, but she knew that woman would want to talk to her. While on the train, Lena had flashbacks of the prior night. As she suspected she realized that she was the one who initiated things with Trey. It wasn't surprising since Lena often couldn't contain her emotions whenever an ER case reminded her of her father. Before she went to the bar, she knew the fallen officer would be a trigger for her. The ER team did their best to try to save him, but the bullet had hit an artery. When she went into the bar, she was looking for anything that could make her forget her own demons.

By the time the train arrived in Manhattan, she felt worse about herself because she knew the way she dealt with her grief was not how her father would want her to act. The most important thing to Lena was to try and live her life in a manner that would make her father proud. In fact, it was because of the night her father passed that she became an ER nurse. Lena had never forgotten how kind the doctors and nurses who tried to save her father were. Initially, she wanted to be a doctor, but that dream was on hold because she did not wish to have any additional student loan debt. She had put herself through school on loans. Although it was worth it, the debt was high, attending medical school would have only made it worse.

Lena met up with Gus at their favorite burrito place a few blocks away from SoHo. Gus was on his lunch break and was dressed in a full NYC police department uniform. Lena loved that uniform. Even though she had lost her father because of his job, she was never anything but proud of his service. Upon seeing Gus, she flew into his arms with tears in her eyes, completely unaware of anyone else in the restaurant. He knew that a police officer had fallen and figured the reason for the call was that she was shaken. Seeing her like this only affirmed his belief, and he tried to reassure her that everything would be fine. Lena broke the embrace when she realized many people in the restaurant were staring at her. It was lunchtime in Manhattan, and the burrito place was always busy then.

As they were waiting in line to order, Gus could sense that Lena was still uneasy. "If your father were here, he would be so proud of you. You can't save everyone. That's just not God's plan."

If only that was the only thing she was upset about. Of course, she was devastated by the poor fallen officer and his family, yet it was more than that. She was ashamed of herself. There was no way that she was going to tell Gus how she chose to handle the aftermath because she didn't want to disappoint him either. Before they could order, the police radio went off, asking all units in the area to respond to a robbery in progress at a jewelry store two blocks away. Gunshots were reported. Gus responded he was on his way and apologized to Lena for needing to leave. Against Gus' protest, Lena insisted on going with him. There was not enough time to argue, so Gus relented. Truthfully, she wasn't sure what she would be able to do, but after the prior night, she needed to know Gus was safe.

Since there was always traffic on the NYC streets, they set off on foot. Even in his late forties, Gus was in great shape and believed he could get to the scene quicker by running. As a bonus, he felt if anyone fled, he would be able to stop them. Lena loved running and had no trouble keeping his pace even though he argued with her all the way there that she should go home. By the time they arrived, several units were already on the scene. The shooter had fled in the opposite direction they had come from, and the police were in pursuit. Gus went into the store while Lena waited on the street behind what was starting to be police yellow tape, feeling relieved that the shooter was already gone. A couple of minutes after Gus left her, another officer asked Lena to help provide medical assistance. Gus told him to get her because they needed her nursing skills until the paramedics arrived. During the robbery, three people were wounded. When Lena entered the store, the officers were busy gathering evidence. One officer was looking through the security footage, trying to get a description of the robber, but he was wearing a mask. What Lena noticed most was the blood on the walls and floor. As an ER nurse, Lena was not fazed by the sight of blood. However, this being a crime scene somehow made her feel a little queasy. There was no time for that because Gus called her over to help a young pregnant woman lying on the floor who had been shot in the chest. She had lost a lot of blood but was awake. Lena rushed over to her to apply pressure to the wound while Gus went to help the man with a superficial wound to the arm. The other victim was shot in the head and died on impact. The woman was very weak but was trying desperately to talk to Lena. Even in extreme pain, the woman was trying to fight for the life inside of her. She had never laid eyes on her baby; however, she was still a mother. Her love for her unborn child was unwavering.

"My baby. My baby." The woman was crying weakly.

As best she could, Lena tried to reassure the woman. "Don't worry. I'm a nurse, and the paramedics are coming. You're going to be fine."

With what little strength the woman had, she put her hand on Lena's arm for emphasis. "Please, please, you have to save my baby."

There was nothing more Lena could do to repair her wound other than keep pressure on it, but there was such a need in the woman's voice Lena was going to make sure she helped her get the best possible care. "We'll take care of both of you. I promise."

That calmed her some, but she was getting weaker by the moment. Lena wondered where the paramedics were because neither the woman or the baby would last much longer. Even with pressure she was losing too much blood. Before the woman lost consciousness, she asked Lena to make sure her husband knew he was always in her thoughts, and she loved him.

After a few minutes the paramedics arrived and took over the woman's care. Lena called the hospital to explain the situation and request they page Dr. Castillo in from his day off. She knew he was the best, and she didn't want to break her promise to the woman. The nurse on the other line was hesitant to call him in, but Lena was insistent.

Lena knew the doctor loved a challenge and wouldn't refuse. "Tell him that the victim is a pregnant woman, and that Lena is requesting him to go to the hospital."

Lena had a flirtation with Dr. Castillo that had been witnessed by the hospital staff. There were rumors about an affair, but he was married. Since Lena believed the vow of marriage was sacred, they were only rumors. If the challenge did not entice him, she hoped the flirtation would. There was an unexplained connection Lena felt towards the woman, which made her want to do anything she could to help.

After the nurse agreed, Lena felt compelled to contact the woman's family. She rummaged through the woman's designer purse to see if she could find information to call the woman's husband. Inside her wallet, she found a driver's license with the name Anne Armstrong on it. After she found out her name, she looked in the contacts of her phone and found the name Luke Armstrong. A man with a strong, deep voice answered, unsettling Lena. Something in the man's tone made Lena aware that he was a man who was used to being in charge. She felt ridiculous that she was a little intimidated by the voice, although she assumed her reaction was because she had never called a loved one with bad news before. Many times, she had been with the ER doctors as they delivered news of a loved one, but she never had to say the words herself. It was hospital policy that only a doctor could update the family on a loved one's condition. She was grateful to hide behind that policy. Unsure of what to say, she quickly regrouped, asking if he was Anne's husband. The voice on the other line explained he was her brother-in-law and wondered why a stranger had Anne's phone.

With a shaken voice, Lena responded. "Mr. Armstrong, my name is Lena McKay, and I'm with Anne now. There has been a shooting, and Anne is on her way to the hospital. I'm going with her, but can you please tell her husband to meet us?"

Instantly, the confidence in the man's voice changed to that of shock with a hint of fear. "Shit! How bad is she? And the baby?"

"All I know is what I have told you. Can you please get the message to her husband?"

"Of course. He's with me now. Just tell me this, though. Is she alive?"

"She is, but that's really all I can tell you. You'll find out more when she sees a doctor."

"Thank you for letting me know."

As the paramedics lifted the woman off the scene, Lena didn't want her alone and asked to ride with them. The paramedics started the IV and did their best to keep her alive while Lena tried to comfort her all the way to the hospital even though she was unconscious. The ER team was outside the entrance awaiting the arrival of the ambulance when they arrived at the hospital. While rushing her into the exam room, the paramedics updated the doctors on her condition. After lifting her to the ER bed, the team quickly went to work on Anne. Lena suited in the yellow smock, ER glasses, and gloves in order to join the team in the room. As they took her vitals and assessed the situation, Lena entered the room. Her presence was a surprise to the doctors, especially since it was her day off. Lena explained that she was the first to treat Anne on scene. She noted that Anne was able to speak at first but quickly lost conscience.

The attendant offered, "She is in shock. We need four units of O-positive stat. Find out what is keeping Dr. Townsend and page Dr. Webster."

Lena needed to know how the baby was and asked. The ER doctor responded that there was a heartbeat, but they needed to wait for Dr. Townsend, who was the OB on call, to really know. The fact that there was a heartbeat relieved Lena and made it clear that the woman relayed that the baby was her priority.

"I'm sure. But you know that the body's instinct is to protect the fetus. She's our first priority."

Dr. Townsend entered, asking what the situation was. She was one of the best OBs in the area and quickly took charge. At close to sixty, she was a no-nonsense woman. Lena quickly relayed

Anne's wishes, knowing full well that Dr. Townsend would indeed take them to heart. Anne was still losing blood quickly, and the ER team was doing its best to get it back in her as quickly as possible. There was so much activity in the room and a lot of chatter about what was needed next. Lena helped Dr. Townsend with assessing the sonogram. The entire time, Lena hoped that Dr. Castillo would arrive before Dr. Webster. A sonogram indicated that no harm had come to the baby, and the age of the fetus would make survival outside the womb difficult but not impossible.

Dr. Townsend asked, "Has anyone notified this woman's next of kin?"

Lena explained that she had spoken with her brother-in-law, who promised to tell her husband. She also said that she had asked for Dr. Castillo to be paged right as Dr. Webster entered.

"Why Dr. Castillo, Lena?"

Lena knew that Dr. Webster was a fine cardiologist, but he lacked Dr. Castillo's insight. Not waiting for a response, Dr. Webster quickly assessed the situation, ordered tests, and told Dr. Townsend to be prepared to take the baby at a moment's notice.

Lena started to interject with Anne's wishes, but Dr. Townsend cut her off with her opinion that they should wait. As they were about to argue their opinions, Dr. Castillo walked into the room. Relief filled Lena when she saw him until Dr. Castillo mouthed that she owed him. It was clear he wasn't there for the challenge but for the flirtation. It didn't matter at that point. All she still wanted was the best for the injured woman. Dr. Webster gave Lena a cold stare. "What are you doing here, Carlos?"

"I was asked to come in as a special favor. Now, what do we have here."

It was obvious who requested that favor. The tension in the room was thick. There was no time for big egos.

The attending interrupted what was about to be an argument. "This woman is our priority. Can we focus on getting her stabilized? Lena, perhaps it would be best if you went to see if her husband has arrived."

Lena knew she was being dismissed and frankly was grateful. After throwing off the ER cover, she went in search of Anne's family in the crowded ER waiting room. There were several people waiting to be seen, but in the corner of the room, she saw two men dressed in expensive designer suits huddled together, speaking with a police officer. In their thirties, they were equally good-looking. Even though they were seated, she could tell that they each were at least six feet. There was no mistake that they were related with their fine chiseled chins and rugged, handsome features. The one distinctive difference between the men was their hair color. One man had lighter brown hair, while the other had deep dark brown hair. As she saw them, the man with the lighter hair looked up at her. Instantly, she noticed his bright emerald eyes looking at her as if they could see through her soul, and a chill went through her spine. As she moved closer, she knew the man with darker hair was Anne's husband. It was obvious from the shattered look on his face. Lena knew that look; it was the same one Lena's mother had on her face the night her father was killed. As long as she lived, she would never forget her mother's face when the doctor said her father had passed. This wasn't about her, though, so she tried to shake the memory. Lena didn't want to interrupt the conversation but found it important to speak with them. She stood behind them, awaiting a break in the conversation. The man with the lighter hair saw her moving towards them. However, it was the first time Anne's husband noticed her. When he looked up, she noticed he had the same emerald eyes as his brother. The difference was that his were softer and filled with despair. Their eyes were the deepest color of green she had ever seen on anyone. Again, she felt a chill as their green eyes scanned her body, wondering why they were studying her so intently. It wasn't until she looked down that she realized her once-pink tank top and denim skirt were covered in blood. Anne's blood must have gotten all over her in the jewelry store, and she could see the horror on their faces. Instantly, she regretted not changing into scrubs before approaching them, but she hadn't realized it was there.

As best she could to sound confident, she reached for the dark-haired man's hand. "Mr. Armstrong." When he nodded, she began. "I'm Lena McKay. I'm the one who was with your wife at the scene and called your brother."

"Yes, of course. I'm Justin Armstrong. How is she?" Justin stood and was barely holding back the tears when he took her hand. Thankful once again that hospital policy stated only doctors could update family members on conditions, Lena was only able to say that the doctors were working on her. She added that a doctor would come to speak with him as soon as possible. It was evident from his nervous expression that her words had done nothing to assure him. Looking into his beautiful, distraught eyes she wished she could tell him everything would be all right, but the fact was that it might not be. Anne's and the baby's conditions were serious. Serious but not hopeless. The baby was unharmed for now and Anne was young, strong, and had so much to fight for. It was obvious the man before her was deeply in love with his wife. As if that was not motivation enough in Lena's eyes, she also had an unborn child to give her extra incentive to fight.

Lena looked for the right words. "Mr. Armstrong, your wife wanted me to tell you how much she loves you. Please hold on to that while you wait. I really should change and get back. Excuse me."

"Please wait." Lena turned. Justin was no longer able to hold back his tears. His voice cracked as he asked his question. "Is that her blood?"

It was a question that Justin already knew the answer to before Lena nodded to answer. Justin felt the world around him collapsing. This woman's outfit was covered with the blood of his lifeline. Anne's wound was clearly bad even if Lena did not offer that as an answer. In complete despair, Justin sat down. He was frightened for Anne and more frightened for a life without her. Even if Luke couldn't relate, he understood his brother's emotions. In support, he put his hand on his brother's shoulder while offering his free hand to Lena and introducing himself as Justin's brother, Luke Armstrong. His handshake was firm and businesslike. Lena thanked him for relaying the message to Justin before excusing herself again. She could feel Luke's eyes on her as she left the waiting room and looked back to see if her suspicions were correct. He was a man who radiated confidence and charm. There was no mistaking that both men were successful as they were well-dressed in expensive suits. Upon seeing him looking at her in that way,

Lena felt an uneasy sensation. From the slight interaction she had with him and the cold stare in his eyes, she could tell he was dangerous. It was not what he said or how he treated her. It was the look in his eyes and aura that made her feel that way. Even though Lena knew his type there was something about him that drew her to him. Whether it was his ruggedly handsome good looks or his demeanor, she had no idea. Whatever made her feel that way, she was intrigued.

Chapter Four

In the waiting room, Justin paced as he felt his world around him collapsing. Every person who came through the ER door into the waiting room made Justin more anxious. In the background, a television played the news with the robbery being one of the top stories. Justin could not focus on that though. He was too worried about Anne. Besides, they were saying the same things over and over again. It was almost the same information that the police officer who came to speak with them relayed. On the wall above the nurse's desk was a large clock which Justin paid attention to. The minutes on the clock moved like hours. While watching the clock, he recited a mantra "Please let her be okay." He prayed to the God Anne believed in, but he wasn't sure existed. All the waiting was killing Justin, so he tried to focus only on positive things. It was hard though. The blood on Lena's clothing kept running through his mind. As he closed his eyes, he reflected on the day he first met Anne. It was love at first sight, at least on his part. They met as undergraduates at Boston College. One night he had attended a fraternity party and drank too much as he often did in those days. While walking home from the party he saw her standing in front of a fountain. She was a vision with long hair and a bright smile shining even in the dim night lights. In his drunken state, he thought she could be an angel. All he wanted to do was touch her. Before he could he started throwing up. Not very gallant he acknowledged. In fact, it was pretty embarrassing, but that story always put a smile on his face, even now. Anne was never one to walk away from anyone in need, so instead of being upset Anne walked him to a bush and rubbed his back while she waited for him to finish. Most women would have been disgusted. Not Anne. Justin knew at that moment he had met his soulmate. Not surprisingly it took her a little while longer to figure it out. In fact, he had to work hard to get her to even agree to a date although she did help him make it back to his dorm room safely that night. Years later when they told that story, she changed it to say that she too knew right away. In spite of their first meeting, their love blossomed. For the remainder of their college days, they could be found together. Even as Justin attended law school, she remained in Boston to work on her Master of Social Work degree. Justin always took pride in being able to win Anne's heart. Without that love, he would have been lost. He would be lost. A page over the hospital intercom brought him back to the hospital waiting room.

Luke watched Justin's suffering intently and felt helpless. He frequently went to the nurse's station for news. The answer was always the same, "a doctor would be out to speak with them as soon as possible." All the while the brothers sat in silence. Luke was never at a loss for words. In this instance, words failed him. He watched the love between Anne and Justin over the years. It was a love that he admired, yet never understood because he himself had never felt that kind of love. Finally, Justin broke the silence with the words that both had been thinking but had been unable to say.

In barely a whisper Justin asked under his breath, "What if I lose her?"

With as much confidence as Luke could muster Luke responded, "You won't. She's strong and has so much to live for. Anne's a fighter."

He didn't know if that was true or even believed it was, but he had to comfort Justin whose face was vacant. It was taking such a long time for someone to come out to speak with them. Plus, they both saw the blood that covered Lena. Luke might not know the outcome for Anne, but the one thing he did know was no matter what he would be there for Justin. There was no way he was going to let his brother go down the self-destructive path he had been on before meeting Anne. Justin wasn't always the confident man he was today. Anne's love changed Justin for the better and Luke was grateful for that. No one understood the need to self-destruct better than Luke because he was also prone to that trait. It was something they both learned having grown up in a house where there was no love. Even at a young age Luke already had one failed marriage that resulted in a child. Although he cared for his wife, he was never in love with her. As Justin was building a future with Anne, Luke's family arranged a marriage of convenience while Luke was in law school. Jessica was from what his father decided was the right family. She was beautiful, wealthy, and educated, but Luke never loved her. He watched how hard Justin fell for Anne. Since he didn't believe he was capable of such love, he agreed to the arranged marriage. It never occurred to him until it was too late that Jessica might fall in love with him. After the birth of their son, Luke tried to reciprocate her feelings, but he couldn't and in the end, the marriage failed. During the entire marriage, Jessica was aware Luke didn't reciprocate her feelings and assured him her love was strong enough for the both of them. Luke wanted to believe that because it was important for his son to grow up with a strong family unit, but he couldn't stop himself from hurting her. Her emotional pain was evident the longer they were together, and she tried to mask it with alcohol. As the light from her eyes diminished, Luke did the only thing he could to save her and his son and ended the marriage. Jessica had begged Luke to stay, however, he knew ending it was for the best. It took several years to become the friends they are today. That friendship has created a happy environment to co-parent their son.

On the outside Luke appeared to have it all. He was more handsome than one would find in a fashion magazine, confident, and successful. What he lacked was warmth and compassion. There were only two people in the world Luke acted differently with; one was his son James and the other his brother Justin. They always got the best of Luke and knew the depth of Luke's love even if Luke himself did not. Justin was equally as striking and successful as Luke. The difference between the two men was the warmth that made Justin's emerald eyes sparkle. Anne put that sparkle there the day she met Justin. As they waited for word on Anne, Justin's sparkle was gone. All Luke could see on Justin's face was loss and helplessness. Seeing Justin like that was hard for Luke. What was even harder for him was not being able to do anything. Luke always took control. In this instance, without all the facts, Luke was just as lost. Silently Luke searched for a way to help. As the story was already on the news Luke thought it might be time to let Anne's parents know and offered to be the one to call.

Justin wasn't ready for that because he knew they would want answers that he didn't have. "No. Not yet. We'll call after we know something more concrete."

"If that's what you want. I can call once we get an update. What the hell is taking so long? Surely, they know something by now. It's been hours. I'm going to go bug the nurse again."

As Luke approached the nurse's station, he noticed three doctors coming out of the ER doors looking in Justin's direction. They all looked somber. Instantly Luke knew the news wasn't good and followed them back to his brother. Lena watched from a distance careful not to be seen by either brother. After being dismissed, she stood outside Anne's room unwelcome inside, but unable to leave without more information. Lena always took great care of her patients. This was different because she felt bonded to this woman. It was something she herself couldn't explain, yet real, nonetheless.

Justin stood with an ill feeling in his stomach because he too could sense that the news wasn't good. Luke arrived first and placed a hand on Justin's shoulder bracing for the news that was about to come. After introducing himself as Dr. Bay, the attending spoke first, delivering the news that both Anne and the baby were in stable condition. His tone was serious but soft. Justin was comforted hearing that both Anne and the baby were still alive. As Dr. Bay continued it became clearer that the rest of the news was not as good. Dr. Bay explained that it was touch and go for a while. They had managed to get her stabilized, although she was still unconscious. Anne was twenty-seven weeks pregnant and by all accounts it was too early to deliver a healthy baby. It's the body's natural reaction to protect the fetus first which endangered her further. At some point to save her they may have to deliver. The bullet was lodged in Anne's chest very close to her heart and she had lost a lot of blood. Surgery was risky but essential. To stabilize her they were giving her several units of blood. At that moment Dr. Castillo introduced himself in a cold matter of a fact manor explaining that he would remove the bullet as soon as she had more blood. He didn't sugarcoat the information as he explained her situation was dire. At that moment Justin collapsed back in the chair and felt sick. Every core of his body ached, especially his heart. Lena could see the pain he was in and could no longer watch. Instead, she decided to go back to the ER room to be with Anne. Even though this wasn't the first time Lena had witnessed a family's torment, this time it seemed so personal. Dr. Castillo was unaffected by Justin's heartache and continued to explain the procedure was Anne's only hope for survival. Justin tried hard to focus on what he was saying, but all he could think of was the word "dire." It wasn't until he mentioned that they would try the procedure without disruption to the fetus that Justin turned his attention back to the doctor. He hadn't even considered the baby. His only thoughts were on Anne and her survival. As he turned his attention back to Dr. Castillo, he heard him say that if the need arose Dr. Townsend was ready to deliver at a moment's notice. Dr. Townsend was kinder as she assured Justin that if she did need to deliver the baby, she would do everything she could to make sure the baby was safe. It was her concern that given the early stages of development, the baby might have a rough start to life, but survival wasn't impossible. There was no reason not to believe that if the baby was delivered early the child wouldn't grow up strong and healthy. If they could wait to perform the surgery that would be ideal, however, that may not be possible to save Anne. All of this was hard for Justin to digest. Just hours earlier everything was perfect. Now they were discussing Anne's and the baby's chances for survival. It really wasn't a choice. Justin agreed to the surgery. First, he needed to see Anne. If he were able to feel her warmth it might make everything okay. He knew no matter what he would feel her love and she would feel his.

"Before we operate, you'll need to sign some paperwork, but there's no reason why you can't spend some time with her now," Dr. Bay said while leading Justin into the room behind the curtains.

When Justin arrived in the ER room, he saw Lena was there holding Anne's hand. She had no idea why she was still at the hospital, especially since it was her day off. There was just something that kept pulling her back to this woman. They had only spoken briefly, yet she felt a strong connection. Tears were in Lena's eyes when she looked up to see Justin entering the room. It touched him to see her there with so much genuine concern. Although her presence made Justin feel better, Dr. Bay was confused to see her with Anne and upset since she had mentioned previously she had just met her.

He knew Lena well and many times witnessed her compassion, but this went above and beyond. "Lena, Mr. Armstrong would like to spend some time with his wife before they take her to surgery. Do you think you could leave them?"

Lena whipped away her tears. "Of course. I'm sorry. I just didn't want her to be alone."

Lena stood up to leave, and Justin spoke. "Wait. Do you know my wife?"

The truth was she didn't and responded. "Not really. Just the moments before the paramedics arrived."

After speaking with the police, Justin had a better understanding of the role Lena played and he was grateful. "The police said you saved her life. I'm not sure how to thank you."

Lena may have attempted to stop the bleeding, but she knew it was Anne's will that was keeping her alive. "You and the baby saved her. She really loves you both. Is there anything I can get you?"

When Lena mentioned the baby, Justin instinctively put his hand on Anne's belly. He could feel the baby kick even though Anne was still. "Forgive me, my love," he said as he leaned down to kiss his wife's cheek. Lena was confused by his words. She didn't understand why Justin would need forgiveness. Justin knew that Anne's first priority was their unborn child, while his main concern was for her life. She loved the baby before they even conceived. It wasn't that he didn't love his unborn child, but he couldn't imagine living without Anne, even if it meant grieving another life.

"She looks so pale," Justin whispered almost so softly that you could barely hear it over the beeping of the machines keeping Anne alive.

Lena leaned in and put her hand on his shoulder, "She lost a lot of blood. That happens, but she is getting the best care possible. I promise you. I'll leave you to her now."

"Ms. McKay, thank you again for everything."

"Lena, please, and no thanks necessary, Mr. Armstrong. You'll be in my prayers."

With that, Lena took her leave, but not before noticing again the distraught look on Justin's face. He was right; Anne was pale and weak. There were no guarantees that Anne or the baby would survive this. Too much had happened in the last couple of days, and Lena desperately needed air before she lost control. Quickly, she went running out of the ER doors. Outside of the ER, the cool end of spring breeze felt refreshing on Lena's face. In the distant background, Lena could hear the sirens of the incoming ambulances. She could take no more and let her grief take over. Lena rolled up into a ball, leaning against the brick wall in a patch of grass. At that moment, she tuned everything and everyone around her out to allow her pain to take over. She needed release and was crying for the family of the fallen officer, the shame she felt over how she handled her grief, and, most of all, she was crying for a woman she just met. That was the part she didn't completely understand. This wasn't the first time she had had to deal with a young person fighting for their life, so she couldn't figure out why she was so distraught over this situation. It wasn't until she felt a warm hand on her shoulder asking if she was okay that she realized she wasn't alone. Embarrassed that someone had seen her in her state, Lena looked up to see Luke. After speaking with the doctors, he went outside to call Anne's parents while Justin went to be with Anne. It was the only thing Luke felt he could do to help Justin at that moment. He knew Anne's parents would be frantic, but the conversation was even harder to have than he anticipated. First, he spoke with her mother, who was so upset she gave the phone to her father. As gently as he could, Luke told him what the doctors said. There was no real comforting way to tell a parent their pregnant daughter was fighting for her life, although he did try to sound hopeful. Anne's father could tell from Luke's shaken voice that he and his wife needed to get to New York as soon as possible. They were planning on leaving Philadelphia, where they lived immediately. After speaking with Anne's parents, Luke called his own parents to update them. Both Justin and Luke were working at their father's law firm when Lena's call came in. His father was already partially aware of the situation. Even though he knew otherwise, Luke hoped that they would be worried and decided to let them know how grave her condition was. In the back of his mind, he had hoped they would come to the hospital to support Justin. Any hope for that died after speaking with his father. John, his father being a cold-hearted man who wasn't capable of showing real human emotion, did as he normally would and offered to throw money at the situation by making sure Anne had the best possible care. Money was something Justin had. What Justin needed was his parents' support. Adding to their benevolence was the fact that their mother had already retired for the evening because she was unable to handle what was happening to Anne. Luke knew that was code for after hearing about all of this, his mother drank a bottle of vodka and passed out. At that point, Luke wasn't certain which call hurt him most. Hearing the pain in Anne's parents' voice was awful, yet his father's indifference really cut him. After hanging up, Luke thought he would remain outside to collect his thoughts before going back inside the hospital to be with Justin. He knew for the moment that Justin needed time with Anne. That was when he saw Lena outside crying. Even though normally he would have ignored her, something about her compelled him to go over to her. Handing Lena a red silk handkerchief that matched his now loosened tie, he asked if he could get her anything. Unlike Anne, Luke wasn't accustomed to caring about strangers. There was something different about this woman that made him want to comfort her. Maybe it was the fact that she had been so kind to Anne. His kindness made Lena sob harder. To no avail, she tried to gain composure, knowing how upset Luke must be. Her large eyes looked up at Luke through tears as she expressed her gratitude for his kindness. In her heart, she knew that she should be asking him if he needed anything, but at that moment, she had nothing left to give. She hadn't asked him to approach her, yet as mortified as she was to have him see her like that, there was a part of her that was glad he was there. The look in her tear-filled eyes compelled him to kneel in front of her and place his arm around her shoulder. As a reflex, she laid her head on his chest while sobbing. With her in his arms, Luke felt a desire to have her closer and held her tighter. She too, felt the pull. Instead of giving in to the feeling, she passed it off to her current state of mind. While crying, she apologized for her behavior, explaining that she had just been through a lot the last couple of days. She felt ridiculous because Luke was going through more now and tried to focus on that while Luke felt something unknown to him. It was compassion mixed with something he couldn't put his finger on. In any case, he felt as if in his arms was exactly where she was meant to be. Even tearstained and dressed in unflattering scrubs, Luke could see how lovely Lena was. It was almost as if she was a fragile china doll. One that was easily broken, and he wanted to take care of her. If they had been standing there would have been a large height difference between the two but sitting against the wall they were eye to eye. Luke wasn't the only one who was having a reaction to her being in his arms. In his arms Lena felt secure, and she finally started to calm down. Once she gained composure, Lena moved to break free, but Luke was enjoying himself and didn't initially let go. For a moment, he forgot where he was and why he was there. It was no time before he remembered what Justin was going through, and he was disgusted with himself for allowing his mind to wander. Slowly, he removed the hand that was around her while keeping the other on her shoulder before asking if she felt better. She did and stood up to thank him again for his support. The cry had provided a much-needed release. Often, she kept things bottled up inside of her. This time, even though she was embarrassed to have done so in front of a stranger, crying was cathartic.

Before she left, Luke asked her a question. "Anne's very bad, isn't she? That's why you're out here, isn't it?"

She was bad, and Lena knew that based on where the bullet landed, the survival rate was low, but she wasn't about to convey that news. "It's not only Anne that brought me out here. I've just had a couple of highly emotional days."

Luke wondered what else was bothering her, but he had to focus his attention on Justin at that moment, even if he was drawn to Lena. "Is there someone I can call for you?"

"No, thank you. After a cry like that, I just need a good night's rest. I hope that everything works out with Anne and the baby. You all will be in my prayers."

She did feel better. Plus, there was no one to call except maybe Gus. Since she knew he would be busy working on the case, she didn't want to bother him. Even though Gus was a great support throughout her life, she was alone, relying only on her father's angel for guidance.

Luke knew Anne was a believer, but he wasn't. He did understand for the believers offering prayers was the best thing they could offer in a time of need. For a moment, he wished he did believe. If he did, he might be able to help Justin more. "Thank you. If there is a God, I'm sure he'll listen to someone as caring as you."

"He'll listen. I just hope he provides the answer everyone wants. Thank you again for your kindness."

Kindness wasn't something Luke was used to hearing in the same sentence as his name, and he offered a slight smile. "I should be saying that to you."

After telling Luke goodnight, Lena started her walk towards the subway to make her way home while Luke watched her walk away. He was still drawn to this young woman and wondered why. No woman had ever made him feel the way he did holding her. When she disappeared, Luke went back into the hospital to tend to Justin.

****

During Anne's surgery, her parents, Martha and Ethan, joined Justin and Luke in the OR waiting room. Justin could see how worried they were when they entered the waiting room. As soon as they arrived, Luke told them that Anne was in surgery. Outside of that, they didn't have any news. They were all anxious for an update from the doctors on Anne's condition. The OR waiting room was different from the one in the ER. In the ER waiting room, there were many strangers, all worried about loved ones. In the OR waiting room they were alone. Even with Martha, Ethan, and Luke with him Justin had never felt so alone in his life. Time just seemed to be standing still. It had been hours since Anne was wheeled into surgery, and they still had no updates. He told himself the longer it took, the better the news would be. Even if he wasn't convinced that was true. Luke mentioned to Justin how concerned their parents were and made excuses as to why they weren't there. He didn't have to lie because Justin knew the truth. He knew Patricia, Justin's mother, was passed out from the bottle of vodka she drank, exclaiming that it was because of her despair over Anne. The truth was most nights Patricia comforted her empty life with alcohol, but at least that night she could use Anne as an excuse. John, his father, felt his time was better spent at the office handling the clients to allow Justin and Luke to be at the hospital. This all was typical behavior of his parents. Growing up, Justin and Luke only had each other. During this crisis and in Justin's youth it was Luke who was there for him. Justin hadn't expected this to be any different. Besides he was too focused on Anne and their unborn child to worry about his lack of parental support.

Anne's parents were surprised by the fact that John and Patricia weren't there. Anne had told them about their indifference, so it shouldn't have surprised them, yet under these circumstances they thought it would be different. Even if they had no regard for Anne, they thought with their grandchild's life at stake, his parents would have made the effort. Everyone was silent, sitting and waiting for word. They were all lost in their own thoughts. Frequently Ethan, who was a minister, would offer a prayer. For the second time that night, seeing how much strength Ethan and Martha drew from a single prayer, Luke wished he was a believer. Anne had such strong faith that Justin wanted to believe too, and he prayed with them. Several hours after Anne went into surgery Dr. Townsend came out to speak with the family. As soon as Justin saw her, he knew they had to deliver the baby. There was no other reason for her leaving the OR. She had a warm smile and congratulated Justin on becoming a father to a beautiful baby girl. The baby was tiny, weighing nearly a pound. To give him hope, Dr. Townsend said she could tell the baby was a fighter. Upon further explanation she mentioned that during Anne's surgery it became imperative the baby be delivered. As it was necessary an emergency cesarean section was performed. Once the baby was delivered it was clear from the way she was kicking and moving her arms that she was fighting for her new life. However, since the baby's lungs weren't fully developed, they had taken her to the NICU where a pediatrician was working on stabilizing her and getting her settled. Justin wasn't sure how he felt at that moment. He was a father to a baby girl. All of Anne's dreams had come true because they were now parents. That was good news, and he should be happy. The problem was all he could focus on was that Anne's life was in danger. Martha needed a distraction and wanted to see the baby. Since she couldn't do anything for Anne, she wanted to be with her granddaughter while Anne was in surgery. That wasn't possible at that time because the doctors needed more time before the baby could have visitors. When they had more information about the baby's condition, a different doctor would come out to update them. At that time, they would be allowed to see her. The doctors had explained that they would only deliver the baby if necessary to save Anne. Justin had to know about Anne. Dr. Townsend tried to be as delicate as possible. The good news was that Anne had made it through the cesarean with no complications. However, they decided to deliver the baby when she flat-lined. While Dr. Townsend was in the operating room, they stabilized Anne and were continuing with the surgery. Martha let out a cry at the words "flat-lined." Ethan held her to keep her from falling. He too had a tear in his eye. They all knew Anne was bad, but no one was quite prepared for the words that Dr. Townsend expressed. Even the news that the baby had survived the birth didn't take away from the emotional roller coaster they were all on. Dr. Townsend expressed her sympathy and hope for a positive outcome before leaving to tend to other patients. There was no way Justin could be happy about being a father when the report on Anne was so disheartening. It was as if he was having an out-of-body experience listening to the voices in the background. He couldn't comprehend anything other than the fact Anne could be lost to him forever. As hard as Luke tried, he couldn't come up with the right words to offer comfort. He too was in a state of shock, but it was his role as the big brother to make sure Justin knew he was not alone, regardless of the outcome. For the next several hours, the waiting room was silent except for the television playing in the background. Anne's shooting was big news. When the story came on, Luke quickly turned that television channel. They didn't need to constantly hear the news of the horror they were living. Luke could no longer take the silence and went to the nurse's station to see if there was further word on either Anne or the baby. The nurse offered to check to see if she could get any information.

Shortly after Luke spoke with the nurse, the NICU pediatrician came out to speak with the family. He introduced himself as Dr. Matthews and relayed that the baby was comfortable in her incubator. Since as Dr. Towsend explained her lungs were not fully developed they had her on a ventilator, but she was fighting hard. Dr. Matthews tried to prepare the family for what they would see when they went into the NICU. The baby was connected to many tubes and machines. Because she was so tiny, it would look like there was a tube connected to every core of her body. Even though the baby was critical, they had every reason to hope because babies do survive being born at twenty-seven weeks. His words of encouragement gave Martha hope for the first time since hearing Anne was shot. They still were uncertain of Anne's fate, however, in her heart she believed her granddaughter would be okay. This was her first grandbaby and knowing that she was weak, Martha needed to be with her. In her heart she knew that was what Anne would want. It was a hospital policy that only visitors accompanied by a parent were allowed in the NICU. Martha was persistent and begged the doctor to make an exception. When that didn't work, she asked Justin to go with her so they could both see the baby to let her know that she wasn't alone in the world. Justin had all he could manage in the waiting room. Instead, he insisted that if Martha wanted to visit the baby, she had his permission. They were unable to make exceptions. Without Justin being there, it wasn't possible for Martha to see her even for a brief time. For the first time since they arrived at the hospital, Luke felt he could do something and offered to call some of his clients who were hospital board members. He believed they would allow her access even if they were annoyed at being disturbed at such a late hour. Dr. Matthews shot Luke a cold stare at his audacity, however, given the situation, he finally agreed to let her visit for a couple of minutes. Thrilled, Martha walked off with a less-than-pleased Dr. Matthews.

Less than ten minutes after leaving the waiting room Martha came back, bragging about what a beautiful baby her granddaughter was. Although her time with the baby was brief, she did manage to get some pictures. Ethan gushed over the pictures, but to Martha's dismay Justin couldn't bring himself to look at them. It didn't go unnoticed by Anne's parents that Justin appeared indifferent towards his daughter. As Martha opened her mouth to say something, Ethan offered that they shouldn't push. With his hand in Martha's, Ethan reminded her that everyone deals with grief in their own way. Justin was just processing everything that happened that day. Even if Martha didn't agree with Justin's reaction, she knew her husband was right. Justin had every right to react in any manner he needed to get him through the night. If this persisted eventually, they would have to take action, but for now, they would leave it alone. Martha and Ethan were talking about how much the baby looked like Anne when Dr. Castillo, looking exhausted, finally came out to speak with them. Everyone rose from their seats and braced themselves for the news when Dr. Castillo entered the room. Luke intuitively knew from the serious look on his face that the news wasn't going to be good. He was a skilled attorney who prided himself on being able to read people's thoughts by their expressions and body language. This time he hoped he was wrong. Dr. Castillo greeted them. As they were already aware, the surgery was touch and go. Anne was out of surgery; however, she was in a coma. After delivering the baby, she hemorrhaged, and they had to revive her again. She was not breathing on her own. Although Anne was stable, she was critical. Through the doctor's arrogance, he declared the surgery a success since they were able to retrieve the bullet. However, given her critical condition, they would need to wait to determine her prognosis. Dr. Castillo reiterated that the next couple of days, especially the next twenty-four hours, would be crucial. Before he answered another page, he told them a nurse would be out shortly to let them know when they could see her. It probably would be several hours, so they might want to go home to get some rest and return in the morning.

As emotional as they all were, there was no way any of them were going to sleep, not with Anne and the baby both in critical condition. They all stood flabbergasted at how quickly things could change. Less than twenty-four hours ago, Anne was a pregnant woman, full of life, but now both Anne and the baby were in separate units fighting for their lives. It was Martha who was first to break and fell into Ethan's arms, tears flowing freely. Unable to believe what they had heard, Ethan too began to sob. Shocked, Justin was just lost in disbelief. He was having a hard time grasping how this all happened. The police had no details other than it was a robbery. Justin had so many questions. The first one being why she was even in the store. How he wished she hadn't been. Not for the first time that night, his world was collapsing around him. Part of him felt like he was still having an out-of-body experience where everything was in slow motion, while the other part hoped it was all just a nightmare. When he woke up, he would again be in Anne's arms. In some ways, Luke felt as helpless as Justin. He was a man who took charge in every situation, but this was beyond even his control. At that moment, all he could do was try to show his brother that he wasn't as alone as he knew Justin felt. Even a wordsmith like Luke couldn't make Justin feel better. Nothing could except Anne's and the baby's recovery. As much as he wished he could, Luke could not make that happen. He wished he could tell Justin that Anne and the baby would be fine. It would be a lie though because no one knew that for sure. The only thing he could think of doing to lighten Justin's heart was to offer a congratulatory hug for becoming a father. His life changed for the better the day his son was born. Now Justin would get to feel all the joy the fatherhood could bring. Justin appreciated the attempt, but the joy wasn't something he was able to feel at that moment. All Justin could feel was a sharp feeling in the pit of his stomach that things would never be the same. Ethan interrupted Luke and Justin by asking that they all join hands to pray. Even though neither Luke nor Justin were true believers that night, they prayed as never before, hoping that their prayers would be answered.

Hours went by as the family waited for permission to see Anne. During that time, Justin wondered if his family would ever be whole again. Even if the baby survived, without Anne, there would be a hole that could never be replaced. If Anne survived, and the baby did not, the grief of losing the baby might change Anne. In his darkest moments, he wondered what would happen if he lost them both. He would have no reason to live. It was after three in the morning when a nurse came to take Justin to Anne. Upon entering the room, he saw all the machines keeping her alive and was shaken. His beautiful Anne looked so weak and pale while struggling to get back to him. In his eyes she was still his beautiful wife. He wouldn't lose her or their baby. As he took Anne's hand, he tried to tune out the beeping sound of the machine while talking to her about their love story. When he told her about their daughter, he realized that she would be mad that he was with her and not the baby. He assured her he would see their daughter soon. Honestly, he had no idea how he would face seeing his daughter so weak without Anne. For Anne and his daughter, he would have to get the strength.

In the room Justin would occasionally drift to sleep, dreaming he was with Anne, still pregnant in their penthouse. For a moment when he woke, he would forget all that had happened. The noise from the machines quickly drew him back to reality. Anne wasn't with him the way he had dreamed. She was lying there still with the machines keeping her with him. He put her hand on his face. There was never a time when he needed her strength more. Determined to be strong for her, he again prayed, asking if there was a God to watch over Anne and their baby. Never had he wanted to believe more in a higher power. Later, he fell asleep again to the beeping of the machines. Although they were harsh, he managed to find comfort in them as it meant that Anne was alive and with him.

****

After leaving the hospital, Lena took the subway back to her apartment, still wrecked from the past couple of days. On the train, she couldn't get the image of Justin's distraught face out of her head. The way Justin looked reminded her of her mother on the day the doctors told them her father had passed. To fight the images, she tried to drown her thoughts with music from her phone. It was no use. Justin's eyes kept haunting her. As she looked around the busy train, she noticed that people were going on with their normal lives. Some of the riders were laughing, excited about new prospects. Others sat quietly reading or with their eyes closed. The world was continuing while Lena was lost in her own little piece of hell. While walking back to her apartment, she stopped at a church she passed every day. Even though Lena hadn't gone to church in a while, she believed that her father's angel guided her there. Often, she felt his presence and believed he sent her signs of guidance. The night he died, she believed he came to speak with her and told her that he would always be there. The only person she shared this belief with was Gus. Gus was the only person she shared anything with. Since her father passed and her mother was unable to recover from his passing, Gus was all she had. The beautiful old church was filled with colorful handcrafted stained-glass images. On the altar was a large crucifix. For the first time in a couple of days, she felt a sense of peace as she knelt in front of the altar. Immediately she turned to light candles for the family of the fallen officer, one for Anne, another for her baby, and the final one for Justin. With everything that had happened she needed her father more than ever. After she lit the candles, she sat in a pew to pray. With no other explanation than faith she felt her father's angel with her. "Daddy, I'm so sorry. I wanted nothing more than to make you proud and live my life as honorable as you did, but I struggle every day. Last night I saw my eyes the night you passed away. They were in a boy who was told his father was never coming back. Like me, he tried to be strong but was overcome with grief. Today, I saw Mami's eyes. This man whose eyes looked like Mami's needs his wife desperately. Please Daddy, please help these people. Help me to deal with these events. I feel you around me all the time. All I ask is that you hold me close now and put in a good word for these people. Even though I know you watch over me, I miss you every day and know my life would be so different if you were here." Talking to her father always gave her a sense of comfort.

While Lena was in church, it began to rain hard. As soon as she saw the rain, she smiled. This was a sign Lena thought to herself. "Heavenly Father, you are crying with me." To Lena walking in the rain was freeing. It was exactly what she needed even though by the time Lena arrived back at her apartment she was drenched from head to toe. Quickly she removed her soaking wet clothes and replaced them with dry ones. It finally occurred to her that she hadn't eaten all day and was starving. As she ate a bowl of cereal, Gus called to check on her. Although he hadn't realized she had stayed at the hospital so long, it was the first opportunity he had to see how she was. He was working diligently to find the man who shot Anne and the other two. She learned that the man with the superficial wound was taken to the hospital, but he was already released. Lena could tell by Gus' voice that something was wrong and questioned him. One of the worst parts of the job was informing the family of a death. It was Gus who had to tell the jeweler's family he would not be returning home. The jeweler had been married for forty years. He made a promise to his wife that he would find the person responsible. Lena knew all too well that finding the person responsible would give all the families much-needed closure, but it wouldn't bring back those who were lost.

She remembered every moment of the trial of the man who killed her father. For days she sat with her mother as her mother stared at the man who took her husband. The killer was eighteen, only eight years older than Lena was when she lost her father. According to his testimony, he never meant to pull the trigger during the robbery. He was so high on drugs and desperate for money, he didn't even know that the gun he held was loaded. His lawyers argued that he wasn't in his right mind because of his drug use and, therefore, wasn't guilty of second-degree murder. The jury disagreed. During his sentencing, he looked directly into Lena's eyes, and she saw his fear and sorrow. If he hadn't been responsible for her father's death, Lena might have felt bad for him. For years, she couldn't forget his look or his mother's face when they sentenced him to life. It was as if his mother felt the same pain Lena felt. She was innocent, and even at an early age, Lena understood that. In one single moment, his life and the life of his mother changed forever. Just has her life had. The system was not easy on cop killers, and he was stabbed to death in prison shortly after his sentencing. Often, Lena wondered how his mother felt when she heard the news of his death and was sympathetic to her pain. As an ER nurse, she has witnessed firsthand the effects drug use has on people. Often she wondered if he had lived if she would've had the strength to forgive him. Exhausted after hanging up with Gus and eating, Lena quickly fell into bed and drifted to sleep.

Chapter Five

The next morning Lena woke up before the alarm. All night she dreamt of Anne and Justin. Even as she dressed for work, she was unable to get them out of her mind. The subway ride did nothing to change that either. She tried to listen to her music and think of other thoughts, but Justin's eyes haunted her. When she arrived at work everyone was still talking about Anne and Justin. Typically, Lena didn't pay too much attention to hospital gossip, but as the ER was slow that morning Lena couldn't help but listen to what the nurses were saying. It wasn't just a topic among the other nurses, the hospital was working hard to contain the barrage of reporters who were trying to get the story on the high-profile family. Lena had to know what the outcome was. When it was time for her break she went in search of Dr. Castillo. Part of her knew that finding him was a bad idea because she knew he felt she owed him something, however, the connection she felt to that woman made her unable to stop herself. Her time in the church gave her the strength and determination to know that no matter what Dr. Castillo wanted from her there was no way anything would happen. Lena learned Dr. Castillo was making rounds in the ICU and went in search of him. As soon as she arrived at the ICU, she saw Justin. He had changed out of his formal suit and was wearing jeans and a grey T-shirt. From his wet hair, it looked like he had just showered. Although he looked more comfortable his facial expression was serious and his good-looking face distraught. Instantly Lena knew things had not gone well. He was standing outside of Anne's room looking horrified. As she approached, she could hear doctors and nurses working on Anne. One voice Lena recognized was Dr. Castillo as he yelled "Clear." For a moment Lena thought of leaving, but she couldn't walk away from Justin alone and looking helpless. She put on her best smile and approached him, but he didn't respond. He was too focused on what was happening in Anne's room. The commotion in the room sounded so bad that she felt it was best he didn't hear everything. She put her arm around his waist to lead him back to the waiting area. He tried to tell her he couldn't leave; however, she assured him when there was news the doctors would find him. The vacancy in his eyes showed he wasn't fully comprehending what she was saying. Yet there was something about Lena being there that was so comforting that Justin went with her. She looked for Luke hoping he would be able to assist her. Instead, she looked at the television in the waiting room to find Luke issuing a statement to the reporters that the family had no comment. He was obviously trying to keep the reporters at bay. Lena searched for comforting words. Since she didn't know what happened with the baby, she didn't wish to bring that subject up. Instead, she sat holding his hand assuring him that the doctors were doing everything they could for Anne. Her words meant nothing to him although he was grateful to have her there. Justin watched again as the clock moved slowly awaiting answers about his beloved wife. Dr. Castillo finally came into the waiting room to see Lena with Justin. The look he gave her clearly showed that he wasn't happy with the scene, but Lena didn't care. He was married and she was just trying to offer comfort to someone in obvious pain. Feeling brave, Lena shot Dr. Castillo an irritated look back. Lost in his own thoughts, Justin was oblivious to their exchange and stood when Dr. Castillo entered. Anne had a seizure. They were able to stabilize her condition, but she was being taken for a CT scan to determine the damage. Until the results were back, they would not know if any brain damage had occurred. They were still dealing with a lot of unknowns, but he would update Justin as soon as he knew. Unable to process anything further Justin collapsed at the words "brain damage." Justin tried to focus on the fact that she was stable. Unaware of the latest setback Luke came in as Dr. Castillo finished speaking with them. He was dressed in jeans and a black T-shirt. Even if Luke didn't know what happened he could see Justin's despair and put his hand on Justin's shoulder. Instantly he spotted Lena and was surprised and oddly comforted. He offered her a half smile. As Justin was still processing, Lena told Luke the update. Luke was in shock and asked how long the CT scan would take. Dr Castillo was a cardiologist, and he wanted assurances that the top neurologist would be brought in to consult. Although irritated at Luke's command, Dr. Castillo assured him Anne was receiving the best possible care. That included a neurological consultation. Lena knew that was true, however, she was also startled by his arrogance and tone. While Luke was trying to help Justin, he picked up on the tension between the doctor and Lena. He didn't know exactly what was happening between them and wasn't even sure why he cared but was acutely aware. The important person was Justin and that was where he needed to focus his attention. When he looked at his brother, he was reminded of a lost boy who was upset when their father berated him. Luke was always more apt to take on John's words while Justin took them to heart. Their father never hit them, although John could be ruthless with his words. Even now John felt the need to control them. Anne had broken John's power over Justin. Without Anne, Luke worried that Justin would always look like a lost boy. Lena's break had long since been over and she had to get back to work. She excused herself. Dr. Castillo wanted the opportunity to get Lena alone and told her he would walk with her since he was headed that way. Acutely astute Luke again sensed the tension between Lena and the doctor. It was evident from her body language and her facial expression that she didn't want to be with him. He asked the doctor to wait a couple of minutes while he asked some additional questions. Then he gave Lena a look that told her to leave now while Dr. Castillo was distracted. The smile she gave Luke said it all and quickly she left.

****

On Lena's way back to the ER, she ran into Dr. Townsend who confirmed that Baby Armstrong was residing in the NICU. Once the baby was admitted to the NICU she had no additional information. Lena was relieved the baby survived. A couple of hours later a fifteen-year-old girl gave birth early in the ER. Lena offered to escort the baby up to the NICU to have him checked out. The baby appeared in good health, however, given the age of the mother and the uncertainty of prenatal care, the doctor felt it better to have the baby examined in the NICU as a precaution. Knowing that even as hospital personnel Lena didn't have access to the NICU, she took this as her chance to see Baby Armstrong. For some unexplained reason, it was important to her to see the infant herself. While she was in the NICU, she saw an older woman knitting by an incubator. Even though she had never met Anne's mother, she knew instantly it was her because Anne looked so much like Martha. Lena sneaked a glimpse of the tiny baby. There was a cord coming out of every part of her small body, yet her energy made Lena believe that she was going to fight to stay with them. At least that was what Lena hoped. To not break the rules Lena went back to work.

****

Several hours later Anne's CT results arrived. Dr. Castillo gathered the family in his office to hear the results. They all sat around a round redwood oak table to hear the news. Their moods were all somber, but still, there were glimpses of hope in Anne's parents and Justin's eyes. There was no way to sugarcoat the news, so bluntly Dr. Castillo told them that the news wasn't good. The results of the scan determined that there had been a lot of damage to Anne's brain. They felt there was very little brain activity if any at all. Another doctor in the room interjected first, introducing herself as Dr. Lee, a neurologist. Dr. Lee pulled out the scan to show them what part of the brain had been impacted. She was much softer in her explanation and was compassionate even if she agreed with Dr. Castillo. It was her opinion they should wait a couple of days to do another CT scan. If the results determined there was still no brain activity as they suspect they will the family should consider taking Anne off life support. Dr. Lee went on to ask if Anne had a living will. Justin couldn't believe that they were discussing a living will or the possibility of taking Anne off life support. Adamantly he refused to discuss it further; she was not lost to him. His feelings of helplessness turned to rage that they could even consider giving up on his wife. He stormed out of the office to be with Anne, still certain she would find her way back to him. After Justin left, Dr. Castillo turned to the others in the room offering his sympathy. They didn't need to decide yet, however, they had to consider if Anne would want to live the rest of her life on support. Anne's parents couldn't hide their pain as they clung to one another crying. Even Luke felt a tear fall down his face. He loved Anne and knew she wouldn't want to live her life on machines, yet there was no way he could ask Justin to let her go either. She was his life. If he asked Justin to give that up, he felt he would lose his brother too.

In Anne's room, Justin was unable to process what the doctors had just told him. Anne was there. There was no way she was lost to him forever. Fearing Anne would sense his emotional state, Justin left Anne's room. Unaware of where he was headed, he found himself in the hospital chapel. There wasn't much to the chapel. It was small and plain-looking with white walls, but often patients and their families would retreat there. Justin didn't care what the chapel looked like. He needed a place to find solace and think. Even though Justin wasn't raised with religion, Anne was unwavering in her belief. Anne was always right even if Justin didn't admit that to her. Feeling completely lost he began to cry out for assistance. He was fighting for his life and prayed. As tears streamed uncontrollably down his face he promised if God helped him, he would become a true believer.

After Lena's shift was over, she was off for three days. That was the benefit of having a three-day work week even though the shifts were twelve hours long. Even after a long shift, her mood was still unsettled. When she was most upset, she would look for comfort from male companionship. It was a quick fix that usually resulted in her feeling worse about herself. This time she was determined she would find another way to deal with her emotions and make her father proud. The brief time she was in the church the previous day had given her some much-needed clarity. She was proud that she had managed to divert Dr. Castillo's advances all day. Instead of going to the local bar, she decided she would go home to watch a romantic comedy. First, she needed to go to the chapel for a little extra support. When she arrived, she saw Justin making every bargain with God. Feeling that she was interfering she wondered if she should leave. There was something about the way Justin looked that told her she needed to reach out to him. Instead of leaving, she went in to sit down beside him. Justin could feel Lena's presence even though he didn't acknowledge her at first. Finally speaking Justin asked Lena if she believed in God. Lena answered absolutely.

"How can you? Aren't you surrounded by grief all day?"

"Some days more than others but working here you also see a lot of miracles too."

"Anne believes. I'm not so sure, but I need a miracle now. Do you see miracles often?"

"It depends on what you consider a miracle. If you mean the birth of a baby or a man who walked away from a major car accident with a broken rib, then yes, I see miracles daily."

"The doctors say Anne won't recover. I can't allow myself to believe that. Now would be a good time for one of those miracles."

Lena was disheartened to hear that news. She wanted the CT scan to come back clean. She had to offer Justin comfort. "You have one. She's tiny and struggling, but she's alive fighting to get home to you."

Justin was surprised by her words. She reached out for his hand and asked if he had decided on a name for the baby. Justin shrugged his shoulders, indicating that he hadn't. His thoughts had been mostly on his wife, not his baby. With his apparent indifference to the question, she wondered if he had seen the baby. Unable to hide the panic in her voice, Lena asked him if he had. As he shook his head that he had not, Lena tried to fight her own tears of anger, knowing that he was already distraught enough. That had to be rectified.

In a gentle voice, Lena pleaded with him, "I know how worried you are about Anne. I understand that, but you have a daughter too. Daughters need their dads. Trust me, I know. Your wife made me promise to help her baby and now that same baby is struggling for her life. You can help her. She will feel you."

In every sense of the word, Justin felt defeated. "I can't. All this is just too hard. I just don't have the strength without Anne."

"What do you think Anne would say to you if she heard you talk like this?"

Justin gave a light smirk as he knew what Anne would do. "She would kick my ass."

"Well, I'm too small to do that. I am willing to go with you. Honestly, I got a brief look this afternoon when I brought a newborn up and would love a closer look."

With that she stood, holding out her hand, urging him to walk with her.

****

Luke was frantically looking for Justin after the meeting with the doctors. The most logical place for Justin to go after he stormed out was Anne's room. When he wasn't there Luke searched all the places in the hospital that he thought Justin might be as he didn't want Justine alone. He knew Justin was hurting and wouldn't wander too far from Anne. In a final attempt to find Justin, Luke went to the NICU. As soon as he got off the elevator, he was surprised when he saw Lena and Justin walking towards the unit. Luke knew that Justin had been too involved with Anne to think about the baby and thought to himself that was progress. He was afraid if Justin saw him it would interrupt, so he stood back to observe. It seemed that this woman had a positive effect on Justin. Every time Justin was at his lowest, Luke would find him with her. Since Luke had no idea how to help Justin, he appreciated someone else's help. Justin looked stronger than he had in the doctor's office and for that he was grateful.

On the way to the NICU Justin told Lena about Anne's stubbornness. Even though Justin had wanted to find out the sex of the baby, Anne was insistent that there are so few wonderful surprises in life the sex of the baby should be one of them. They were laughing about all the ways Justin tried to find out and Anne's determination. As Luke looked at them, he couldn't help but notice what a beautiful smile Lena had. When she laughed her whole face lit up like Christmas. It was very different from the sad eyes that she had shown him the night before. She had changed out of scrubs before going to the chapel and Luke appreciated the way her behind looked in her jeans. Briefly, he remembered how she felt against his body. Quickly he changed his thoughts to Justin, feeling a little guilty that his mind wondered.

As Lena and Justin entered the NICU, they were told they had to put on a robe, mask, and hat before they could see the baby. It was important that the baby not be in contact with any germs. They were also told to scrub their hands before entering. When they finished suiting up, Justin froze at the door. He was unable to walk to the incubator. Lena gently pushed him forward, telling him that Anne would expect him to look after their little girl. There was nothing more that Justin wanted than to honor Anne and he forged forward. At the sight of his daughter in the incubator, Justin again froze. She was so tiny and the most beautiful thing he had ever laid eyes on. It was love at first sight. He didn't care about her size, or the tubes hiding her beauty and was overcome with emotion. "She looks just like Anne," Justin said with barely a whisper. He reached to put his hand in the slots of the incubator so that he could touch her. She was so warm under the heat lamp. Lena leaned forward to the incubator telling Baby Armstrong that she was an incredibly lucky girl to be so loved. The NICU nurse came over to talk to Justin. She had a kind mature face and assured him that although the baby was small, she appeared to be strong. So far, she has had to deal with minimal complications. Often premature babies born at twenty-seven weeks face a lot of difficulties that his daughter currently doesn't appear to have. Relief filled over Justin's face as he bent down and kissed the incubator whispering to his daughter to keep up the good work. Now that the baby was a reality he was overcome by love for her. He and Anne created this little person that would always be a part of them. Tears of joy filled his eyes as he told his daughter how much he loved her. Justin wanted to promise that Anne would be there soon, but he didn't ever want to break a promise to his daughter and wasn't sure it would be true. At that moment he wanted the baby to know that he was there and always would be.

Luke observed the whole scene from a window in the NICU. For the first time since learning of Anne's prognosis, he felt Justin might be okay. Lena looked up to see Luke and waved him in. When Justin saw Lena wave, he looked out the window and was excited to introduce his daughter to his brother. After Luke was germ-free, he joined them to see his new niece. Shortly after Luke's arrival, the nurse told them that it would be better if they didn't stay too long. Even in the incubator, a baby can be excited by company. It is important for a baby to know she is loved but in short visits. They all decided to leave as the nurse requested. The visit revitalized Justin who went to tell Anne about their baby. Secretly, he hoped this would give her the strength to prove the doctors wrong.

Once Justin left Luke filled Lena in on what the doctors had said. Although Lena listened attentively, she already knew what the doctors said, and her heart ached for the entire family. She knew that someone could get lost from a broken heart. It happened to her mother, and she feared the same fate for Justin. That would mean his baby would suffer the same fate she had. The early years of the baby's life were going to be enough of a struggle. With no mother and a lost father, she didn't stand a chance. As upset as Lena was for the baby, she also saw Luke's despair. Not only was he grieving the loss of Anne, but he was also terrified of losing Justin. With no idea how to make things better Luke did the one thing he never did and asked for advice. He witnessed the positive effect she had on Justin and at that moment needed help. As he asked, his jaw tensed to hold back his emotions of sadness and fear. She could tell how much he loved his brother and knew that all this was difficult for him too. All she could offer was reassurance that he was doing everything he could just by being there. For emphasis, she put her hand to his face. Luke leaned into Lena's touch, surprised by how right it felt. It was obvious that Lena cared deeply. Although he still had no idea why. They were virtual strangers after all, yet somehow her connection with them was effortless. The mood was broken by the vibration of Luke's phone. It was a call he needed to take, so as much as he didn't want his time with Lena to end, he excused himself.

When Lena left Luke, she had no idea where she was going. She was tired but felt a pull to check on Justin before she left. She needed to make sure that he was truly feeling better before she could take her leave. Outside of Anne's room, she listened as Justin excitedly told Anne how much their daughter looked like her mother. The love in Justin's voice was evident and Lena was reassured. As she was about to leave, she saw Dr. Castillo approaching her. Negative butterflies rose in her stomach, and she tried to think of a way to avoid him. It was no use. He saw her and was headed straight for her. When he was in front of her, she smiled trying to excuse herself by saying she was headed home. Dr. Castillo knew her shift had ended hours ago and was irked to find her again with Justin or in his vicinity. He was going to have his time with her and put his hand on her arm. Chills and not good ones went down her spine at his touch. It was weird because they had the flirtation, but now she felt pressure.

"Lena, wait a minute. I was just going to check on Anne and then go home for the night. Perhaps I could entice you to go have a drink with me. That will give you the opportunity to repay the favor."

Dr. Castillo was using his most sultry authoritative voice. Lena had never planned to take the flirtation beyond that and the way he had acted the past couple of days was unsettling. A fact that only solidified her resolve that nothing would ever happen. It had been an exhausting couple of days, and she explained that all she wanted was to sleep. He opened his mouth to say that there was no need for her to sleep alone, but before he could Justin came out having heard voices in the hall. For the first time, Justin realized Lena's unrest at being around Dr. Castillo. He eyed Dr. Castillo with ire and turned to Lena.

"Thank you for tonight. You were right. It's what Anne would want and what I needed. I appreciate everything you have done since the beginning of this nightmare." He turned to Dr. Castillo in almost a warning, "She's a very special lady." It wasn't what he said to Dr. Castillo as much as the unwritten message in his voice that Dr. Castillo understood was Justin's way of saying leave her alone. Dr. Castillo understood that Justin was from an affluent family, however, he wasn't about to let him intimidate him. In his mind Lena owed him, and he wasn't about to let that go.

Only Gus had told her she was special in an exceptionally long time. His words made her smile, and she returned the compliment by saying Anne and his baby were incredibly lucky to have him. He insisted he was the lucky one as he walked back into Anne's room. Their exchange further enraged Dr. Castillo who couldn't understand why Lena had become so involved with this family. She had always been compassionate, but not to this extent. The thought that she was connected to another man infuriated him. Again, he insisted they have that drink. Before she could answer Luke approached them. He wanted to say goodnight to Justin before leaving for the night. To his surprise and delight, he saw Lena in the hall. He wasn't thrilled to see her with Dr. Castillo. His feelings went beyond knowing Lena was uncomfortable with the man and even more than not liking his arrogance. Luke genuinely did not like seeing Lena with any man and he was going to end the tension he witnessed.

He ignored the doctor and approached Lena directly. "I am glad you waited. Let me say goodnight to Justin, and I'll give you that ride I promised."

Although Lena was confused by what he said, she understood he was trying to help her. "No problem. Take your time. I will be waiting here."

For the first time since approaching them, Luke acknowledged Dr. Castillo's presence with a smirk. It was a pissing match and Luke intended to win, he thought as he went into Anne's room. Since Luke had wanted to spend more time with Lena, Dr. Castillo's presence helped him out too. On the ride, he hoped to hear her thoughts about Justin, but he knew in his heart that was not the only reason. No other woman had affected him the way she had, and he wanted to know more about her.

All Lena could feel was relief. Luke's offer, although she did not think it was genuine, it gave her the out with Dr. Castillo she wanted. Dr. Castillo wasn't deterred. While Luke was busy Dr. Castillo made it clear to her that he would soon collect on what she owed. It was hard for Lena to believe that she ever felt anything but disgust for him. She was about to tell him off when Luke came back out to the hallway asking if she was ready to go.

Lena looked at Dr. Castillo with spite and said that she was more than ready to go before the two walked down the long hallway to the elevators. In the elevator, Lena turned to Luke. "Thank you for the save. When we're outside, I'll head for the subway."

That wasn't what Luke wanted at all. "No need. It's late and after everything you've done for us, I can take you home."

Lena was surprised and a bit confused, "You don't have to do that. I'm happy to be there for Justin and Anne. The subway will be fine."

Luke really didn't like that idea. The City late at night for a young woman can be dangerous, especially for someone as attractive as Lena. "I wouldn't be a gentleman if I let you do that. Where do you live?"

Gentleman was not the vibe Lena got from Luke. He had been nothing but kind to her, however there was something about him that said he was no gentleman. Not in the way Dr. Castillo was not a gentleman, but in a good, dangerous way that she couldn't resist. "Brooklyn."

"I love Brooklyn. What do you say?" The truth was he knew very little about Brooklyn, he just wanted the opportunity to spend more time with her.

Since Luke offered her a rare smile that made his beautiful emerald eyes twinkle, she could not refuse his offer. At that moment she wasn't sure she would be able to refuse him anything. Justin made her feel comfortable. With Luke, there was a charge between them that she was having trouble denying.

As they walked towards his car Luke was wondering what was going on with Lena and Dr. Castillo and decided to ask. "What exactly is going on with you and the doctor?"

It was a question that Lena wasn't prepared to answer even if she should have been. Luke had seen her reaction to Dr. Castillo.

Even though Lena knew he deserved an answer she wasn't used to sharing with anyone except Gus. Even with Gus, she was guarded.

Immediately after Luke asked the question, Lena's body tensed. As much as he wanted to know the answer, he didn't want to ruin their time together and quickly changed the subject when they arrived at his car. Lena knew the brothers were well off, so she shouldn't have been surprised to see the red Porsche in the parking spot, but she was. It was the nicest car she had ever seen up close. Her face couldn't hide her excitement.

Luke smiled at her reaction and opened her car door. He loved the fact he could read what she was thinking from her facial expressions. "Your chariot Madam."

As she entered the car Lena said, "Nice car."

The car was one of Luke's prized possessions and he couldn't hide his pride. "It is. Isn't it?"

As he closed the car door, Lena felt the soft leather of the black car seats against her skin. It was as soft as a baby's bottom. While Luke walked to the other side of the car, Lena noticed how gracefully he moved. He was a tall man standing over six feet, but not at all awkward.

When Luke was in the car, Lena offered her gratitude for the ride. Although Luke was not typically the man who went out of the way to help people he barely knew, he was happy to drive her home and told her so. He kept telling himself it was out of gratitude, yet deep down he knew it was more. The truth was that he wanted to get to know her better.

It had been another long emotional day. Although Lena typically enjoyed the subway ride using it to decompress from her day, a ride on that day was exactly what she needed.

Unbeknownst to them Dr. Castillo angrily witnessed the whole exchange. He had followed them out of the hospital determined to find out what was really going on and he wasn't at all happy to see what he did. In his mind, Lena was his and he did not like anyone who would attempt to get in the way one bit. At that moment he vowed to stop whatever was happening as soon as possible.

The ride was silent except for the dance music playing on the car radio. Lena was comfortable with the silence because she knew they would have nothing in common. He was clearly wealthy and sophisticated while she was a nurse who lived in Brooklyn and had a ton of student loan debt. They were from different worlds. Even though she felt a charge, she knew there would be nothing for them outside of the bedroom.

Luke on the other hand was searching for the words. She was different from all the other women he encountered. Most of the women he knew had an agenda. That was fine with him because he knew how to act with them. Lena cared. Lena was genuine. The way she was with Justin and Anne, it was obvious that it was true. It was rare to meet someone with a pure heart. Anne also had a pure heart. The two women looked nothing alike, however in so many ways Lena reminded him of Anne. Anne had gone to one of the best colleges and was polished. Luke could tell from Lena's clothes and how she carried herself that Lena was not refined. What you saw is what you get even if she had secrets. That was one of the things he liked best about her. He liked the fact she was different from everyone else he knew. She also presented a challenge to him which was another thing he found interesting. Luke was used to women throwing themselves at him. He was a rich, successful, eligible bachelor who frequently made the most eligible list. Normally women had no trouble letting him know they were interested. Luke wasn't accustomed to making small talk. He never had to.

As they rode through the Brooklyn Battery Tunnel Lena noticed Luke's long fingers on the steering wheel and his defined chin with perfect a nose. She marveled at how much he and Justin resembled one another. Right down to the sadness in their beautiful emerald eyes. Luke could feel her eyes on him even if she was playing coy. Secretly he was thrilled she was not completely unaffected by his looks. Suddenly traffic came to a halt. Luke braked hard and the two jerked forward. Instinctively Luke put his long arm across Lena to block her from going forward. As he put his arm across her chest, he was rewarded with her right breast being cupped straight into his hand. Luke lingered a bit longer than needed. Having him touch her in that way put charge throughout Lena's body. Even though she knew it was wrong, she didn't move away. Through her tight t-shirt and bra, he could feel her nipple harden. Luke's lower body reacted to her as well. With regret, Luke removed his hand and apologized for the quick stop. He wasn't really sorry and if she were honest Lena was not sorry either. The removal of his hand felt wrong as they both wished this could have been a lot more.

After the bridge they were in Brooklyn and Lena gave Luke directions to her apartment. Luke knew Brooklyn had turned into an up-and-coming neighborhood for young professionals though he rarely left the Manhattan scene. Luke had assumed she lived in one of those neighborhoods, but the further they drove away from Manhattan he realized that was not the case. On the corner of her street was a man who was clearly selling drugs to a young girl.

There was graffiti drawn over the brick walls. Some graffiti could be considered art, but others were more sexual in nature. Along the building were homeless men and women trying to sleep or were passed out. It was too hard to tell.

Upon seeing her rundown apartment complex Luke was shocked and a little frightened for her safety. "This is where you live?"

It wasn't that he felt superior, but Lena misinterpreted his expression and tone as disgust and not what he was feeling. "Not everyone can drive a Porsche Mr. Armstrong." Using his formal name at that moment felt right. It was only moments ago he wasn't so high-class, and she wanted to remind him of that fact while she opened the car door to get out. "Thanks for the ride and the feel."

Luke could tell she was annoyed even though he didn't understand why. The building didn't look safe, and it was late. He was not going to let her walk to her door alone even though he was aware she had done it many times before. Without stating his intentions, he began to walk Lena up.

Lena was offended and wanted him to leave. She knew they were from different worlds, but it didn't stop her for a moment in the car thinking what it would be like to be with a man like Luke.

After his reaction to her life, she knew that could never happen. She liked where she lived and in fact, was proud of what she had accomplished, so she was not about to let him put his nose down at her. "Aren't you afraid for your car?"

Luke tried to lighten the mood by shrugging and saying, "The car is insured. I wouldn't be a gentleman if I let you walk to your door alone."

His flippant attitude wasn't going to warm her. "You weren't such a gentleman when your hand was squeezing my tit."

This was not going well, and Luke needed to try a different approach. "No one is perfect although your breasts are close. If I recall you weren't exactly making me remove my hand."

His charm was working, and Lena had to fight back her smile. After all, he was right, she enjoyed the feel of his hands on her. "Like I said no gentleman. I'd ask you in, but it's late. Thanks for the ride."

Luke was disappointed to be leaving. He thought about extending his visit with questions about how he could help Justin, but he could see she was tired. At times on the car ride, he could see her fighting back the sleep. Instead, Luke said, "It was my pleasure."

Once again, referring to the feel, it was Lena's turn to be flippant. "Yes, it was. Goodnight."

This banter while entering the building and walking up three flight of steps was a turn on for Luke. When they arrived at her door, he could no longer fight what he was feeling for her. As they reached her door, he turned her to face him and pulled her into him for a kiss. At first, she was startled, but it felt so right. In fact, it felt as if nothing else could be more right in that moment. His lips were tender, and she passionately returned the kiss with their tongues entwined with want and need. They were breathing fiercely with their hard bodies pressed against one another. She could feel his desire press into her and her own lust made her vagina call out for more. Luke felt as if he could not pull her close enough as he started moving his hands to her behind. As much as she wanted him, Lena knew she would have to break away and did. Instantly her body ached, however a man like Luke would not be interested in anything other than a one-night stand with a woman like her. Normally that would be okay, but not this time. After her time in the church, she vowed to respect herself and her body. To not use sex as a mechanism to forget pain. She also feared the intensity between them would cause her pain and she was protecting herself from getting hurt. As her body yearned to feel that connection again, she quickly took her leave before she changed her mind. It would not have taken much persuasion on his part, and she knew that before closing her apartment door, leaving Luke confused. Perplexed Luke stood motionless outside her apartment having never felt so connected to anyone. On the other side of the door, Lena leaned against the wall wondering what had just happened. Her body was telling her to run after him because it would be hot between them. The feel of his lips upon hers would not soon disappear. She needed release. While using her vibrating friend she thought of emerald sad eyes, long fingers, firm hands, the hot kiss, and fell into a deep orgasm.

****

By the time Luke arrived at his spacious two-story apartment on Sutton Place, he too needed a release. The entire ride home he thought of the way Lena's lips felt against his and the perfect fit of her breast in his hand. As a man, he understood why the thought of her body pressed against him made him excited. What he didn't understand was why he kept thinking of her smile. All thoughts of Lena made him desire female companionship. There was an extensive list of women Luke could call to take care of his primal needs. Most recently the one he called frequently was Tabatha, a redhead with a stylish bob cut and curves that went on for days. Luke had represented her in her divorce a couple of years back. Although he recognized that she was a social climber who married for money, he had obtained a large settlement for her, and she was no longer in need of money. She was often the call he made when he needed a distraction. Luke liked to play sexual games and Tabatha was more than happy to role-play. Tabatha hoped one day she would be more than just a sexual partner, however for the time being she was pleased to oblige Luke when she got the call. As soon as she arrived, she greeted Luke with a warm kiss stating that she was happy, he called. With no gentleman's intention, he kissed her back fiercely, leading her up the stairs to his room. The intensity was different from the one he shared with Lena, but so was his connection with Tabatha. That was odd to him because he just met Lena whereas he had known Tabatha for years. Luke wasn't going to dwell on that. At that moment Tabatha was there, and Lena wasn't, and he had needs that had to be satisfied. In his room, Luke demanded Tabatha take off her clothes slowly. As he watched her undress he was still haunted by images of Lena. Tabatha was a beautiful woman, but she lacked Lena's warmth. It was Lena who Luke really wanted that night. To forget Lena, Luke threw Tabatha onto the giant red satin sheet king-sized bed and climbed on top. There was nothing gentle about their encounter. They fucked hard while Luke envisioned Tabatha as Lena. Their naked bodies slammed against one another at a fast pace as they panted trying to reach their sexual peak. When it was clear that Tabatha had reached hers, Luke found his release with his body falling on top of hers. As selfish as Luke was, he always made sure that his bed partner was equally as satisfied as he was. With Tabatha, he found his release, but mentally he was still thinking of a time when it would be Lena in his bed. Silently he questioned if he could fuck Lena the way he had Tabatha. He knew it would be intense but there was something about her that made him want to be less gruff. Instead of basking in the afterglow of their sexual encounter, Luke thought about how long Tabatha would need to stay before he could ask her to leave. She understood their relationship boundaries, however, that didn't stop her from trying to push the limits by trying to cuddle with him. They didn't have that relationship and Luke wanted to make sure she again received that message. After Jessica, he didn't believe he was relationship material and made that clear to everyone he was involved with. To make sure she was clear, Luke got out of bed to put his boxer shorts on. He was sending a message while using work as an excuse to not hurt her feelings. Luke was selfish but tried not to be cruel. It was believable as Tabatha knew that Luke had been with Justin at the hospital for the past couple of days and had a lot to catch up on. Tabatha understood that and tried to ask about how Anne was. The news reports hadn't been forthcoming on her condition. Even though he knew Tabatha and Anne were social acquaintances, Luke didn't trust Tabatha's concern was real and was not comfortable sharing information. The family was very protective, and Luke saw the lengths Tabatha was willing to go to for social standing during the divorce. He could see the headline "Source close to the family says Anne is brain dead." It was one thing if the hospital leaked the information. It would have been another if the media released the story because of him. He shrugged off the question and kissed her cheek before telling her to lock the front door on her way out while he retreated to his home office. That did not please Tabatha one bit who was searching for a way to connect with Luke outside the bedroom. One day she thought to herself they would be more, however, Luke's mood changed after she asked about Anne. She realized it wasn't time to press the issue.

Before Tabatha left, she stopped by Luke's office to kiss him goodbye hoping he changed his mind. He had not and escorted her to the door again, telling her goodnight. Her disappointment was evident, and he wondered how much longer he could keep her as one of his pleasure women. While he pondered the question, he poured himself a glass of whisky and headed back to his office. It was not entirely a lie that he needed to get some work done. Before all of this, he and Justin had been working on the biggest case of their careers. The case had taken a backseat to Anne but work still needed to be done to prepare. Time was short and their client needed them. Luke needed to focus. Even though Justin was his priority, he couldn't completely ignore his other responsibilities. Plus, he knew John had limited patience even with his boys. If

Luke couldn't help Justin emotionally, he would keep their father at bay. It was only a matter of time before John insisted the brothers return to work. Most fathers would understand that their son's life had been turned upside down and would give them the time they needed to recover. Not John. Luke knew John didn't have a heart and he feared he was just like him. The only people Luke could let into his heart were Justin and James. He was convinced that he needed no one else although being around Lena the past couple of days made Luke question if that was true.

Chapter Six

The next couple of days Lena was off, and she tried to remove herself from the hospital drama. That task was impossible. During the day, it was hard to avoid because the news was constantly reporting the same details. Gus was working day and night to find the person responsible. He would frequently check in with Lena, and it was difficult not to ask about the progress of the case. Gus would share what he could, but some details were confidential. What she could deduce is that the leads were drying up, and this may be unsolved for a while. At night, Lena's dreams were haunted by the thoughts of Justin and Anne. Watching Justin was like looking at her mother all over again, although she hoped for everyone's sake, he was stronger. When she wasn't dreaming of Justin, her dreams were of Luke. Those were the ones that haunted her the most. Thoughts of Justin and Anne were like reliving her past. It was a past she tried to forget, but it was still a big part of her. The dreams of Luke were of a new emotion. One she didn't fully understand the meaning. If the dream had been of a sexual nature after that kiss, she would have fully been able to appreciate the meaning. Instead, when she dreamed of Luke, she was frantically searching for him. It was like something out of a movie as she was wearing a long pink flowing dress running through a forest. She would look behind every tree until she found him. As soon as she did, something awful would happen. The closure was always different but tragic in nature. One time, when she was lying in his arms, she was shot and bleeding out. Another time, he turned into a vampire and bit her neck. No ending was logical, but as the ending was always of her getting hurt, she understood the message. Her subconscious was telling her to stay away from Luke. He was going to hurt her. It was something she already knew, so the dreams only solidified her belief, even if she wished things could be different. That was the part that was even more complicated because she never desired the "true love" others yearned for. She saw what losing it could do to a person and wanted no part of that, and questioned the significance of her dreams .

When Lena was awake, her main goal on her days off was to keep busy to not focus on anything Armstrong-related. She had only known both brothers for a short time and could not fathom why they were taking up so much of her thoughts. It was her time off and her time to decompress. For Lena, exercise was the best medicine. Every day she would run to the gym that was located a mile from her apartment to work out for a couple of hours. Her gym had a punching bag, and since Gus had made her take self-defense classes, she would use the bag to practice and get rid of pent-up frustration. She wouldn't leave until she was at the point of exhaustion, only saving enough energy to walk back to her apartment. While she walked back to her place, she would analyze her dreams even though she would try to think of other things, there was no escape. All her life Lena had been a loner. There were people that she went out with on occasion, mostly other nurses, but no one she truly called a friend. After everything she had been through in her childhood, trust was a big issue for her. Until recent events, the only person she had a connection with was Gus. That was why she was having a tough time understanding the instinctive pull she had towards Anne, Justin, and their family. She always had compassion for her patients, but one of the reasons she liked being an ER nurse was triage. She could help the patient without getting too emotionally involved. This time it was so different. Even on her days off, she found it difficult for her to fight the urge to go to the hospital to check on them. If she had shown up, they might have thought she was odd or a stalker, so she resisted. The connection she felt with Justin and Anne was powerful, but despite the warnings of her dreams, there was no denying that there was sexual chemistry between her and Luke as well. On night two, when she couldn't sleep, Lena let her curiosity take over. She decided to look up the Armstrong family on the internet. There was a lot of information on their involvement with various endowments and charities. It didn't surprise her that Anne was involved with several children's causes. After reading the information about Anne, Lena believed that she was the type of person that Lena could have been friends with or at least someone she would have liked to have known. That was rare for Lena, and she could understand why Justin was so in love. From what she read, Anne was a beautiful person inside and out. In addition to the Armstong philanthropy work, there were several stories that featured the brothers' high-profile cases their law firm supported. One case in particular caught Lena's attention. Several years back, in what must have been early in Luke's career, he and John defended a wealthy businessman accused of embezzlement. Their client was accused of taking millions of dollars from people's retirement funds. From all the evidence presented in the article, Lena couldn't believe the man was found not guilty. Luke was able to get him off on a technicality. When she finished reading the article, Lena was appalled. The man was guilty, and all those innocent people lost their savings, but nothing happened to him. There was story after story of innocent people who lost everything. The article was making her angry, so she decided to switch to looking at images. The first images that appeared were of Anne and Justin. Their obvious love for one another beamed through the pictures. Lena recognized that love. It was the way her mother and father looked at one another before his death. The idea of that and what Justin may have lost sent a teardown Lena's face. That kind of love is not replaceable, and Lena felt awful Justin may have to find that out now. As she was about to close the laptop, an image caught her eye. It was a picture of Luke and Jessica Armstrong together. Lena was frantic as she had no idea Luke was married and continued her search to find more. She was no home wrecker and hoped Luke hadn't omitted something so important. Relief filled her when she learned Jessica was Luke's ex-wife. Upon reflection, Lena realized her panic was more than about not wanting to break up a marriage, the idea of Luke with another woman impacted her in ways she didn't happily accept. Even through an image, her heart pounded at the site of Luke. There was no denying his good looks, but the pull was so much more than looks. This was getting her nowhere, and she decided her fact-finding mission should end. As she closed her laptop and went into bed, Lena began to wonder what someone looking her up on the internet would find. She was too young when her father died to be featured in any of the stories. Outside of that and her hospital affiliation, there probably was nothing there. No spring break gone wild or crazy images of college parties. For that she was grateful. All of her demons were hidden inside her.

****

As promised, after a couple of days, the doctors took Anne back in for more tests. In his heart, Justin believed Anne was getting better. Even if his head was telling him otherwise.

Everyone else started to accept what they believed was inevitable. Anne's parents prayed with her daily, hoping that she was at peace. At one point Justin felt her squeeze his hand, but the doctors said that it was a reflex action. For Luke, watching his brother in so much pain was devasting. He tried to get Justin to see that there had been no improvement, but when he did, he would see Justin's eyes lost and couldn't continue. Within a couple of hours, after the tests were finished and the doctors analyzed the data, the family was called back into Dr. Castillo's office to meet with him and Dr. Lee. They were all seated around the same table in the same chairs as they nervously awaited the news that was about to come. This time it was Dr. Lee who spoke first. In a sympathetic tone, she relayed the information that as anticipated Anne's condition had not changed. Everyone in the room was silent. It was one thing to know something in your head, it was another thing to hear it as a concrete fact. Luke broke the silence by asking for a second opinion. To his request Dr. Lee mentioned that she had already consulted with two other neurologists who concurred that Anne didn't have any brain activity. It was time for the family to think about what Anne would want and to consider taking her off life support. Vehemently Justin refused, claiming the tests were wrong. Ethan wrapped his arms around Martha as they sobbed. They knew Anne would not want to live that way and planned to convey it to Justin when it came time, but first they had to process the fact they were going to lose their baby. Dr. Lee told them all how sorry she was. She had met Anne once at a hospital event and really liked her. Luke knew the doctors were asking Justin to do the impossible by taking Anne off life support. Once Anne left this earth Justin might not recover, but he also agreed with Martha and Ethan that Anne wouldn't not want to live like that. Before the test results came back, they had conversations without Justin present to determine what Anne would really want. Anne was filled with life and love. That woman lying in the bed was not Anne.

As Justin was arguing with the doctors that something else had to be done, Ethan collected himself enough to put his hand on Justin's shoulder. With tears in his eyes, he began to speak, voice breaking. "Son. It's time. We must let her go and be with God now. She gave us all so much her entire life. She'll always be with us. She will be there when you look in the eyes of your daughter. When you need advice, it will be her voice you hear. As much as we want to keep her with us, we can't be selfish. Her work on Earth is complete. Now she has work to do in heaven."

Justin could not believe his ears. How was it so easy for Anne's parents to give up on her? "What are you saying, Ethan? She has us. A daughter. We need her. There's no way her time is done. She's alive and in there somewhere. I know it, and God needs to wait."

"You have no idea how much her mother and I wish that were true, but we must accept this. Justin, Anne wouldn't want to live like this. Not for you, us, or that beautiful baby. We must do this for Anne."

Deep down Justin knew Ethan was right. Anne was always so active and would have hated the machines and being confined to bed. Visions of Anne smiling and laughing ran through Justin's head as he considered what Ethan was saying. He looked at Martha with tears flowing down her cheeks, who nodded in agreement with her husband. It wasn't as if they were telling him anything that he didn't already know. He just couldn't believe she was really gone. As much as it hurt him, he couldn't be selfish. Justin would do anything for Anne, even if it meant letting her go. This was going to be the hardest thing he ever had to do. Reluctantly, he signed the paperwork to take her off the life support. Dr. Lee suggested that they spend the next couple of hours saying their goodbyes.

Immediately the family went to spend their final moments with Anne. Justin wanted so much to have Anne meet their baby, but that was impossible. The baby was too weak to be moved from the NICU, and Anne could not be moved from the ICU. While the family gathered, Luke took the time to call Jessica to make her aware of what was happening. During their marriage Jessica and

Anne had become close, and that relationship continued after the divorce. Luke wanted to give her a chance to say her final goodbyes if she wanted.

In Anne's room, each family member took a private moment to say their goodbyes. Martha went first. She sobbed as she remembered holding her daughter in her arms for the first time. That day she had never experienced that much love in her life. Her only regret was that her granddaughter wasn't well enough for Anne to experience that feeling. Ethan came in as Martha lost full control. He hugged his wife and kissed his baby girl's head while telling her how much he loved her. Even though God was calling her home, there would never be a day that he didn't miss her. Ethan told Anne that he and Martha would look after their granddaughter but hoped she would look after everyone from above. Before leaving the room, they prayed for her salvation while tears rolled down their faces. In his career Ethan had counseled parents on the grief of losing a child. Having never gone through it himself, it was difficult to relate to, but now he understood their pain. He loved his little girl more than she could ever have known. As Anne's parents left the room, they told her to rest in peace.

Outside of the room Ethan put his arm on Luke's shoulder, giving him the signal it was his turn. Luke had so many things he wished he had said to Anne before this happened. Most importantly, he wanted to thank her for saving Justin and for giving Justin a life filled with happiness. No matter how brief, Justin would always have those memories and feel that love. With her gone, Luke promised that he would be there for Justin and their baby. There was really nothing left to say except that he loved her too. Before leaving, Luke kissed Anne's forehead and told her if there was a God he knew she would be with him.

When he walked out of the room, he saw Jessica standing there. She was crying and ran into Luke's arms as soon as she saw him. They had been able to push aside the bad things from their marriage for the sake of their son, and Luke was glad she was able to come. When she gained her composure, he released her and said it was her turn. Jessica was out of town when this first happened and had not seen her previously. To prepare Jessica, Luke took a moment to let her know how weak Anne looked, hooked up to all the equipment that was keeping her alive. Nothing could prepare Jessica for how Anne looked. When she saw her, Jessica again began to cry. Luke squeezed her hand and asked if she would be okay. Jessica nodded that she would be, and he left them alone. Anne was her sister, and Jessica had no idea how to handle this, so she did the only thing she could think of doing. She went straight to her bed with her make-up case from her purse. There was no reason that everyone had to remember Anne looking this pale. As Jessica applied her make-up, she told Anne how much she meant to her. She couldn't have made it through her divorce without Anne. For that she was extremely grateful to her for always being there. Anne could have turned her back on Jessica, but she didn't. Although Anne never bad-mouthed Luke, she supported her by listening, arranging spa days, and encouraging her to date. Anything that would help Jessica move on. As she applied the make-up, Jessica imagined Anne laughing at her for doing that. She knew that vanity was not Anne. That was more her. It did make Jessica feel like she was doing something for Anne, and that helped Jessica even if Anne wouldn't have cared. When Jessica was satisfied with Anne's appearance, she left the room. As soon as she saw Justin, she hugged him tightly because she didn't have words. She knew her pain was only a fraction of what Justin was feeling, and there was nothing anyone could say to lessen it for him. He returned the hug and stated he was grateful she came. As his nephew's mother she would always be family and have a place in his heart too. It was Anne who made him see that.

Justin could see Anne as he held Jessica and knew what she had done. He gave a slight smile because that was so Jessica. When Jessica left the room, it was his turn. The entire time everyone was with Anne Justin had been thinking about what he would say. There was so much that he wanted to tell her, and no way to do it in a short amount of time. He began by expressing that she was the most amazing woman he ever met. She could never know the depth of the love he felt for her. In his heart, he knew she would have been an amazing mother and loved their daughter with everything she had. Justin made a promise that their daughter would grow up knowing how much her mother loved her. He would make sure of that. As he said his goodbyes, he once again urged her to fight. To prove the doctors wrong. She had so much to live for, and he wasn't sure he could do it alone. Their daughter needed her. If she was tired and needed to leave, he would make sure their love would live on in him, and he would do his best to make her proud. As he kissed her lips for what might be the final time the doctors entered, and the entire family came back. They all wanted to be there with her as she left Earth, hoping that she would feel the love. There was silence in the room as they turned off the machines until Ethan said another prayer. All eyes were on Anne. Martha held one hand while Justin held the other. Justin had become accustomed to the beeping sound and found the silence deafening. In his mind, he still was urging her to fight. It was almost as though Anne heard him because seconds later, she began to breathe on her own. Justin had his miracle or so he believed. He placed her hand against his face, relaying that he knew that she wasn't ready to leave yet. Everyone was astonished. Jessica placed her hands on Justin's shoulder while Luke and Anne's parents pulled the doctors outside the room to see what this meant. They too were hopeful this meant that Anne would recover and wanted to hear it from the doctors. Dr. Castillo was very cold to Luke after seeing him drive away with Lena and couldn't hide his bitterness. He addressed only Anne's parents by saying that Anne surviving without life support did not mean that their diagnosis was incorrect. Dr. Lee saw the coldness with which Dr. Castillo was explaining and interjected. The family was hopeful, and she knew she had to be delicate. Gently, she explained that although she was surprised at this outcome, it sadly did not mean Anne would recover. Some patients with severe brain damage are capable of living without life support. Unfortunately, that didn't mean Anne wouldn't live in a constant vegetative state. Although uncommon in these instances, they would take the wait-and-see approach. She apologized as she told the family it was only a matter of time before she passed away. That time frame could be one day or ten years; she didn't know. Her bullet wound was recovering nicely, and soon the hospital would need to release her. The family needed to figure out the next steps. Dr. Lee continued by saying there were recovery centers equipped to care for people in Anne's condition. As the family digested what they were being told, Luke wondered how he would tell Justin. For the first time in days Justin had hope. How was he going to take that away from him?

Before taking leave both doctors apologized that the news wasn't better. Dazed and confused, Martha decided she needed to be with her granddaughter and left to do just that. The baby was making a lot of progress, and everyone was thrilled. At this point there was only one setback. She had a hernia and needed surgery but made it through perfectly. The baby was a real fighter. Martha needed to feel Anne's life would go on. To say goodbye and get hope only to have the hope crushed seemed cruel, and Martha needed something that would give her hope again. That was Anne's baby.

When Martha left Ethan told Luke that he needed to go to the chapel to pray for guidance. He felt the same way Martha did and chose to seek guidance from a higher power. Luke tried to ask for guidance about the best approach with Justin, but at that moment, Ethan was drained. He couldn't offer advice when his own emotions were everywhere. Luke understood. Anne was his child, and Luke could only imagine the devastation he and Martha felt. Still Luke knew he was facing a major problem. He had no idea how to tell Justin what they had learned, and he wasn't even sure he wanted to. If Justin held onto hope, he was still with Luke. Before crushing Justin again, Luke decided it was time for him to look for a specialist in this area. They were at a highly rated hospital, but new research happened daily. Maybe he could find someone who was working on emerging research. Money was no problem, and Anne deserved a chance if there was one.

****

After Ethan returned from the chapel, he ran into Luke. Ethan felt calmer and offered to speak with Justin about the next steps. That is when Luke told him about his decision to find a specialist to seek his own second opinion. He further explained that Justin's hope had been renewed, and he did not want that taken away until they were positive there was no room for it. Since the doctors were convinced, Anne wouldn't survive being taken off life support, it was possible they were wrong about that too. Ethan wasn't sure he could handle another disappointment. Even though he appreciated Luke's tenacity and knew his heart was in the right place, Ethan warned Luke about giving more hope that might not materialize.

That was understood Luke knew he needed to tread lightly and wanted to speak with someone he could trust. The first person he thought of was Lena. She had a medical background, and she seemed to really care. Plus, he trusted that she would keep this confidential. The last thing Justin needed was reporters circling around him. Once the decision was made, Luke did not want to wait another minute to get the information he needed and went to the ER to seek her out. It had been some time since he had seen Lena, and he was excited at the prospect of seeing her. He genuinely wanted her advice, but he also knew as someone with hospital connections he could ask anyone for help. It was her that made his heartbeat faster, and he could not wait to see her again. While in the ER, Luke learned that Lena was not scheduled to work. That didn't work for Luke, and he felt an urgency to see her again. He tried to tell himself that it was because of his desire to start his search for a specialist, but the truth was he hadn't been able to get her out of his mind. In desperation, Luke drove to Lena's apartment. The entire way he thought about their kiss. It had been the one thing that had been getting through this dire situation. She was the bright spot, and he needed a fix. Silently he thought it was interesting Martha had the baby, Ethan had God, and Lena was what he needed to cope with the day. He only knew her for a short time, so it was odd that he felt that way, but he did. Since traffic was terrible, he had plenty of time to think about what he wanted to say. What he really wanted to do when he saw her was grab her and make her his, but he had to focus on the goal. There would be time for his desires later, and he was determined that there would be time one day.

As he drove through her neighborhood, he again wished she didn't live there. He hated the idea of her walking the streets alone at night and wondered if he should offer to buy her a car for all her help. If he did offer, he knew she would not accept. From what he had seen, she was one of the very few people in the world who were pure of heart. By the time he arrived at her apartment, he had planned exactly what he was going to say to allow him to ask for help while still seeming in control. The truth was for the first time in Luke's life he was not in control, and he hated that feeling. It was not just Justin's situation that made him at a loss. His feelings for Lena were also foreign. As hard as he tried, he could not get control of any of them, and it was torture. When he knocked on the door, there was no response. Distressed he went back to his car to wait for her return. The neighborhood looked no better in the daylight. All he could think about as he waited was Lena living alone in an unsafe neighborhood. He wondered if he could find a way to better her living conditions. While trying to understand his thoughts, Lena started walking up the sidewalk. It was obvious from the way she was dressed that she was coming back from the gym. The tight yoga pants and a half-tank top showcased every curve and left nothing to the imagination. As he looked at her outfit, desire filled Luke. He tried to get control by focusing away from her body. When he did, he noticed that her hair was up which brought his attention to her neck. Luke could not help but marvel at her beauty. There was no way he could bring himself to look away while he remembered their kiss and felt his member growing firmer. As he stared Luke began to wonder what her face would look like in mid-orgasm, calling out his name in pleasure. While watching her enter her apartment complex, Lena put the bag of groceries she had been carrying down to look for her keys in her gym bag. After she found them, she bent over to pick up the bags. That was Luke's undoing. It was not the time to have his way with Lena. Instead, he quickly called Tabatha. He was in the mood for role-play and asked her to pick up some scrubs before meeting him that night. She was to be at his house at seven. Without hesitation, Tabatha agreed. Luke knew that she was becoming attached, and the time to move on was close. It just wasn't the right time.

By the time Luke had gained enough composure to walk into the building and knock on Lena's door, Lena had entered the shower. He could hear the water running through the door. Luke attempted to focus on the paper-thin walls rather than on Lena in the shower. That was impossible because he knew beyond that door was Lena naked with glistening water droplets. Every fiber of his being wanted to walk in and join her in the shower. He had to stop himself for two reasons. The first was that he had no idea if she was feeling what he was feeling. The second and most important was he was there for Justin and not his needs. Even though his body ached with desire, he needed to focus more on the task at hand. There was nothing more important than Justin and Anne. After a few minutes, he heard the water turn off. During his drive over and wait he practiced what to say a thousand times but was still unsure what to say when she opened the door. Part of the problem was that he was not sure what the main ask was. He knew that he wanted to learn about clinical trials that could help Anne.

However, he knew he needed more than that. Luke needed her advice on how to help Justin as well. When he felt enough time had passed, he knocked on the door.

Lena wasn't expecting company when she heard the knock. Her initial reaction was that it was a solicitor, or someone lost because it was rare that she had company. In fact, no one besides Gus and the occasional one-night stand ever visited her apartment. Before cracking the door open, Lena had put on a short satin red robe that was barely covered. She hadn't intended on letting anyone in, and the robe covered enough to shoo whoever was at the door away. As she cracked the door open, she was surprised to see Luke. Instantly she wondered if something had happened, but if it had, she was curious why he was there to see her. In her bewilderment, she forgot what she was wearing and fully opened the door. Luke stood in awe of how attractive she was, even fresh from the shower without a stitch of make-up. The robe she was wearing barely covered, and her toned legs were in full view. Although it was tied shut, there was enough cleavage to make him realize the robe was all she had on while her hair fell long and wet from the shower. For a long moment Luke forgot why he was there. His only thought was to push her against the wall and have his way with her. It took all his restraint from doing just that. As Lena followed his stare, she was made aware of what she was wearing. She knew she should be embarrassed, but she was very satisfied with the way he looked at her, full of desire. Instead of putting on more clothes, she decided to have a little fun with him. It was her robe, and she knew how much she could get away with without showing too much. As she asked what brought him there, she slowly allowed one end of the robe to fall to show her naked shoulder. The effect it had on Luke was visible as she could see the want in his emerald, green eyes. She was affected by him too. Luke was dressed in a tight black T-shirt that clung to the ripples in his chest and a pair of khaki shorts. It was obvious that he took good care of himself. Of course, she already knew that having felt his firm arms around her a couple of times. The attraction between the two was evident, each having their own secret fantasies about ravaging the other. Lena knew Luke was dangerous, and although she was okay with teasing, she knew she could never allow herself to take it too far. On the other hand, Luke was fighting his attraction because he could sense this woman was different and was not sure how far he wanted to take things. That, in addition to the fact Luke's priority needed to be Justin gave him the strength to look away and fight his carnal urges. It was Luke who broke the gaze first. Sensing that the game of silently daring one another was over, Lena invited him to sit on the futon while she went into the bathroom to dress. Before she left the room, she offered him something to drink, which he declined. It was easier to talk to her while she was not in the room, so Luke took the opportunity to begin his story about recent events at the hospital. Initially Lena was too lost in her disappointment of breaking the connection to comprehend what Luke was saying. It wasn't until he said that Anne had been taken off the respirator that she started to pay attention. Half-dressed in only a tank top and panties, Lena came out of the bathroom shocked and full of concern. She knew that Anne was critical and that the doctors were thinking that she would not recover. However, she had no idea that they had decided to take her off life support on that day. Secretly, a piece of her heart broke because she could feel how devastated Justin was even without seeing him. This time it was not what Lena was wearing that made Luke's heart flutter. It was the look of genuine sadness that made Luke want to pull her to him. He thought to himself, "pure of heart, just like Anne." Lena needed to know how Justin was and what the plan was as Luke continued with the fact that Anne was still alive. Lena knew that was not unheard of but said it was rare and mentioned it to Luke.

Her response was exactly what Luke was thinking. "It is rare. That's why I am not convinced the doctors know what they are doing."

Lena knew the hospital had some of the best doctors in the world. No one is perfect, but what he was thinking was unlikely.

"Luke Dr. Lee is top of her field, and Dr. Castillo may be an ass, but he definitely doesn't like to lose patients."

"Understood, but there must be some clinical trial somewhere that I can get Anne in."

"Maybe, but Luke, this really isn't my area. I'm an ER nurse. I don't even work in neurology. I wouldn't even know where to begin to tell you to go. Surely, you must know plenty of doctors that would be more helpful than me."

That was a true statement. In his social circle, he knew plenty of specialists, but it was her he sought out because it was she that he trusted. In Luke's world, trust didn't come easy, and he wondered at times if she had ulterior motives. The fact was she could have already sold her story to the media but had not made him choose to believe she was genuinely concerned. Also, as a lawyer he prided himself on being able to sense when someone was lying, and she gave no indication of that. "I do, but you know Anne's case better than any of them and …" Lena knew what he was about to say before he could say it. She was inexplicably vested in this family. Instead of letting him finish, she suggested that the best place to start would be in Europe. If there was a clinical trial in the U.S. that might help Anne she was confident that Dr. Lee would be aware and offered to see if she could get Anne in.

As Ethan did, Lena cautioned about getting Justin's hopes up. If two of the best doctors in the country were saying they needed to consider long-term care, that is something Justin needed to think about no matter how hard. Even though Luke understood what she was trying to say, he also knew for the first time in days Justin did have hope. His wife survived against all odds, and that gave Justin the evidence that the doctors were wrong. Lena could see that it was not only Justin who had hope renewed. As much as he didn't want to admit it, Luke was also hopeful. If he didn't he wouldn't be looking for a clinical trial. Deep inside, she understood why they were holding on to that. She wanted that for them as well but was trying to be realistic. She saw what a broken heart could do, and she wondered how many times Justin's could break without completely shattering. Without revealing too much about herself, she tried to explain that someone needed to prepare Justin for what was the probable outcome. More than likely what Dr. Lee said was correct. As much as he didn't want to admit it Luke knew she was probably right. He also recognized that Lena seemed to be the only person who was able to get through to his brother. Everyone was trying to help, but whatever she did was what he needed. For that reason, Luke asked if she would talk to Justin about the next steps. It wasn't that she didn't want to help.

In fact she wanted nothing more, but in this instance, she wasn't sure what she could do. She barely knew him and Justin was struggling, so she thought it should be someone close to him that helped. On the other hand, no one understood what Justin was going through better than her. No matter who spoke with him in the end, it was only Justin who could decide when it was time to pick up the pieces. There was a baby involved, and she had promised Anne to fight for her baby. Lena knew it was to fight to save her, but she also felt compelled fight for him to be the father Anne believed he could be. In addition, Luke looked so desperate she couldn't say no. She liked it when Luke dropped his facade and showed his vulnerable side. It almost made her believe he was not as dangerous as she believed him to be. Lena knew that she had to try to help Justin and agreed to go with him.

As soon as she agreed to go to the hospital with Luke, she realized that she was only half dressed and went to the bathroom to finish. Luke felt better that she was going to talk to Justin. This time while Lena was dressing Luke looked around her apartment and realized how small it was. He looked at her kitchen and wondered if there was room for one person in there. There was no sitting area, only the kitchen and bedroom. Luke thought that her whole apartment would fit in his living room. As he continued his exploration something on her night table he had not seen before caught his eye. Lena had left her vibrating friend out from the evening before. It was not like Lena to forget to put it away, but since she never had company in her apartment, she didn't worry if she had. When Lena came out of the bathroom, she caught Luke eyeing her friend and was embarrassed. She hoped they could leave without calling any more attention to it. "I'm ready. Let's go."

Nodding at the device Luke and with hope in his voice he asked, "No boyfriend, huh?" It was really his way of trying to figure out if she was single and hoped he would get the response that he wanted.

Instantly Lena regretted not putting it away. She knew Luke would have to make a comment and choose to be equally flippant. "Who needs a man when I have something that make me come every time without a lot of hassle? Can we go now?"

Lena walked towards the door. Before she opened it Luke gently took her arm, emerald eyes fixed on her blue eyes. "Then I guess you've not been with the right man. A man who knows what he's doing would make you never want to use that again."

His touch and comment sent shivers down Lena's spine. When he released her to open the door, she instantly missed his touch. She was frozen as she pondered once again what it would be like to have Luke naked on top of her. Or would she be the one on top, she wondered? Either way she was convinced it would be hot. Part of her wanted to kiss him and throw him back on the futon to test her theory. His eyes were so dangerous and filled with lust. He smiled slyly as he saw her reaction to him. It was satisfying to know she was as affected by him as he was to her.

"Coming," Luke said as he walked out. Lena wanted to respond that she was about to but decided against it.

In her mind someone with the wealth and social status of his family would only be interested in a quick lay with someone like her. She was broken and damaged and knew that a relationship with someone like Luke was out of the question. Not that Lena was looking for one. There was something about Luke that made her feel like it was more than just sex. Still her dreams cautioned her against it. Lena had changed into a denim mini skirt and grey tank top with sandals. As they walked down the steps of her building, she felt his eyes skimming the back of her body. It gave her a jolt to know that she was desirable even if it could go nowhere. After all, she probably paid less for her entire outfit than Luke had his shorts. Luke opened the door to the complex so that Lena could walk through. When he did, she again marveled at his long fingers, thinking they were probably very skilled. "Stop it," Lena thought to herself. Once they were at the car, Luke again opened the door and waited until she got in to close it before getting in the car himself. Lena didn't realize that men outside the movies opened and closed doors for women. As odd as she thought it to be, it did make her feel special. In the car Lena noticed the music Luke was playing was much different from the dance music the other night. A woman was singing about swinging it. "Who is this?"

"Ella Fitzgerald."

Lena shrugged, "Don't know her, but it's nice."

Luke smirked because he was surprised. He also wondered how young she really was. He was guessing mid to late twenties, but he didn't know for sure. "Really. You don't know Ella Fitzgerald. She's only one of the best singers of all time."

Offended Lena responded snidely, "She can't be that great. I've never heard of her."

With a hint of laughter in Luke's voice he asked. "And who do you listen to? Who would you consider a great?"

Lena tried to think of someone who spoke to her heart. "Well since you are asking, I really like Bruno Mars."

Luke smirked. "Bruno Mars and Ella Fitzgerald are not even in the same realm Lena."

Chastised Lena responded, "You're right. We both know who Bruno Mars is while you are the only one in the car who knows who this Fitzerald lady is."

Luke had to laugh. As crazy as it was it was a valid point, however he could tell from the way that her arms were folded over her chest that she was defensive. The conversation had taken an awkward turn and Luke wanted to change that. It wasn't that he was trying to be rude. In fact, he was genuinely interested in her taste in music when he asked. Luke thought it was best to change the subject. "Thank you."

Her defense mechanism was still heightened. "For what?"

"For helping Justin. I hate to admit it, but I'm at a loss as to what to do. I've watched you together. You seem to always know exactly what he needs."

His admission caught Lena off guard. She wanted to tell Luke that she had no idea how to help and what a disaster she had made of her own life. Since he had so much faith in her she kept quiet. No one except maybe Gus ever had so much confidence in her and it was nice to have another person feel that way about her.

At work Lena was an accomplished nurse who always knew what to do for her patients. In her personal life she was somewhat of a train wreck and was grateful for the fact that Luke had not sensed that even after their encounter the first night. Silently, she wondered if she was better at hiding it than she thought. Then she remembered everything Luke had been going through and decided he was just too preoccupied to notice.

When they arrived at the hospital, Lena became a little nervous. She had no idea what to say to Justin. There was no way she wanted to encourage him to lose hope, especially if Luke was going to try and bring in a specialist. There was a reason Anne held on after the respirator was turned off. Luke studied Lena as she seemed lost in thought and asked what she was thinking. Lena shook her head in response, indicating that she didn't wish to share. Even though Luke wanted to understand her better, he didn't press. It was clear she wasn't someone who liked to share. That was something they had in common. Luke never wanted to let anyone into his darkest thoughts either and he had many. Especially about women. With her it was different. Never would he have considered going to a woman that he didn't know well before to ask for advice. Let alone help. All of this was foreign to him as he was navigating new territory.

Ethan was alone in Anne's room when they entered. He asked Luke for a private moment with him, so Lena went in search of Justin. Ethan wanted to discuss the specialist idea further. Martha wasn't handling these events well and he wanted to make sure until they found someone, they not mention it to either Martha or Justin. Before Luke arrived, Ethan had tried to speak with Justin about moving Anne to a facility, but as expected he shut him down. The fact the Justin was unwilling to even entertain the idea was not a surprise to Luke. That is why he brought someone he hoped would be able to help Justin cope. Ethan wasn't sure it would work, but at that point he was willing to try anything.

Dr. Castillo saw Lena enter the waiting room looking for Justin and decided to follow before she could escape. She was bent over the water cooler, helping herself when he entered. He enjoyed the view from behind and placed his arm on top of the wall above her. This startled Lena as she hadn't expected anyone else in the room.

"Lena, we have some things we need to discuss in private."

He was right she needed to bite the bullet and tell him they worked together and that was it. It was for that reason that she agreed to go back to his office with him. As soon as they arrived Dr. Castillo closed the door. Lena began with as much respect and candor as she could muster. She knew he was a superior, so she couldn't be outright rude. Lena also understood that she had initially encouraged him by their flirtation and asked for a favor, but that didn't give him the right to think she owed him anything. Plus, he was married a man.

"Dr. Castillo I appreciate everything you did to help Anne. That's where it ends though. We won't be having drinks or anything else together. You're a married doctor and I'm a nurse here." She paused for a moment to assess his reaction. By his tightened jaw she could tell it didn't go as she had hoped. With as much courage as she could muster she started to walk out of the office. At the door she stopped to say, "I hope we can maintain a working relationship, but that's as far as it will ever be."

Before she could open the door to leave, Dr. Castillo spoke. He was clearly annoyed. "If your finished I want to explain this to you." He moved closer while Lena moved back. "You asked for a favor. I don't do favors unless there's something in it for me. By pulling me into this case you put my reputation on the line and I'm damn well going to collect what is owed."

Lena could not believe her ears, who was this man in front her? How had she not noticed what a pompous ass the man before her was? She knew he was arrogant, but this took things to a new level. As she was about to tell him exactly what she thought of him he landed an unwelcome kiss on her. When she was unable to push him off her, she tried to shake him lose, but his hold was too tight.

"You know I can make you feel so good. This playing hard to get act was a turn on at first but it is getting old."

Angrily and with a bit of panic Lena shouted, "This isn't a game. Let me go."

In his mind he was getting what was owed and threw her down on the black leather sofa in his office while claiming they had waited long enough. Before Dr. Castillo could get on top of her, Lena kicked him hard in the groin. He screamed in pain that she was a "little bitch" while she ran out of his office as quickly as she could. As she was running out Justin saw her. He was going up to Dr. Castillo's office to speak with him at the request of Ethan. Instantly he recognized Lena's duress and called out to her. Without thinking, Lena ran right into his arms shaking and crying. Justin could feel her heart beating rapidly as she sobbed and did not let her go. With Justin's arms wrapped around her Lena felt safe. Safer than she had felt in a long time. Even more than when Luke held her. She relished the feel of his arms as he calmed her down. He was physically strong. When he held her, she believed no one could hurt her. As she was in Justin's arms, Dr. Castillo recovered from her assault and came out looking for her. It didn't take Justin long to realize that whatever had upset Lena had to do with Dr. Castillo.

Justin released her long enough to ask, "What did he do to you? Did he hurt you?"

Lena gave a half smile remembering that it was she who had hurt him. It could have gone a different way if Gus had not insisted, she take self-defense lessons. It was one of the many times in her life that she was grateful for Gus. She wasn't ready to share and responded the best way she could. "No. Not really."

Justin wasn't about to let this go. He already wasn't a fan of Dr. Castillo's and could sense she was hiding something, "What do you mean not really? Did the asshole touch you?"

At this point Lena had regained her composure and wanted to forget what had just happened although she was more confident in her resolve to avoid him at all costs, "I'm fine. Just forget about it."

Justin had no intention of forgetting about anything. As Dr. Castillo approached them, Justin released Lena and walked towards him. He didn't have the full story, but he knew Dr. Castillo's type. The doctor was a self-entitled asshole. There was no way he was going to let him walk all over Lena. In a firm voice he warned Dr. Castillo to stay away from her. If he didn't he would make sure that the hospital board was made aware of his actions. Dr. Castillo knew the Armstrong family did have the clout to make the threat a reality and walked straight past Lena in a huff. The look in his eyes made Lena shutter because she knew he was a man who was used to getting his way. If the rumors were true, she wasn't the only nurse he had pursued. She did seem to be the only one who refused the advances through. Although Lena was grateful for Justin's protection, she wondered if he hadn't made things worse. Dr. Castillo was a respected doctor at the top of his field, and she was just an ER nurse.

On his way to Justin and Lena, Luke passed a very angry Dr. Castillo. As soon as he saw Lena's face, Luke knew something had happened. Her usual tan face was pale, and from the mascara stains under her big, blue eyes it was clear she had been crying. Her body was tense while Justin was clenching his fists in anger. It was obvious Luke had missed something, and he wanted to know what it was. Justin wasn't even sure what the story was. Lena wasn't about to explain to either one of them what just happened even if she was grateful for the interference. Instead of recanting the event she excused herself to the bathroom. She needed time to process what had happened in the office. In the bathroom she washed her face to fix herself up and clear her head. In the mirror, she saw that her eyes were swollen from crying, but it was the look in her eyes that gave away her fear. She knew that look; it wasn't the first time she felt so afraid. That was a long time ago though. Lena was no longer a scared fifteen-year-old girl; she was now a woman who could protect herself. Quietly and with some amusement she wondered why both Armstrong men didn't think she was insane. She had been there to help Justin while he was the one who helped her instead. After this scene, she thought he wouldn't listen to anything that she had to say.

Concerned, Justin and Luke waited in the hallway near the bathroom. While they waited Luke pressed Justin for answers. All he could reveal is that Lena looked terrified when she came running out of Dr. Castillo's office. As Justin spoke, Luke could feel the anger register deep inside him. It appeared that Justin was feeling the same way. His face was tense like he wanted to hurt something. Luke was happy to see something other than the lost look on his brother's face and knew his brother's compassion was still instead of him. His heart hadn't changed, and relief filled Luke.

When Lena was fixed up, she left the bathroom hoping that by then both Justin and Luke had left. She was humiliated she didn't want to see either man. No such luck, they were both exactly where she left them. Rapidly she exited, walking opposite where they were standing. Although she was honored by their concern, she had no intention of discussing this with virtual strangers. All she wanted was air and space. Since she knew it was inevitable she would see Dr. Castillo again she had to think of what the best way to handle it was. They saw her leave and this time Luke went after her. With genuine concern Luke approached Lena as she waited for the elevator. He put his hand on her arm and asked if she was okay. His touch was gentle, but because of what had just happened Lena didn't feel the charge she had the other times he touched her. All she wanted to do was leave.

His question about her being okay loomed. It was a trick question. Was she okay? It felt like she hadn't been truly okay since the night her father died. Luke wouldn't understand and even if he would, she wasn't about to test the waters. "I'm fine. I just need to go home."

There was no confidence in her response. Clearly something had happened, but as much as Luke wanted to know what it was, he needed to make sure she was fine even more. "I brought you here, so it's only fair I take you home."

As much as she appreciated the offer, she couldn't see herself sitting in a car with him or anyone at that moment and declined, saying she needed time alone.

When the elevator doors opened Lena quickly stepped in while Luke followed. He wasn't about to accept her response. Luke was used to being in control. The last several days had presented a real challenge for him. Luke could not save Anne, help his brother or niece and at that moment he was unable to even get this woman to accept a ride home. Of all the things that he could not control he damn well was going to see to it that this woman got home safely. As the door opened Luke was stopped by a hospital board member who was a client. He was hoping to get information on Anne. All Luke wanted was to be with Lena, but before he could excuse himself from the elderly gentlemen she was gone. He quickly ran to the garage where his car was to see if he could catch her.

By the time they left the hospital it was dusk. Through tear-filled eyes Lena looked at the sky almost hidden by the tall New York City buildings. She wondered how in the face of everything she had experienced the past week there was still such beauty in the world. The thought made her smile because it gave her a sense that everything would be okay. "Thank you, Daddy. I feel you here," she whispered to herself as she entered the subway station. The subway was more crowded than usual, so she had to stand. "Lena," someone called out from the crowd. When she looked around, she saw Trey moving toward her. "Great. As if things weren't bad enough," she thought to herself. Trey gave her a huge bear hug. To her surprise, he acted as if they were old friends as he asked her how she had been. It was odd, but since she had been the one to wrong him, she went along with it. After exchanging pleasantries, they continued to talk about music and his job. Trey was a welcome distraction and by the time the subway came to Lena's stop she felt better. It was nice to have some idle conversation.

"This is me. It was nice seeing you again." This time she meant it.

It wasn't goodbye as he responded, "I'm getting off here too. I'm going to meet some friends at the bar we met at. Do you want to join?"

Lena pondered the invitation. It might be exactly what she needed, but she needed to make sure Trey understood she had no interest in a repeat of what happened the night they met.

Trey's response was one of amusement and teasing. "You mean the night you don't remember. I think you'll be safe."

At that Lena smiled and agreed. His playful banter was a welcome change from the seriousness of the last several days.

The bar was on the corner of Lena's apartment complex. At the opposite end of the street was where Luke had seen the drug deal. It was a dive bar, but a lot of young people went there to forget their troubles, play some pool or shoot darts. Lena felt comfortable there and was looking forward to a carefree night.

By the time Luke had his car and left the parking garage he missed Lena. Instead of driving her home, he found himself waiting outside her apartment building wanting to make sure that she arrived safely, not fully understanding why he cared so much. When he saw Lena walking, he realized that she wasn't alone. "Who the hell is this mother fucker," he thought to himself. She seemed familiar with him, but he was relieved to see that she was not overly familiar with him. They were walking closely, conversing, however they weren't touching in any manner. Lena and Trey were laughing as they walked past her apartment to the corner bar oblivious to the fact Luke was staring intently. He watched every move wondering why he had been reduced to a stalker. Even though he wondered what was happening to him, he couldn't look away. For a minute Luke contemplated going into the bar. Since he knew there would be no other way to explain his presence other than he was there to see her, he had to consider his next move carefully. As he sat with conflicted emotions, his phone rang. It was Tabatha wondering where he was. Joyce, the housekeeper, let her in and she was anxious for Luke's arrival.

With his thoughts on Lena, Luke had forgotten about Tabatha. Momentarily he thought about telling her that he couldn't make it after all. Since there was not much he could do with the Lena situation, he decided to go home because she was there already. The entire drive back to his apartment visions of Lena haunted him. He saw her face when he found her with Justin and imagined their kiss. What upset him most to think about was the smile she had when she was walking with that man. It was a beautiful smile. More upsetting was it was not for him. As hard as Luke tried, he couldn't get her out of his head.

Tabatha was ready and waiting for Luke in the bedroom when he entered the apartment. As Luke had requested, she was dressed in scrubs though she found that odd. Tabatha thought the naughty nurse role would suit her better if she were dressed in a short, tight uniform instead. The doctor would come in and see how naughty she was. He would punish her before taking her all night. Even though Tabatha thought the scrubs were a weird idea, it was Luke's fantasy, and she was willing to comply. Luke in no way felt the way he thought he would with Tabatha in the scrubs. Instead of taking his mind off Lena all it did was further remind him of her and what she might be doing at the bar. Luke's normal insatiable appetite for sex was lost. At least it was for Tabatha. He apologized for changing his mind using that he was too worried about Justin to focus on having a good time as an excuse. Tabatha was not about to leave. She insisted that she had the medicine that would make him forget his troubles while slowly undressing. After she was naked, she moved closer to Luke to pull down his shorts and boxers to take hold of his manhood. While she caressed him Luke shut his eyes and again began picturing Lena. Once his member was firm Tabatha started kissing the rim. As her mouth and tongue circled, he found himself picturing the way Lena's breast felt, her tight behind and abs, her smile and her beautiful eyes. With those thoughts Luke found his release in no time. Still keeping his thoughts on Lena, he threw Tabatha to the bed and kissed her passionately. To keep the fantasy a reality he closed his eyes. As soon as he pictured Lena he slowed and was gentle. This wasn't the first time when they were having sex that he pictured Lena. On their last sexual encounter, he did the same thing. The first time he pictured Lena it was about animal lust. This time there was more to it. He was genuinely concerned for Lena and allowed that emotion to show through in his sexual encounter with Tabatha. It reflected in the way he touched and kissed Tabatha. Once they both found their release, Luke opened his eyes. His images had been so clear that briefly he was surprised it was Tabatha in his bed. "What is this woman doing to me," he thought to himself. In Tabatha's mind they had made love. Finally, she felt as if after all this time their relationship was heading in the right direction. She had no idea the role playing was not about her. When she kissed the pecks of his chest Luke tensed up. Even though she sensed it, she assumed it was her imagination and continued to snuggle into his chest, still feeling that they had never been closer. While Tabatha was lost in her thoughts Luke again wondered how to get rid of her. When he realized it was after ten, he excused himself to check his phone to see if Justin had called. It wasn't just an excuse because he was genuinely worried about Justin. Even though Justin hadn't called, he told Tabatha that Justin needed him to get back to the hospital. That was the perfect excuse to get her to leave. She was very understanding and even offered to go with him, which he declined.

Once Tabatha was gone Luke tried to lose himself in his work. His father wanted results, but he was too distracted with Justin and Lena. While writing a legal brief Luke found himself wondering what Lena was doing at that moment. As hard as Luke tried to focus on work, he still found himself getting dressed in jeans and a blue button-down shirt and heading back to Brooklyn.

****

At the bar Lena was having a great time with Trey and his friends. She found herself saddened at the way she and Trey had met because he was a great guy. With their history there was no way to pursue a normal relationship other than friendship. Even that was tricky after sex. There were six tables in total at the bar with a dance floor in the middle. The bar itself was old and wooden with ten bar stools. To the left of the bar was where people shot darts. In the back there were two pool tables. That night the bar was only mildly busy, but Lena was having so much fun she didn't care who else was there. Since Tequila usually got Lena in trouble, she found herself drinking beers and playing pool with the guys. Lena was an experienced pool player and beat everyone in the group at least once. It was nice to not think about the dramatic turn her life had taken even if it was only for one night. Trey was ruggedly good looking and very attentive to Lena. One of Trey's friends was an up-and-coming comedian. He kept the group laughing with his jokes and stories from his act. Will, the comedian, told Lena that he was opening at The Comic Strip in a couple of weeks and invited her to the show. Since there was no band or DJ that night no one was dancing. As much as Lena loved to dance on that night it did not matter. When "last call" came Lena found herself disappointed that the evening would soon be over. All of Trey's friends and Trey walked Lena home on their way to the subway station. After they reached her complex, she hugged each one goodbye. Trey stayed behind and told his friends he would catch up to them. It was clear that Trey liked Lena as he leaned in to kiss her cheek goodnight. The kiss was gentle and tender. For a moment she thought about inviting him up. Instead, she gave him her number. As she added it to his phone, she assured him that if he called, she would answer. When Trey offered to walk her up to her door, she declined, thinking that it could be dangerous for their blossoming friendship. It was after two in the morning and Luke observed the whole interaction from the street in his car. It seemed to him that there was something going on between the two of them but he was relieved to see Trey leave without even a goodnight kiss. He had been waiting outside her apartment for the better part of an hour and was thrilled Lena was going to bed alone.

As Lena opened the door to her complex Luke couldn't stop himself from calling out to her. She turned to see Luke standing in the shadows of the night lights. The lights accented the highlights in his hair and Lena thought he was the most handsome man she had ever seen. At that moment she wanted to go running into his arms and kiss him passionately. She would have done just that if she hadn't sensed his hesitation. It was clear Luke was apprehensive as he moved towards her. He was cursing himself for calling out to her because he had to make an excuse for being there at such a late hour as she questioned him.

"What are you doing here? Did something happen to Anne or the baby?"

Usually, Luke was able to think quickly on his feet. All that seemed lost in the presence of Lena. Every excuse he could come up with made him seem like the stalker he was. There was no way he was going to tell her the truth, which was that he just wanted to see her. To be near her. "No everyone is the same."

Relief filled Lena, but she was more confused than ever. "So, what are you doing here?"

Luke said nothing but continued to move towards her. From his silence Lena assumed that he was there to continue their sexual banter. After what happened with Dr. Castillo, she knew she was not in the right state of mind to make any decisions about Luke. She was worried the temptation of his presence might be too much for her to resist. More than that she feared she had become too emotionally involved and would not allow herself to get hurt. "Luke, wait. Don't take another step. I can't do this with you now. Please leave."

All Luke wanted to do was pull her into an embrace and he continued to move forward. When he was in front of her, she stepped back. He was upset by her move. "Please listen to me for one second?"

It was a long night, and she was in a good headspace. She didn't need Luke to mess that up. "I really can't do this with you. Not now. Not ever. I think it's best we just stay in our separate corners of the world. Please just let me be."

Luke was confused. Outside of being a slight stalker, he had no idea what he did wrong. "What? Where's this coming from?"

"Why are you here?" She asked exasperated.

"I wanted to make sure you were, okay?"

"At two in the morning. Come one Luke. The only reason that a man shows up at a woman's house at this hour is for a booty call. It's been a long day. I need to go to bed alone."

She turned to open the door. He wanted to tell her that she was misunderstanding why he was there. If he could just touch her, she would know. Even if that was what he was thinking the words wouldn't come out of his mouth. Her message was clear, and he stood on her stoop watching her walk up the stairs to her apartment. To his disappointment she never turned to look back. Luke was hurt and walked towards his car more confused than he had ever been in his life. He tried to reassure himself as he reached his car, "It was better that way." At least now he could focus on his priorities; Justin and work. Finally, he could get his mind off Lena.

From the window inside her building Lena watched as Luke drove off. She had such a great evening after the afternoon ended up so badly. After her conversation with Luke, she was once again upset. Even though she knew it was for the best if she stayed away, telling him it still hurt. She didn't want to go down that dark path she was in several years ago. For a moment she thought of calling Trey back. That wasn't a good idea either and she decided she should go to bed alone. After tossing and turning for hours she finally fell asleep. Around 4 a.m. she was awakened by a nightmare. It was still dark outside, and she was alone in her apartment. She turned on her bedside light and rolled up in a ball while crying. It had been several years since her last nightmare, but it was just as terrifying. When she used to have them as a teenager Gus would come running into her room to comfort her. As an adult, she was all alone.

At the age of fifteen it was clear Lena's mother was no longer able to take proper care of her. That was when Lena went to live with Gus. Gus had promised Lena's father that he would take care of her and her mother. He did the best he could by them, but Lena's mother fell apart after her father's death. No matter what he did, he couldn't get through to her. Many times, Lena would hear him pleading with her mother to get control of her life. He knew Lena needed a mother, but she was too lost herself to be there for Lena. After deciding there was no way to pull her to the light, Gus concentrated his attention on Lena even though he would never fully cut her mother from his life. The promise he made to her father was too important, yet he knew Lena needed him more. He had helped her through a very dark time. No matter what, Gus was there for her, and she knew it was coming from love and not the promise he made. If hadn't been so late she might have called him. He had a way of getting rid of the nightmares. However, it was late, and she knew he had been working around the clock to solve Anne's case. There was no point in worrying him because of a nightmare. He would know something had happened to trigger them and she wasn't mentally in a place to explain. Alone she grabbed her bear that the ER nurse had given her the night her father died. It was the only thing she had from her childhood. She kept it nearby. In a way she felt closer to her father when she held it. That gave her comfort, and she was able to go back to sleep.

****

Unable to sleep once he was home, Luke went into his home office to research clinical trials in Europe. His office was one of his favorite rooms in the apartment as it had a large window with a view overlooking the City which somehow made him feel powerful. The desk he had was a family heirloom given to him by his maternal grandfather who meant a great deal to him. On the desk was a picture of him, Justin and his son James on vacation at the family home in St. Thomas. As he looked at the picture, he remembered it was Anne who had taken it. She was a big part of a lot of his happy family memories. James loved Anne. They all did. Somehow, he had to try to make things right and started sorting through the list of clinical trials on vegetative states the law firm's research department provided. After his conversation with Lena, he had asked them to look at all the neurological clinical trials they could find. The one with the most promise was being conducted by a doctor in France. This doctor's treatment seemed to have a great success rate on people with severe brain damage. Quickly he e-mailed the doctor to make an appointment to discuss Anne. As an extra incentive he hinted that there might be financial gratification to assist in funding her continued research. After the e-mail was sent Luke was exhausted. With no desire to walk upstairs, he laid down on the leather sofa in his office. This wasn't the first time he slept on the sofa so there was always a blanket hanging around the back. He pulled the throw blanket over him and quickly fell asleep. That night he dreamt of Lena's blue eyes. It was not the sexual dreams he was used to having. Instead, it was almost a slide show of all their encounters. From the first moment he held her outside, to their kiss and lastly the look on her face when she saw him standing outside her apartment that night. All the images were there.

Chapter Seven

When Luke awoke in the morning, he was visibly aroused. That was not uncommon. What was uncommon was the unsettled feeling he had. He couldn't understand why this woman had consumed so many of his thoughts. He needed to get her out of his head. His thoughts were interrupted by a knock on the door. It must have been later than Luke thought because his housekeeper had already arrived at the penthouse and came into the office with coffee, eggs and bacon. As Luke drank his coffee, he noticed that he had received a response from the doctor who had agreed to meet with him. In the email she offered no promises about adding Anne to her trial, however, she did agree to look at her medical records. Even though Luke knew he could have the records sent, he thought a trip to France might be exactly what he needed to get his head straight. While he was in France, he could appease his father with meeting with a couple of their international clients, and sent an email to his secretary asking her to schedule the meetings. He also requested that she make his travel arrangements as he was planning on leaving later that day. With everything in place Luke headed to the hospital to see Justin and gently let Justin know his plan. If there had been another way to get the records without getting Justin's hopes up, he may have considered it, but since he had the power of attorney it was Justin who had to make the request.

****

It was odd. Until this happened Luke had spent very little time at the hospital. He would go there for an occasional meeting with a client who was a board member. Now he felt as if he knew every square foot of the building he hoped never to visit again. Initially, Luke sought Justin out in Anne's room. When he didn't see him there, he went to the NICU. It was there that Luke found Justin with the baby who was getting stronger every day. While Justin was looking at the baby Luke noticed he seemed so much lighter. The color had returned to his face and there was even a hint of a smile as he looked at his beautiful daughter. It was clear he was hopeful. As soon as Justin saw Luke in the window, he waved him in. While Luke dressed for the NICU, he thought about the best way to approach the topic.

Luke didn't want to do anything that might be detrimental to Justin's emotional state, so as he explained his plans he warned not to be overly optimistic. "I'm not making any promises, but I'll see if there's something this doctor can do for Anne. I think it's time we find a new doctor anyway. Dr. Lee seems okay, but Dr. Castillo is a total asshole."

To that Justin agreed. He was thankful that Luke wasn't giving up and hugged his brother out of gratitude. Everyone else he spoke with was telling him that he shouldn't have hope. It was a relief that someone else was still fighting too. Justin was grateful to Luke for exploring other options, although it wasn't surprising since Luke and Anne were the only people he could ever truly count on. Even if it didn't work out Justin was still appreciative Luke sought this specialist out. It was the first time since Anne coded that someone besides him was being positive, and Justin believed that together they might be able to help Anne. That meant agreeing to get her records from Dr. Castillo. At the mention of Dr. Castillo, Justin thought of Lena. "Did you catch up with Lena yesterday? Is she okay?"

Luke shook his head, "I couldn't catch her." He didn't want to lie, but he also didn't want to share with his brother that he had been reduced to a stalker. To change the subject Luke said that he was short on time. "Are you going to be okay while I'm away?"

That was an interesting question as Justin wondered if there was no more Anne if he would ever be okay again. He didn't want his brother worried, "Luke, Ethan and Martha are still here. I'll call you if there is any news. I need you to do this trip. If there is any way this doctor can help, I need to know. Don't worry about me. Just keep me updated."

Luke knew what Justin was saying was true and handed him a card with an email address for Justin to have the records sent as soon as possible. It would be best if the specialist had time to review her records before they met in France.

Luke had one stop to make before his trip and that was to find Dr. Castillo. Even if Lena didn't want him in her life, there were still some things they needed to discuss. He needed to ensure Lena was protected. He didn't have far to look because Dr. Castillo was in his office. First Luke told him about the specialist. To that Dr. Castillo arrogantly responded that it was a waste of time, but it was his money to waste. He was glad Luke was leaving and believed without his interference it would finally be his time with Lena. It was clear Dr. Castillo didn't like Luke as much as Luke didn't like him. Condescendingly, he explained any request for records would have to come from Justin. Luke wanted to wipe the smug grin off of the doctor's face but refrained from doing so because he was still Anne's doctor, even if he hoped that would soon change.

In a serious and forceful tone Luke spoke, "Justin will make the request, and I expect your full cooperation. There's something else we need to talk about."

Dr. Castillo knew Luke wanted to talk about Lena. It wasn't a conversation he wanted to have. "I agree to get the records to your specialist if your brother issues a request. Now I'm a busy man and feel we have nothing else to say to one another."

Dr. Castillo motioned to the door for Luke to leave. That was not going to happen until he had his say. "I'm not quite ready to leave yet. You and I have something else to talk about."

The doctor responded, "We are both busy men and besides my patient who is really not your concern, we have nothing to talk about."

His smug attitude was not a deterrent for Luke who lowered his voice and got close, "I know what you are doing to Lena McKay and the harassment stops now. I have many influential friends at this hospital and believe me you do not want to make an enemy out of me."

And there it was. The threat Dr. Castillo was prepared for, "I have no idea what she told you and frankly I don't care. You can't believe her. The woman is unstable." He could tell Luke didn't believe and continued, "I'm sure with your influence you could get her medical records. Go ahead. Check. I was the attending physician when they brought her in bleeding and full of pills. Once that got out no one would believe her or you."

This information caught Luke off guard even though he pretended otherwise. That didn't excuse the behavior Luke had witnessed and he still felt protective of Lena. Before leaving Luke threatened, "You want to try me go ahead. I'm a very powerful enemy and I'll bring you down."

Although he gave nothing away to the doctor, Luke had to question the validity of Dr. Castillo's information. Truth be told he knew very little about Lena. She appeared out of nowhere and seemed to be everywhere. If she was unstable, he had to know. She was getting close to Justin and as vulnerable as Justin was at that point, Luke needed to look out for him. In his heart he knew that there had to be some explanation. He was excellent at reading people. Maybe she was different but not unhinged. As much time as they had spent with her, there was no indication that the doctor was telling the truth. Still, he had to know and called a private investigator the law firm uses to perform a background check on Lena.

****

The next morning Lena was still shaken by her nightmare. The first thing she did when she woke up was call Gus. Even though she didn't want to tell him about her nightmare because he might ask questions about what triggered them to return, she needed to hear a caring voice. It wasn't until Gus asked her what was wrong that she realized how shaky her voice was. He knew her so well that she should have known better that she would be able to hide how upset she was from him. As much as she wanted to reassure him that all was well, it wasn't the truth. She needed someone to talk to and finally broke down and told him about her nightmare. Gus was immediately concerned and asked the question she dreaded. There was no way she wanted to tell him about her altercation with Dr. Castillo. If she did, she knew he would confront the doctor and make everything worse for her. There was no way out but to lie and tell him that she had no idea what caused the nightmares to return. Lena hated lying to Gus because that wasn't how their relationship worked. This time she told herself it was for everyone's protection. She would handle Dr. Castillo on her own. That didn't mean it was easy for her to lie, and she hesitated as she questioned if she should. From the pause Gus knew that she was holding information back from him. He also knew her well enough to not push her. What he did suggest was that she go back to speak with her survivors' group. Even before he could get the words "survivors' group" out Lena cut him off. She wanted to put her past behind her. Not relive it.

Many nights when Lena was fifteen her mother's live-in boyfriend came into her room to force himself on her. The thought of him touching her was unfathomable and she would fight. Oh boy would she fight, but he was much larger and stronger than she and he would always win. Some nights she would just let it happen because there was no point in trying to struggle and she didn't have the strength. Her mother never heard her scream because she passed out. One night after he left her, she felt so alone and decided to end her life. She couldn't take another night of the fat slob, naked on top of her smelling of cheap booze and cigarettes. All she wanted was to be with her father. In his arms, she was loved and safe. When she was sure her mother and the bastard were both asleep, she went into her mother's bathroom and found some of her sleeping pills in the medicine cabinet. This had been something she had been thinking about doing for a while and had researched the best way to take her life with the least amount of pain. The sleeping pills would provide peace while splitting her wrists would make sure it happened. After taking a handful of pills, she cut her wrists. All she could think about was soon her suffering would be over. As she was drifting and covered in blood, she felt she owed Gus a goodbye. He had been good to her, and she knew he would be upset. Over the phone her voice was weak as she thanked him for everything. Gus knew instantly that something was wrong. He tried to keep her on the phone as he put on his police siren and drove to her apartment, but she had fallen asleep. He made it to Lena's apartment in record time. When he arrived, he knocked, but there was no answer. Terrified, he broke the door down. By the time he arrived, Lena was covered in her own blood. After calling for an ambulance he started CPR. At that point, her mother woke up wanting to know what had happened. She rode with Lena to the hospital while Gus and her mother's boyfriend followed. The doctors worked for hours pumping her stomach and repairing the damage. While they worked on her, they discovered that she had been raped. Once the doctors stabilized Lena, they shared their findings with her mother and Gus. It didn't take a detective to know what had been happening. He had noticed a change in Lena's demeanor. Initially, he passed it off as teen hormones, but with this new information, everything made sense. As Lena's mother sat puzzled, Gus threw her boyfriend against the wall warning him that as soon as Lena woke up, he was going to take great joy in arresting him. The entire time Lena's mother was quiet. Furious Gus pleaded with her to put her life back together. Lena needed her more than ever. A single tear fell down her cheek indicating that she heard what he was saying, but that was the only sign. When Gus threatened to take Lena if she couldn't, she stood up and asked him to help Lena before leaving the hospital. He tried to stop her, but she was determined. That was the last time Lena saw her mother.

Lena could never forgive her mother for not being there to support her when she needed it the most. The next several years Lena spent picking up the pieces of her life. Her mother didn't try to make contact after she left the hospital that night. For the first ten years of her life, Lena was happy. She was loved and had parents who adored each other. Anyone looking in would be envious of their family. All that changed the day her father was killed. The day she lost her father was the day she also lost her mother. Lena never understood why she wasn't enough for her mother to fight the darkness, but that she would have been able to forgive. There were times when Lena was taking care of her mother from one of her drunken nights when Lena felt sorry for her. The first year after Lena's father's funeral Lena's mother was in a deep depression, unable to leave her bed. She lost her job and would stare at the ceiling of her bedroom wrapped in the flag that they were given at the funeral. It was heartbreaking for Lena to see because she knew her father wouldn't want that for them, and she loved her mother. She had hoped her mother would get stronger and was willing to take care of her until she did. Before her father's death, she and her mother would cook together. As such, at a young age Lena was skilled in the kitchen, and Lena would prepare meals using the food that Gus would bring to the house. All that was in the hopes that she would eat to get her strength up enough to return to Lena. The dance classes and soccer that had been a part of Lena's life before her father passed ended because she had no way to get to the activities. There was no joy in Lena's life, only sadness. After school, she would do her homework and then watch television. It was almost as if her mother didn't exist. With her mother losing her job they lived off social security and the money that was left by her father's insurance. At times the electricity in the apartment would be shut off, so Lena learned how to access the bank account to pay the bills online. Gus worried about Lena and her mother and would visit frequently. He would always have something for Lena when he did, but he could see that this was no way for a child to live. Many times, he would try to coerce Lena's mother to help herself and even found a grief counselor to visit their apartment. Nothing worked.

The only time her mother seemed coherent was at the trial of the man convicted of killing her father. Together Lena and her mother sat in the cold courtroom and listened to every detail of that night play over and over. Occasionally her mother would cry, but for the most part she was stoic. They had already known the events leading up to her father's death. What they didn't know was why and what happened before and after. The trial was supposed to give them closure. It didn't matter what the verdict was they were broken, and nothing would bring her father back. After the guilty verdict, her mother started drinking. At first, Lena was happy that her mother was out of bed, but she would come home drunk and often would spend the night passed out on the cold bathroom floor. Lena would clean her up and get her to bed before scrubbing up the mess she had made in the bathroom. It was no life for a child, but she always held on to the hope that one day she would have her mother back.

When Lena was fourteen her mother brought Alan home to live. Lena knew that she never loved Alan the way she had her father, but he was someone for companionship. At night they would get drunk together. Six months after he lived with them Lena started looking more like a woman. At first, he would make comments, but then one night Alan came into her room after her mother passed out. He smelled like cheap alcohol and cigarettes. He violated her in so many ways and threatened to hurt her mother if she told. This went on for almost a year before Lena attempted suicide. While he was forcing himself on her, Lena would try to focus on happier times. Often, she prayed for her father to help her, but it never came until Gus found her that night. Lena was certain that Gus would never understand how grateful she was to him for helping her. He saved her and she loved him as much as she could love any human being. It was Gus who held her when she had a nightmare and took her to therapy. He also enrolled her in self-defense classes to make her feel safer. Since Lena had loved dance and soccer, Gus encouraged her to try out for the school play and join her high school soccer team. When Lena got the lead role in the school play, Gus had a front row seat. He also attended as many soccer games as his schedule would allow often trading shifts with other officers to be there. Gus was her rock. Slowly he helped

Lena put the pieces of her life back together. She never doubted he loved her. Although they never spoke about it, Lena also knew that Gus was still trying to help her mother pick up the pieces of her life. After Lena woke up in the hospital, Alan was arrested for sexual assault. He made bail and disappeared before the case went to trial. With Alan out of the picture, Gus had hoped Lena's mother would get the help she needed. She did not. Still, he never gave up on her, even though Lena did. It hurt Lena so much that her mother never tried to contact her. Eventually, she decided that it was for the best and had to move on with her life as if her mother had passed away too.

In all her nightmares, she was fifteen and unable to fight off an attack. The attacker in her latest nightmare wasn't Alan, it was Dr. Castillo, but he still felt and smelled as disgusting as Alan. Even though she knew she was no longer a helpless teenager, the realism of her nightmare still left her unsettled. The fact that they had returned made Lena worry that she was headed back down a dark path. Gus was still there urging her to talk to someone. She knew that this time she needed to deal with things herself. Maybe all these events were a sign that she had to face the demons of her past or maybe it was a test. Either way, she was determined to be strong. She was no longer a child. If there was one thing in life she had learned was that the one person you can depend on is yourself.

****

In France, Luke met with the specialist who as promised had reviewed Anne's medical records prior to his arrival. Dr. Barre was a middle-aged, petite woman who greeted Luke kindly. She spoke perfect English. Even if she hadn't it wouldn't have been a problem because Luke spoke fluent French. Her lab was located in a major Parisian hospital. They met in her office which didn't look any different from the one Dr. Castillo had. On her desk were pictures of her children. She had explained to Luke that she understood his pain. Her research was personal because her son, who is now fifteen, had a horrible accident riding a bike when he was ten. He hadn't been wearing a helmet and was left with severe brain damage. She had dedicated her life to helping others in similar circumstances. Through her research, she had been able to help her son. He was not one-hundred percent, but the progress he had made in her trial was encouraging. Luke could see her passion and understood her dedication. If he had been a doctor, he too would have dedicated his life to finding answers. After Dr. Barre told her story, she spoke of the specifics of Anne's case. Unfortunately, based on Anne's records she didn't believe her to be a candidate for her trial. At Luke's urging, since she was planning on attending a seminar in the United States in the next couple of weeks, she did agree to come early to evaluate Anne herself. Dr. Barre cautioned that sometimes the damage was just too severe for any treatment to work. It wasn't the answer Luke had wanted, but was grateful she would evaluate Anne herself. Instantly, he wondered what this news would do to Justin. Dr Barre's research was the most promising trial he found. If she couldn't help, he wasn't sure anyone could. At least he was encouraged by the fact she would evaluate Anne herself even if it did have something to do with his mention of funding for her research. As he was leaving, he decided when speaking to Justin and Ethan he would be completely forthcoming with everything that the doctor said, as to not give them false hope. Even if he was cautious, he knew Justin would hold on to that hope as long as he could. Ethan was more of a realist. Maybe it had something to do with his faith and believing Anne would find peace in the afterlife which made him more apt to deal with the circumstances. If that was the case, he wondered why Martha wasn't equally as apt. It didn't matter what it was Luke's main concern was Justin.

****

When Lena awoke the next morning, she was apprehensive about going back to work because she knew she would have to face Dr. Castillo. Her conversation with Gus had made her feel better. After a day of cleaning, going to the gym and cooking for the week, Lena didn't have another nightmare. Her fear was that going back to the hospital might end that. Even if she could avoid him on that day, eventually she would encounter him unless she left her job at the hospital. That was something she wouldn't do. In addition to loving her job, she would not give him that power over her. Since seeing him was inevitable, she wondered if she could ever be comfortable with him again. That did not seem likely. The best she could hope for was to remain vigilant about avoiding him until he was bored with her or finally received the message. While she readied for work, she listened to empowering music. One of her favorite songs for psyching herself up is "Invisible" by Pat Benatar and she played it repeatedly. If her neighbors heard her, they were probably annoyed but she didn't care. When she heard that song, she really did believe she could do anything, and she was pumped to get to work. That changed the closer she got to the hospital. The entire subway ride into the City, she became more nervous and thought of ways to avoid Dr. Castillo. It was a big hospital. If she stayed in the ER setting, she would be fine. It was if she ventured to other parts of the hospital that she had to worry. She had spent so much of her time focused on Dr. Castillo she barely had time to think about Luke and his odd behavior. On the one hand, he was protective and sweet, but it was on the other hand that she knew he was dangerous for her. While she was avoiding Dr. Castillo, she thought it best to avoid Luke too.

Fortunately, the ER was busy that day. There had been an explosion at a building site and there were many casualties. All the hospital staff was focused on trying to save lives. It left no time for her mind to wander, and she liked it that way. This was why she became an ER nurse. To focus on helping people, not to deal with soap opera drama. At one point she did hear Dr. Castillo's name paged. Just hearing his name made her nervous, but there was no time for her feelings, especially since the page was not for Lena's patient. That meant she didn't have to interact with him which made her happy. The day went very quickly. Several of her patients had been admitted, however, all had survived. At one point Lena caught sight of Dr. Castillo, but with all the police around questioning victims about the explosion he didn't dare approach. Lena hadn't shared much about her life with her co-workers. The one thing everyone knew was that she was the daughter of a decorated police officer and NYPD treated her as one of their own. On her breaks, she was able to catch up with some of them. Not much was known about what caused the explosion. They were leaning towards a gas leak. What they weren't sure of was if the gas leak was accidental or if someone with a grudge caused it. The owner of the building had received some threats, so it was an ongoing investigation. Often Lena wondered if she shouldn't have followed in her father's footsteps and become a policewoman. She loved her job, but the investigative side always thrilled her. In what seemed like no time at all her shift was over. Most of the patients had been moved or released and the ER had quieted. After transitioning her remaining patients to the next shift of nurses, she went to the locker room to change into a pair of jeans and a white T-shirt. As she was changing her mind wandered to thoughts of Justin, Anne, and Luke. Being in the hospital made her wonder if there had been anything new. The last time she was there she was supposed to talk to Justin. With everything that happened she never did. Since she knew Dr. Castillo was in surgery after she changed her clothes, she knew it was safe to spend some time in the chapel to pray for them and to ask for guidance. When she arrived at the chapel, she immediately saw Justin in tears. He wasn't praying but looked as if he wanted to. She knew he wasn't a believer or at least convinced there was a higher power, but he looked so sad that she knew he wanted to be. Even though she considered giving him his privacy to be alone with his thoughts, she found herself going over to sit next to him on the hard wooden bench. He was lost in thought and didn't realize she was there until he felt a hand on his shoulder.

"Justin. What happened?"

He looked up at her with his sad eyes and pale face. She could tell that he was frightened."Is it Anne?"

Justin shook his head. "No Anne is the same. It's the baby."

Silently Lena wondered how much more this man was going to have to endure. With genuine concern, she asked, "What happened to the baby?"

"She had a setback. Something with her heart. She's in surgery now."

"What happened?"

With total panic in his voice, he responded, "I was with her and the monitors started going crazy. They kicked me out to examine her. The next thing I knew they said she was being taken to surgery."

Lena tried to reassure him, "I'm sure the doctors explained to you that premature babies sometimes have setbacks. It doesn't mean that she won't be okay. In fact, I'm sure she'll be fine. Are you alone? Where is Luke?" Lena didn't think he should be alone.

"Anne's parents are at my house. I didn't want them to worry until I knew something, so I didn't call them. Luke's in France visiting a specialist."

The fact that Luke was in France surprised her. He must have taken her advice about looking for trials being conducted in

Europe. At that moment Justin was the important one. "Don't you think Anne's parents should know?"

He loved Anne's parents, but they were of different opinions about all of this, and Justin needed space. "They will, but to be honest I don't think I can handle having them here right now."

Lena knew she couldn't leave him alone in his fragile state. His emerald eyes were filled with tears, so she asked if they could pray together. When he nodded in agreement, Lena asked God to look over the baby and protect her. She also asked that he look over her family and give them strength. After she finished, she again tried to reassure him. "You know babies are a lot stronger than we give them credit for being. I've seen a baby that fell down a flight of stairs with barely a scratch. I can't say the same for the panicked mother though." Justin gave her a slight smile indicating that he heard what she was saying. Hoping to distract Justin, she decided to change the subject to a happier topic. "What did you decide to name her?"

That was something he and Anne were supposed to do together, and it didn't seem right picking without her. "I haven't picked a name. I was hoping. Well."

He didn't need to finish that thought. Lena knew what he was hoping for. "I think I can guess what you were hoping. Surely you and Anne had talked about names when she was pregnant?"

"We talked about it a lot. The last names were Jake for a boy and Madeline for a girl. Madeline is a good name but doesn't seem to fit now."

"Madeline is a beautiful name." She knew what he was saying though. "You need to give her a name that sounds as if she's prepared to fight like Grace or Hope."

Lena could tell that Justin was considering what she said. There was a crinkle in his forehead as he thought. Finally, he smiled a real smile. "What about Faith? I really could use some of that now. We all could."

Lena returned his smile. "Faith Armstrong. I like it. Once she's out of surgery you should tell the nurses you've chosen a name, and they'll have it put on her birth certificate."

Justin did feel better. As if everything with Faith would be okay and he knew Anne would approve of the name. She always had faith. There was something about Lena that gave him strength. "I need to go back to wait for the doctors to update me. I don't want to intrude on any of your plans, but will you come back with me and wait?"

Lena couldn't deny him his request. In fact, it was something she wanted to do. She knew if Dr. Castillo saw her with Justin, he wouldn't approach her. With Luke in France, there was no danger there either. Not that Luke was dangerous in the way Dr. Castillo was, but to her heart, he could be. Together they left the chapel and went to the waiting room. The waiting room was in the pediatric wing of the hospital. It was cheerier than the one Justin had waited for when Anne was in surgery. The walls were painted yellow and there was a small table and chairs with children's puzzles and books on them. Lena joked that they should read while they waited. Since Justin was feeling stronger, he commented that now that he was a father it might not be a bad idea. The latest children's books were foreign to him. That made Lena smile, commenting that she was sure he could catch up. They were only in the waiting room for about thirty minutes when the doctor came out to speak with him. The surgery was a success. They were able to repair the small hole in Faith's heart with no complications and she was back in the NICU resting peacefully. Finally, some good news. Justin was so elated that he hugged Lena tightly. As she did the last time Lena felt safe in his arms and she wished the feeling wouldn't have to end.

"I told you she was strong. Now you had better go and give that little lady her name."

He excitedly released her, "I will." Before he left, he turned to her and said, "After my daughter has her name. I know it's late, but have you had dinner yet? Faith is out of danger, and I would like some company while I eat

Lena couldn't think of anything she would rather do and nodded when he asked her to wait for him there.

After twenty minutes Justin came back and took Lena to a Chinese Food restaurant that was within walking distance of the hospital. It was a brisk walk and Justin commented on how nice the summer air felt. He hadn't been outside much the last several days and it was nice to take a walk in the fresh air. Lena joked that he didn't like the smell of bleach. It was the first time that she could remember hearing Justin really laugh. Faith was out of danger, and he was happy. For the first time, Lena believed that he would be okay. As the host sat them, Lena offered some suggestions as to what to order since she was a frequent customer. It occurred to Lena that all she had eaten that day was yogurt and was starving. When she told Justin that he also realized how hungry he was. They decided to start with a Pu Pu Platter followed by entrees. Lena ordered chicken with broccoli while Justin had crispy beef.

Over dinner, Justin told Lena how excited he and Anne had been for the baby. It took Anne some time to convince him, but once he found out she was pregnant he was never happier. They wanted three kids in total and had so many plans for their family. Lena listened intently seeing how happy Justin was thinking of Anne and Faith. For a moment, Lena saw the relaxed, carefree Justin that Anne had probably fallen in love with. It wasn't that thoughts of his situation were out of his mind, but after the success of Faith's surgery, Justin finally had something real to hope for. Listening to Justin talk, Lena began to understand how lucky Anne was to have had someone who loved her so much. Justin realized he knew very little about Lena. He asked her why she decided to become a nurse. The answer was simple. When she told him about her father's passing, Justin began to realize a little more about why he felt that she really understood his pain. She did know because she too had been through it. Only she was the Faith in the equation. Suddenly he felt he understood her better. Lena also shared something with him that she never shared. She hoped to go to medical school one day. There was just something about Justin that made Lena completely at ease. He was just as good-looking as Luke, however Justin's demeanor was so different. The dinner lasted just over two hours. For a moment, they both forgot their troubles. When the check arrived, Lena offered to pay half, but Justin insisted it was the least he could do. Before they left the restaurant Justin offered to drive Lena home. That was not necessary, she was happy to take the subway. The idea of her taking the subway alone late at night made him uneasy, but she assured him she did it all the time. That didn't make him feel better, but he decided not to argue. They had a nice time, and he didn't want to ruin it. Plus he wanted to check on Faith before going home. As they were saying goodbye, Lena offered to check up on him after her shift the next day. Justin smiled and kissed her cheek goodnight. He told her he appreciated everything.

****

The ER the next day was much less eventful. Lena thought often of Justin and Faith. As she was lost in thought, Dr. Castillo snuck up behind her. He forcefully whispered that he needed to speak with her. Although she wished he would leave her alone, she couldn't argue with that. They needed to talk, but not for the reason he thought. It was time to end this once and for all. After what happened last time, she had no intention of being alone with him and suggested they get coffee in the cafeteria. There was always a lot of commotion in the cafeteria. Lena knew he would not try anything there with all the people around. She had a break in fifteen minutes and would meet him there. Dr. Castillo sensed a change in Lena and wasn't sure he liked it. She seemed more in charge. That was something he would have to correct as he wanted to be the one in control. On the way to the elevator, Lena rehearsed the conversation in her head. She was prepared again to tell him there was no chance ever. In the cafeteria, Lena tried her best to hide how nervous she was and sat with him at a table he had already selected. Even though he apologized for being rough with her on their last encounter, she felt it lacked conviction. There was something in his eyes that defied his words. It was best not to challenge him. For that reason, Lena accepted his apology. That was when he told her that she should call off her attorney. If she wanted to fight him, he would destroy her. As he said that she wondered if Justin, Luke or maybe both spoke with him. The last thing she wanted to do was make him angry and insisted that she had no idea what he was talking about. It was obvious by the surprised look on her face that she was not lying, so Dr. Castillo told her about his conversation with a person he called her "latest tryst." Instantly, Lena knew it was one of the Armstrong brothers. There was a part of Lena that was honored that either Justin or Luke had gone to such lengths to protect her, but she could tell Dr. Castillo was not at all pleased. While she remained seated, he stood to walk behind her and placed his hands on her shoulders. Lena tensed up at his touch and began to tremble when he whispered in her ear. "Call off your guard dogs Little Girl. I know everything about you. I was there that night and will destroy you if you or he pursue this."

Shocked, flustered, and terrified Lena asked what he meant. Something about the smile he gave as he walked away told her everything she needed to know. In barely a whisper she said, "Oh my God he knows. How? Was he really there? That's not possible." As she was considering what she had just heard, she thought about the age difference and realized Dr Castillo could have been working in the hospital that night. While she was lost in thought, she felt a hand on her shoulder. Quickly she turned around to see Justin who had witnessed the end of the exchange standing behind her. Her tanned skin was flushed, and he knew she was upset even though her words said she was just tired. That wasn't the first time he witnessed the negative reaction Lena had to the doctor and he really wanted to be able to help her. It was obvious that she wasn't ready to talk to him about it though. Gently he told her that friendship worked both ways. As good of a friend as she had been to him, he would be there to return the favor should the need occur. That was nice to hear, but she was still processing what she had just heard and told him she needed to get back to work. A million things ran through her mind at that moment, and until she herself understood what he was talking about for sure, there was nothing anyone could do to help.

The ER was not busy enough for her to get her mind off her conversation with Dr. Castillo. She needed answers and wondered how to get them without asking him directly. At the end of her shift, she found Justin who had been worried about her all day in front of her. In his hand were irises as a thank you for getting him through Faith's surgery. He did want to thank her, but he was also worried and wanted to check on her even if he didn't say that. Lena was beginning to know him well enough to understand the hidden meaning. It was a sweet gesture, and it did make her feel better. What Justin didn't know was irises were the flowers her father would bring her as a child. Of all the flowers he could have picked, he chose that one and Lena took it as a sign that her father was watching out for her. The idea that her father was there spiritually if not physically always made her feel better. Out of instinct, she gave him a big hug as a thank you. Instantly, she regretted it because she could hear the other nurses in the background gossiping about what they thought was going on between her a Justin. She knew they were all aware of her flirtation with Dr. Castillo and now this. It wasn't her reputation she was worried about. It was his. Justin had done nothing wrong, and he was going to be the product of hospital gossip at least until the next item of interest came along. That wasn't fair and it made her release him. Justin was oblivious to all the chatter and was just happy the gesture put a smile on her face. With the flowers came an invitation for dinner, which Lena really wanted to accept, but she could see her co-workers inching closer to figure out what they were talking about. She turned him away and started walking down the hallway to escape the nosy people before accepting. The condition was they met at of the hospital entrance after she changed.

When Lena met him thirty minutes later, she had changed into a floral sundress. In the moonlight Justin noticed how lovely she was, however, did not think that it was appropriate to comment. At dinner, he was hoping to get her to confide in him and he didn't want anything to stop that. They had decided on a pizza place that Justin knew and walked towards the parking garage. Justin drove a black Lexus SUV, a very different car from the red Porsche Luke drove. His black leather seats were as plush as the ones in Luke's Porsche. It was just a very different type of car. He too opened the car door for her, but there was something different about it when it came from Justin. When Luke opened the car door, she felt like he was trying to impress her. With Justin, it felt like he was just a gentleman. Everything about Justin was so sincere and she enjoyed the comfortable feeling of spending time with him. That was a rare feeling for her, however, it was one she was beginning to really cherish. There was no doubt in her mind this was what a real friendship was about. Most men wanted something from her. Justin was too in love with his wife to want anything from her but company. That made the relationship easy and uncomplicated. Even the night she spent with Trey she had enjoyed, but the fact that they had sex had made her more guarded. This was just nice. She did notice that, unlike Luke, Justin didn't have the radio on and thought maybe it was because Anne was still a news topic even if the stories had slowed. By the time they arrived at the restaurant Lena was famished. She had not eaten all day, and the aroma made her stomach growl. Dr. Castillo had mentioned that she should call her lap dogs off and she wondered if it was Justin or Luke who had talked to him. At the table, she tried to figure it out. There was no subtle way to ask, so she asked him if he had talked to Dr. Castillo. Justin was hopeful that he was going to get more information. He offered that he had issued a warning. She thought to herself that she should be mad, but she knew he was coming from a genuine place and only thanked him. Before Justin could ask any more questions, Lena changed the subject to Luke's trip. Justin took the hint and told her, "He went to meet with a specialist. Then he had some work to do for our firm. He will be back later in the week. At least his being there is keeping my father off my back for the time being."

At the mention of a father, Lena was surprised. Even though she had seen in her research that they worked for their father, she had never given the fact that he wasn't around any thought until Justin mentioned him. Then she found it strange. "What do you mean by that?"

Justin could see the confusion on her face and went on to further explain. "Dad is a hard ass. Forgive the language. It's just the best word for him. Work is the most important thing in his life. He thinks I'm letting my clients down by not being there for them."

Lena couldn't believe that his father wasn't understanding the situation. "Surely your father sympathizes. I mean he's your father."

"You don't know my father. He's about as supportive as he can be. He feels that returning to work would do me some good. I've promised I'd return to the office on Monday at least part-time. Honestly, I don't know how I can focus on anything outside of the hospital, but who knows, maybe he's right? What about you? I guess your parents would be more supportive."

"You already know about my father. At one time both my parents would have been a great source of comfort. Not so much now. As I told you before my mother never recovered from my father's death. She's here physically, but her soul died the night my dad did." Lena reached over to put her hand on Justin's. "It's very important for Faith to know regardless of what happens with Anne she's loved. Little girls need their daddy's."

Tears threatened Lena's eyes as she spoke to Justin, but she was able to fight them off. Justin reached over to caress Lena's cheek. Sometimes she seemed so tough. Other times he could feel how fragile she was. Maybe fragile was not the right word because it was obvious from everything that he knew about her, that she had been through a lot at a young age. Obviously, she was a survivor, however, she felt things so much more than most of the other people he knew. In some ways, she reminded him of Anne. Anne cared so much for others. "I promise you and Anne that I'll be the best father I can. No matter what happens. Every child deserves that."

Lena leaned into Justin's touch. Normally she didn't want to be comforted when she was emotional, but Justin made her feel she could trust him. His emerald eyes looked at her with such warmth and sincerity. The waiter brought the pizza breaking up the tender moment. Lena instantly missed Justin's touch. A thought she brushed off to her emotional state. While they ate their dinner they talked about safer topics. Lena told interesting stories about the ER and Justin talked about the marathon he had just run. During a lull in the conversation, Justin thought again about broaching the subject of Dr. Castillo. Since Lena seemed more relaxed, he decided against it. For that night they were just two friends sharing stories.

This time when Justin offered to take Lena home, she accepted not wanting her serene feeling to end. On the way, Justin mentioned he had wanted to buy a Porsche like Luke, but Anne thought this would be a better family car. "She was right," Lena thought to herself. Even in the night lights Lena could see his face light up as he talked about Anne. Justin was always good-looking, gorgeous in fact, but when he spoke of Anne he was luminous. For the first time in her life, Lena wanted what Justin had with Anne, even if it was cut all too short. She had spent her life avoiding relationships because of what happened to her mother. As they drove to her apartment Lena was certain that Justin would not break the way her mother had; she wouldn't let him. He had become too important to her to let him escape to the darkness. When they arrived at Lena's apartment Justin walked Lena up to her door and kissed her cheek.

Before he walked away, he reminded her that they were friends. "Friends can tell each other anything without judgment. If you ever want to talk about anything, I'll be there."

He waited for a response, but none came. Lena knew he was referring to Dr. Castillo. They had a lovely time, and she knew they were friends, but she had to wrap her head around things before she could talk to anyone. There was a part of her that considered using him as a sounding board. A bigger part of her didn't fully trust anyone enough to tell him her darkest secrets. She had already shared more with Justin than anyone else besides Gus. It would take time for her to get to the point where she shared the rest. If she ever did. Not to mention that Justin already had so much to deal with. She didn't want to burden him with her troubles. "Thank you." She was sincere and Justin understood the meaning. He wasn't about to press her, so he left. Lena had off the next day and would figure out her next steps then.

Chapter Eight

After her conversation with Dr. Castillo her nightmares returned. Due to a restless night's sleep, Lena woke up late. She had to know if Dr. Castillo knew about her past. The only way she could think of without talking to him again was to ask Gus. She had to be careful about what she said to Gus because she wasn't prepared to divulge everything to him just yet. That was going to be difficult because not only did he know her well, but he was also trained at getting the truth out of people. Gus answered on the first ring. After they exchanged pleasantries, she asked if he remembered the name of the doctor who treated her. That was the only way she believed he would know. It could have been possible because the age difference between the two would put him early in his career. She knew Gus would recall all the details of that night. Although in his late forties, Gus never forgot anyone or anything. His mind was trained for police work, and he recalled that it was a Spanish guy was the attendant when they brought her into the ER. When Lena asked if his name was Dr. Castillo, Gus wanted to know if this conversation had anything to do with the return of her nightmares. He assumed she was dreaming about that awful night in the hospital. It was a question that Lena had prepared herself for and responded that she was trying to figure things out. Recovering her memory was the first step. There was nothing Gus wouldn't do to help Lena, so he confirmed that the doctor's name was Castillo. Silently, Lena thought "That bastard. All this time he knew." She was a mixture of emotions from angry to horrified. Most of all she felt violated. The only thing she did know was that she wasn't going to let Dr. Castillo get away with destroying her. After she got her answer, she abruptly ended the call before he could ask her any additional questions.

As angry as she was, she decided she needed to confront Dr. Castillo, but not at the hospital. It had to be on neutral territory. At that moment, she realized that Dr. Castillo worked out at Jumba, which was where Trey was a trainer. Jumba would be the perfect place to get her control back. No one was ever going to take that from her again. Lena and Trey had been trading texts since the night at the bar. They had agreed to keep their relationship platonic at her request. Even if he was disappointed when she explained to him that she wasn't in a place to have any other type of relationship. He did agree that he enjoyed her company and would like her to be a friend. She felt comfortable with him, so it was no effort to call him to ask him a favor. After she found out from Trey that Dr. Castillo was scheduled to attend a spin class that night, she needed him to get her a guest pass and reserve a space for her in the same class.

He was happy to help her but wanted more information. "What's going on?"

"I just need to sort some things out with him"

He could tell from her voice that there was something wrong, "I'll get you the pass, but whatever is wrong you can count on me to help you with it."

At that moment Lena felt lucky to have met Trey. He was just the type of friend she really needed. Not just because he agreed to help her, but because he was so concerned about her. In fact, she was beginning to really see how important friends are. For years she was alone, now she was grateful for both Trey and Justin.

****

Several hours later, Lena entered the gym. As promised Trey was waiting for her at the front desk. Lena was happy to see him and greeted him warmly. Jumba was an elite gym much nicer than Lena's. On the tour Trey provided Lena saw how the other half lived. Her gym was very basic while Jumba had the best equipment, complete with private televisions on each of the aerobic equipment. In the locker was a private hot tub and sauna. After changing into her workout shorts and top, Lena went to the room Trey told her was the spin room. Intentionally she arrived early to make sure Dr. Castillo saw her. She was contemplating leaving due to her increasing nervousness. As she was about to forget her plan, Dr. Castillo walked into class. At the sight of him, anger took over. She needed to follow through with what she had decided to do. There was no way she would let her fear deter her. After he chose a bike, she sat on the one next to his. Dr. Castillo noticed her immediately. He thought that he had finally reached her and was excited. Lena's workout clothes showed all the curves of her body and Dr. Castillo took instant notice. The entire class Lena made sure that Dr. Castillo would keep focus on her which he of course did. In fact, he hardly took his eyes off her as her body glistened with sweat from their exercise. After class ended Lena waited until everyone left, except Dr. Castillo, before she made her move. In her most sultry voice, Lena spoke to him. "So, doctor if you know everything what are you planning to do about it?"

As she suspected he would, Dr. Castillo was buying everything she was trying to sell. He was so arrogant. She wanted to wipe the smirk off his face as he spoke to her, but there would be time for that later. He leaned in close in response to her question. "Nothing as long as you're a good girl or a bad one. It makes no difference to me."

"What about confidentiality?"

"I don't need to break the code. All I need to do is plant doubt about your mental state. Your suicide attempt is a matter of record. The Board could find out without my interference. Play along like a good girl and you won't get hurt."

"And your wife? Will she get hurt?"

"She won't know."

Dr. Castillo leaned in to kiss Lena. Although she returned the kiss, it repulsed her, but she needed him to think that she was into it. Slowly, Dr. Castillo started moving his hand down her sweaty body. It took all her strength not to quiver. "Can we go somewhere, doctor?"

"My wife is out of town. I live a couple of blocks from here. Forget the shower. I plan on getting you very sweaty. Let's go now." He was surprised by the sudden turn, but he thought he had gotten through to her and wanted to act fast before her watchdog returned.

"Give me a couple of minutes. I need to thank my friend for getting me the pass here."

"I'll be up front. Don't be too long."

Dr. Castillo was breathing hard. As Lena walked away, she thought about what a disgusting pig he was. She really wanted to wash her mouth out to get the taste of him off her. Dr. Castillo was so into this that she began to worry if she could handle this alone. By the time she reached Trey, she decided she needed his help and asked him for it. For him to agree she had to offer him an explanation. Once she explained to Trey that Dr. Castillo was blackmailing her for sex, he offered to take care of him for her. That wasn't what she wanted because she needed to make sure this ended that night and believed her plan would work. Her plan was for Trey to follow them and wait outside the door. If he heard screams, he needed to call for help. Trey didn't think it was a good idea. There was no time to change the strategy, she needed to know if he would agree or not. Either way, she was going to do this. Even though he was wary of her plan, he still agreed to help because he didn't want her doing it alone. It might be too dangerous without some back-up. Trey knew the doctor's reputation at the gym. Many of the female trainers had refused to work with him because he couldn't keep his hands to himself. That combined with what Lena had said made him worry about her safety.

She and Dr. Castillo walked hand in hand back to his apartment. His touch made her feel sick, but she was determined to follow through with her plan. It was time for her to take control of her life again. If her plan was to work, she would have to find a way to stomach his touch and pretend she was enjoying herself. Fortunately for her, he was so arrogant she would have to vomit on him for him to realize how his touch repulsed her. It gave her some comfort to know that Trey was going to act as backup if things went awry. The one thing that Lena hadn't considered was that Dr. Castillo would live in a secure building. When they arrived, and she saw the doorman she knew Trey would have trouble getting into the building. At that moment she wondered again if she could follow through with her plan, knowing that there was a possibility she wouldn't have Trey there. It was too late to back out now. Her plan had gone too far. In the elevator, panic took over Lena, although she tried not to show it. She needed a drink for courage and to hopefully allow enough time for Trey to get to the door. Inside the spacious apartment at her request, Dr. Castillo went to the kitchen to get a bottle of wine. While he was getting the wine, Lena unlocked the door and looked around. The large apartment was as she imagined it would be. It was decorated beautifully with expensive leather sofas, plush white carpets and plenty of expensive-looking trinkets. The walls were painted in cool neutral colors. Around the room were various pictures of Dr. Castillo with an attractive woman Lena believed was his wife since she had never met her. Lena took a closer look at the picture. Silently, she noticed that his wife looked like she had a lot of work done. No one's boobs were that perfect. Not to mention the fake tan and hair color. She looked every bit the trophy wife and Lena felt bad for her. Since they had no children or animals there were no pictures of anyone else. Before he returned with the wine, Lena peaked through the door hole hoping Trey was in place. He was not. As she started looking away, relief filled her when out of the corner of her eye, she saw him getting off the elevator.

Trey had run into one of his clients as he entered the building. He made up a story about being there to see if his girlfriend was cheating on him. Since she had just gone through something similar with her husband, she gladly vouched for him. Lena was still standing at the door when Dr. Castillo came out of the kitchen with two glasses of wine.

He eyed her suspiciously, "Planning an escape?"

More like your demise Lena thought to herself as she responded, "What gave you that idea?" Dr. Castillo handed her a glass and nodded at the door. She had to think of something believable so as not to alert him. "I thought maybe I heard your wife."

"My wife is at a spa in Connecticut. No chance of that."

Lena guzzled the wine like it was a shot. That was for courage. "Then we won't be interrupted."

Seductively, she approached him. It was the moment he had been waiting for, and he pulled her into a kiss before leading her to the guest bedroom. At least he had some class so as not to take her to his marital bedroom because this one had a very plain décor and was empty except for the expensive furniture and brass bed. In the bedroom, he kissed her passionately, while she faked arousal and started taking off his clothes. She wasn't sure how far she could take this but felt a lot safer with Trey outside the door. When he was dressed in only his boxers, Lena pushed him on the bed. Slowly she undressed to her bra and panties. Dr. Castillo salivated. His excitement was evident as she took a scarf out of her bag. In her most sultry voice, she explained that tying him up had been a fantasy of hers. His arrogance overwhelmed her as he agreed. Not once did he question if she had ulterior motives even after she had refused him so many times. Briefly she wondered how someone so smart could be so dumb. After he was tied up, she slowly pulled off his boxers. He was so turned on. To ensure that he was securely tied up Lena leaned in to kiss him while tugging on the scarf. After her assessment that he was secure, she again went to her bag. This time she pulled out her phone, got in bed next to him, and began taking pictures of them together. He was naked while she had very little on. A light bulb went off in Dr. Castillo's head and he tugged at his restraints. He was furious as he yelled, "What the hell?"

"Just a little piece of insurance that you will stop fucking with my life. That's right I'm taking back control. Our conversation at the gym was recorded and now with the pictures your ass is mine."

After snapping several pictures, she quickly dressed to leave. She wanted to get out of there as quickly as possible. Dr. Castillo tugged, trying to break loose while spewing profanity at her and telling her that she wouldn't get away with this. The odd thing was she wasn't scared. He was raging and she was just wondering what she had ever seen in him. As she was walking out the door, Dr. Castillo broke free and lunged at her. That surprised her and she screamed as loud as she could. It was so loud Trey heard her through the door. He barged into the apartment and ran towards the commotion. When Trey came into the room, he saw Dr. Castillo manhandling Lena as they were fighting over the phone. To the surprise of Dr. Castillo, Trey grabbed him to throw him against the wall. He had no idea that Trey had been outside and wasn't prepared for anyone other than Lena to be there. Angrily, he went after Trey. That was a mistake because Trey was stronger, and put Dr. Castillo in a choke hold to give Lena to enough time to leave. As she was leaving Lena the room screamed, "Don't fuck with me again or your wife will know exactly what kind of pig you are!"

Minutes after Lena was outside the building, Trey joined her. Since he didn't have a scratch on him, she wondered what the doctor looked like and asked. Trey smiled and let her know that once she left the apartment, he simply released the doctor. She looked at him quizzically and he laughed, telling her that he may have threatened his surgical hands if he went after either one of them. She knew that threat would put him in his place. The one thing Dr. Castillo valued was his surgical skills and he would do anything to protect his hands. A sense of relief filled Lena as she sighed, "This is finally over." While her plan was being executed, she was calm. Once it was over, she was visibly shaken. Trey could see she was upset. He wrapped his strong arms around her and offered to take her for drinks. All Lena wanted was a shower. Dr. Castillo's touch lingered on her body, and she wanted to wash it away. He could understand that and escorted her back to Jumba where she could freely use the showers. She didn't seem steady, so he thought she shouldn't be alone.

Inside the locker room, several women were changing after a hard workout. Lena wondered how many of them had been harassed at work or had been a victim at one time or another. If she was to believe the statistics at least a couple of them had. It wasn't a pleasant thought, but she was proud of herself for not allowing herself to be the victim this time. As she entered the shower, she thought about how to keep the proof safe. She didn't go through that only to lose it. The water from the shower burned across Lena's naked body as she scrubbed vehemently to get the feel of Dr. Castillo off her skin. She finally felt in control and it was an exuberant feeling. Allowing the doctor to touch her was worth every bit of the satisfaction she now felt. After her shower, she felt better and dressed.

Trey was waiting outside the locker room when she left. He was a real friend which was something Lena didn't have many of. After all, he put himself at risk simply because she asked him to. She knew she owed him an explanation as he asked what he was blackmailing her with, she just couldn't answer yet. When she was evasive, he didn't press. He didn't want to be lied to and he could see from her smile that she was feeling better. That was the important thing, and he smiled back. At that moment she really loved him. Not in the way you love a lover, but as a true friend. "I'm so grateful to you."

He wrapped his arm around her shoulder. "One day I hope to understand why, but since you're not ready to give it, let's just go have some fun." They left Jumba walking arm and arm towards the subway.

She wasn't in the mood to party, but she also didn't want to be alone either. "I'm not sure I'm up for a night out. Any chance we could grab a bottle and watch a movie?"

"I know just the place. We can go back to my apartment." Lena's face said that she was not certain that was a good idea either. "Don't worry. If you get tired you can sleep in my bed. I'll take the couch."

She loved that he understood her without words. "That's not necessary. I can sleep on the couch, but hanging out at your place does sound like fun."

The idea of staying with a friend was comforting. On the subway Lena briefly questioned herself if she made things worse. Dr. Castillo was extremely angry. She wondered how or if he would retaliate. This had to be done because she needed leverage. Since Dr. Castillo didn't want his wife to know what a cad he was, this was her way of protecting herself. That didn't mean he wouldn't try and find a way to get even. If he did, she would be ready. Trey could see she was lost in thought. Although he was curious about what she was thinking, he allowed the silence as they rode to his stop.

Like Lena, Trey lived in Brooklyn. He lived in a nicer part, but not one of the affluent neighborhoods. He had a two-bedroom apartment that he shared with his roommate, Will, who was performing out of town for a couple of days. The apartment itself looked like a typical bachelor pad. It was clean, but not overly organized and had very little décor. The best item in the house was a big screen television that took up much of the sitting area. That night the drinks flowed freely. They started with vodka and then moved on to whatever else was in the house. It was the antidote Lena needed as the two laughed the night away talking about some of Trey's clients and other drunken night stories. Initially, Lena tried to stay off the topic of their one-night stand, however the more they drank the funnier how they met became. Trey's feelings were no longer hurt that she didn't remember him. He felt what was important was the friendship they now had. Although as a joke he requested if any of his friends asked, she tell them he was the best she ever had. That night Lena realized how much she cherished his friendship and was grateful they could get beyond the awkwardness of how they met. Usually, her one-night stands are exactly that and she never saw them again. Trey was different and she was thankful. Even though Trey was still curious about the Dr. Castillo situation, he decided to let her explain when she was ready. After several hours of drinking and laughing, they both fell asleep on the couch. Lena never explained the whole story.

****

The next morning Lena awoke with a raging headache and in Trey's arms. During one of their drunken conversations, they decided it would be a good idea to make copies of the photos and recordings. Lena thought of asking Justin to hold onto a set. It was her belief that Dr. Castillo would never go after Justin the way he would her or Trey, since she feared retaliation. When she left Trey's she quickly went home to change into a black strapless maxi-dress and sandals before she headed to the hospital to see Justin. On the subway she wondered what she should tell Justin when he asked what he was holding for her. Even though she was involving him and knew he cared, she knew he had enough to worry about. She didn't need to dump more on him but believed he wouldn't be as accepting as Trey. By the time she arrived at the hospital she decided to ask Justin to hold it and offer a retainer to keep her confidence. She didn't have much money, but hoped he would help her at a discounted rate.

To her surprise she worried for nothing because he too trusted her enough to do her a favor with no questions asked. All she had to say that what was in the envelope she was asking him to hold would help her with her Dr. Castillo problem. Whatever it was she handed him, allowed her to be much stronger and that was good enough for Justin to want to help her. Without question he put the envelope in his pocket and told her he would take it to the safe in his home office later. It wasn't that he wasn't curious, he had just known enough about Lena that she shares when she is ready. In this situation she wasn't ready. Aside from that he was preoccupied by the fact that the specialist Luke found was examining Anne. When he mentioned that to Lena, she started to apologize for being insensitive. She had no idea that the specialist was arriving that day and hated that she was making him deal with her problems while he was going through so much. He stopped her apology by reminding her that they were friends, and he appreciated the distraction. As she was ready to take her leave, Luke approached with his cell phone glued to his ear. At the site of Luke, Lena felt an electric charge. He looked delicious; dressed in tight jeans, a white shirt with a black jacket. His eyes were locked on hers as he ended his phone conversation. He couldn't believe how happy he was to see her and smiled at the sight of her. "Lena. How are you?"

She wondered why he had to be so good-looking and tried to hide the fact he made her nervous in a good way. Not the Dr. Castillo creepy way. "Nice to see you, Luke. How was France?"

Luke was surprised to find out that she knew about his trip. Obviously, Justin had told her. For a minute he thought about saying it would have been better if she were there, but stopped himself. "As always Paris was amazing. It was also prudent. Did

Justin tell you about the doctor I brought back with me?" While in Paris, Luke couldn't believe how often he thought of Lena. When he sat at a café he wondered if she would enjoy the food. If he passed a store window, he would wonder what Lena would look like in that dress or skirt or especially that negligee. He thought Paris would help to escape his thoughts of her, but it didn't work. She was all he could think about.

"He did. That's great." Lena turned to Justin, "I really hope you get the answers you want. I'm praying for you. Thank you for your help." She needed to leave. There was something in the way Luke looked at her that filled her with nervous energy. Not because she was afraid of him, but because he seemed to be seeing into her soul. She knew she would never feel as comfortable around him as she did around Justin. They just had too much chemistry.

In addition, to her feelings for Luke she was very worried that she would run into Dr. Castillo. If the specialist was evaluating Anne, she knew he was probably not too far away, and she was quickly making her leave. Eventually, she would have to face him, but she needed more time. That was too much to hope for. As soon as she left Justin, Lena ran into Dr. Castillo while waiting for the elevator. He was obviously furious. Without saying a word, he pushed her away from the elevator and into the supply closet.

It was clear he no longer was playing, "Listen here you little bitch. You're going to give me everything from yesterday."

Lena tried not to show her terror. If she screamed it would draw attention that she didn't want. Yet she knew he could overpower her. Before Lena could open her mouth to say something sassy, Luke busted into the closet to ask if there was a problem. As he was asking Justin why she thanked him, he saw Dr. Castillo force Lena in there. Luke knew Lena didn't want to be around him and took action. Before either could answer he pinned Dr. Castillo against the wall with his elbow across the doctor's neck. Luke reminded Dr. Castillo that he warned him to stay away from her. It was Luke that Dr. Castillo was referring to and she was grateful. There wasn't time to think about that yet. She needed to make her escape while they both were distracted. Fortunately, the elevator door was open as she ran to it. At that point, she didn't care if it was going up or down. It was just taking her off that floor and that is what she cared about. Fortunately, it was going down. Air was what she needed and left the elevator to run outside to get it.

In the supply closest Dr. Castillo moved to go after her. Luke wasn't about to let that happen. Again, he issued a threat to stay away from Lena. He was back in town, and if the doctor wanted Lena, he would have to go through him. Luke was bigger and stronger than the doctor. Dr. Castillo tried to break away telling him this was none of his concern. He simply was trying to help Lena after all he reiterated that it was she who was mentally unstable. It had been a long time since Luke had felt such rage. The last time was in an argument with his father. No matter how angry he was at his father, deep down he loved him. There was no love for Dr. Castillo, and he wasn't sure what he would do if he let even a little bit out. It was best to walk away. Before doing that, he issued another stern warning to start treating Lena with respect. This wasn't the first time he had told the doctor to back off. Since he didn't listen, he would need to ensure the doctor knew his threats weren't idle. That would come after the specialist gave the assessment of Anne. Still furious, Luke returned to Justin who wanted to know why he took off so abruptly; especially since he could tell by Luke's mood he was enraged. After taking some deep breaths, Luke explained what had transpired. At that point Justin began to worry about Lena. He couldn't leave to check on her while Anne was having tests, however, that didn't mean he wasn't concerned. In a short amount of time, she had become important to him. Justin turned to Luke, "You need to go after her to make sure she's okay. I think she really needs someone now."

Luke was torn. He didn't think Justin should be alone; however, he saw Lena's face and was also worried about her. When Justin insisted because there was no way to know how long the specialist would be with Anne and how long it would take for her to give the results, Luke decided to look for her, but not before ensuring Justin would be okay. "Are you sure? I hate to leave you alone."

"Yes. It'll be hours before I get the results. She needs a friend right now. I can't leave, so you must. Trust me. If I know she has a friend with her, I'll feel better."

Luke still felt bad about leaving him, but Justin was relentless. "Promise you will call me as soon as Dr. Barre comes to speak with you."

He nodded, "I will. Just go and let her know that I'll do as she asked."

"What did she ask you to do?"

"I'm not exactly sure, but I am protecting something for her. Please just go and catch her. Luke, she needs a friend. Understand?" Justin's message to Luke was clear. He wanted to make sure that Luke didn't make a pass at her. That wasn't exactly the last thing on his mind as the chemistry between them was real, however on that day he just wanted to make sure she was okay. He knew from experience that too much time had passed to catch up with Lena at the hospital. Luke set out on foot to see if he could catch her before she got on the subway.

As he was looking for her, he thought about the dossier on Lena he received while he was in France.

Name: Angelina Ryan McKay

Age: 25

DOB: September 25, 2000

Address: 2501 Irving Avenue, Apartment #10, Brooklyn, NY

Relationship Status: Single

Occupation: Emergency Room Nurse

College: NYU. Mega Cum Lada. [Com Laude]

Parents:

Father: Ryan McKay deceased died in the line of duty on September 25, 2010. Police Officer.

Mother: Camilla McKay. Multiple arrests for drunken disorderly conduct. No convictions.

Guardian: Agusto Costas former partner of Ryan McKay. Guardianship April 13, 2014.

Luke was curious as to why if her mother was alive Lena had a guardian. Other than that, he found nothing out of the ordinary from the report. There had to be more. According to Dr. Castillo Lena was troubled at one time. It was important that he knew what Dr. Castillo meant and asked the investigator to probe further.

****

At the subway station, Luke found Lena sitting on a bench trembling. Several trains came and left, but she didn't move. Luke sat next to her. She was in her own world and didn't notice. On her arm was bruising from where Dr. Castillo had grabbed her. "Mother fucker," Luke thought. There was something about the way she was acting that made Luke feel as if this situation wasn't entirely about the altercation with Dr. Castillo. Lena had clearly gone into a protective mode. She was not allowing outside influences to affect her. Dr. Castillo told him he was there the night the paramedics brought her in and implied that she tried to kill herself. What he didn't understand was why. He saw the report and wondered if it had to do with a dysfunctional mother and why she had a guardian. At that moment the why didn't matter. Seeing her like that impacted him in ways he didn't understand. All he wanted to do was ensure that she was safe. As he wrapped his jacket around a shaking Lena, Luke tried to talk to her. Eventually, Lena looked at him. Tears filled her big blue eyes, but they looked vacant. Luke was genuinely concerned. He decided the best thing to do was get her out of the subway station to some place she would feel cared for. He put his arm around her waist to lead her out of the train station back to his car.

As Lena felt the warm air on her face she began to come out of her protective state. She leaned into Luke and held him as though he was her lifeline. Luke assured her that he wasn't about to let anyone hurt her again. His desire to help her became a need. "Come on," he told her still holding her tight. Gently he put her in his car and started to drive. Suddenly Lena completely snapped out of her catatonic state and realized what Luke had witnessed. Everything from the night she met Trey had caught up with her and she began to laugh hysterically. Nothing about her situation was funny, yet that was all she could do at that moment.

Luke had no idea how to respond as he had no idea why she was laughing. "What's so funny?"

Through her laughter, she responded, "Nothing. Everything. I don't know." Suddenly she realized how crazy he must think she was and stopped laughing, "You shouldn't have followed me. Justin needs you."

Luke pulled over to the side of the road to look at her. Her eyes were swollen, and her cute perky nose was as red as Rudolph's. "I had to. You looked like you needed a friend. Is there someone I can call for you?"

Lena thought about Gus and then Trey. Gus would only worry and want answers, and she had already involved Trey too much, so she shook her head no

"Do you want me to take you home?"

Lena again nodded no. Home to be alone with her thoughts was not a good idea. Plus, she knew her nightmares would return for sure. They didn't come when she was with Trey, but she couldn't impose on him again. Even though she had no idea where to go she still needed to go somewhere. "Just let me out. I'm better now. I'll be okay. Don't worry, I can take care of myself. I've been doing it for years."

Her words didn't match the look on her face and Luke was not comfortable just letting her out. "Why don't I take you back to my house to talk and maybe have a bite to eat?"

"That's not necessary. Really. I'm fine. I just need some air. Go back to Justin. He's the one who needs you."

"Justin has Martha and Ethan. Plus he wanted me to find you."

Lena was a little disappointed to think he went after her for Justin and not because he wanted to. "You came after me for Justin?"

Luke didn't mean to imply that he wasn't concerned. "No, I came after you to check on you. We were both thought you could use a friend."

"Are we friends?" It was a serious question because until that moment Lena hadn't thought that they were. He had helped her, but she just didn't see him like she did Justin or Trey.

It was a fair question. One he wasn't sure of either. Outside of Anne and Jessica, Luke didn't have female friends. Anne was his sister-in-law, and Jessica was the mother of his child, so they had to be friends. "I'd like to think so. Why don't we go back to my place and have dinner?"

With no other options, Lena nodded in agreement. Even though she felt better, she didn't want to be alone.

During the twenty-minute ride back to Luke's his cell phone rang five times. The first time it was his father whom he assured everything in France was on target. Next was Tabatha. Luke didn't answer that one. She had called many times while he was away, and he never picked up. The third was a client whom he told he would have the contracts to them in the morning. Justin was the fourth call. Luke told him the situation was under control. Grateful Justin let him know that the doctor wouldn't give him any information until the morning. There was no point in him returning to the hospital until then. That made Luke feel better, as he did want to be with Justin when he received the news. The last call came as they were pulling up to the apartment building garage. It was James who he was excited to speak with. Lena wasn't surprised to find out Luke was a father. She had read it on the internet. What did surprise her was how his face lit up when he talked to him. It was the first time that she saw a hint of Justin in his eyes. The look Luke had when speaking with James was the same look Justin had when he was talking about Anne. The call ended with Luke telling James that he loved him and would see him soon. Lena smiled at how warm Luke was when he spoke to James. Luke had a rough exterior with most people. Until that moment the only person she had seen him truly unguarded with was Justin. That was the side of Luke that Lena really liked. It was the side that he had shown her since he saw her at the subway station. Realizing that Luke may be more like Justin than she initially thought, Lena began to feel more comfortable being with him.

When they entered Luke's apartment Lena could see why he assessed her place with such apprehension. It was huge. It was even bigger than the apartment that Dr. Castillo had. She had a hard time believing only one person lived there. As soon as they entered a woman whom Luke introduced as Joyce greeted them warmly, asking if she could get them anything. Joyce was a plain looking woman in her early forties. Lena could tell by the kindness in her voice that she had a strong affection for Luke, and he returned the sentiment. It was not sexual, but one of mutual respect. Luke had gone straight from the airport to the hospital without eating anything and was starving. That was all Joyce needed to hear. She hurried off to make them dinner. Luke led Lena into a large living area with burgundy walls and asked if she would like something to drink. The bottom floor of his apartment was very open with plenty of windows. They were up high, although Lena hadn't noticed on the elevator how many floors to the complex there were. The room was tastefully decorated; however, it lacked what some would say was a "woman's touch." There was no warmth in the rooms. Lena could tell that it was the house of a single man. In the next room, Lena saw Luke had a big screen television complete with theater and game consoles. It also had a large pool table and a bar. The room had every toy a man could want. As she assessed his apartment, it suddenly occurred to Lena that by Luke bringing her there he may have certain expectations. Even though he gave her no indication that sex was on his mind she couldn't imagine any other reason she was there. From her internet search, she knew Luke had a reputation for being a womanizer. Although she had imagined what having sex with Luke would be like many times, with everything she had been through that day she didn't think it to be a good idea. Instead of taking the drink, Luke was offering, Lena asked where the nearest subway station was.

Luke was confused. "I thought we were going to have dinner?"

Lena abruptly blurted out, "I can't have sex with you tonight." The words came out before Lena could stop herself.

Luke spit the wine from his mouth as he laughed. After seeing how surprised he was by her statement she wanted to die. Clearly after what Luke witnessed the attraction was over. Suddenly, she felt disappointed. Luke could feel her retreating, which was the last thing he wanted. Slowly, he moved towards her. "I'd be lying if I said I hadn't thought of having sex with you, but you're not in the right frame of mind tonight. So tonight, I thought we could eat and maybe have some fun." In a move that even surprised Luke, he lifted Lena's face and kissed her red lips chastely. "When we have sex, it'll be at a time when we both can enjoy. Trust me you'll enjoy it."

For a moment Lena was lost in a trance as Luke's lips were so soft. The kiss offered her what she needed. She was also thrilled that he said "when they had sex" as if it was a forgone conclusion. Joyce interrupted the conversation by announcing that their dinner was ready. While they walked to the kitchen, Lena felt uncomfortable as she sensed Joyce was eyeing her warily. She wondered how many women Joyce had cooked for. The kitchen walls were painted white with dark blue granite counter tops as a contrast. There was a dark wood kitchen table set for two by a large window that overlooked the skyline of New York City. It was dusk and the view was amazing with all the colors of the sunset shining through. Had this been a date it would have been a perfect romantic setting. Luke pulled a chair out and invited her to join him at the table. Lena's stomach growled as she realized how hungry she was. In the morning, she was too hung over to eat. After she was in a hurry to get to the hospital and hadn't eaten all day. Joyce quickly excused herself from the room so that they could have privacy. The aroma from the fettuccini alfredo filled the room as Luke opened a bottle of white wine Joyce had set on the table. Over dinner Luke filled Lena in about the clinical trial Dr. Barre was working on. She hadn't offered much hope, but Luke deemed her to be Anne's last chance at recovery. He was nervous about hearing the result because even though he had issued caution, Justin had so much hope about this. During dinner, Luke sensed that Lena had let down some of her barriers. As much as he wanted to know what the story with Dr. Castillo was, he feared it would ruin the mood and didn't bring up the topic. Instead after dinner, Luke suggested they watch a comedic movie. Lena was feeling much better and agreed. They settled in the room Lena deemed Luke's man cave, although when she said that Luke cracked a joke about what his real man cave was. It was the first time in a long time that Lena blushed, which made them both laugh. Seeing her laugh made Luke feel things he didn't think he was capable of feeling. Her smile was so beautiful. All he wanted to do was capture that moment. In the emerald green room that matched his eyes, they sat close to each other on the leather sofa despite the fact that there was more than enough room for at least five other people. As the evening slipped into night, Lena was exhausted. Before the end of the movie Lena fell asleep while resting her head on Luke's chest. "Sleeping Beauty," Luke thought as he ran his fingers through her soft brown hair. She looked so peaceful that he didn't want to wake her. Instead, he decided to carry her upstairs to his room. While in his arms one side of her dress fell to reveal one of her naked boobs. To Luke's delight, she wasn't wearing a bra. What he had held in his hand the night he drove her home was suddenly in plain view. It was killing him not to touch it or pull the other side of her dress so that they were both visible. He was no gentleman, yet he also couldn't take advantage of her either. When he laid her down on his bed, he decided she would be more comfortable in one of his T-shirts which he placed over her dress. To his surprise, she didn't wake up. Luke tried not to look as he pulled her dress down, however as the dress fell in sight was a view of her black lace panties. "Damn," Luke thought as he quickly placed the covers over her well-toned body. After she was settled Luke took a shower and did the only thing that would allow him to get through the night; masturbating with the images of Lena he came in record time. As Luke climbed into bed, he marveled at how that night felt like a date. Since his divorce Luke hadn't dated. He attended social functions with women for pretenses, but he never considered them his date. Luke wasn't even sure that he ever dated Jessica either. She was selected by his family to be his wife. During their courtship, they would attend formal events and have sex. Lots of sex. There was no real connection there. That relationship continued even after they were married. Jessica knew the way Luke liked it and let him have his way with her. Now that they were co-parents, their relationship was better than it ever had been. His night with Lena was so different. It was more of the way he imagined Justin and Anne would have spent their evening. Initially Luke thought it would be awkward having a woman share his bed. It was something he had avoided doing since divorce. To his surprise, it wasn't. In fact, having her there was oddly comforting. Soon after getting in bed, jet lag took over and he was asleep.

****

The next morning Lena woke up just as the sun was rising. Luke's room was painted the same blue as the granite kitchen countertops and there was sunlight trying to come through the blind covered windows. For a second Lena was disoriented and forgot where she was until she saw Luke lying in bed next to her. When she closed her eyes to think about how she ended up in his bed, she had a vague recollection of Luke carrying her up the stairs and putting her in there. Briefly she wondered why in an apartment that had several rooms, he chose to keep her with him. The reason really didn't matter as she stared at the man next to her quietly snoring. Even his snoring was controlled she thought as she giggled. While looking at Luke in his sleep she could see how young he really was. When he was awake, he always appeared to be so much older than his actual age. It wasn't that he had wrinkles or grey hair that made him look older. There was something about the way he carried himself and the fact that he always seemed so stressed that he did. With everything that was going on, he had a reason for the stress, but even in the pictures on the internet you could see his stress through the fake smile. Now at peace, he looked around thirty-three. His age wasn't the only thing she noticed. Luke wasn't wearing a shirt and Lena could see his well-defined bare chest and rippled arm muscles. Even though she knew nothing had happened, she realized she was wearing a long T-shirt that she knew she hadn't changed into and felt a little awkward. She wondered if he looked at her the way she was looking at him and also questioned if he was completely naked. For a moment she considered how she would feel if he was. One way or another she wanted to know, and she slowly lifted the covers to find him in red silk pajama pants. That was not the only thing she found. She also noticed that he must be having quite a dream because he was clearly aroused. Briefly, Lena wondered what it would be like to wake up with him as his lover. From the look of things Luke had the right equipment to make someone very satisfied. Part of her wanted to find out, but the more rational side of her realized it was those thoughts that got her into trouble. Instead, she decided it was best she left before something happened. As to not wake him, she quietly got out of bed, while looking for her clothes. They were folded on a chair near his dresser, and she tip-toed over to grab them. On his dresser, Lena noticed a picture of Luke, Justin and a little boy whom Lena assumed was James on a fishing trip prominently displayed. Lena thought it was funny, that was the only picture she had noticed in his house. Not that she had seen every room, however, she had seen enough to know it was mostly vacant. She couldn't help but notice how happy the three of them looked and it brought a smile to her face to see both Justin and Luke that way. Nature was calling and she needed a bathroom. Surely in a room this size there was one attached, she just needed to find the right door, she thought to herself. The first door she opened was a full walk-in closet about the size of half her apartment. On one side of the closet there were expensive designer clothes and shoes. She couldn't believe one person needed that many clothes, however it was what was on the opposite side of the closet that caught her attention. There were all kinds of handcuffs, restraints, paddles, floggers. It was a smorgasbord of sexually kinky toys. Lena looked over at Luke to make sure he was still sleeping before walking in to take a closer look. Honestly, she couldn't believe her eyes as she went across the items wondering how someone so refined could be into that life. It was out of character or so she thought. Suddenly she felt uncomfortable being there. Not just in the closest but with Luke in general. He had acted as nothing but a gentleman, however with her history the idea of any of that made her want to leave the house. Aside from their different worlds, she could see they would not even be compatible sexually. The thought was disappointing. Still, it was better she found that out before they took things to the next level. The second door she tried was the bathroom where she washed up and dressed as fast as she could. He had been so nice to her, so she decided to write and leave a thank you note on the pillow she had slept on. The note explained that she needed to leave to get ready for work. That wasn't a lie. She did have to work. Lena waited until she was outside to put her shoes on and arrange an Uber so that she would not wake him. If she had woken him, he she knew he would have insisted on driving her home. At that moment she didn't think she could be around him anymore. After Luke was so sweet the previous night, she had thought maybe they could have something. Not after what she saw. All those thoughts disappeared.

Luke awoke an hour later. By that time the sun had fully risen. He felt well rested; better than he could remember ever feeling. Since his divorce, Luke hadn't liked to sleep in the same bed with a woman. It wasn't that he was opposed to sharing a bed, but after sex, it seemed too intimate. He never wanted to give the woman he was with the wrong idea. Normally he liked to wake up alone, but not that morning. Immediately he realized Lena wasn't in his bed. All sorts of negative thoughts went through his head as he went in search of her. Instead of finding her, he found her note and wondered why she didn't wake him as he would have been happy to give her a ride home. When Luke looked up from the note, he noticed that his closet door was ajar which was odd because he always made sure the door was closed. Once he walked over to it, he instinctively knew she had been in there which was the reason for the quick departure and the note. While he was thinking about the situation the phone rang. It was Justin who sounded nervous about Anne's test results. Dr. Bare was his last hope for Anne's recovery and in a couple of hours he would have his answer. The thought was nerve wracking. The other reason he called was that he wanted to know about Lena. She had been on his mind, and he needed to know if she was okay. Luke told Justin about how he found Lena at the subway station. She was so upset he brought her back to his house where she fell asleep. Justin was cross with Luke before he clarified that nothing happened between them.

Jessica had shared many tales with Anne about Luke's controlling ways. Because of that, Justin knew way more about Luke's preferences than he wanted. Even without the details, Justin knew with women, Luke was trouble. At first Luke wanted to argue that he had no idea what Justin was referring to, but deep down he knew Justin was right. There was something different about Lena though. When he saw Lena at the station, it was clear she had been hurt. Instead of wanting to take advantage, Luke felt protective. All he wanted to do was make sure she felt safe. That had never happened before. The feeling of protectiveness over a woman was foreign to him and he knew he would do anything to make she was never hurt again. This wasn't a topic he wanted to discuss further. It hurt him that Justin thought so little of him, even if it was justified and he had been wondering what these feelings towards Lena were. All of it was too much and what was important was Anne. Because of this Luke quickly changed the subject back to her. Although Anne was never far from Justin's thoughts, it was nice to worry about something else even if it was only for a short time. They were going to have to find out if the specialist could help so they agreed to meet at the hospital in an hour. Even though he was going to meet Justin, Luke intended to hurry to the hospital with the hopes of being able to speak with Lena before the meeting. He needed to find out why she left abruptly even though he had an idea. It was killing him that she may be feeling anything negative about him. In ten minutes, he was showered, dressed, and ready to walk out the door. He hoped the drive would help him think about what to say because again he was at a loss. All he could do was first gage her reaction to him. They were comfortable the night prior and if anything was different, he would know immediately.

While on the way to the hospital, the private detective he hired to investigate Lena phoned. Since Luke was driving, he put the phone on speaker. "Luke Armstrong."

"Mr. Armstrong as you asked, I did some further digging on Angelina McKay."

"Hold on for a moment." Luke put the phone on mute. He was at a crossroads; he wanted to know more about Lena, yet somehow it seemed like an invasion of her privacy. "Screw it," Luke thought and put the phone back on speaker. "Tell me what you have."

With that, the private investigator started his story. "When Angelina was fifteen, she was admitted to the hospital for an apparent suicide attempt. After she was released, Augusto took guardianship of her. There was an arrest warrant issued for her mother's boyfriend Alan Smith. The charges against Mr. Smith were for physical and sexual assault. The guy skipped town before the trial and was never found."

The investigator had confirmed what Luke had already suspected. Lena had been assaulted. In her despair she decided that she would rather take her own life than deal with it anymore. Luke's heart ached for her. The thought of anyone going through that as a child was horrifying. The fact that it was Lena's past made it painstakingly awful. "And the doctor who treated her? Was it Dr. Castillo?" Luke asked the question even though he knew the answer. He just needed confirmation. "One of them Sir."

"Any idea where the bastard boyfriend is?" Luke was furious. Dr. Castillo had known everything she had gone through and still behaved like a dick. "Bastard," Luke thought. His thoughts were interrupted by the investigator saying that he didn't know where Alan was. As much as Luke wanted justice for Lena, as long as Alan stayed away, Luke believed she was safe. Too much time had gone by for him to still be interested. All he could do about Alan at that moment was tell the investigator to keep looking for him. The investigator could do things that the police couldn't even though he knew that the entire police department was on the lookout for him. What he could do now was make sure that Dr. Castillo ended the blackmail.

The call had Luke so upset, he knew it wasn't the best time to seek out Lena. He wasn't sure he would be able to hide his feelings if he ran into her. Instead, he went directly to look for Justin while plotting his next steps to inflict pain on the "good doctor." Justin had also been restless and went to the hospital early. He was with Ethan when Luke found him. Martha was unable to handle any more bad news and elected to stay with Faith. Luke could deal with Dr. Castillo later. At that moment his focus had to be on Justin and Anne. Dr. Lee had agreed to allow them to use her office for the meeting. She was very interested in the research and had chosen to work with Dr. Barre on this in the hopes of learning something new that could help her patients as well. The office was very similar to Dr. Castillo's office except she had pictures of her two daughters everywhere. Before Dr. Barre entered the room,

Justin looked at one of Dr. Lee's pictures. It was her daughter at a dance recital. He could tell because of the costume she was wearing. He wondered what it would be like to attend Faith's recital; if he would sit in the audience alone or if he would have Anne at his side. Luke could see his brother's melancholy mood and tried to reassure him. They were all startled when Dr. Barre and Dr. Lee greeted them about twenty minutes after they arrived. Their faces were serious and that concerned Luke as he thought if it was good news their faces would be lighter. This research was Justin's last hope. In all the clinical trials he examined it was the only one that could remotely help Anne. Dr. Barre began by offering her apologies in a thick French accent. That wasn't a good sign. Luke, Ethan and Justin braced themselves for what was to come next.

"I have run the tests and spoken with Anne's doctors." She paused because she did understand Justin's pain. "I'm sorry but your wife is not a candidate for my trial. I had hoped that when I arrived here, I would have found her a candidate, however, I have to agree with her other doctors. Unfortunately, I believe your wife will be in a permanent vegetative state."

The words "permanent vegetative state" ran through Justin's head many times and each time it felt like a knife was being stuck deeper and deeper in his heart. There was nothing else he could do.

It wasn't that he hadn't heard the words before, he just had hope. Now there was none, and the reality sank in. His face went completely pale as tears ran down his face. Ethan had been as prepared as a father could be for the news. His strong religious belief would get him through. That didn't mean that he hadn't hoped too though, and his pain was also apparent. As Luke looked at Justin and Ethan, he felt guilty for having even given them a glimmer of hope. If he had left it alone maybe they wouldn't be in so much pain. He knew that wasn't true. It just would have come earlier, yet it was hard for him to witness. The room was completely silent as everyone digested the news. Dr. Barre really wished the news was better, but sometimes doctors are powerless. She did wait in case the family had questions. After a couple of minutes, Ethan stood to join Martha in the NICU. He needed to tell her the news. Before he left, he asked Justin if he would be okay. Again, Justin questioned what that word really meant. He would live, but would he be, okay? At that moment he didn't think that would ever be possible again. Not without Anne. Luke stood to walk Ethan out and assured him that he would take care of Justin.

"I need to get Martha back to Philadelphia. We need to get back to our church and start to heal. We'll be back to help Justin when Faith comes home. I had explained this to Justin this morning before the meeting, but if Justin or you need anything please call us."

Luke knew all of this was too painful for them too. He was a father, and he couldn't imagine ever hearing those words spoken about his son and hoped he never would. "I will. Thank you and I'm sorry this didn't have the outcome we wanted."

"My boy. At least you did something. None of this is your fault. I just pray that they catch the real person responsible soon. Take care of yourself and Justin."

After Ethan left Dr. Barre asked if either brother had any questions. Neither Luke nor Justin did. She couldn't do anything to help. That was self-explanatory. As she turned to Luke before leaving, he assured her that he would keep his word and send the money he promised to fund her research. Just because it couldn't help Anne, it didn't mean it wasn't important. Justin sat at the conference table unable to move, looking as if someone had just knocked the wind out of him. Deep down Justin had a feeling she wouldn't be able to help, but he wanted so much to believe this would be his miracle. With that gone there was nothing left. Luke too felt the loss and went over to his brother to hug him tightly. "I'm sorry. I really wanted this to work."

Still in shock, Justin didn't return his hug. Nothing could console him at that moment. He was numb. After a few minutes he told Luke he needed to be with Faith and stood to walk away. Luke knew if anyone could help at that moment it would be Faith, but what was next? When Justin was gone Luke thought about going to see Lena to ask her advice. More than that he wanted to see her reassuring smile because he thought that would help with his nightmare. It wasn't just Justin who lost Anne; they all had. After learning everything he had about Lena, he was worried Justin could be right about him possibly making things worse for her. Luke wanted better for Lena since he couldn't give her the love she deserved. She needed someone like Justin. Instead of going to see Lena, he went to Anne. It was better for both of them.

Luke knew Anne couldn't give advice, but he hoped she would speak to him through her energy. "Oh Anne, please help me with Justin. He needs me now more than ever and I've no idea how to help him. I wish you could tell me what to do."

Luke sat for a while, willing Anne to answer. As expected, she did not.

****

For the first time ever, Lena seriously considered calling in sick from her shift. She was feeling better about what had transpired but still had no idea how to handle Dr. Castillo. When she arrived at the hospital, she checked the schedule to learn it was his day off. Instantly relieved, Lena was able to focus all her attention on her patients even though thoughts of Luke kept popping up. Each time she remembered how gentle he was with her, she would remind herself that he was dark, dangerous and off limits. Knowing that the specialist was meeting with Justin that morning, Lena wondered what the outcome was. Justin had been a good friend to her, and she was worried. She decided after her shift was over, she would check on him. Lena said a silent prayer asking God to let Justin get the outcome he wanted. "Justin is such a good man. Please help his family"

While Lena was at the computer checking some lab results, she heard a familiar voice. When she looked up, she saw Justin. One look at him, and she knew he had not had good news regarding Anne.

His voice was weak and barely a whisper, "How did you get through it? You told me that your mother didn't. How did you?"

Her heart broke for him. She had to really answer truthfully. "I'm not sure I have." She picked herself up, but the triggers were there, and the pain returns without warning. It was an honest answer, but he looked so devastated that she wanted to take him in her arms to assure him everything would be fine. That he would be okay, but she wasn't even sure that it was the truth. Lena came out from around the desk taking his hand. "What do you need?"

"Anne." Justin lost his ability to hold back the tears he had been fighting. Lena hugged him. Unlike with Luke this time he put his arms around her and sobbed. "I can't do any of this without her. How do I do this?", he said as he cried.

All Lena could do was reassure him, "I'm here. I'll help you. I promise."

Justin released his hold on her and wiped his tears. "I'm sorry."

"You have nothing to be sorry for, especially after you have seen me cry so many times. I still have two hours left on my shift. Then we can really talk. In the meantime, why don't I call a social worker so that you can discuss your options?"

At first Justin responded that he wasn't ready. With encouragement from Lena, he changed his mind. The doctors wanted to release Anne, and he needed to know the choices. Lena paged the hospital social worker to the ER while Justin sat in the waiting room trying to process that he would be living a life without Anne. When Linda Hampton, the social worker, reached the ER, Lena explained Justin's situation. She thought it would be easier for him if she gave Linda the information first. Lena also prepared her that he might not be ready for the full conversation. After introducing Justin to Linda, Lena wondered if she should have Luke paged to assist. If her shift was over, she would have gladly sat with him, but since she had patients that wasn't an option. Justin hadn't asked for Luke, so she decided against it.

Linda talked to Justin for over two hours about treatment facilities and support groups. She mentioned that there were even groups that would help Justin prepare for life with a premature baby. The thought of Anne being in a facility and not with him was too overwhelming for Justin. By the time they finished their discussion Lena's shift was over. After she changed out of her scrubs, she met them in Linda's office.

Overwhelmed and exhausted Justin looked at Lena. "I want her home with me."

Lena understood how he felt. If it was her father, she would have wanted him home with her and her mother. She looked at Justin to see what his eyes were telling her and could see it was important to him. "If that's what you want Justin, I'll help you."

Lena took Justin's hand and squeezed. He was immediately comforted by her presence. At that moment having Anne at home was the only option Justin could accept.

Lena took control because she knew it wouldn't be easy, but they could move Anne home, "Linda, can you tell us what Justin will need?"

Linda was shocked. "Lena, you know that Anne will require around the clock care. A facility would be better."

"Who says? This is what Justin wants, and he knows what Anne needs better than we do. Can you please give me the lists of homecare providers? I'll help him get it set up."

Justin knew she understood and was grateful to her. He could tell Linda disagreed with his decision; however, she did hand them the list. Before leaving the office Lena assured her that if this did not work out, Justin could always consider a long-term care facility. It just didn't need to be now.

Outside Linda's office Lena turned to Justin, "Have you eaten today?"

He had to think before answering. In the morning, he was too nervous and after the news too upset. "No."

The answer didn't surprise her, and the truth was she hadn't eaten anything but yogurt all day too. "You need your strength so let's go get something to eat. We can talk about how to get Anne home."

Justin agreed and they walked to the parking garage. Honestly Justin didn't feel like talking even though he did feel better having Lena there. Knowing that she had suffered a great loss made it easier to be with her than anyone else. They went to Lindies on Broadway because often he and Anne would eat there after the theater. On that night he felt it was important to be somewhere he felt connected to Anne. A worried Luke called several times while they were together. Justin wasn't ready to talk to him or anyone besides Lena and didn't answer his calls.

After they ordered Lena decided to break the silence. They needed a plan as the hospital would insist on releasing Anne in the next couple of days. "Do you have enough space for you, Anne, Faith and more than likely a live in nurse?"

"Yes. Space will not be a problem. The penthouse is quite large."

"Penthouse of course," Lena thought to herself. Judging from where Luke lived it was probably very spacious. "Oh good. You'll need to hire a nursing service. One that will allow for around-the-clock care. You'll also need a medical bed and"

Justin cut her off. He was trying to come to terms with the loss of Anne and his head was spinning. "I just want her home. Can you help me with the details? I'll pay you."

She wanted to help because she liked him and was Lena little offended at the offer of money. "I thought you said we were friends."

Justin didn't understand, "We are."

Lena could see the confusion on his face. "Friends help each other. At least that's what you told me the other night. I don't want your money. It would be an honor to help you out."

Hurting her feelings was the last thing he wanted to do. "I'm sorry if I offended you."

"Look I don't want you to think that I am crazier than you probably already do, but I think that God or the angels have put me in your life for a reason."

Justin looked curiously at Lena. He had never expressed those thoughts before, although he wondered why he had such a connection with a stranger. Justin was just starting to believe in the existence of God. Even though he wouldn't have worded it as Lena had he understood. Lena saw his face looking at her with interest and continued. "I think that by helping you, I'm supposed to bury my own demons. I haven't figured it all out yet, but I feel connected to you and will do everything I can to help."

"I feel the connection too. I just never considered it was God or the angels pushing us together." Justin pulled out his phone from his pocket as it vibrated. "It's Luke again. Let me just tell him I'm alive. Then I want to continue this conversation."

Justin answered and told Luke that he needed time to process. He left out where he was and the fact that he was with Lena which made her briefly wonder why. It wasn't important. It just made her curious.

As soon as he hung up, Justin went back to his conversation with Lena. "I'm not sure if you're right about you being put in my life for a reason, but I'm glad you're here."

Lena smiled a true smile; one that lit up her face. "I'm glad too."

Justin remembered something else she said. "Why would I think you're crazy?"

"I think I have given you plenty of reasons to think that. If I didn't know me, I would think I was."

"Not me. I would still think that you're an angel."

Even though he was in so much pain Justin always knew what to say to make Lena smile. She wished she could have that effect on him. He barely spoke during the meal except to say that Ethan and Martha were leaving soon. He loved them, but in some ways having them around made it harder. They were clearly upset. Yet they wanted to make sure that he knew God was taking care of her. It was supposed to be comforting. For him the only thing that would make him better was if God granted him a miracle. Lena understood that. Justin needed to adjust to his new normal and he had to deal with it the way he needed. Not the way others felt he should. The entire meal Lena wondered if bringing Anne home was really the best idea. She also believed that Justin would one day have to move on. Even though she silently questioned his decision, she really believed that he needed to deal with his grief the way he wanted to. When the meal ended Lena reached for the check to pay her half, however Justin wouldn't hear about it. Paying the check was the least he could do. It was late when they finished, so Justin insisted on driving Lena home. Driving with Justin was very different than driving with Luke. Luke always had music playing while Justin never did, and Lena wondered why.

She decided to mention it. "I'm surprised that you don't like music."

Justin was caught off guard but decided to give an honest answer. "It's not that I don't like music. In fact, Anne and I are or were big dancers. It's just a lot of songs remind me of her. I don't want to get upset and hurt someone, so I just drive in silence."

"I get that. My dad used to play Angelina for me when I was a kid. It was years before I could listen to that song. Even today when it comes on it makes me sad. Although sometimes I play it just to make me feel close to him again."

"Angelina, why?"

"Lena is short for Angelina. My dad was the only person that ever called me that though."

"Angelina. That suits you because as I said earlier you might just be my angel."

His response made her blush, and she was grateful he couldn't see it. She thought to herself "if he only knew me, he wouldn't think that."

The ride was quick, and Lena hated the silence, so she tried to make small talk while staying away from subjects that might upset him. She thought a safer topic was flowers and wondered what prompted him to buy her irises that day. His reasoning was that they reminded him of her and Lena explained that her father used to buy them for her. That was a surprising piece of information, and they further acknowledged how connected they were.

Once she was home, Justin escorted her to her apartment. The brothers were so different, yet there were some similarities, and she could tell they were both well bred. They both opened car doors and wanted to see her home safely. Even if she wasn't sure that Luke had the best intentions by walking her to her door, she knew Justin only wanted to make sure she was home safe and sound. When they walked up the stairs, they were surprised to find her door wide open. "Wait here," Justin ordered as he entered the apartment to look at around. Since the apartment was so small it wasn't hard to see if the person was still there. The only room with a door was the bathroom. In no time he came back out to get her and confirm there was no one there. Even though the invader was gone, the place was ransacked. Everything was out of order. The pillows and blankets were thrown on the floor and her drawers were open. As she looked around, she was devastated that someone could do this. Lena didn't have much, so nothing was missing as far as she could tell. The way the apartment was left it was clear that the person who broke in was looking for something. If they wanted to rob her the only thing of value was her computer and TV. Both were still there, but the computer screen was open, and she never left it that way. It looked like someone went through it. Once she realized that she was not robbed, she knew it must have been Dr. Castillo who broke in looking for her evidence. Quietly she whispered his name. It was hard for her to believe that things had gotten this out of hand. This man was someone she had worked with for years. She questioned how she had not noticed how unhinged he really was before all this. How no one had noticed. All of this was really making her question her judgment.

Justin's words interrupted her thoughts. "I think we should call the police."

He was reaching for his cell phone when Lena told him that she didn't think that it was necessary. Something had to be done, but she feared calling the police would make all this worse.

Justin had heard her say Dr. Castillo's name. "Why you think it was the asshole doctor? Does this have to do with the envelope you gave me?"

Lena looked up at him to see the concern on his face and knew she could trust him. She closed her eyes and just spit out the words because she needed someone to talk to. "He was blackmailing me, so I turned the table. What you have in the envelope is a recording and some pictures. I never thought he would go this far though."

Justin wondered what he was using for blackmail but decided if she wanted to share she would. Whatever it was she went through great lengths to make sure he couldn't use it. He wondered if the reason she didn't want to call the police was because of the information he had on her and not what she had done. It didn't matter. He had no intention of leaving her alone. The evidence was safe in his home office, so he knew that the doctor didn't find what he wanted. Justin was worried he would return. "If you won't let me, call the police then pack a bag. You're staying with me tonight and we will figure things out."

Lena shook her head no. "What about Anne's parents?"

Justin looked at his watch. "I told you they were leaving. Their train left to go back to Philadelphia about ten minutes ago." Justin looked at the mess and waved his arm around. "Look if you think there's any way, I'm leaving you alone here tonight with the possibility that he could come back. Well, that's not happening.

Now please pack some things. We can start getting ready for Anne's move home. I promise we'll figure out how to deal with Dr. Castillo."

After some persuasion Lena finally agreed. She could tell he was concerned, and truth be told she was worried as well. Lena chuckled thinking that the previous night she stayed with Luke, the night before with Trey, now with Justin. "This is getting ridiculous," Lena thought. All of this because of a man she had worked with for years. He was a doctor. A healer. Surely, he would not hurt her.

On the way to Justin's, he asked what information Dr. Castillo was blackmailing her with. It was truly perplexing for Justin as he felt he knew Lena. She had been so kind to him. If there was such a thing, she was his angel. Nothing she could tell him would change his opinion of her. He just needed the information to figure out how best to deal with Dr. Castillo. Without getting into the details Lena told him that Dr. Castillo knew something about her past. When she was a young girl, she had done something innately stupid. Dr. Castillo knew about it. Now he wanted her sexually. Truth be told before all of this they used to flirt with one another. Lena thought they were being playful, but he took it to the extreme and she had no idea he knew anything about her past. Justin could tell that what she was hiding was painful. Even though he wanted to know, he felt the best way to handle this with her was to not pressure her too hard. Again, he believed that she would let him know everything when she was ready.

****

Justin's penthouse was very different from Luke's. There were happy photographs everywhere that told a story of better times. The photograph of Justin's and Anne's wedding prominently displayed on the mantle over the fireplace instantly drew Lena's attention. They looked so happy. Lena wished she had known Justin before all of this. Even in a photograph it was obvious from the sparkle in Justin's eyes how much he loved Anne. She in turn looked at him with such admiration that Lena could feel the love they shared. It was both touching and heartbreaking as Lena knew Justin was going to have to face his life without her. Justin caught Lena looking at the wedding picture and told her it was the happiest day of his life. He never thought anyone as wonderful as Anne could love him. On the day of their wedding, he felt that he could accomplish anything if he had Anne by his side. That feeling never left him even after all the years of marriage. Sadness filled his face as he realized how different a life without Anne would be. Everything Lena was going through was nothing in comparison to what Justin faced. Her heart ached for him as he stood there staring at the photograph. It occurred to her that maybe he could use some alone time to process the day's events and told him that she was exhausted. He was too and showed her to the guest bedroom. Like the rest of the penthouse the room was decorated in warm colors. It was painted in a light yellow with a pale blue and yellow duvet comforter on the large king-size bed. The room was the size of most of her apartment. Justin showed her the attached full-sized bathroom and a cabinet where she could find fresh towels. Before closing the door and saying goodnight he asked if she needed anything. Lena wondered what could she possibly need and responded no.

After leaving her Justin went to his room to call Luke. Luke was happy to hear from his brother and answered immediately. "Justin, thank goodness."

Justin didn't want to get into anything about Anne and said, "I need information on Dr. Castillo."

Luke was perplexed as to why he was asking about Dr. Castillo. When he left all Justin was focused on was what Dr. Barre had said. Now he was asking about Dr. Castillo. It didn't make sense unless something else had happened to Lena. Luke couldn't hide his hatred towards the man in his voice. "Why? What has the bastard done now?"

Justin figured that when he became Anne's doctor Luke would have him investigated. Trust wasn't something Luke gave, and Justin knew that. That was why he went to Luke with this; however, he wasn't about to betray Lena's confidence by telling Luke why. "I just need the information. Can you help me or not?"

Luke was genuinely worried. Even though he decided to stay away from her to protect her, he wasn't going to let the doctor hurt her either. "If he has hurt Lena again," anger filled his voice.

"What do you mean hurt Lena again." He knew that she was upset by Dr. Castillo the prior night, but he was now wondering if he hurt her and what Luke knew. Justin was going to have to share some information for Luke to do the same. "Lena's fine. She's in my guest bedroom, but there are some things that I just need to understand."

The idea of Lena being with Justin and not him felt like a needle going through his heart. "What do you mean she's there now?"

"Something happened tonight, and I think Dr. Castillo may be behind it."

The tone Luke's voice went from concern to anger. "What did the bastard do?"

Justin felt like he was betraying Lena by discussing this even though he knew his brother wouldn't repeat anything. "All you need to know is that she's fine. I just want to make sure she stays that way."

"Don't worry I'm already looking further into his past. I did a background check when he became Anne's doctor, but I think there's more going on than him being a good doctor."

At some point they were both going to have to share what they knew, but it was clear Luke was also trying to protect Lena's confidence. Justin wondered what she had shared with Luke. "Why?"

"He made some comments to me about Lena's sanity and after last night. I just thought it was a good idea."

"What did he say?"

Luke thought about telling Justin what he had learned of Lena's past, but decided against it feeling that Justin was dealing with enough. The fact that he wasn't wallowing in self-pity relieved Luke. "Not much, but it was enough to question him."

"So, you'll let me know what you find out?"

"If I find anything useful, I'll let you know. Now how are you? Where did you go after the meeting with Dr. Barre?" Luke's main concern was for Justin. They had barely spoken after their meeting with Dr. Barre and Luke was worried, he might be lost in grief.

"I met up with Lena. We talked about what to do about Anne. Luke, I want her home with me. Lena has agreed to help with the transition." Justin wanted Luke's approval, even though he was going through with his plan regardless of what Luke thought.

It made sense to Luke that Justin had gone to Lena in his time of need. He was glad Justin was feeling better, but worried he was becoming too attached to Lena. It was clear Lena was good for Justin, he just wondered if it was healthy. So many times, she had been able to pull Justin from the darkness. Normally he would do anything for Justin which is why he wondered why it bothered him if Justin was attached to Lena. Luke had spent the day thinking of her. Everything about her made him want to be with her more. All these feelings were new to him. Realistically it shouldn't upset him she was helping Justin, yet it was. None of it made sense especially since Justin was still so committed to Anne. The proof was the fact that Justin wanted to move her home. Luke couldn't express his apprehension about the idea of having Anne home over the phone and simply told Justin that he was glad he was feeling better. Luke did wonder with Anne at home if Justin would be able to move forward and pick up the pieces of his life.

****

Later that night Justin woke to blood curling screams. Instantly, he jumped out of bed and ran to the guest room where Lena was. There he found her curled up in a ball looking childlike and scared. As he questioned if he should touch her or not, he went over to her. At first Lena didn't recognize him and screamed. "Get away! Don't touch me please!"

He knew the scream was not directed at him even though he was who she was yelling at. "Angelina, it's me Justin."

After he said it was Justin, Lena began to snap out of her state and opened her eyes. Once she recognized him, she leaped into his arms. He could still feel her shake as he held her tight. In his protective arms, Lena was instantly soothed as he always made her feel safe. As shaken as she was Justin considered there was more going on with her than Dr. Castillo and he recalled Luke's words. Even with the nightmare, Justin refused to believe that she might be unstable. Something must have happened to her and he hoped that she would share what so that he could help. Justin knew about her father, but as upsetting as that was for her this was a different kind of trauma.

In his arms, Lena whispered through her tears, "He was here."

She wasn't making sense, although he did look around the room to see if there had been someone there. "Who was here? Dr. Castillo?"

Lena shook her head, "No Alan."

Justin was puzzled. "Who's Alan?"

Lena realized there was no way Alan had found her at Justin's and slowly started to calm down. The story of Alan wasn't something to share was ready to share. It was a pandora's box that she hoped to never open again. "No one of importance."

Justin wanted her to confide in him. Not for him but for her. He had entrusted his deepest thoughts with her and hoped she would be able to do the same. "Angelina, you can tell me. Trust me."

Lena wanted to tell him everything. She did, but talking about it and opening old wounds was just too hard. Justin sensed her apprehension and started to put the pieces together. Obviously, Alan was someone who hurt her tremendously. She didn't need to say anything to him to draw his own conclusions. Lena was in no shape to answer questions. Instead, he reassured her. "No one will hurt you here. I promise."

Lena knew that was true. No one knew she was there and would even look there for her. Plus, she hadn't seen Alan since that awful night and hoped to keep it that way. "Don't worry. It was just a dream. I'm better now. I'm sorry I woke you." She needed to change the subject before Justin asked any more questions. "This really is a nice room. Perfect light. Is it where you want Anne to be?"

The room wasn't what Justin wanted to talk about. He really wanted to understand the nightmare and know what Alan had done to her; however, it was clear Lena wasn't ready, so he went along with her. "I haven't decided which room. Are you tired? Do you want to go back to sleep, or would you like to see the possibilities?"

"I'm not really ready to go back to sleep but understand if you're tired."

Justin didn't sleep well without Anne and was happy to distract Lena from her thoughts. "Let's have some tea and I'll show you around."

Lena figured Justin as a coffee drinker. The offer of tea was a welcome surprise. He offered his hand to Lena to escort her to the kitchen. In the kitchen Lena noticed that Justin was only wearing pajama bottoms that hung from his hips in just the right way. The fact that he was bare chested was a surprise because she hadn't realized it earlier. Once she did, she could help but look. His chest was not as broad as Luke's, but his stomach was as cut and his chest defined. "Anne was a lucky woman," Lena thought to herself. She admired Justin's physique, while sitting on a bar stool under the salmon granite countertop. While looking, she noticed that he moved gracefully although it was clear he didn't spend much time in the kitchen because he didn't seem to know where anything was. He opened several of the oak cabinets looking for the tea before finally finding it and was excited when he did.

Lena smiled at him, "You don't spend too much time in here, do you?"

Even though it was true, Justin was a little embarrassed, it was so easy to tell. "Well, we have a housekeeper and when she's off Anne usually does the cooking." It once again occurred to him that even that was going to change. When he spoke, there was sadness in his eyes. "I guess I'll have to learn though."

Lena didn't want to bring up a painful topic. Again, she decided to change the subject. "How long have you lived her?"

"Anne and I bought the place after we got married six years ago."

They must have married at the age she was now. That was surprising to her as she was nowhere near ready to consider spending her life with anyone. At her age she hadn't even had a serious boyfriend let alone contemplated marriage. "Wow. You must have married young?"

Justin's eyes softened. "Angelina, when you know it's right. You want the rest of your life to start as soon as possible. We waited until I passed the bar though."

Justin calling her by the name her father used surprised her, even though that was her name. "Why are you now calling me Angelina?"

Justin shrugged. "I think it suits you better. Angelina my angel."

Lena smiled although she knew that she was no one's angel. Suddenly she had an idea that might solve both of their problems for a little while anyway. "You know I could take a leave of absence from work for a couple of weeks to make sure everything gets settled." He needed time to get Anne settled and it would allow her time to think about what to do about Dr. Castillo.

The idea of having her there was comforting to Justin. He was excited by the suggestion because he would not be alone. "You would do that and stay here?"

It was as much for her as it was him, but she didn't want to come across as needy. "If you need me to. Yes."

"Could you afford that?" Justin didn't want to offend her again, yet he had seen where she lived and thought having no salary might be problematic. He was right, it was a problem. Lena had a large amount of student loan debt plus her rent, but after she made the point of telling him she would help him because they were friends, she didn't want to tell him money was an issue. Her face said it all. Justin read the look. "What I meant to say is I would love that, but only if you accept a salary. I know we're friends, but I don't want to put yourself in jeopardy either."

This time she was grateful for the offer of money. Politely she accepted the offer. "It's settled. I'll tell the hospital tomorrow. Now where did you want Anne to stay?"

Both of their moods instantly changed. The idea brought comfort to them both, and they felt lighter. After the tea was ready, Justin offered a tour of the penthouse. "I'll show you around. You can tell me what you think is best."

Lena agreed as they took their cups. The penthouse was very large; along with the room that Lena was sleeping in there were six other bedrooms. All were nicely decorated in warm earth tones. She had already seen the living area and the kitchen, so Justin skipped through them on her tour. The room next to Justin's was being decorated for the baby. Anne wanted the baby near their room. Since they didn't know the baby's gender the room was to have a zoo theme because Anne always loved seeing the animals at the zoo. Wistfully Justin continued that Anne loved all of God's creatures. Even after everything when Justin spoke of Anne, he still had a sparkle in his beautiful eyes. It was obvious that he loved to tell Anne stories, however, often as he remembered where Anne was his eyes would turn. The sparkle would be replaced by complete and utter despair. Witnessing that always made Lena's heart ache for him. It also made her sad that Anne would never know she had a daughter. She hoped there was a part of her that did, but they will never know for sure. The only thing she could do for them was to make sure the transition was seamless. It reassured him when Lena promised to make all the arrangements for Anne's return because it meant he didn't have to think about it. They decided the room next to the baby's would be the best place for her. That room has excellent lighting from a large window with a view to the City. Even at night you could see the moon and the City skyline. It was beautiful and they agreed was where Anne would be happiest. As a bonus it was close enough to Justin and the baby where her presence could still be felt. Silently, Lena once again thought eventually Justin would have to move on, but not until he was ready. Until that day she was happy to help him and hopefully get him adjusted to his new normal, as painful as that might be. With the room decision made, Lena told Justin that they should rest. She could see how tired he looked, but he was still concerned about her. "Angelina, if you ever want to talk."

Although she knew what he meant and was grateful, she really didn't want to get into it anymore that night. She did feel better and didn't want that to change. "Thank you. Maybe one day, but right now we need to focus on getting Anne home."

Wishing each other goodnight they went their separate ways. Lena slept with the lights on that night. Even though Justin made her feel safe, she still didn't want to risk another nightmare.

In his room Justin paced unable to sleep. He was glad Anne would be home soon, yet understood his life would be forever changed. It was hard to imagine that he would never laugh, dance, or eat with Anne again. That thought was overwhelming and why he struggled to sleep. Eventually he did lay his head down and drifted off with the thought that Anne would soon be home.

Chapter Nine

The next morning Lena and Justin had a pancake breakfast that Mrs. Warner, the housekeeper, prepared. The idea of a housekeeper was foreign to Lena. Even though they were probably the best pancakes Lena had ever eaten. Normally she didn't eat breakfast, but with Justin it just seemed right.

Mrs. Warner was a kind lady in her late forties. Although attractive, she was dressed maternally. As Justin explained to her that Lena would be staying with them a while and why, Lena could tell she wasn't entirely comfortable with the idea, even though she chose not to comment. Lena wasn't sure if it was because she was protective of Justin or if it had something to do with Anne. The one thing she knew was that Mrs. Warner was very warm with Justin, but politely cold with her. She also couldn't help but notice the way she was eyeing Lena suspiciously. After what she had been through in her life she was used to being guarded, however, the mistrust that Mrs. Warner showed her made her feel uncomfortable. She tried to think about she would feel if she were in Mrs. Warner's position. If someone she cared about came home with a strange woman and said that woman was now living there, she too might be worried about someone as vulnerable and wonderful as Justin. Even if she understood, the way Mrs. Warner looked at her was awkward. To get her mind off of Mrs. Warner, Lena thought it was best to discuss their plans for moving Anne home. "It'll probably take a week to get Anne released. I'll finish my shifts this week. Then I'll take the leave."

"Will you stay here while we make arrangements?" Not only did he enjoy her company, but he also feared her going back to her apartment alone.

"There's no need. Once Anne is here, I'll stay until everything is secure." Lena didn't want to be a burden. She knew Justin was concerned and thought he had enough to worry about without her nightmares. It was also time she stopped letting her fear take over her life. Lena had felt great that she was able to put Dr. Castillo in his place and really wanted to get that feeling back. If she could get the control back, she knew the nightmares would stop. In her life she had given too many other people control of her emotions. Justin was disappointed but pretended to understand. In his head he decided if she wanted to return to her apartment, he would make some security adjustments to protect her.

As they were finishing breakfast Luke entered. He wanted to check on Justin and truth be told he had a sleepless night worrying about both Justin and Lena. Mrs. Warner greeted him kindly and immediately prepared him some pancakes. Even though Luke knew she had stayed there, he didn't want her to know that he and Justin had discussed her. He feigned surprise as he looked at her at the breakfast table. "Lena, what are you doing here?"

Justin eyed him suspiciously as he asked the question. Lena hadn't been prepared to see Luke. Her first thought was that she looked a mess while he looked delicious. He was dressed in a grey pin striped designer suit while she was wearing boxers and a tank top. Once she got control of her faculties, she wondered how comfortable she would be living at Justin's with Luke coming and going frequently. When she agreed to stay that thought didn't occur to her. She too tried to play nonchalant as she answered his question. "My apartment was broken into. Justin was kind enough to let me stay."

That was news. He knew something had happened, but having her home invaded wasn't what he was prepared for. When he spoke with Justin, he had assumed that it was another run in with Dr. Castillo. Nothing like what really happened. Concern filled his voice. "Are you okay?"

"I wasn't there, and nothing was missing. Just a little shaken I guess." Lena got up from the table to put her plate in the sink, "If you two will excuse me I'll get dressed and Justin we can go to the hospital together. Nice to see you, Luke."

When she was no longer in the room, Luke wanted details about what happened. Justin didn't share much, only that Lena believed Dr. Castillo had broken in to retrieve what she had handed him in the envelope. "Do you know what was in the envelope?"

"Nope. All I know is that she felt it gave her security and Dr, Asshole didn't want her to have it."

"Did you ask what the hell this thing is about?"

Justin shrugged. "She'll tell me when she's ready. Besides I have a feeling there's more to this than Dr. Asshole."

Luke already knew what it was, "You may be right, but our immediate problem is what to do about the asshole."

"I haven't figured that out yet. We have some time, since Lena will be taking a leave of absence to help with Anne."

That was news to Luke. He had known they had grown close but hadn't realized how close they had become. It also brought him back to the real reason for his visit. He had come over to try to persuade Justin out of moving Anne back home. "Do you really think having Anne here is a good idea?"

He really did. In fact, he couldn't imagine anything else since he had been told it was a possibility. "This is her home. There's no other place for her to be."

Luke knew Justin was thinking with his heart not his head. "She's going to need constant care. How are you going to handle that?"

Justin understood Luke was worried, he just wasn't going to change his mind. "Lena is going to move in here for a while to help get things settled. We've discussed this. Don't worry everything will be okay."

From a reason that was unclear to Luke that statement didn't make the idea a better one. "If Anne's coming back, don't you think that you'll need to hire a nursing service and not rely on Lena?"

"That's part of what Lena will handle. Dad wants me back at work. I'll still need to spend time with Anne and Faith. Having Lena here is the best solution for my piece of mind. At least with her here I know Anne will be well cared for when I'm not here."

It was news to Luke that Justin was thinking about going back to the office. "Are you ready to go back to work? I've been handling everything."

"I know you have and honestly, I'm not sure if I am. I do know I need to do something. I've put everything on hold. I'm going to have to figure out what my life will look like now. Faith deserves that." He had fallen completely in love with Faith. It would be very easy for him to give up without Anne, but Anne wouldn't want that, and Faith needed him whole.

Lena's return to the kitchen interrupted their conversation. She was happy to hear that they weren't discussing her situation, but Anne. When she entered the room, all eyes were on her. It was apparent that they both thought that she was attractive. Fresh from the shower Lena's long wet curly hair flowed over her shoulders. She was wearing short, ripped jean shorts that showed the firmness of her legs and behind with a white lace baby doll shirt that was low cut. The lace of the body of the shirt was see through. If you looked closely as Luke did, you could see that she had a diamond piercing on her belly button. Briefly Luke wondered what else he would see if he explored the rest of her body. Lena walked to her purse on the kitchen counter and bent over to get a hair clip from it. While Luke was enjoying the view, Justin felt guilty for looking and quickly turned away. As she pulled her hair into a loose bun, Lena told Justin she was ready to go to the hospital. The way Luke was looking at her ignited feelings that she needed to push aside because she couldn't get her discovery about him out of her head. Before they went to the hospital, Justin needed fifteen minutes to shower and dress and excused himself, while asking Lena to talk to Luke. "Can you please explain to Luke what our plans for Anne are? He's concerned."

Although Lena didn't want to be left alone with Luke because she didn't trust herself, there was no other choice. "Sure."

As soon as Justin was out of the room Luke wanted to know what her thoughts of Anne returning really were. "Do you really think that it's a good idea for him to move Anne back here?"

Luke was still unable to take his eyes off her. They were piercing and made Lena feel desirable. As calmly as she could she addressed him. "I think right now this is what Justin needs. If it's too much, he can have her moved to a treatment facility later. This is all his call, and we need to follow his lead."

From her inability to make eye contact, it was obvious Lena was uncomfortable in Luke's presence. The question wasn't upsetting. It was the pull she felt towards him that made her want to run away. Her body was telling her to run to him and let him make her forget everything for a little while. She knew that if he touched her, she would be lost. The attraction was that strong. Her head was saying "dark and dangerous run." For once she was choosing to listen to her head over her body. No matter how hard it was.

Luke sensed her nervousness. He decided that she was shaken over Dr. Castillo. "Did you report the break-in?"

There was no point. She knew who and why. What she didn't want was for Gus to get involved. That would make things worse since he was so protective of her. "No. Nothing was missing."

Having been to her apartment Luke knew that Lena had nothing of value in there. He had seen that for himself. Even her computer was several years old. He was hoping if he asked the right questions she would confide in him. "So, if nothing was missing, what do you think it was about?"

She wasn't about to share with him. If she couldn't tell Justin, she certainly wasn't going to share with Luke. Nonchalantly she responded, "Not sure."

"Ready," Justin came out saying before Luke could ask a follow-up question. Luke saw the way Lena looked at Justin. There was so much affection in her eyes and her facial features were softer as they interacted. The look she gave Justin was very different from the way she looked at him, which was more of a nervous expression. She was nowhere near as relaxed. Even though she and Luke had chemistry, it was evident she was also developing feelings for Justin. It was also clear that Justin was returning her affection. The idea of that should have made Luke happy. It didn't. Instead, he felt a twinge of jealousy. Because of that he offered to go with them to the hospital. They both turned to Luke surprised when he offered and questioned why. It was a simple explanation. To accept the idea of Anne going to the penthouse, he needed more information. As such Luke thought it was best Lena rode with him to further discuss the plans. The idea that Luke was trying to accept his decision made Justin happy as he hoped Lena could put Luke's mind at ease. Justin believed to Lena's dismay that it was a good idea for Luke to talk to Lena. The last thing Lena wanted to do was ride to the hospital with Luke. There was no way for Lena to decline without suspicion and agreed.

During the short ride to the hospital, a fidgety Lena explained Justin's plan. He wasn't really interested in the details because he knew Justin's mind was made up no matter what Luke thought. When Justin told him about the idea, he had that same look he had as a boy when there was nothing that would make him change his mind. For the most part Justin was easy going, but there were times when there was no swaying him and this was one of those times. Luke knew better than to even try. What Luke really wanted was time alone with Lena, even though he sensed she wanted to be anywhere else. "Why do I make you uncomfortable? I thought the other night we were becoming friends. Then you left without a word."

Lena was going to try to downplay her feelings. "Uncomfortable. I don't know what you mean. I left you a note so that I didn't wake you."

"I saw the note, but it's pretty clear you don't want to be around me. Are you embarrassed?"

After everything she had been through embarrassed was the last thing she was. Maybe if she were in a different place mentally, she would be, but in this state she wasn't. "Should I be?"

"There's no reason to be."

"Well than why would you think that?"

"Maybe the way you're acting around me now."

This conversation wasn't what she needed, and she really didn't know what to say to him. Luke was Justin's brother and they both wanted Justin's happiness. "There's just a lot going on now." Lena couldn't wait to get out of the car. Luckily, they were pulling into the hospital parking garage. As soon as Luke parked the car Lena jumped out.

"Lena, wait!" Luke feared he wouldn't have another chance to speak with her alone. He really did want to know why she left abruptly and why she was now so nervous around him. Although after the way she was acting, he suspected his closet had something to do with her change in attitude towards him. "If you're going to be living with my brother. We're going to see each other. I need to know why you are so nervous around me?"

Lena didn't turn to face him out of fear she wouldn't be able to lie or deny her feelings. The nervousness wasn't about Luke, it was her electricity towards him that she knew could destroy her. "I'm not nervous. Look I can't deny there's a physical attraction, but I know you're bad for me. I think we should keep our distance from each other when at all possible. I understand that my living with Justin complicates things. We should try though."

Luke already knew that was probably true but having her say it made him want to persuade her otherwise. Maybe he wasn't as convinced as he initially thought. "Bad for you? How?"

With her back still to him, she replied, "Look, you're just too dangerous."

Her statement hurt him even if Luke knew it was true. Jessica could attest to that. "Please look at me." Luke needed to see her face when he said that next thing. He had to make sure she understood what he was saying was the truth. Slowly, she turned because as kind as he had been to her, she owed him that much. "I would never force you to do anything you didn't want." The thought of forcing himself on anyone was repulsive to Luke. All his sexual encounters were completely consensual.

Even though she saw the sincerity in his eyes she still had to be strong. She knew he wouldn't have to force her. She would be a willing participant. It was after that worried her. "I really can't do this now. I need to go to the Administrator's Office. Tell Justin I'll meet him in Anne's room in an hour."

Before Luke could say another word, she ran off. He thought about chasing her, but thought better of it because he didn't want to appear obsessed, and he definitely didn't want to frighten her. Luke stood for a couple of minutes in the garage wondering if he was obsessed. She filled a lot of his waking moments. Even now he was standing, wondering how he could put her at ease with him. That suddenly became very important to him, which was odd because that wasn't how Luke thought. He never cared about making someone comfortable with him. In fact, he prided himself on intimidating people. That is what made him an excellent lawyer.

He thought about it all the way up to Anne's room. Before Luke let Justin know he was there, he listened to Justin tell Anne she would be home soon. It was heartbreaking because Luke could almost feel Justin's pain. He had never experienced that kind of love but watched Justin with Anne long enough to understand their love. Luke interrupted their one-sided conversation to relay Lena's message.

Although Justin was grateful for Luke, he wanted to be alone with Anne. "I know you have other things to do than be here. Go spend some time with James."

Luke eyed him suspiciously. "Are you sure?"

"Go. Give him a hug from Uncle Justin and Aunt Anne."

Uneasy, Luke turned to leave. Before Jessica and Luke told James about Anne they wanted more information. Since the doctors had no hope of recovery, it was time for James to know. It was going to be a hard conversation. James loved Anne very much and would be devastated. Luke envisioned James would have all kinds of questions, but Luke wouldn't have the answers. They didn't know who did this or why it happened. Nor did he completely understand why Anne was there physically, but not mentally. He hoped Jessica thought of a way to explain what happened to James, even though he knew Jessica well enough to know she was leaving it up to Luke. As Luke was getting on the elevator, he ran into Lena who was getting off. She saw he was headed down and asked if he was leaving. When he answered that he was, he saw the relief in her face and was disappointed by her reaction. Unable to help himself, he gently took her hand. "It could be great between us. I'm not the dangerous man you think I am."

As he stepped into the elevator, Lena felt the charge from his touch. There again was an internal conflict. Her body was telling her that maybe he was right, while her head still said stay away.

*****

Lena and Justin spent the day together making plans, interviewing nursing agencies and purchasing items. They learned that they could have everything ready with Anne moved in four days. Since there was a lot to do in a short amount of time, they agreed that Lena would stay with Justin. Justin took her back to her apartment to get some more of her clothes. There were already new locks on the door which Justin had arranged when he thought she would return there, however the apartment was still a mess. Initially, Lena started to clean it up, but stopped herself because she was too disheartened. She loved her little apartment. It had been more than a home; it was a safe haven. With the invasion it was violated and tainted like so many other things in her life had been. Instead of cleaning up she took as much as she thought she would need and left.

Justin wanted Anne's room painted in her favorite lavender color. Since they were unable to find a painter who could get it done on such short notice, they decided to paint it themselves. Justin had never painted anything before and was looking for Lena's guidance to help him get the job done. Before starting they hired movers to take the bed that was already in the room to a storage unit within the penthouse complex. Anne required a hospital bed and there was no need for the one that was already in the room. Once the room was emptied, they began to get the paint ready. First Lena told him that they needed to tape the trim and ceiling. There was no time for extra work. Since both were in good condition, there was no need to repaint. Justin teased her about having a second career as a painter. She laughed as she told him to just do as he was instructed. After taping the room, they began to paint. It was clear from how Justin looked at the roller, he had no idea what he was doing. To help him out Lena stood from behind him, while holding his arm showing him in slow motion what to do. In such a close proximately to Justin, Lena was able to smell how wonderful his aftershave was. For a moment Lena found herself wishing that he was available but knew his heart belonged to another. After several minutes Justin got the hang of it and Lena let him move independently. The lavender was a soothing color. While painting Lena mentioned that since the room had been painted a pale green before they changed it, they were going to need new drapes to match the new color. All Justin wanted was to make Anne comfortable. He agreed because he knew Anne would want the drapes to match the room. The mood had become somber, and Lena decided music would make the job more fun. To make sure the music didn't remind Justin of Anne, Lena decided to put on salsa music. She had a feeling they had never salsa danced together, and the music reminded her of better times. Her parents loved to dance. With no culture of his own her father embraced everything about her mother's Latin culture including the food and music. While painting Lena moved her hips to the rhythm of the beat in an expert manner. While Lena painted carefree, Justin was very intent. He moved at a slow and steady pace so that he wouldn't make any mistakes while also enjoying the music. They enjoyed each other's company telling stories and teasing one another about who was the better painter.

With Chinese food in hand, Luke and James entered the penthouse. They heard the music and went to see what was happening. Luke was instantly drawn to Lena with a roller in her hand bending over to get more paint shaking her backside as she moved to the beat of the music. She had changed into an old white tank top and light blue gym shorts. As Luke studied her he had visions of them painting each other, naked. He would eventually take her with her backside sitting on top of him as he moved. Her breasts would fit perfectly in the cups of his hand while she screamed with pure pleasure. His visions were so vivid that he found himself getting hard and had to excuse himself before anyone noticed.

Justin introduced Lena to James. James was an adorable five almost six-year-old boy who looked like a mini version of his father. The only difference between them, aside from their height and body structure, was that James' eyes were blue, not green like Luke's. Jessica and Luke had told James about Anne and with the innocence of a child he had a lot of questions. "Is this where Aunt Anne will stay?"

Justin loved his nephew and as hard as all of this was on him, he had to help James too. "It is. What do you think buddy?"

James scrunched his nose. "It's kind of girly."

Lena and Justin laughed at his perspective. "I guess it is, but Aunt Anne is a girl."

"Dad said that she won't be able to talk to me anymore. I'm going to miss her."

"Me too. She'll always be with us in our hearts. She loved you James. Now you'll have to tell your new cousin about how wonderful her mom was."

Lena marveled at how great Justin was with him. She knew the conversation was painful, but he did his best not to make it that way for James.

"Don't worry Uncle Justin. I'll be a good big cousin."

Justin smiled. "I know you will."

When Luke was composed, he returned to the room to announce they had Chinese food. Since the walls were covered with one coat of lavender, Lena and Justin decided to take a food break. Over dinner James enthralled them with tales of kindergarten. He spoke about a school play his class was doing. To his disappointment he had gotten the part of Humpty Dumpty when he had wanted to be the Big Bad Wolf in the Three Little Pigs. He spent a great deal of time showing them what a convincing wolf he would be. They all had to agree that he would have made an excellent wolf. James was such a delightful child that Lena fell in love. The feeling was mutual as she laughed at all his jokes. Many times throughout dinner Luke tried to catch Lena's eyes. Even though she was drawn to him, she did her best to keep focus on James. When dinner was over Justin opened another bottle of wine for the adults. The brothers started to talk about their boyhood misdeeds while James went to play video games. About thirty minutes later James was bored with playing games by himself and asked Lena if she would play with him. His father's looks weren't all James had inherited from Luke. He also had his charm. When he asked Lena, she couldn't refuse. They all decided to play a football game. Lena and James were an unbeatable team against the brothers. Anyone looking at the four that evening would think that they didn't have a care in the world. For one night they didn't. At midnight Luke carried James, who had fallen asleep to the car while Lena and Justin went to their separate rooms.

Chapter Ten

The next day Lena worked her final shift before taking a month's leave. Everyone in the ER wondered why she was going on extended leave. There was no one that she was close with and didn't wish to share. All she offered was that it was personal, and she would be back in a month. In an envelope left at the desk was a message claiming she had lost her leverage. It wasn't signed, but she knew it was from Dr. Castillo. Lena was surprised by this note in no way. She knew Dr. Castillo would assume he had taken everything from her apartment and her computer. What he didn't count on was the copy that was in Justin's safe. After a lot of consideration, she decided she didn't want him to believe he had gotten the better of her. Smugly, she dropped a letter off with his secretary. Her unsigned letter read:

Dr. I know you're celebrating that you have all proof but make no mistake I'm smarter than you give me credit for. There's another copy in a safe place you will never find. Lose sleep wondering where it is and know you will NEVER have me.

The ER was filled with people who had minor injuries that day. Lena felt gratified to know that when Dr. Castillo read her note he would be upset. She was even happier that it would be a month before she had to deal with the fallout. By then he surely would have moved on. In the mist of everything Trey called. It had been several days since she had seen him, and she was happy to hear from him. He was interested in hearing how things with Dr. Castillo ended up. Since she was at work, she couldn't provide an update. All she could do was thank him for his help. He was happy to do it and wanted to know if she wanted to go to a beach party his friends were having the next day. It sounded like fun and Lena wanted to go, but thought she should check with Justin first to see if he needed her for anything even though Anne wouldn't be home yet. It was a tricky situation that was new, and she didn't quite understand the boundaries.

Justin also returned to work. It was hard for him as people stared almost as if they were waiting for him to break. All day Justin heard the whispers behind his back. Many offered their condolences. That was particularly hard on Justin because he was still trying to come to terms with everything and wasn't ready for people's pity. No matter how well-meaning they were. It seemed like a lifetime had passed since he was last there. To avoid gossip, Justin sat in his office with his door closed, starring at a picture of Anne. He was just about to leave for the day when he received Lena's text about the beach party. Justin wasn't a selfish person and told her to have fun. There was a part of him that was jealous. Not because she wanted to go to a party but because she was able to be carefree. He longed for the days when he and Anne would play on the beach. Anne loved the beach, but her fair skin had to be completely covered in sunscreen, or she would burn easily. The last time they were there Anne fell asleep. Her bathing suit had ridden up and exposed her naked behind. Justin smiled at how he teased her about her awkward sunburn. While he was lost in his daydream, John walked in with Luke to discuss the big case that they were working on before Anne was shot. Understandably, Justin was having a hard time focusing on work. Luke noticed Justin wasn't paying attention and adjourned the meeting after he assured their father, they had everything under control. That appeased John a little.

After her shift Lena went in search of Justin in Anne's hospital room because he had offered her a ride home. Lena listened as Justin told Anne how much he loved her. Lena never thought about getting married or starting a family. The idea of loss had always been too painful. Watching Justin with Anne made her again wonder about how amazing someone loving you that much would be. Not that she thought she would find it. The important thing was Justin wasn't going to let losing it break him the way her mother had. He was using it to get stronger and Lena believed Anne was holding on to give him that strength. She also thought that once Anne knew Justin was strong enough, she would let go. That was the only real way he would be able to get on with this life. Until that day Anne would always have a hold on him. Lena felt guilty for her thoughts and was grateful that no one could read her mind. When Lena entered the room Justin smiled brightly at her. Every time he gave her that smile it melted her heart. It was the first time since the first day that Lena had seen Justin dressed in an obviously expensive suit. His black suit and white dress shirt were accented with a lavender tie. Lena understood the significance. "I am ready," Justin said leaning over to kiss Anne's check.

On the car ride home, they discussed their day. Lena told him about the interaction with Dr. Castillo. Justin assured her the copy was in the safe. Even if he figured out it was Justin who had it there was no way he would get past the building security to recover the evidence. For that she was grateful. After he reassured Lena, Justin told her about how he was unable to concentrate at work. He felt so uncomfortable being back. Even though everyone was well intentioned, their actions made it harder. Before he could get depressed, he proudly relayed the progress Faith was making. If Faith kept doing as well as she was, the doctors thought she could be home in a little over a month. That was wonderful news. Silently, Lena marveled at how normal things with them were. They were discussing all the day's events as if they had known each other for years, not just several days.

At the penthouse Mrs. Warner had prepared a ravioli meal for them which she left on the warmer. Lena put the plates on the table while Justin opened a bottle of wine. The ravioli smelled delicious and tasted even better. Lena was starving and ate every bite, while the two sat at the table eating and drinking wine. It was Justin's turn to be grateful that he had her company to enjoy dinner with, instead of eating alone, wallowing in despair. The dinner conversation was light until Lena decided it was time to talk about something that might be painful for Justin but needed to be said.

She bit her lip and pushed the words out. "I have to talk to you about something, but I'm not sure you're ready."

Justin had hoped it was about her. "I thought we'd already established that you could talk to me about anything."

"This isn't about me. It's about Anne's clothes."

Justin looked confused, "What about Anne's clothes?"

"Well, I think that we should move them to her room. It would make it easier for the nurses. Not everything just, the basics. I can help you move them tonight if you like."

That hadn't occurred to Justin. He was just adjusting to not having Anne in his room and he wasn't ready to think of parting with anything belonging to her. It wasn't as if they were leaving the apartment, but having all of Anne's things in his room made him feel comforted. Often, he would go into the closet and take out an item like Anne's favorite sweater just to smell it. Her lavender perfume smell was still on many of her things. When Justin wanted to feel Anne, he would take an item of clothing, hold it close while closing his eyes. For a moment, he could picture her with him. Justin still needed that, even if he had to agree that moving them would be more practical. While Lena had offered to help, he couldn't bear the thought of having someone else touch Anne's things, even Lena.

"No, I need to do it myself. I'll do it tomorrow while you're at the beach."

It was apparent that Justin was lost in thought after their conversation. All of this was so painful for him and Lena understood. Before she went to her room, she gave him a big hug telling him that if he needed to talk, she would be there. The gesture was comforting and appreciated. Losing any part of Anne was impossible for Justin to face.

****

Luke decided a pleasurable, carefree night with Tabatha would be just what he needed after the last several days. When Tabatha arrived at his apartment, he immediately escorted her to his bedroom. It had been the first time since Luke went to France that she had heard from him, and she was happy to oblige especially since she believed their relationship had reached a new plateau. After his visions of having Lena from behind, he decided they would play out his fantasy. He asked Tabatha to put on a long brown curly wig. Since she loved role play, she quickly agreed. Once Tabatha stripped while wearing the wig, Luke grabbed her into a hard kiss and threw her on to the bed. She asked him how he wanted to play. Luke told her that he wanted to play hard. That was her cue as she knew what he meant and told him that she had been a very bad girl. Excited, he asked how bad she had been. After she responded that she had been very bad, Luke told her that he thought she needed to be punished harshly. Luke then told her to get up and bend over the bed after he went into his closet to pull out a paddle to issue a harsh punishment. With her behind crimson after a paddling, he put the paddle down and he felt in between her legs. Tabatha liked it rough and was very wet. He removed his pants taking her from behind as he had in his fantasy of Lena. He knew it was wrong, but in his head, Lena was riding him. The wig only helped with the allusion. In the bedroom, Luke liked having

Comment
but "allusio
better choi

all the power over the women he sexed. Tabatha was always willing to oblige. After looking at the color of Tabatha's behind, he wondered if he could do that to fragile Lena. During his thoughts about Lena, Luke became softer and more caring while having his way with Tabatha. In Tabatha's mind they were making love while Luke was completely lost in his thoughts of Lena. Slowly, they found their release. Luke held Tabatha close until he opened his eyes and realized who he was really with. When he did, he released her, wondering again what Lena had done to him. There was no way he could treat Lena the way that he had Tabatha or most of the other woman he had bedded. She was special. Through Luke's internal battle he decided that he had to try. He wanted Lena at any cost. When Luke looked at Tabatha, she was grinning from ear to ear. She had started to worry that maybe the last time they were together she misunderstood, but this time she knew his feelings towards her had changed. To get to leave Luke told her he needed to do some work. This time Tabatha refused to leave because in her head things had changed between them. She was determined to spend the night and stayed in the bed, while she assured him she would be waiting when he returned. Luke was confused because she always took the hint. Hours later when he returned to his room, she was still in his bed. Aggravated, Luke told her that he needed his rest and turned off the lights. When Tabatha moved to cuddle,

Luke turned over. It was a move that confused Tabatha, however she was not deterred. With his back to her, Luke dreamed of Lena.

****

Lena woke up early to run in the morning. There was something so relaxing about an early morning run. Just Lena and the music on her iPhone. It was early summer. The warm air hit Lena's face as she ran through the streets of New York to Central Park. There were many joggers out that morning, but Lena paid them no attention even as one male runner tried to talk to her. She was focused on losing the images of Dr. Castillo, Luke and Justin. In an attempt to drown her thoughts out, she turned up the music on her phone and began to run harder. As she hurried her pace everything that haunted her seemed miles away. By the time she made it back to Justin's, she was exhausted, sweaty and more relaxed than she had been in a long time. Also having just worked out, Justin was seated having breakfast. Mrs. Warner had prepared him an omelet and asked Lena if she wanted one. Lena didn't like to eat much after running, so she asked if she could have a yogurt that Mrs. Warner quickly got for her.

Justin smiled as she entered the kitchen. "Were you out running?"

"I did a couple of laps around Central Park." Before sitting at the table Lena marveled at how unfair life was. After her run she was glistening with sweat with her ponytailed hair frazzled. She was very aware of how bad she looked. While Justin, who had also just worked out in his black tank top and gym shorts, looked like anything but a mess. In fact, he looked hot. Justin's words brought her back to reality. "One of my favorite places to run. Maybe next time we could run together."

She liked that idea. "Did you used to run with Anne?"

Justin laughed. "No Anne hates or hated to run. In fact she hated any exercise that wasn't tennis. Do you play?"

"No. Tennis is more for you country club types. I like hard pavement."

Justin laughed again. Anne was anything but a country club type. "So what time are you going out tonight?"

"Well, the party is at Jones Beach. My friend told me he would pick me up at two. We have the medical supplies being delivered today. I won't be leaving until after that. Listen Justin, I think it might be best if I slept in my own apartment tonight. I'll probably be getting back late and plan on letting my hair down. If you know what I mean."

"Do you really think I'm that old? Believe me Angelina, I get it and to be honest unless you have other plans, I would prefer that you come here no matter how late. That way I know you'll be safe."

"You don't need to worry about me."

Justin stood up and kissed her forehead. It was an innocent kiss but sent tingles down Lena's spine. "Right now, I need to know my angel will be here to guide me. Believe me wanting your safety is not so unselfish."

With that Justin went to get dressed for work. Lena sat dumbfounded thinking how sweet Justin was. Within half an hour, Justin was ready for work dressed in a navy-blue pin stripped suit with a vest and red silk tie. The vest hugged tightly against his strong physic. Lena couldn't decide whether he looked better in his gym clothes or his suit. Either way he was a good-looking man.

"I'll be back before you leave today. I have a lot of work to do moving items."

"Are you sure you don't want help?"

"Thank you, but this is something I need to do alone."

When Justin left Lena decided it was finally time to call Gus. She didn't know how he would feel about her living situation and hated the idea of him disapproving. When he answered, Lena filled him in on the edited version of events. As she feared Gus was not pleased initially and expressed his feelings, until she explained she felt her father had sent her there. At that point he could no longer argue. Gus knew Lena often looked for signs from her father. He wasn't sure he believed it, however it seemed to give her strength, so he never expressed his uncertainty. Besides it was nice to think Ryan was looking after his daughter. As a police officer he knew the Armstrong family reputation well. He wasn't at all comfortable with the idea, yet tried to be open-minded once Lena mentioned Ryan. More importantly, Gus wanted to know about her nightmares. She assured him they were gone. Since that first night at Justin's, she hadn't had any other. He made her feel safe and she was confident they were gone for good. There had been no update on who shot Anne although Gus was now operating under the impression it was a targeted attack. So far there has been no proof of that. It was just his gut feeling. Lena hoped he was wrong and decided not to share that with Justin or Luke until he had something. They ended the conversation with Lena promising to visit soon and telling him she loved him. Gus had a rough exterior, but every time he heard those words from Lena he melted. Even though she wasn't his blood, in his heart she was every bit his daughter as Ryan's. After they hung up Lena was excited that the conversation had gone better than she expected.

****

At the law firm's offices Justin informed Luke, he needed to leave early because he still had a lot of work to do to get ready for Anne's arrival. Before he went home, he first wanted to go to the hospital to see Anne and Faith. Luke could see that there was something else on Justin's mind and inquired as to what it was. Justin's eyes began to fill as he discussed his afternoon plans, telling Luke that he had to pack up some of Anne's things and move them to her new room. It was evident that it was going to be a difficult task. "Is Lena helping you?"

"No, she offered but this is something I should do in private. Since she's going to a party today, I thought it would be a good time."

Luke tried to act nonchalant. "Lena's going to a party?"

Even though Luke decided he would pursue Lena since Justin disapproved, he was trying to cover up his intent. It was obvious Justin and Lena were growing closer. As much as he wanted his brother's happiness, he felt he had to have Lena for himself. It wasn't going to be easy. There were so many obstacles including him and his inability to commit. This time with this woman Luke believed he could be different. He felt something so powerful for Lena that he couldn't define. The time to act was now while Justin was still so dedicated to Anne and before he realized how he was beginning to feel for Lena.

Justin sensed something odd in Luke's question and suspiciously answered. "She and some friends are headed to Jones Beach for the day."

This time Luke was unable to hide anything. "Male friends or female?"

Irritated Justin sternly commented. "Luke, you promised you would stay away. She's fragile."

Again, Luke tried to act nonchalant. "Just concerned that's all."

"Yeah. Concerned huh? I don't know the specifics, but she did mention a guy picking her up. Just let her be."

"A guy" Luke thought and needed more information. Since Justin was becoming suspicious Luke decided to change the subject for now. "I know you want to go through Anne's things alone, but you'll probably be wrecked afterwards. How about a man's dinner tonight? I could bring a pizza and beer. We could watch some movies. Just bros hanging out."

It was an offer made from genuine concern even if there would be a bonus in it for Luke. Justin knew going through Anne's things was going to be difficult and appreciated Luke's offer, although after their conversation he questioned if supporting him was all Luke wanted to do that night. Not wanting to think badly of his brother, Justin agreed that an evening with Luke might be what he needed after a hard day.

****

When Justin arrived home, Lena was standing in the kitchen wearing navy-blue bikini top and white shorts. She was waiting for Trey and decided to get a bottle of water for the ride. Feeling guilty about looking, Justin had a hard time not admiring her body. He could see the glistening of the diamond stud on her belly button. It had been a while since he had been with a woman, but seeing Lena half naked was bringing up feelings that he quickly shot down. Lena smiled knowing that Justin was trying not to stare. It was nice to know that he wasn't completely unaffected by her. Justin began to loosen his tie as she greeted him. Since he seemed so uncomfortable Lena reached for a blue tank top that was on the kitchen counter.

As she began to put it on Lena spoke. "The bed came. I have all the bedding and new drapes set up. You should look."

"Thank you. I will. How does it look? I want Anne to be happy in her new room."

"I think you'll be happy and believe she would be too."

Justin was having a hard time looking at Lena and tried to focus on anything but on the vision of her half naked. "Have a great time tonight."

Justin had to leave the room to get his impure thoughts out of his head. After he was gone, Lena yelled that her ride was there and wished him luck with everything.

Outside the penthouse building Trey was standing at his friend's car. He hugged Lena tightly when he saw her. Lena was happy to see Trey and his friends Mark and Will. It had been some time since she had had a carefree day and knew being with Trey was going to be a lot of fun. They asked Lena about her living arrangements and commented that the new apartment complex was very different from the place they dropped her off at after the bar. When she told them she was helping a friend whose wife was in bad shape, they left it alone. On the hour and a half drive to the beach, Will entertained them with jokes from his comedy act enlisting input for his big show. Traffic was moderate for New York. When they weren't listening to Will, they were singing along to old Journey songs. The 2006 Honda Accord they were riding in was so different from Luke's Porsche or Justin's Lexus, but Lena felt more comfortable than she had been in weeks.

It was a beautiful day when they arrived at the beach. The warm summer air felt better with the cool breeze of the beach. Since Lena didn't own a car or even drive, she didn't get to the beach often, but she loved it. Some of her favorite family memories from before her father passed were of them spending the day at Jones Beach. Her father would always bring a kite. They would try to fly it as high as they could. Later her father would play with her in the water. Even though she grew up in Mexico Lena's mother wasn't one for swimming. She did, however, pack the most wonderful picnic lunches. Being at Jones Beach made Lena feel closer to her father. Even with Lena's olive complexion the sun was hot, so Lena asked Trey if he would mind putting sunscreen on her back. Trey obliged while quietly reminding himself that they were just friends, even if he wanted more. The last time he saw Lena she was in bad shape, and he had to know how everything was. It wasn't the day for any negativity. All he needed to know was that she was fine. She didn't want anything to damper her day and decided to go in the water. As she threw off her shorts to run into the water, she yelled back that everything was great.

Trey and his friends stood on the beach for a minute with their mouths open watching the vision that was Lena. Once they recovered from being dumbstruck, they joined her in the water. Since it was early in the season the water was cold. There was a storm in the Atlantic, so the waves were strong and great for body surfing. As petite as she was Lena was thrown many times running into Trey on several occasions. Trey didn't mind. Slowly, the others arrived at the beach. There were twelve in total. Later in the day they set up a volleyball net to play beach ball on the plush sand. Lena and Trey were an unbeatable team. They worked together in perfect unison, beating the other teams. On the final match of the day, they celebrated their win with a hug. Trey held Lena a little tighter than needed, making Lena question if he wanted to be more than friends. As much affection as she had for Trey, the thought of more than friendship wasn't something Lena was prepared for at that point. She had too many men in her life to contend with at that moment, although she did have to admit they did have chemistry in bed. Plus, he was a great guy. If their relationship had started differently maybe she would be interested, but for the time being all she wanted was a good friend. Trey could tell from her body movements what she was feeling so he playfully removed his baseball cap to put it on her head while laughing as he did it. The mood was instantly altered to the playful, serenity Lena was enjoying. As the sun set they marveled at the beauty of the colors on the horizon. Somehow a sunset on the beach always seemed more beautiful, especially since the buildings in the City often hid the beauty. At nightfall they set up a bonfire and enjoyed roasting hotdogs and marshmallows while drinking beer. There was a cool breeze in the air causing Lena to get a chill. Since Lena had not brought anything heavier than a tank top, Trey offered his sweatshirt. The sweatshirt was way too big for Lena but somehow felt just right. Mark was a Deejay and brought dance music. When the music started everyone danced on the beach under the stars. Trey and Lena danced closely. It was hard for Lena to determine if she was growing feelings for Trey or if it was the beer. In order to be sure, she decided to wait until she was sober to make that determination, so she kept him at bay. His friendship had become very important to her. It wasn't something she wanted to end because of another drunken night. Everyone was having so much fun as the day continued into the late hour of the night.

****

Many times, while packing Anne's things, Justin questioned if he should put away more than the essentials he packed for her room. There were items he knew she would never need again like her evening gowns from the various charity events they attended. Even though she wouldn't wear any of them again, each one held a special memory for Justin. He looked at the long backless black evening gown and remembered the night she told him she was pregnant with Faith. It was right before an important event for a new center for underprivileged children. Before they left, she pulled out a teddy bear she had bought for the baby. The bear wore a shirt that said, "proud papa." That was exactly what Justin was from the moment Anne told him she was pregnant. As frightened as Justin was about becoming a father, he wanted nothing more than to share that experience with Anne. When Justin closed his eyes, he could still see how happy they both were that night. It seemed like a lifetime ago not just a mere seven months. Again, he wondered how he would go through life without Anne. Not her body because that would be with him, but her. Everything about her that made her so special to him was gone. Justin fell to the bed feeling alone as he stared at a picture of Anne and him on the nightstand. He knew Anne wouldn't want him to wallow in despair. She loved him very much and he needed to honor that love by picking up the pieces of his life. The problem was he had no idea how to do that without Anne. As painful as it was, he knew the first step to doing that was to continue with the task at hand. He had to take her things to her new room.

After all the essentials were moved, the room was ready for Anne's arrival. Justin sat in a chair that was by Anne's new bed for hours wondering what his new life would be like. As he started to drift off, Luke arrived with pizza and beer. It was a welcome distraction that only Luke could provide. While eating pizza and drinking beer, they discussed the fun times they had with Anne. Luke reminded Justin of the first time he met Anne. They didn't hit it off initially. Especially after Luke, who didn't know who she was made a pass at her. Once Anne discovered Luke was already engaged to Jessica, she really gave him a piece of her mind. Anne wasn't one for mincing words. Justin had to calm her down by telling her the engagement was a business arrangement. Years later they would laugh about that. As much as Anne grew to love Luke, she always believed he should have done better by Jessica. For Justin talking about Anne with someone who knew her was comforting after a rough day. After they ate Luke suggested they play the football game they had played with Lena and James. He was determined to get better at it than James and Lena. The distraction was just what Justin needed to forget for a little while. Moving Anne's things was difficult. That was compounded by the guilt he felt for feeling the hint of desire he had when he looked at Lena earlier. She was in no shape for a relationship and his heart still belonged to Anne. Justin thought about telling Luke. He wrongly thought Luke would encourage him to act on it because Luke would, but that wasn't what he needed. His energy needed to be on Anne and Faith. Justin was oblivious to Luke's feelings for Lena. Luke would never have told Justin to act on his primal instincts with Lena. He wanted her for himself. After midnight

Justin was exhausted and went to bed while Luke told him he would sleep on his sofa because he drank too much. Even though Justin offered one of the spare rooms, Luke said the sofa was better. He was anxious about the fact Lena wasn't home yet and wanted to wait for her. The beers were only an excuse to do so. On the sofa Luke wondered what was keeping Lena. He didn't like it at all that she was out with another man. Finally, around one-twenty Luke heard voices in the hallway. Immediately, he jumped up to look through the peek hole. Lena was in the arms of the man Luke recognized as the one from the night before he went to France. Anger and jealousy ran through his veins as he watched this man hold his Lena. They weren't doing anything, but he was carrying her while trying to unlock the door. It was obvious Lena was drunk and looked like she was about to kiss Trey when Luke quickly opened the door intentionally interrupting what looked like a tender moment between the two. Lena laughed when she saw him. "Nice to see you, Luke. Luke, Trey, Trey, Luke."

Although disappointed, Trey motioned to bring her into the penthouse while Luke stood aside "Nice place you have here Luke. Where's your room Lena?"

"You don't have to carry me. I can walk. Oh, and this isn't his house it's his brother's."

Trey turned to Luke and told him Lena had twisted her ankle before leaving the beach. He didn't think it was broken, but she was having trouble walking. That explained why she was in his arms; however, Luke certainly wasn't about to let him bring her to her room. "Put her on the sofa. I'll take it from here."

Trey gently put Lena down and kissed her cheek telling her he would call her later. Luke watched with his fists clenched to control his outrage. As Trey approached the door, Lena called for him to wait. On one foot she hopped towards the door to give Trey back his sweatshirt. When she took off his sweatshirt her bikini top was dislodged. Lena was too drunk to notice until Trey bent down to tie it back up. She giggled. "Oh well, nothing you haven't seen before."

As Luke heard what Lena said, he scowled. It wasn't that he thought she was a virgin, but he didn't like at all that a man she had been with was touching her now.

Trey smiled and yelled back to Luke, "Take care of her for me man."

As Luke nodded Trey again kissed her cheek before leaving. After Trey left, Lena turned to Luke. "I need a shower. Goodnight."

She started hopping on one foot towards her room. This was Luke's chance. So many emotions were going through his head as he went to carry her back to her room. She tried to tell him she was fine, but he would not hear it. Once they reached her bedroom, he put her on the bed and commanded her to wait there while he went to get a chair for the shower. Hobbling and commenting on Luke's grumpiness, Lena went into the bathroom for the shower ignoring Luke's command. He was gone a little longer than he wanted because he had a hard time locating a chair that could go in the shower. By the time Luke returned with the chair, he heard a very drunk Lena fall while she was trying to hop out of the shower. Quickly Luke burst in to find Lena naked lying on the floor laughing. If it had been another time he would have enjoyed the view. On that night she was clearly too drunk. He wrapped her in the towel and lifted her back to the bed. Luke was angered by the fact she didn't do as she was told and snapped, "I told you to wait."

His serious tone was funny to Lena. Jokingly she said, "My hero."

Even though she was kidding, Luke couldn't help but smile. He wanted nothing more than to be her hero. After he put her back on the bed, he went to her drawers to get her some clothes before handing her a pair of lace panties and a T-shirt. Lena put on her panties. In her drunken state she removed her towel before putting on her T-shirt. This time Luke looked at her perfect naked breasts, longing to pull her into an embrace. Before he did, he needed to know what Trey meant to her. "What did you mean when you said it was nothing that guy had not seen before? Is he your boyfriend?"

Ever honest when she was drinking Lena answered, "No. Not a boyfriend. We met at a bar and well he came home with me. At first, I didn't remember him, but now I think it's the best thing I ever did because now we're good friends."

That was not the answer Luke wanted. Annoyed he asked, "Do that often?"

Lena could feel his disapproval and sarcastically answered. "What? Screw men I meet at bars? Is that any of your business? Besides I read about you, Mr. Armstrong. You are in no position to judge me."

Her comment caught him by surprise. As much as he hated to admit it, she was right. Still, he hated the idea that she had been with Trey. "You can't believe everything you read."

"Normally I wouldn't, but I saw your closet."

Lena had no filter when she was drunk. She had just confirmed what Luke had dreaded. He had already known, but there was no denying it with her omission. Luke had to decide how to handle this. "What you saw is a preference. It has nothing to do with you."

"And my sex life has nothing to do with you. I never told you I wanted you. You told me one day you would bed me, so your preference does have something to do with me."

Luke moved so close to Lena that she could feel his breath on her neck sending chills to her spine and tingles in other areas of her body. "You can't deny you want me too. I can tell by your body's reaction to me and the look in your eyes. It will happen with us. For now, you need to lay down while I get you some ice for your ankle."

Once Luke left the room, Lena heard her phone buzzing from the pocket of her shorts. She hopped over to where she dropped them on the floor. It was a text from Trey asking if she was okay and telling her he had a great time. She texted back that she did too. Luke entered the room and saw her standing.

As he walked over to her, he chastised her, "Dammit. Do you ever do what you're told? Do I need to tie you down?"

"You would like that, wouldn't you? Sorry, that's not my thing. In fact, I have a secret." This time Lena leaned close to

Luke's ear and whispered as he picked her up to put her in bed. "It would really freak me out."

Lena's words resonated with Luke. He knew what she had been through and understood some of what she saw could upset someone who had such a traumatic experience. "Oh, Sweetness."

Luke let go of the anger altogether and caressed her face. He helped Lena back into bed. Taking the extra pillow from the bed, he placed it under her ankle and put the ice pack down. By the time he got her situated Lena passed out.

She looked like an angel. He wanted nothing more than to climb into bed with her. Again, he caressed her face, "No rough play for you. I could be different for you. I know I could. I just have to prove it to you."

Luke went back to sleep on the sofa. While he laid there, he asked himself why she had to see what was in his closet and how to put her mind at ease. He had just promised her things could be different with her. That left him wondering if he really could change for Lena. No matter what he wanted to try if she would give him a chance. After that night not only did, he feel he was competing with Justin, there was also Trey to contend with. Justin was too wrapped up with Anne, so he was safe. Trey on the other hand was a different story. Luke saw the way he looked at Lena. It was not a look of friendship. He fell asleep contemplating his next steps. In Luke's dreams Lena hobbled onto the sofa to apologize. When he motioned for her to sit next to him, she took her shirt off and put her mouth on him. He could feel her soft lips. Slowly he moved his mouth down her neck to her breasts and sucked one at a time. She moaned in appreciation as he continued his journey south while she caressed his hard member. Gently he placed his hand underneath her panties while slowly teasing her clitoris. Right before she slipped in an orgasm, Luke was awakened by a loud noise. "Mother fucker" he heard a scream. Lena woke up and was in dire need of a bottle of water. In the kitchen she stepped on her ankle the wrong way and screamed in pain. Upon hearing Lena's duress, Luke lunged into the kitchen to find her sitting in a chair drinking water. He had leaped so quickly to check to see if Lena was okay, he forgot that he had been in the middle of an erotic dream. Luke was dressed in only boxers and his member was visibly saluting.

As he stood in front of Lena, she was at perfect eye level. Lena looked at it and then at his face and then back down. "Pleasant dream?"

Luke was not at all embarrassed. After all, he had just seen her completely naked. "It was. You were enjoying it too."

Lena tried to be nonchalant, but Luke looked hot standing there half naked. His long member saluting her was enough to send shivers down her spine. Luke had been right earlier. She did want him. It was taking everything she had not to reach out to him. All that was compounded by the fact he just admitted that he was dreaming about her. Feeling a little flustered, all she could manage to ask was, "The dream was about me?"

Luke could see from her reaction that she wanted him. Confidently he commented, "I would be willing to act it out for you now if you were so inclined."

Luke moved towards the back of her chair. With the back of his hand, he moved slowly from her neck to her shoulder. Lena leaned into the touch. Her reaction made him happy. He bent down to where she was sitting. Normally it wouldn't have occurred to him to ask, but he felt it was only right. "How drunk are you?" He looked right into her eyes. Her beauty was breathtaking.

She was drunk, but the feelings she was having weren't because of that. "Does it matter?"

It should, but Luke had wanted this for too long and could no longer resist. Slowly he kissed her ear to her neck. This time it was Lena who couldn't resist and pulled him into a passionate kiss.

Gently Lena ran her hands down his bare chest to his happy trail. She started to go lower when Luke picked her up to bring her back to her bedroom. Each one had been having fantasies of the other and they poured all their desires into the kiss. In her room, he placed her on the bed quickly removing her shirt. The sight of her almost naked at his mercy, made him groan in appreciation. As in his dream he began kissing her neck, moving south. This was so much better than he had envisioned until Lena broke the mood. Breathlessly, she asked, "Do you have a condom?"

Luke looked at her surprised "What! No. Aren't you on the pill?"

She started to push him off and shook her head. "No. It's my protection against diseases. The only way I can be sure that I won't do anything too stupid that I can't recover from. Remember I'm a nurse and have seen what can happen without a condom."

Until that moment he hadn't even considered someone as honest about her sexuality would not be on the pill. He knew not every woman was, but it had been his experience that most were, "Shit! Fuck! Really?"

At his reaction she fully pushed him off her because it wasn't going to happen. As soon as she did their bodies yearned for one another. There was an ache that needed to be filled. The feeling was so intense that Lena wanted to tell him to forget about the condom. The fact that she knew some of his history with women and that it was clear he did not practice safe sex, stopped her. As much as she wanted him, she had to be smart. In her mind, even though she was disappointed, she was proud of herself for not allowing this to go further. It showed that even drunk she had self-control and started to dress. Luke collapsed on the bed trying to think where he could get a condom. It was not as if he could ask Justin and if he could since Anne was pregnant, Justin probably didn't have one. He wanted her more than anyone he had ever wanted in his life. Deep down he knew he didn't want her that way. Not if there was a chance, she might regret it later because she was drunk. Their first time together had to be when they both had clear minds. With her clothes back on Lena put her head down on his bare chest. He kissed her head before she drifted to sleep in his arms. Luke caressed her cheek promising that one night they would not stop. She would be his. Until then he would go to sleep on the sofa.

Chapter Eleven

The next morning over breakfast Luke told Justin about Lena's ankle. Intentionally, he left out the other details from the prior night. Justin was worried and immediately went to check on her. When Justin knocked on the door, Lena had just woken up with a horrible headache and was half surprised Luke wasn't still in her bed. She wondered if it had been a dream or if it was real. If it was real was, she disappointed that he wasn't there. Fortunately, Justin's knock interrupted her thoughts. Justin couldn't hide his worry as he entered after she said to come in. Before she explained that she was fine, he went over to her to look at her ankle. His concern was sweet, and Lena was flattered. Although Lena didn't want the fuss, Justin insisted on looking at it. When he lifted her leg, his touch was so gentle. "It looks bad. Let me take you to the hospital."

"I'm a nurse. Trust me it is just a sprain."

"And they say doctors make the worst patients. Doctors have nothing on stubborn nurses. It's really swollen and badly bruised. I really think you need an X-ray."

"Honestly my head hurts worse than my ankle. I'm good. I just need to stay off it. Don't worry so much."

He could see that he was not going to win this argument. After all she was a nurse and experienced with injuries. Instead of trying to rationalize with her, Justin left the room to retrieve some Advil and a cold bottle of water. Within a minute he was back and instructed her to take the medicine. As her head was pounding, she gladly accepted the gesture, even if she knew he was trying to treat her injury and not her hangover. The water was exactly what her dry mouth needed.

As she was drinking, Justin spoke. "I was planning on working late tonight because Anne comes back tomorrow, but I can just work from home."

Lena didn't want him to change his plans. All she wanted was to go back to sleep and get rid of the hangover. "Don't be silly. I'm a big girl. Go to work. I'll be fine. I just need to take it easy for a day. Then I'll be good as new."

Suspicious Justin asked, "Are you sure?"

"Yes. Go."

Justin looked at her skeptically, but didn't argue further. "Mrs. Warner will be here if you need anything and I'm only a phone call away."

Only Gus had fussed over her in a long time. It was a nice feeling to know that someone else cared. "Thank you. I'll see you when you get back."

Before Justin turned to leave, he reminded her to call him if she needed anything. He wasn't at all comfortable, leaving her in a delicate state, but he had to trust that she knew what she needed. When Justin came out of her room, Luke asked about Lena. Justin explained that even though he thought she needed a doctor, she refused. Luke was relieved to know that she was not just stubborn with him and silently smiled. As Justin was preparing to leave for the office, Luke explained that he needed to go back to his house to change before meeting him there. As soon as Justin left to go to the office Luke went to check on Lena. He didn't bother to knock and cracked the door. She was laid up so what was the worst thing that could have happened if he walked in? If he knocked, she had the opportunity to tell him to leave and he needed to see for himself that she was okay. "How are you?"

As soon as she heard Justin leave for the office, she knew that she would be seeing Luke because she heard their voices in the hall. "Embarrassed." There was nothing about the previous night she didn't remember. Even though she wished she had woken up in his arms, she was still grateful they stopped before things went too far. In the light of day, she still knew they were not a good idea.

Luke smiled that smile that reached his beautiful emerald eyes. "Why?"

Lena hated that he was playing coy. She knew he knew exactly why she was embarrassed, but he wanted her to say it. "I said and did things last night that I shouldn't have."

"The things you said were all true. As for the rest, I don't think we did anything that I didn't want except stop. Have dinner with me tonight. I'll show you that I'm not the monster you think."

"I don't think you're a monster. After last night I think you should know that."

"Dinner then?"

As much as she wanted to say yes, her head was telling her that going out with Luke wasn't a good idea. The attraction was too powerful. "We're not a good idea."

After the prior night, Luke thought they were past that, but he wasn't going to give up. He needed to sway her. "It felt like a good idea last night."

"Do you believe in signs?"

That question came out of nowhere. Even though he had an idea of what she meant he still asked. "What kind of signs?"

"When something leads you in a certain direction."

"No, why?"

She wasn't surprised by his response. "I do and the signs are saying we're not meant to be."

Luke laughed, not realizing that Lena was serious. When he saw her face, he could tell she was. "I'm sorry, but I believe in facts. The fact is nothing has ever felt as right as having you in my arms did last night."

She couldn't argue with what he said. It did feel right. That wasn't the point because she worried it felt too right. "My dreams, the lack of a condom, the interruptions. They are all signs. We're not a good idea. Please respect that."

He moved so close to her that Lena could feel his breath. Having him so close threatened her resolve. In a sultry voice Luke responded, "I'll give space for now, but one day soon Sweetness, I will have you."

After his words, he bent down to kiss her lips chastely. At that moment she knew he was right. If only he weren't so dangerous for her. It wasn't that she believed he would hurt her physically as others had in the past. Her fear was for her heart as she had never been so drawn to another man before. Even with her one-night stands and flirtations, she knew what she felt for Luke was different than anything she had ever experienced. That knowledge terrified her. The right thing was for her to stay strong. She just wasn't confident she would be able to, which was why before Luke left the room Lena wanted to respond that it wasn't going to happen. She even opened her mouth to say it, but the words didn't come out.

****

Most of the day in bed Lena drifted in and out of sleep. Even though her head and ankle were hurting badly, she knew she was also exhausted from all the recent events. It felt great to know she was in a safe place. Safe if she could keep her resolve to not have sex with Luke. It was wonderful to feel that way for once in her life. For a short time, all her problems could be pushed aside. Plus, for the first time in a long time she had friends. Real friends that cared. Trey had called to check on her ankle and Justin was so sweet. It was a nice feeling even with the Luke situation.

Throughout the day Mrs. Warner checked on her. Justin left strict instructions that she was to make sure she had everything she needed without getting up. Mrs. Warner was still cold, but Lena felt a slight thaw in her attitude. When Lena was awake, she watched mindless television to keep her thoughts on safe topics. It didn't work as her thoughts often wandered to the men in her life. After seeing Justin's love for Anne, Lena yearned to have that. It was odd for her to be thinking this way as she never thought she would ever want that. Love destroyed her mother, and she always pushed the idea of that aside. Being with Justin had made her realize that the risk was worth it. Her feelings for Justin were strong in a different way than her feelings for Luke. She knew with Justin she could have something real if he could move on from Anne, but she knew it was too soon for that. If time was the issue, it would be okay. The problem was she wasn't sure any other love would be first in his heart, and she wanted someone to feel the way about her that he did Anne. In contrast to her feelings for Justin, the physical yearning for Luke was powerful. Her body craved his touch. That had never happened before. She wondered if the danger around him was part of the appeal. From everything she read, Luke wasn't into relationships. Even if he was ready, all the women he dated were high society. That was not her as she struggled to pay rent and her student loans. A relationship with him could crush her. Then there was Trey. The relationship started off strange, but he was a good man. Lena could see herself living a perfectly happy life with him. They had a great time together and he treated her with nothing but respect even after learning a lot about her. Lena wondered if maybe the friendship could grow into more. Maybe they could have a future together. Lost in thought and more confused than ever Lena fell back asleep until she was awakened by a loud banging noise in the living area. She hobbled out to see Justin was home. It was late and it was obvious he was in a bad mood. He was grumbling something that she could not quite make out. It was clear from his facial expression that he was frustrated. Lena had never seen him like that and wondered what had happened.

When Justin turned to see her standing there, his spirits immediately lifted. "How's the ankle?"

Lena looked at him to try and read his mood. "Better thank you. You seem off. Are you alright?"

Justin sighed, "It's just my father. Nothing to worry about. He could put a playful puppy in a bad mood. Have you eaten?"

Lena smiled. "Yes. Mrs. Warner took very good care of me today. I think she said there's a plate in the refrigerator for you."

"Thanks. I ate already at the office and I'm exhausted. If you don't need anything, I'm going to bed."

"I'm good. Goodnight."

As they were about to go their separate ways there was a knock on the door. It was Luke and John with some important business to discuss. They also didn't look happy. Lena was surprised they were there. It was after ten and Justin had just left them. "It's all falling apart," Lena heard John say.

"I'll leave you then."

"Wait. Before you go. Dad, this is Angelina McKay. Angelina this is my father, John Armstrong."

He was as good looking as his sons, but he had no warmth to him. That was obvious from the suspicious way he looked at Lena.

Nervously Lena held out her hand and responded, "Pleasure to meet you, Sir."

John graciously accepted, telling her that the pleasure was his. As Lena left the room, she heard John tell Justin he could see why work wasn't his priority. It was Luke who interjected that his comment was out of line. Justin had enough on his plate. He didn't need John adding to it. Even though Luke would have defended Justin anyway, Luke was upset by John implying that Lena was with Justin. Lena overheard John's briskness towards both his sons and was thankful that she hadn't met him earlier. His sons were good men. Both men, even Luke. Just because she worried about her heart didn't mean that he was a bad person. In contrast, it was that she was worried about falling too hard for him and him not feeling the same way. John's attitude towards them was completely uncalled for. Aside from that how dare he think that about her. He didn't even know her. After meeting John, she couldn't wait to go back to her room and leave them, hoping she wouldn't see a lot him and feeling sorry that they did.

****

In the middle of the night there was a knock at Lena's door. Half asleep she responded to enter. Since it was still dark it was hard to see who it was, but her body knew it was Luke before her eyes did. Even half asleep her body gravitated to him. As he approached her, she sat up to see what he wanted. Through the moonlight she could tell he looked exhausted, and she could smell the slight scent of alcohol although he didn't appear drunk.

Luke sat on her bed without looking at her. "I have no idea what you are doing to me. I can't stop thinking about you. This is something I have never told anyone before, but I need you."

Lena's heart melted a little. He expressed exactly what she had been feeling, yet she knew it had been a hard night for both Luke and Justin and she wasn't sure if what he was feeling was because of that. "I'd be lying if I didn't say I'm having a hard time not thinking about you too, but we talked about this in the morning. Whatever is happening between us is not a good idea."

He turned to face her and took her hand. "You're so wrong. Let me show you how good we are together."

Lena considered what he said. "Luke, I can't. I need time to think."

Luke wondered if her real reason was Justin. He had seen the way she looked at him. Even his father noticed something between them. "If this is about Justin, don't hold out for him. Anne will always have his heart. He may find love again and I hope he does, but it will always be a shadow of what he had with her. I'm the one that can give you everything you want."

She knew Luke was right about Justin. What he said only confirmed what she had already thought. Luke could sense that she was considering his words and decided not to push his luck. Instead, he kissed her chastely and said, "think about it" before leaving her room.

Thinking about it was all she had done. If only things were different, she thought. As she fell back to sleep, she wondered if he was sincere. Luke didn't seem like a man who was vulnerable and what he had just shown her was exactly that. That night she had a vivid dream of passion unfolding between them. Their bodies were bound together passionately, and the dream was so real she could feel her own orgasm. Except when she awoke to the buzzing sound of her alarm, she realized it was her own hand that had caused her pleasure. The dream had seemed so real, and her body ached for him even after her release. She knew that she would have to do something to stop her yearning for him though she was not sure what. There was no time to think about that because it was Anne's homecoming, and she needed to make sure everything was perfect. Although she and Justin selected a twenty-four-hour nursing service, she was determined to supervise homecare until Justin felt comfortable.

After showering she went to the kitchen where Justin was already having an omelet for breakfast. The circles around his beautiful eyes showed he must have been up all night or at least most of it. She wondered if they were from his father or the fact that Anne was returning. Justin had been so confident that Anne should return to the penthouse, however now that the day was here, she wondered if he had second thoughts. "Good morning. Big day."

Justin had been lost in thought and hadn't noticed her arrival until she spoke. When he saw her, he smiled. "Hi Angelina. Did you sleep well?"

She loved that smile even if this one did not reach his eyes. That troubled her. "Yes, but it looks like you didn't. Are you worried about today? If you are having second thoughts…"

Justin cut her off before she could finish. "It isn't that at all. Anne belongs here. I haven't changed my mind. It's this big case I'm working on. Could mean millions for the firm. And Dad, well he is Dad." Justin wanted to change the subject. "How's your ankle?"

"Better." It was a bit of a lie. Her ankle still hurt, but she didn't want Justin to know. "Are you ready for today?"

Justin shrugged. "Today my life changes again. Is anyone ever ready for that? The only thing I know about this awful mess is that she would want to be home. It's the only thing I can do for her now." Lena understood exactly what he meant. If this was her father, she wouldn't have wanted him in a home somewhere with strangers caring for him. At least this way Justin could make sure Anne had the best possible care. "I need to be at the hospital in an hour to sign the final paperwork. Then the ambulance will bring her here."

"Do you want me to go with you?"

It was going to be a hard transition for Justin to make. So many times, he and Anne talked about coming home after the baby was born and how happy they would be. This wasn't at all the way they planned it. Within a couple of days their happiness was obliviated. Not only was Anne coming back in a vegetative state, but Faith was also unable to come home. He was alone even with Lena there. This would probably be one of the most difficult days of his life and he felt he needed to handle it alone. "I appreciate the offer, but I have to get used to doing these hard things on my own."

She could see the sadness in his eyes as he left the room to get dressed. Lena began to pray. "Dear Heavenly Father, please give Justin strength and courage. His journey will be a long one. Help guide him. Daddy, please watch over this family today."

****

It was early afternoon when Anne arrived home. By the time Justin returned Lena, the nurse and the paramedics had Anne situated in her new room. They had put all the finishing touches on the room and Justin had moved some of Anne's favorite trinkets there. One new one was a framed picture of him holding Faith. It was prominently displayed on the table next to the bed. As soon as he saw her settled, Justin's face was filled with relief. He immediately went to Anne and kissed her to welcome her home. Everyone in the room knew that her physical body was home, but the spirit that Justin loved so much was gone and could almost feel his pain. Even though Justin was coming to terms with the situation, he still had vivid images of her holding Faith and them being a family. So much of this was still not real for Justin. There were some machine that the hook-up needed to be finalized before the transition was complete. Lena assured Justin that Anne would be cared for while he went off to call Anne's parents with the update. They had urged Justin to no avail to put Anne in a long-term care facility because they knew Anne would want him to move on with his life. Justin knew how much they loved Anne and couldn't understand how they could tell him to move forward. She was still alive. As long as Anne was, he would dedicate his life to her as he promised the day they married. It wasn't just for Justin that they felt this would be bad for. They were also worried about Faith because they wanted her to hear stories of how vivacious

Anne was, not see her in a coma. The one thing Justin did promise was that as Faith grew older, he would reassess having Anne home. If in any way he thought it was detrimental to Faith, he would move Anne. For now, Faith was too young, and Anne belonged at home.

After his call Justin returned to Anne's room and asked for some time alone with his wife. They had set up monitors in all the penthouse rooms so that any sign of trouble could be heard instantly. Justin wanted to make sure that no matter where they were in the penthouse, they would be aware of any trouble. After the nurse left the room, Lena briefly watched as Justin tenderly cared for Anne fluffing her pillow and making sure she wouldn't be cold by placing a blanket over her. There was no mistaking his pain. Lena wished that she could make it better, but knew the only thing that could do that was Anne awakening. Since that wouldn't happen, Lena went to the kitchen with the nurse to go over details. While she was reviewing the list of Anne's medications with the nurse, Luke entered. He was dressed in a grey suit with a white shirt and was loosening his red silk tie while walking towards Lena. As he approached her, Lena had a brief vision of her dream and felt flustered.

Luke could feel her body respond to his presence and smiled. "Hello Lena. How did the move go?"

She couldn't look at him out of embarrassment. There was no need to be self-conscious because he had no idea what she dreamed about, but she was and hoped the nurse didn't notice. The nurse didn't because at the sight of Luke, she was paying more attention to him than Lena. Once Lena noticed her reaction to Luke, she wasn't happy. "Anne is settled. Justin is with her."

Luke knew that even with Lena and the nurse in the penthouse Justin would be with Anne. "How is he?" His concern was genuine as he agreed with Anne's parents that this was a mistake. Selfishly he liked the idea that this gave him more access to Lena, he just didn't think it was what was best for Justin.

"As well as you can expect." Lena had seen a mixture of emotions in Justin. "Happy. Sad. I'm not sure."

"I'll bet. We have some work to do. Do you think you could sit with Anne? It'll be another late night."

"Of course. That's why I'm here. That is if he will let me."

Mrs. Warner entered the kitchen interrupting their conversation and stating that she would have dinner ready at six, which was in a couple of hours. She wasn't surprised to see Luke and asked if he would be joining them for dinner. Lena wondered how often Luke joined them for dinner as Mrs. Warner made it seem like a regular occurrence. If it was often her resolve was going to be harder than she originally thought. After Luke said that he would be, he asked Lena to lead the way to Anne's room. He knew where it was but rather liked the view from behind. As they walked down the hall, Lena could feel his eyes on her. Without turning around, she could feel his eyes removing her running shorts and crop top. The thought both excited and terrified her. It was taking everything she had after her dream to not jump into his arms and forget everything she believed to be true. To get her mind off things she decided to focus on Justin by reminding Luke that Justin waited a long time for this. He may want his time alone with Anne. If this case hadn't been so important Luke would have granted him that, but they had already lost a lot of time. When they arrived at Anne's room and knocked no one answered. Slowly, Luke cracked the door open to find Justin was asleep in the reclining chair, looking relaxed and young. It was hard to believe this was the same man whom Lena knew. "Anne's presence in the home must be a comfort to him," Lena thought. Neither of them wanted to wake him and Luke motioned for them to leave the room while he shut the door. "He needs his rest."

"Are you going to let him sleep?"

"For now, but you can help me. We're working on a big case. I can't give you the details, but you can help organize things. That is if you aren't doing anything."

Lena really didn't have any plans, and she thought if it would help Justin, she should at least try to help even if it was just an excuse for Luke to spend time with her. From her search she knew the law office was large and there were probably plenty of better-qualified people at the office who could do what he was asking Lena to do. Once they were in Justin's home office, Luke handed Lena a stack of papers. She looked at him puzzled. "You do know I know nothing about law."

"Don't worry. The paralegals have put these documents in order. What I need you to do is highlight any reference to Moore Pharmaceuticals in the phone records."

"That doesn't seem too complicated."

"Good then get to work," Luke commanded while playfully tapping her on her behind. His touch was all Lena needed to reignite her feelings in her dream. She grabbed his wrist after his swat and looked him in the eye like a sultry vixen. Lena meant the move to be a warning, however it had the opposite effect. Neither made a move, but both were hoping the other would, while keeping eye contact. As she was about to give in and kiss him, the bells on a cuckoo clock in the office chimed bringing her out of her trance like state. In her mind it was a sign that moving forward wasn't a good idea.

"I'll help, but only because it will help Justin. Not because you commanded it."

Luke gave her a playful smile that again made Lena want to push her lips against his tender lips. Many times, since their kiss she thought about how it felt to kiss him and longed for that feeling again. Instead of giving in to that feeling, she went to work highlighting as requested. While Lena highlighted, Luke reviewed some other documents. Occasionally Lena would catch him staring at her and would smile.

After about an hour Luke could no longer take the silence and spoke, "How's your ankle?"

It was odd to Lena how invested everyone was in her ankle. This wasn't the first time she had sprained something in her adult life, but it was the first time so many people expressed concern. "Better. Well, manageable."

"Are you still in a lot of pain?" She nodded yes and Luke smirked. "Serves you right."

His response caught her off guard and she snidely responded. "What do you mean by that comment?"

"You should've taken better care of yourself and not gotten so drunk with virtual strangers"

"Trey isn't a stranger. He's a friend." This conversation was not going to get them anywhere and Lena could tell Luke was baiting her. She wasn't sure why he was, but she knew that was his strategy. Instead of playing his game, Lena decided to change the subject. "Is someone suing Moore Pharmaceuticals? We use their pain medicine at the hospital. Are you for or against the company?" She wanted to change in subject, but she was also curious.

"We're representing Moore." As Luke responded, Justin entered. He no longer looked like the carefree man whom they saw sleeping an hour earlier. Now he looked like a man who was carrying the weight of the world on his shoulder and was surprised to see Luke and Lena together in his office. Luke could see his apprehension and offered that Lena was helping with the case. Although Justin didn't say anything with Lena in the room, he still didn't understand because the job she was doing was one that any of the paralegals in the office could handle. In order to get the answers, he asked Lena to check on the nurse who was with Anne. It was obvious that Justin wanted time with Luke, and she excused herself. While she was leaving Luke asked if she was coming back. With uncertainty she nodded that she would return. However, she could tell that Justin wasn't exactly happy to have her help with the case which was confirmed by Justin saying it wasn't necessary. Luke disagreed and was insistent that her presence was helpful. To avoid further awkwardness, Lena left the room saying she would let them hash it out. She was happy either way.

With Lena gone, Justin questioned Luke. "What's going on? She doesn't need to do this. That's what the trained paralegals are for."

Luke knew Justin was right. Not only did they have paralegals, but they also had medical consultants at their finger tips. That didn't mean he was going to surrender though. "This is a tough case and she's a nurse. I thought she could offer a new perspective. A medical one."

In Justin's mind it did make sense. They had been struggling to come up with a strategy for the case and with Lena's ER background she might be able to offer something new. It was worth a try. "Okay. Maybe you're right, but I don't want to take advantage of her kindness."

Taking advantage was just what Luke had in mind. Just it wasn't of her kindness. He needed to use this time to get close to her. "You worry too much. Let's get to work. There's a lot to be done. By the way how is it with Anne being home."

"I know this sounds odd, but it is a relief. She isn't my Anne. and I know that. I just can't explain the peace having her here brings me."

Justin was right. Luke didn't understand, however he realized it wasn't for him to understand, and he probably never would. What he did like is that Justin felt more at peace even if he knew one day it would all change again. For now, it was the small victories Luke thought to himself.

After dinner and a bottle of wine Lena did return to help them. Together they worked well into the night. The mood had become more relaxed since Justin first entered the room. They put several strategies on a whiteboard in Justin's office, but none of them seemed like the right approach. Lena didn't understand why someone would sue Moore. She understood that there was an opioid crisis and had often witnessed the effect in the ER, but it wasn't the pharmaceutical company that prescribed them. They were made to help people with extreme pain. Plus, the drugs came with warning labels. That was an interesting theory. Since the hospital was also a client of their firm, they didn't think that was the best argument either. What they needed to do was prove that it was the fault of the person suing. Without knowing who the other party was, Lena felt that seemed harsh and felt they would come across as heartless if they decided to go that route. Luke joked that they were lawyers, they didn't have a heart. As soon as he said it, he regretted it because he was trying to show her otherwise. It didn't matter. Now that she knew them, she knew it wasn't true. Justin wore his heart on his sleeve, and she had seen the way Luke was with Justin and James. Just because she feared for her heart, it didn't mean he didn't have one. At two in the morning Luke and Justin felt that they had done enough work for one day and called it a night.

Chapter Twelve

The next several days were more of the same. Since Justin wanted to be home for Anne, Luke would come over to work in the afternoon. Lena looked forward to the break in the day and enjoyed spending time with the brothers. As time progressed, Lena began to wonder how much longer her presence in Justin's home would be necessary. Everything with Anne's care was running smoothly and she started to think it might be time for her to move out and go back to work. The thought of moving out made Lena melancholy. For the first time she felt like she had a family again. Gus always tried, and she loved him as much as she did her father, it was just he didn't make it seem like a family. They were a duo. Not really a family. This was different. They were not related, but Justin provided her with much needed security. The problem was the longer she stayed the harder it would be for her to leave. She had to talk to Justin about moving out before she became more attached than she already was. One day before Luke came over, she decided to broach the subject with Justin. Justin immediately dismissed the idea saying that he was eventually going to have to return to the office and would feel more comfortable having her there. Since she wasn't ready to return to her life yet, she agreed to stay. Shortly after their conversation, Justin was called into the office. His father needed a progress report on the Moore case and his presence in the office was mandated and not requested.

About an hour after Justin left, the doorbell rang. Lena answered the door to find James and a well-dressed woman standing there. Instantly, Lena recognized the woman from the pictures she had seen on the internet. She knew she had to be James' mother Jessica. As they were about to make introductions, James, who was excited to see Lena ran to her to give her a big hug. After their night together, James was taken with Lena. The feeling was mutual. Jessica followed James into the penthouse and introduced herself. She was a beautiful woman dressed in a silk green dress with black shoes. Her hair and make-up were done perfectly while Lena was wearing shorts, a tank top and her hair in a ponytail. Next to her Lena felt very under-dressed.

Although polite, Jessica addressed Lena coldly. "Lena, it's a pleasure to meet you. I'm Luke's ex-wife Jessica. Is he here?"

"Sorry he's not."

Annoyed, Jessica asked, "What about Justin? Is he here?"

"No. His father called him into the office for a meeting. I assume Luke is there too."

"Perfect." She sounded more annoyed. "That will take hours. My regular babysitter is sick, and I must get to an appointment. I know Luke had been working here and was hoping he could take James."

"Luke isn't here, but James could hang out with me if he wants."

James was excited at the idea of spending the day with Lena. "Can I mom? Please."

Jessica considered it as she was in a bind, but she didn't know Lena and was cautious. "James, I don't want to impose on her."

Lena thought the idea sounded like fun. It would at least give her something else to focus on than her own problems. "It's no imposition. I enjoy spending time with James."

"I wouldn't normally leave him with a stranger, but you aren't one to Justin and James seems to like you. Are you sure you don't mind?"

"I think it'll be fun."

Jessica turned to James. "James, can you give us a moment alone please? I need to have grown-up time with Lena." James went into the family room to watch television. When he was out of the listening range Jessica began. "Anne was one of my best friends, and James loved her too. I know she's here, but I don't want James to see her this way. If he stays, will you please keep him out of her room? It's hard enough for me to understand. I just don't think he could."

It never crossed Lena's mind to take James to see Anne. Even if it had, she wouldn't without Luke or his mother's permission. "Children are more resilient than we give them credit for. With that said I understand your feelings and promise to keep him away."

Jessica's eyes began to fill, and her attitude softened. "How is Anne?"

It was clear that she loved Anne. With compassion, she responded. "I'm sorry there is no change."

"No change," Jessica quietly said with sadness in her voice. As if recovering she continued, "Well, as long as you don't mind, I do appreciate your help. Please tell James I'll see him later."

Before Lena could respond Jessica was out the door. Although she was emotional about Anne, after Jessica's aloof attitude towards her, Lena understood why Luke and Jessica were divorced. It could not have been all Luke she thought, before going to check on James.

The two had a great day even though Lena didn't feel comfortable leaving the penthouse. First, they played the football video game. James was excited at how good they had become and mentioned that he couldn't wait to play his father and Uncle Justin again. They would beat them badly this time. When they became bored with the game, they decided to bake chocolate chip cookies. Mrs. Warner had everything they needed stocked in the kitchen. Although she offered to bake the cookies for them, Lena suggested it would be more fun if they did it themselves. While they were preparing the batter, James was extremely inquisitive. He asked all kinds of questions about Lena's childhood and wanted to know if she used to bake with her mother. She used to make all kinds of foods with her mother when she was his age. Often it was hard for her to think about the times when she had a real family. Before her father passed away, she and her mother were so close. Her father worked odd shifts with late hours, but her mother always made their time together special. One of her favorite things to do with her mother was bake. Lena's father had a sweet tooth. They would try to surprise him by trying all kinds of new dessert recipes to see what he thought. He always told them that they had outdone themselves even if the experiment was a failure. They were good times, and Lena couldn't help but smile as she shared them. So many times, throughout her childhood she longed for the simpler times. They just never came. That wasn't something she would share with a five-year old though. Her thoughts were interrupted when a sad James responded that he never did anything like that with his mother.

Lena wanted to make him feel better. "I'm sure you do many fun things with her though. Baking isn't for everyone."

"Not really. When mom and dad divorced, mom was sad all the time, now she's just busy. I have a great time with dad when I see him. We do lots of fun things, but baking isn't one of them either."

She smiled at the thought of Luke baking. If Justin's familiarity with the kitchen was any indication of how Luke was in there as well, she didn't think he would be baking with his father any time soon. "We should save some cookies for your dad and Uncle Justin."

James' mood was instantly lifted. "That would be really cool."

After eating several cookies dipped in milk they decided to play "Go Fish." James tried to be slick by trying to divert her attention from his cards. In some instances, he asked for cards to get her to ask for different cards than what he was holding. Lena wondered if that was a trick he learned from Luke. She could see Luke doing that as well. As it started to become dinner time, Lena realized Jessica hadn't said what time she would return. Even though Mrs. Warner inquired about dinner, James begged for pizza which they ate while watching Spiderman. James loved the movie except during the kissing scenes where he closed his eyes. Lena laughed when he did, but he insisted that just ruined a perfectly good movie. In so many ways James reminded her of Luke, although she knew from experience that Luke had no problem with kissing. Lena began to wonder if Luke was ever that innocent. She smiled when she thought about what Luke must have been like as a child. With no word from either Jessica or Luke, eventually they fell asleep on the sofa around ten.

Jessica had asked Luke to bring James home when he finished working. Even though Luke tried to leave the office earlier, he was unable to break away from his meeting with his father. When Justin and Luke walked into the penthouse Lena was asleep sitting up with James laying on her lap. At the sight of them on the sofa together Luke thought what a lucky boy James was. It was an innocent scene, but Luke would like nothing more than to be lying on her lap. Not necessarily sleeping. Justin looked at Luke wondering what he was thinking.

Justin broke Luke's train of thought. "What a nice picture."

Luke smiled. "It is. I hate to wake them."

"I need to check on Anne, but if you want to leave him here you can."

"No, Jess wants him home. Thanks though. See you tomorrow."

"Goodnight Luke."

As Justin left the room, Lena woke up to sleepily greet Luke. Luke bent down to pick James up while quietly thanking Lena for watching him. It was her pleasure, and it really was. Lena never considered herself to be a kid person. There were many who were treated in the ER, but this was the first time she could recall spending time with one outside the hospital. She marveled at how much fun she had with James. Before Luke could sweep him up James excitedly awoke. "We made cookies and saved you and Uncle Justin some."

"You did?" Luke looked at Lena as she shook her head indicating that they had. "That's great buddy, but Uncle Justin is with Aunt Anne and it's late. Mom wants you home so I will come back and try one tomorrow. Go get your stuff Little Man."

James looked disappointed. Lena understood exactly what he was thinking. It was clear Luke hadn't noticed, so Lena interjected. Walking towards the kitchen Lena said, "They'll be better today. Come on. Do you want milk with your cookies?"

Luke was still oblivious. In his mind it didn't matter when he tasted them until he noticed his son's excited face. That's when he decided to follow them to the kitchen.

"You have to dunk um Dad. That'll make them taste extra good."

Luke smiled at his son's face, while agreeing to have milk and reaching over to take a cookie from the plate. As Lena went to get the milk, Luke took a bite while James watched. When he told them it was the best cookie he ever tasted, James was elated. Luke enjoyed seeing his son so happy more than the cookie which he did finish and even took another. "Hey, can you get your stuff Little Man? I need to get you back to Mom's."

James skipped out of the room proudly as Luke looked at Lena. "Looks like my boy had a great time. Thanks again."

"No problem. I enjoyed myself too. He's a great kid."

"I guess despite his mother and me. Not because of us."

James had spent the day telling her how much he loved spending time with his father, so his comment was bewildering, "Why do you say that?"

Luke moved towards Lena and put his hand on her face. With sadness he spoke his regret. "Because you're not completely wrong about me. I almost destroyed Jessica. We had an arrangement made by our parents. I didn't realize she felt otherwise until it was almost too late. When I realized it, I ended it before she was too lost, but James was already born. My father ruined my mother, and I didn't want that to happen to anyone because of me."

Lena couldn't tell if Luke was trying to warn her off or reassure her that he wouldn't let things get that carried away again. It was obvious he felt bad about how things with Jessica almost turned out. That was reassuring to Lena. "How long have you been divorced?' She knew the answer but liked the vulnerable side of Luke.

"We ended it when James was a toddler. I don't think he even remembers."

Lena knew from her conversation with James that wasn't the case, but she could see how bad Luke felt and didn't feel the need to kick him when he was down.

Luke's hand moved from Lena's face to her shoulder. He was about to bend down to kiss her when James came back saying that he was ready to go. Luke whispered, "Another time." James leaped over to give Lena a big hug asking if he could come back the next day. She returned the hug warmly expressing that he could come back any time. The moment was tender as Luke witnessed how great she was with his son. He had always kept his personal life separate from James to protect him. This was different. His feelings for Lena were different and knowing that James liked Lena only made Luke want her more.

When they left Lena went to check on Anne and Justin. James had asked Lena a lot of questions about Anne, but she had done as Jessica requested and kept him from the room. In Anne's room Justin was seated on the recliner next to the bed holding her hand. He turned as Lena entered the room. "I'm not sure how to do this."

Lena didn't understand where this was coming from. Justin seemed so content having Anne home. She thought it must be a moment of weakness. "You're doing fine."

"No, I'm not. When I leave, I can pretend for a brief time. Then I feel guilty because I'm not always thinking of her. When I come home, I can't wait to see her, but she's not my Anne. I have no idea where this all fits. I just know I miss her so much." Justin's eyes were filled with tears. Lena's heart ached as she cradled him in her arms while he wept. "Not very manly of me to cry, is it?"

"I don't think it's about being manly. You're hurting. Every day you still put one foot in front of the other. You're here for Anne and you're here for your daughter. That's what being a man is about. Not whether you need a release sometimes." Lena released her hold to make sure she could look him in the eyes as she made her statement. There was so much sadness there. To help him she wanted to kiss away his pain. Making a move like that wouldn't be welcome and she restrained herself.

With her words of encouragement Justin began to gain his composure. "Thank you, Angelina. Having you here is such a great comfort." Justin knew the answer but decided to ask anyway. "Has there been any change with Anne?"

Lena wanted to tell him her vitals were stronger and she would probably wake up soon. That wasn't the case, and she had to be honest. "Sorry no."

No change was better than a turn for the worse. "I guess that's good news."

"How's Faith today?"

The thought of Faith did make Justin happy. It was obvious how much he loved her. "She keeps getting stronger, thankfully."

"I'm glad. If you're feeling better, I'm going to give you some privacy."

"I am. Thank you again. I'm going to stay a little while longer, but goodnight, Angelina." As she turned for the door Justin added, "Oh and Angelina thanks for taking care of James today."

"He's a great kid. We had fun."

"He is a lot of fun. I can't wait for him to meet Faith."

Lena looked forward to that too. It was late and Lena wished him a goodnight.

****

That night Lena dreamed of Anne lying in the jewelry store, helpless begging Lena to save her unborn child and to let her husband know she loved him. In her dream, Anne's spirit rose from her body to tell Lena to watch over her family. Lena woke with a jolt in a cold sweat. Her dream didn't frighten her like one of her nightmares, but it seemed real. So real in fact that she wondered if Anne was really trying to communicate with her. She believed her father often communicated to her through signs, however he was an angel. It wasn't possible for Anne to try to speak to Lena. The more Lena thought about her dream, she realized even if Anne wanted Justin to move on, there was no way he was ready to. Her mother had found other lovers but was never able to give her heart away again. There was no one who could ever replace Lena's father. If she ever took her relationship with Justin past friendship, she knew he wouldn't be able to give her his whole heart. As Luke said the other night, Justin's heart was with Anne. If she pursued him, she would only end up hurt. The more she thought about her dream images; Luke came into her mind. Luke appeared to be so closed off except with James and Justin. Although often Luke was tender with her, he had only expressed an interest in a sexual affair. Normally she would be fine with that, but the one thing she learned from all of this was that she wanted more. Not only did she want it, but she also now felt that she deserved it. While she was having an internal conflict the alarms in Anne's room went off. Lena ran into Anne's room to find the nurse already there and checking her vitals. For a moment Lena again considered if her dream was real. Maybe Anne had visited her in her dream. There was no time to contemplate that, she had to know what was happening. Justin was in a frenzy worrying about what the alarms meant. He was pacing back and forth begging for Anne to be okay. The noise from the alarm was so piercing that Lena turned the monitor off. Since Anne's vitals had been strong earlier, Lena wondered if one of the leads had come off or gone bad. As she went to check, she expressed her thoughts to Justin. It wasn't until the nurse confirmed that there was no change in Anne's vitals that Justin began to calm down. Lena started to change the leads, while the nurse continued to monitor her in case something changed. Even with the diagnosis that everything was fine, Justin was still visibly upset. The thought of losing Anne completely terrified him. As Lena changed the leads, she tried to calm him by explaining that it was just one of the technical issues that they had discussed could happen.

The explanation allowed Justin to breathe again as he recalled their conversation, and his handsome face began to relax. He still needed reassurance. "Are you sure she's, okay?"

She smiled. "Trust me."

"I do. More than anyone."

The crisis was averted, and the leads were all changed. Lena was there to make sure everything went smoothly. "I'll stay with her a little while. Go get some rest."

There was no way he could sleep after this. "I don't think I can. My heart is racing."

Lena placed her hand over his heart feeling the rapid beat. His bare chest felt hard against her hand. For a moment Lena considered what Anne had said about taking care of Justin and wanted desperately to kiss him. To take away the painful look in his eyes. This wasn't the time because Justin needed his friend to comfort him, not a sexual partner. As she hugged him his bare chest was pressed against her camisole, and he could feel her skin against his. For a second, he too wanted to kiss her. As the thought entered his head, he felt overwhelming guilt and quickly pushed the thought aside. Anne was his life. They held each other for what seemed like hours. Suddenly, they realized the nurse was watching them. Embarrassed, they broke the hold. Justin took Lena's hand. "You go to bed. I'll sleep here with Anne tonight."

"Isn't that why I'm here?"

"I'm beginning to think you're here to keep me together."

Lena left because she knew he really did want to be with Anne and wondered what her dreams would be like after such a crazy night. With an abundance of emotions, Lena had difficulties falling asleep, often speaking to her father, looking for guidance.

Chapter Thirteen

The next morning after Justin left for work Lena went to Anne's room in search of answers. All night she had questioned if Anne had really tried to send her a message. If she was, she wondered what she wanted her to do. It was hard to believe that Anne thought Justin was nearly ready to move on. The logical assumption was that Anne was telling Lena to help him and Faith through the transition. That was exactly what she was doing. Anne looked peaceful in her lavender bed but couldn't give her the answers Lena longed for. It was odd to Lena how close she felt to Anne. They had only spoken for five minutes and there she was with her family and in her room. If Anne hadn't been shot, there is no way she would have met any of them. It wasn't as if they ran in the same social circles, yet she couldn't feel closer to them. Because the situation was so dire it wasn't as if Lena could say she was happy it happened. However, she would be lying if she didn't say that she was grateful to have Justin and even Luke in her life. Since Anne could offer her no answers, the only thing Lena could do was promise that she would always be there for Justin and Faith. She hoped if Anne was trying to communicate with her that would put her mind at ease.

Since she was feeling restless and knew the nurse had everything under control, Lena decided to go for a run. Her ankle was finally feeling better, and she needed to collect her thoughts. The warm morning air felt wonderful against her face. From the time Anne had returned home; Lena hadn't left the apartment much and the fresh air was a welcome change. There were so many things Lena needed to sort through, and she was using this time to think. The more she thought about things the harder she ran. She continued her punishing pace for miles through Central Park. It wasn't until she stopped to catch her breath that she noticed the throbbing ache in her ankle. The pain was so penetrating that walking several blocks to the penthouse was a difficult task. As she hobbled back through the busy streets of New York City, she heard someone call her name. When she looked up, she saw Luke who was dressed in a back suit, white shirt and red tie leaving a coffee shop and walking towards her. After her run she was acutely aware of how awful she looked and smelled. He was the last person she wanted to see, being covered in sweat, no make-up and hair a mess. The problem was it was too late. He was walking towards her, and she was in no shape to run away.

Luke had seen her limping from the coffee shop window and could tell that she was in pain. "Lena. What's wrong?" He called out, voice filled with concern.

To avoid contact, Lena tried to pretend like she didn't hear him, however he was persistent. So much so that she couldn't escape him. "Hey Luke. I'm fine. Just heading back to the penthouse." She didn't turn to face him and kept walking.

Even though she tried to walk as normally as possible, it was still obvious that she was in pain. He figured she had reinjured her ankle. "You don't look okay. Is it your ankle?"

His concern was nice, but she didn't want to talk to him about it. "I'm fine. I just overdid it a little on my run."

For a nurse he wondered why she would take such little care of herself. Even if it was only a sprain it would take longer than a couple of days to heal. She should know better and disapprovingly he asked, "You were out running on that ankle?"

The way Luke looked at her made her annoyed. She turned to face him no longer caring how bad she looked and put her hands on her hips" "It was feeling better."

Luke smiled at her feistiness. "My car is around the corner. Let me take you home." He went over to lift her.

The idea of him carrying her made her nervous. Any time Luke touched her the reaction her body had was overwhelming. At first, she thought about declining the ride altogether, but her ankle hurt too much. "I appreciate the ride, but I can walk to the car."

"You're so damn frustrating. Why won't you let me help you?" It was a fair question. One that Lena had to consider. Was it because she was used to doing things on her own or was there something else? Luke was being a gentleman, and she was in trouble. "You're right. I'm sorry. I guess I'm not used to leaning on people. I can walk, but if you don't mind giving me your shoulder, I would appreciate it."

Although Luke didn't voice it, he thought to himself "progress" and happily walked over to Lena to offer her his shoulder. As soon as he did, she understood exactly why it was hard to accept help from him. Their chemistry was undeniable. She tried to fight it, but as soon as she was near him it was a battle she feared she would lose. Fortunately, the car was nearby, so the electricity wouldn't last long. On the way back to the apartment Luke tried to make conversation. "Thank you again for watching James the other night. He couldn't stop talking about you."

The thought of James made her smile. "He's a great kid and we had fun. I was happy to help."

"Let me get this straight. It's okay for you to help others, but when they try to return the favor, watch out."

"Sarcasm does not become you. Besides I said I was sorry. Have I not thanked you enough Sire?"

Luke laughed. "Now who's being sarcastic?"

The ride was short. As soon as they pulled up to the building Lena hopped out of the car, hoping Luke would head off to work. That was not the case. He handed the doorman his keys and motioned to help her into the penthouse.

"This isn't necessary. I know Justin left for work hours ago, so you must be late."

"Here we go again. If you must know, I had a meeting at the coffee shop. I was leaving when I saw you. I don't punch a time clock Lena. I can and will help you up to the apartment."

"It's fine," Luke cut her off before she could say another word. "Don't say another word. I'm helping you and that's final."

The elevator ride to the top floor seemed to take forever. Luke had his arms around Lena and tried many times to make eye contact, but she couldn't allow it. If they locked their eyes, she knew she would give into her desire for him. Instead, they rode the elevator in silence with her avoiding eye contact. As soon as the doors to the penthouse opened, Lena again tried to get rid of him. "Thanks again. I just want to take a shower and put my foot up, so have a good day."

In a half serious tone Luke asked, "You want company in the shower? I could scrub your back."

The first word to pop into Lena's head was yes that she wanted him to join her in the shower. Who wouldn't? He was a God and with him next to her she was at his mercy. Fortunately, she was able to stop herself from replying to that. "Why Sire that was no gentlemanly offer?"

"It wasn't meant to be, but seriously I was half kidding. Of course, if the answer was yes, I would be happy to oblige."

"I think you know the answer."

"Then I shall help you to your room and get a chair for your shower."

As Lena sat on the bed she thought about this new side of Luke. He wasn't his typical intense self. Instead, he was playful. It was a side that she liked, but didn't see often. Her phone vibrated from her shorts while she was waiting for him to come back with the chair. It was Trey calling to remind her about Will's comedy show. She still needed to check with Justin but was excited to go. Luke entered the room while she was on the phone with Trey making plans. Gone was the playful side of Luke. His emerald eyes turned to ice as jealousy went through his veins. He didn't like one bit that she was making plans with another man and was unable to hide that fact. When the call ended Luke asked, "Was that the one-night stand?"

Lena didn't take his comment well. It was obvious his mood had shifted, and Lena was disappointed to see intense Luke. Determined, she rose from the bed to hobble into the bathroom. Before she left the bedroom she turned to Luke, "How dare you. You have no right comment on anything about my private life when yours is what it is. Listen, thanks for your help. Now go to hell," she shouted as she slammed the bathroom door.

Luke wasn't about to let her have the last word and opened the door as she was getting undressed. "It's okay for you make snide comments on my sex life, but honey bringing strange men home from a bar to fuck hardly makes you an angel."

Lena was standing in only her sports bra and panties as she yelled back, "Who are you? One minute you are a knight in shining armor and the next this snide asshole. Now just go!"

Everything she said was right and Luke knew it. It was just so hard to stop himself from commenting. He was jealous and not used to feeling this way about a woman. They had made so much progress over the last couple of weeks that he did not want it to be ruined. There was no way out of this except for honesty. After taking a deep breath to control his temper, Luke approached a half-naked Lena. "Everything you said is right. I'm sorry. You just do something to me, and I can't stop myself from feeling it when I think of you being with another man. I want you so badly that it's all I think about."

Lena's mouth dropped. She wasn't expecting that response. He could see that what he said impacted her and touched her face. When she leaned into his touch, he pulled her into a tender kiss. For Luke it was a kiss filled with emotion. One he hoped would show how he really felt about her. There was something between them besides desire. Before the kiss could turn into something more an alarm went off on Luke's phone indicating that he had a meeting in fifteen minutes.

"Damn I have to go, but I want to continue where we left off. I'll be back later." He leaned in for another kiss before taking his leave. As he left Lena dumbfounded in the bathroom she wondered if she should be grateful for the alarm or curse it. Every inch of her body wanted to curse the interruption.

****

Lena spent most of the day trying to interpret what had happened between her and Luke. There was no denying that after their kiss if his alarm hadn't gone off, they would have spent the day in bed. Maybe that would have been a good thing as it might have allowed them to get each other out of their minds. Once he had her, Luke would surely lose interest. The question was, would she? It was after seven when Justin returned home from work, filled with concern. As they were leaving the office, Luke had told Justin the ankle portion of what had happened to Lena. He wondered why Luke had waited so long, but they really had not had a free minute. Immediately upon his arrival he went to Lena's room to check on her. She was lying in bed flipping through a fashion magazine that must have been Anne's because she found it in the apartment.

Justin was happy to see her off her ankle and made a joke, "Let me guess you only read that for the articles."

Lena laughed. "Well, you have to learn somehow. What girl doesn't need to know what belt to wear?"

Justin smiled. "You know I'm a little mad at you. You never told me that your ankle was still sore."

Everything was so easy with Justin. "It wasn't. That's why I went for a run. I think I just over did it."

"How far did you go?" Justin sat on the bed. Lena moved her legs to make room. He took the leg with the bad ankle to examine it.

"About three miles. I was trying to sort some things through and just didn't realize how far I'd gone until it was too late."

"That explains it. What were you trying to work out?"

"Nothing of importance now." She couldn't tell him about her dream, her growing feelings for him or her undeniable attraction to Luke. As they spoke Lena wondered why it couldn't always be this way with Luke. Luke was such a chameleon. One day this tender, playful man and another a complete control freak. Justin nodded and left the room. When he returned, he had crutches and an ace bandage. Gently he lifted Lena's foot again to wrap it.

"You know this is not a fair relationship. I share everything with you, and you only give bits and pieces. Talk to me. I think you'll find I can be a good listener."

His gentle touch even at her foot sent shivers down Lena's spine. Lena knew she had to respond because she couldn't shut him out or lie to him. "I dreamt of Anne last night."

That wasn't the answer he expected. "Oh." Justin stopped what he was doing to look at her. She had his complete attention as she continued. "I know it was just a dream, but it seemed so real. In it she asked me to take care of you and Faith."

Justin was confused. "And that's why you were running?"

"Not entirely, but I was wondering what it all meant."

"Angelina, I'm not sure about your dream, but I do know that you do take great care of Faith and I. In fact, I'm not sure how I would have gotten through any of this without you." Lena smiled as Justin finished wrapping her ankle and handed her the crutches. "Do you know how to use these?"

"I work in an ER. I think I can handle it."

"Okay, but let me know if you need some advice. I'm a real pro!"

That was a story she wanted to hear. "Really do tell."

"You wound me by laughing at my pain, but if you must know it was a skiing accident when I was 22. Well, it was more of a drunken ski lodge accident, and it wasn't pretty. I broke my leg and was laid up for six weeks. Anne was a saint for taking care of me." His eyes showed that his mood was melancholy as he remembered better times with Anne. Lena wanted to lighten the mood by asking if he had eaten. When he shook his head and said that he hadn't, they decided to go to the kitchen to see what Mrs. Warner had left for dinner. On crutches Lena went to the kitchen while Justin went to check on Anne before joining her in the kitchen where he opened a bottle of wine.

"How's Faith?"

The topic of Faith always lightened Justin's mood. "Beautiful. Growing stronger every day."

Lena was a little disappointed she hadn't seen Faith in a while. "Maybe we should start preparing her room."

Justin brought over the prepared plates while Lena joked about how confident he now was in the kitchen. That brought a smile to Justin's face as he sat with Lena at the table.

Mrs. Warner left pasta primavera for them and Lena was starving. "Umm. This is good. I need to ask you something."

The last time she said that she wanted him to move Anne's things. Apprehensively he responded, "Yes."

"Saturday night a friend of mine is performing at The Comic Strip. Do you think it would be okay if I went?"

He was relieved, "Angelina. You don't need my permission to have a life. I want you here in case, but also understand you need to have fun."

"What about you? Why don't you come? I promise you will have a lot of fun. My friend is very funny."

"Thank you, but I'm not ready yet. It's just too soon."

"Well, when you're ready to blow off some steam let me know. Listen there's one more thing."

"Yes."

"It'll be late when the show is over. I don't like taking the subway alone that late, so I'm going to crash at my friend's house. I'll be back early to check on Anne and you can call if there are any problems."

"If you want, I can pick you up."

"That's okay Dad. Unless you think you'll need me."

"I'm Dad now. I guess this is good practice, but I see your point. Go have some fun."

After dinner was finished, the plates were cleared and Anne was suitably checked on, they decided to watch a movie. It was a stupid movie, but Justin declared it one of his and Luke's favorites. Sometime during the second movie Lena yawned, and Justin told her to lie back while he elevated her foot with a pillow from the sofa. Within minutes they were both asleep. Lena's head was resting on Justin's chest while he had his arm around her when Luke, who had promised he would be back walked in to see them asleep snuggled on the sofa. Again, his blood boiled with jealousy. It was innocent enough, but Luke didn't want any man touching Lena even if it was his own brother. He picked up a book and dropped it loudly. The noise startled them, awake. "Luke," Justin said removing his arm as Lena sleepily sat up. "What are you doing here?"

"I told Lena I would come by to check on her after work." Luke was eyeing them coldly, realizing Justin had wrapped her ankle and picked up some crutches. Naturally Justin had taken good care of her, Luke thought to himself. The worst part of the realization was that she probably allowed him to without a fight. Snidely Luke commented, "Looks like you have things under control though."

Lena rose from the sofa, grabbed the crutches and announced that she was going to bed, but not before checking on Anne. Justin nodded. He could tell Luke had something on his mind. Before she left the room Lena turned to Luke and thanked him for his concern, but she assured him she was fine. In response Luke wished her well. When Lena was gone, Luke was determined to find out what he had walked in on. "Did I interrupt something?"

Justin was confused as to what was going on. He was surprised to see Luke and had no idea why Luke was looking at him disapprovingly "Huh. Oh no. God no." Justin protested.

Luke could tell that although nothing had happened Justin wouldn't have minded if it did. Luke pressed trying to see what his brother's feelings really were.

Justin answered honestly. "She's a very special girl and let's face it attractive. I'm not oblivious to that. In fact, if I'm to be honest, I've thought about it. Who wouldn't? I mean look at her. She's the whole package, beautiful, smart and kind. I just couldn't do that to Anne or Angelina for that matter."

Luke placed his hand on Justin's shoulder. He was torn because he wanted to encourage Justin to move on. Just not with Lena. He loved his brother and had to do the right thing by him. Gently Luke offered, "Justin, Anne isn't coming back. She would want you to be happy."

As the brothers were talking, Lena overheard them mention her. She stopped to listen.

"Great love only comes once. You may be able to fill a void with someone else, but it'll only be great love once. Angelina deserves to be someone's great love, and I already have mine."

Lena couldn't help but feel disappointed as she hobbled on crutches to her room. With tears threatening she resolved that there was no hope for her and Justin. Even though it shouldn't have hurt her hearing those words out loud, it did. At that moment she couldn't deny her feelings for Justin were moving past friendship, especially since her feelings for Luke were so conflicted. Luke was so complicated which is why she believed it better to remain friends with both men than to have sex with either.

Back in the family room Luke was relieved to hear that Justin didn't wish to pursue Lena. He knew if Lena was given the choice, she would choose Justin. She was fragile and Justin was kind and warm. If Luke were to have a chance with Lena, he needed to show her his tender side more often. Episodes like the one they had earlier couldn't happen again. Luke assured Justin he just needed some time to grieve and accept. One day Justin would be happy again. Although he appreciated his brother's words, Justin didn't see how that was possible. All Justin wanted to do was sit with Anne for a while before going to bed. Luke told him that he would show himself out. Even though he hated lying to Justin, he had to check on Lena to see if they could continue their earlier conversation. When Luke knocked on her door, she pretended to be asleep. She was upset and didn't want to see anyone. The best way to avoid him was to do that. When he peeked in her room, he decided to let her sleep. They could continue their conversation later.

Chapter Fourteen

It took a couple of days for Lena's ankle to really heal. All week Justin had tended to her with such kindness. At times she thought he might be returning her growing feelings, but he always pulled back. Lena knew their living arrangement couldn't go on forever. Several times she tried to discuss moving out with Justin; however, he always told her they weren't ready. Anne's care was going smoothly, and Faith wasn't ready to come home yet. That meant Lena really had nothing to do except be there for Justin. Spending time with him only made her feelings grow stronger.

Lena barely saw Luke the rest of the week. Justin and Luke were working hard on the big case and spent a lot of time at the office. She watched James one day. The two of them escaped from the penthouse. First, they had lunch with Gus which James thought was "cool" because he got to play with the police siren. Gus loved meeting James even though he wasn't so fond of his father. James asked all kinds of questions about police work. It was such a hot day that after they had lunch, she took him to her neighborhood in Brooklyn so that they could run through the fire hydrants with the rest of the neighborhood kids. Lena enjoyed spending time with James. He had never been on the subway before and thought his time with Lena was an adventure. By the time Luke picked James up he was exhausted but was also excited to tell his father about his day. Although Luke appreciated Lena taking care of James, he told James it might be best not to tell his mother about his Brooklyn adventure. He knew Jessica wouldn't be happy about him taking the subway or playing in the fire hydrant even if Luke and Justin thought it sounded like fun.

****

On Saturday Luke went over to Justin's to try to entice his brother into playing a game of tennis. After some coercion, Justin agreed, telling Lena he would be back well before she went out. Luke remembered Lena's conversation about going out with "one-night stand" and needed the details which he planned to get from Justin. He knew if he asked her it would turn into an argument. The brothers went uptown to the most exclusive tennis club in town. To play there you had to be a member of the club. Justin used to frequent the place with Anne who used tennis as her only form of exercise. Several of the regulars who hadn't seen Justin since Anne was shot were interested to know how they were. The shooting and various details had been on all the media outlets; however, they had been able to keep Anne's true condition private. Everyone who was important to either him or Anne knew everything. The rest didn't need the details. Although people showed their concern, Justin worried it would lead to gossip and kept his answers evasive. Luke could see his brother's mood falling. To prevent that he ushered Justin away to the courts before anyone else could ask questions. On the tennis court Luke was in rare form. He was using all his pent-up aggression about Lena to make Justin work hard and won all three matches. By the time they finished playing Justin was exhausted.

"I guess you're a little out of shape little brother. Let's grab some beers before heading home. You can buy."

"Sounds like a plan, but I think you can buy."

"No way. Loser buys." Justin laughed and agreed. While they were sitting down, they talked about Faith and James. Luke had recently found out that Jessica was remarrying and told Justin who wondered how he felt about that. The only thing that bothered him was that James was going to have another father figure. He knew when he divorced Jessica that one day she would get remarried. Unlike him she wasn't the type to enjoy being single for long. In fact, he was surprised it took her that long. It was how it impacted James that was his concern. As the very attractive blond waitress brought their beers, she flirted with both Luke and Justin. Luke noticed right away and told Justin a no strings affair could be exactly what he needed. There was no way Justin was ready and quickly told a disappointed Luke he wasn't interested. His heart and body still belonged to Anne. Even if he was ready, he wouldn't be interested in a fling. Anne taught him that he liked being in a real relationship. After a couple of beers Luke casually brought up the topic of Lena going out that night. Justin had seen the way Luke looked at Lena and was wary of his question. When Luke justified it as just a casual interest in how he felt about her going out, Justin told him the only thing he was worried about was the fact she wouldn't come back home that night. Luke tried to play cool. "Why? Where's she staying?"

"With her friend. They're going to The Comic Strip and since she didn't want to take the subway back by herself so late, she decided to stay out."

Luke knew which friend she was planning on staying with and slammed his beer down. "Like hell she is."

That confirmed what Justin had suspected. He knew Luke was interested in pursuing Lena and had to put a stop to it. "We talked about this. You need to keep it in your pants."

Luke tried to cover telling Justin he was just upset that Justin was so nervous about being there without Lena all night. Justin knew he was lying, but since they were having a good time together, he decided not to push. They stayed another hour, and it felt like Luke was getting his brother back. For that he was grateful.

****

After Luke dropped Justin off at home, he called The Comic Strip to purchase two tickets to the show that night. Because he needed a cover, he called Tabatha to see if she was free. The plan was to pretend running into Lena was a coincidence. Tabatha was excited at the prospect of having a real date with Luke. They had been at several society functions at the same time, but never out together. Quickly she went shopping and to the spa for the full treatment. She had read that Jessica was remarrying and thought Luke's change in attitude towards her stemmed from that. It was finally her chance.

Luke knew he was being a bit of a stalker, but didn't care. There was no way Lena was going to spend the night with the man she had a one-night stand with. He was going to see to that. Idly he wondered if taking Tabatha was a good idea. She had been acting weird lately and Luke knew it was only a matter of time before he called it off altogether. For that night she was a means to an end. Luke believed Lena wouldn't be as suspicious of him being there if he was on a date. He had hoped it would be the night he shared his bed with Lena in a non-platonic way. Even if she wasn't ready, it would be fine if he brought her back to Justin's. She was just not going to stay with the "one-night stand" again. Just in case he had his way, he stopped at a drug store to buy condoms. He hated wearing them, but Lena had made it perfectly clear the last time that she had no interest in being with someone without one. There was no way he wanted a repeat of the last time. Luke shuttered as he thought of being so close and then stopping.

****

Around nine o'clock Lena was ready to go out. She was dressed in a black backless cotton dress with spaghetti straps that clung to the curves of her body. Not wanting to take any chances with her ankle she wore black flat sandals. Whenever she went out, she applied more makeup than she usually wore. Her eyes were surrounded by smoky grey enhancing her beautiful blue eyes and her lips were colored bright red. She wore her hair long, curls flowing down her chest. When Justin saw how beautiful Lena looked, he had a hard time taking his eyes off her as she walked in the family room.

"You're going out like that? I mean you look nice, but are you sure you want to take the subway dressed like that?"

"Don't worry Dad. Trey is meeting me downstairs and we're taking the subway together."

Fatherly feelings weren't what Justin had on his mind. Briefly, Justin reconsidered going with her. "Oh, good."

Justin's voice betrayed his words of relief. Lena was enjoying the way Justin looked nervous around her all the sudden. Her earlier worry that she didn't look okay dissipated as she realized that he was looking at her with desire. She knew at that moment beyond any doubt that he was attracted to her. Even still his admission to Luke that he could never love another haunted her. When Trey called to say he was downstairs she quickly said goodnight and assured him she would see him in the morning. Trey was waiting in the lobby for her. His mouth dropped open when he saw Lena. "Damn girl you look hot." Trey, who quickly hugged Lena, was dressed in blue jeans, a white T-shirt and black jacket.

"You don't look so bad yourself. You ready to go?"

"Your chariot awaits or in this case your subway train." He wrapped his arm around her shoulder as they walked towards the subway.

On the subway they caught up with what had been going on in each other's lives. Dr. Castillo had approached Trey at the gym, wanting details of Trey's part in the set up. Trey threatened to release what he knew to Dr. Castillo's wife and hadn't seen him since. Lena apologized for getting him involved, but she was grateful to him for his help. Trey told Lena he could handle Dr. Castillo. The important thing was that she was safe. That meant so much to her. Trey was maybe the first real friend she ever had. She and Justin and maybe she and Luke were friends, but with Trey it was so different. With Trey there was none of the heavy stuff. He was just someone to enjoy spending time with.

When they arrived at the Comic Strip it was crowded. Lena was a little nervous for Will, while Trey and Mark were confident that he would nail the performance. Will had been rehearsing his act all week and they were excited for their friend. This could be a real break for him. As Will's guests they were treated to front row seats. Some of the other people Lena met at the beach party also joined them. It was so comfortable being around them. No one talked about anything heavy. Mostly they talked about jokes they hoped Will would tell and how this performance could make his career. They laughed as they talked about how impossible Will would be once he was famous. On a good day he was difficult, if he made it big his head would swell. Everything they were saying was lighthearted. While they were enjoying drinks before the show, Lena felt a hand on her shoulder. She could tell from the charge in her body who it was even before she looked to see Luke standing there.

Luke couldn't believe his eyes. She was always beautiful, but there was a goddess before him. There was no way Trey didn't see it too and he was more confident than ever that she was leaving with him. Not Trey. "Nice to see you, Lena. I didn't know you would be here."

Lena could tell that it was a lie but tried to act nonchalant so not to alert her new friends. "I didn't know you would be here either."

Lena couldn't help but shy away from his eyes that looked at her as though they were undressing her. Luke was dressed in black jeans, with a white linen shirt left open at the top and a grey jacket. She eyed him hungrily before turning her head. It had been a while since she had been with a man, and he looked amazing. Even if it hadn't been a while, he looked amazing. Out of politeness, not because she wanted to, Lena made introductions.

"Trey, you and Luke have met. Luke this Mark, Stan, Rita, Jake and Jen. Everyone this is Luke."

"Hey Luke," everyone shouted, but Trey didn't look pleased. He had seen Lena with Luke the other night and was feeling protective. Instinctively, Trey leaned over and put his arm around Lena's shoulder. Lena knew exactly what he was doing and was appreciative. She was feeling a little uncomfortable with Luke's presence. As Luke was about to say something to Trey, Tabatha interjected. "Hi baby. Aren't you going to introduce me to your friends?"

She gave him a kiss on the lips. Although Lena felt annoyed by Tabatha, she didn't wish to give anything away or let it ruin the evening. "Hi. I'm Lena."

"Tabatha." Tabatha responded before turning to Luke. "Baby, don't you think we should take our seats."

As they walked away Lena noticed how attractive Tabatha was. Her red hair was fixed perfectly, and her tight blue dress showed her stunning figure. Like Luke, she was in her early thirties. Lena hated to admit it, but they seemed like a great couple. Based on the expensive designer dress Tabatha was wearing, it was clear she had money. Her uppity attitude made it hard for Lena to imagine that she would partake in what she understood were Luke's sexual preferences. There was no more time to think about it because the show was about to start.

Several comedians went on that night. Some were funnier than others, but Will kept the audience laughing the entire time. Throughout the entire show Lena could feel Luke's eyes fixated on her. Although Lena tried to keep her focus on the acts many times, she would look at Luke and catch his eye. It was clear that Luke wasn't interested in Tabatha who was laughing hard at most of the acts and would caress Luke's leg or hand. When she did, Lena would feel a twinge of jealousy, however Luke seemed oblivious to Tabatha. Instead, Luke was making his intentions towards Lena very well known to her. The fact that Luke was so disinterested in Tabatha made Lena happy. At one point Trey reached over to put his hand on Lena's lap. It was an innocent gesture, but when Lena looked over at Luke, she noticed that he looked like he was going to jump out of his chair. Lena saw his reaction, however she was there to have a good time with friends, so she tried her best to ignore him no matter how difficult it was. Silently, she reminded herself that she was with Trey that night. With Trey she could be herself and she needed to concentrate her attention on him. The more Lena tried to ignore Luke the angrier he looked. After the show, Will joined them at the table. The friends continued to drink and toast his performance; ordering some shots which Lena gladly did, feeling that she needed a boost of confidence. With all the laughter at the table it was easier to ignore Luke until she needed to use the lady's room. As she walked away, she could feel Luke's eyes stare at the back of her. Lena wondered how Tabatha could ignore Luke's obvious attention directed at her. Before going back to the table, Lena looked in the mirror to adjust herself and fix her make-up. Even though she knew it was wrong, she wanted to make sure Luke kept his attention fixated on her. Not his date. There was no worry there because when she came out, Luke was waiting there for her by the door. Gently he pushed her to the wall, while he put each hand on the opposite sides of the wall so that she was encaged. With him in such close proximity her breathing quickened. Try as she did, he was all she thought about that evening. Now that they were face-to-face it was hard to ignore her yearning for him.

"Tell the one-night stand to keep his hands off you. Tonight, you're mine."

Of all the things he could have said that would have made her melt in his arms, that was not one of them. She was no one's possession nor did she like his reference to Trey and snapped back, "Don't you mean tonight Tabatha is yours?"

Luke pulled her into a passionate kiss. At first Lena tried to fight him off, but shortly afterwards found herself lost in an endless sea of passion leaving her breathless. Luke whispered, "Come home with me tonight." As much as Lena wanted to, she thought about the fact that she was there with Trey, and he was there with Tabatha. "I can't. Go be with your date Luke. I need to get back to my friends."

"You want me. I can feel it." He was right, she did more than anything at that moment. It wasn't right. Luke was on a date, and she was spending time with Trey. Before he could kiss her again, she went underneath his arms to escape from his hold. Luke wasn't about to give up. As she walked away Luke called out to her, "Don't do this. You need this and so do I. Don't let this feeling slip away."

She stopped walking for a moment. Being with him would fill the longing in her core, but at what cost to her. Using all her strength she went back to her friends. Luke also went back to his table to order a bottle of champagne for Lena's friends. When the waiter brought the bottle, he told them who it was from. Everyone at the table except Trey and Lena turned to thank him.

"Is there something going on with you and him, Lena?" Trey had to ask the question because he could feel the tension radiating off the two of them all night. Lena had to consider the question carefully. There was. She just didn't know what exactly was happening and answered the only way she could even if she wasn't sure, it was true. "Nothing that I can't handle."

"Good." Trey squeezed her hand. That was the last straw for Luke. He was tired of watching someone else touch Lena and decided to congratulate Will on a great performance, leaving Tabatha to sit at the table alone. She wasn't stupid. She knew Luke was interested in Lena. Part of her was jealous, but the other part of her knew he always came back to her. They had reached a new level in their relationship. She assumed he was acting this way because he was frightened of his new feelings towards her. Luke could have his flirtation in the end they belonged together. When he arrived at the table, Trey's friends again thanked Luke for the champagne. They invited Luke to join them at their celebration. Although he declined the invitation, he told Will that he was an attorney for the largest talent agency in New York and would be happy to arrange an introduction. Lena thought to herself how transparent Luke was. She knew he only made the offer to get to her. It did have the effect that he wanted because she was happy that Luke's interest in her might help Will. An introduction would be a great opportunity for Will. Lena was too lost in her own conflicted emotions about Luke to listen to the rest of their conversation but could tell that Will was excited. Suddenly Luke turned to Lena. "There's no reason that you should have to take the subway home tonight. I'll be happy to drop you at Justin's"

Trey interjected, "That's okay man. I have her covered." Trey leaned in to kiss Lena's exposed shoulder after he responded.

Luke's eyes iced over as Lena remained quiet. If they hadn't been in public, there was no telling what he would have done. Since they were, Luke fought to control his rage. "Lena, earlier today Justin mentioned how uncomfortable he was leaving Anne with the nurse for the night. He would feel better knowing you're there even though he wouldn't tell you that himself."

That confirmed that Luke knew she was going to be there, and he wasn't playing fair, bringing up Justin. Tabatha joined the table, put her arm around Luke telling him she was ready to go. Luke's only thoughts were on Lena. He shook Tabatha off and extended his hand to Lena motioning her to join him. "You ready?"

It sounded to Lena more like an order than an offer. A big part of Lena wanted to tell him to go to hell. No one ordered her, but the other part of her wanted to see where this was headed. Actually, she knew where it would lead. Straight to his bedroom because regardless of what Luke said, she knew he was not wanting her to leave with him for Justin's sake. He made his desire for her clear outside the bathroom. It was exhausting trying to fight what she was beginning to believe was the inevitable. Still the way he approached the whole thing made her angry. Luke needed to understand that she was leaving with him because she wanted this and not because he commanded it. That was something she would make clear later. For now, she took his hand, while making excuses to Trey who was abundantly disappointed that she was ending their evening. When she said it was because of Justin, Trey faked understanding. It was obvious there was something going on between the two of them, but since he was in the friend zone he didn't feel it was his place to say anything other than that he would call her in the morning. Trey pulled Lena into a big hug while wondering why she always surrounded herself with jerks. Even with Luke looking disapprovingly, she gladly returned Trey's hug. Before Lena left with Luke, she said her goodbyes and congratulated Will on his performance with a hug. Tabatha wasn't happy Lena was leaving with them either. She knew Luke was interested in Lena, but until that moment hadn't seen her as competition. After all Lena was nowhere near being in her league. Sure, she was beautiful, but it was clear she lacked any social status. To make herself feel better she decided that any pairing they would have would be for carnal pleasure. No real future. Even still she had heard one of Trey's friends mention that he worked at Jumba. Tabatha made a mental note to get to know him better to keep an eye on the situation.

With Tabatha in the car, they drove in silence. All that could be heard in the Porsche was the sound of dance music coming from the car radio. Much to Tabatha's dismay Luke drove her home first. As Luke explained, he was bringing her home first because he needed to speak with Justin about something important. She pretended to believe the lie but knew Luke well enough to know he was going to make a move on Lena. Instead of causing a scene Tabatha made it clear to Luke that he had better make it up to her. Even though he had no intention of doing so, Luke agreed. When Luke got out of the car to open the door for Tabatha she leaned in for a kiss. Luke turned his head so that all she got was his cheek. That stung a little. She had worked too hard to get Luke and had no intention of losing him to a child. If looks could kill, the one Tabatha gave Lena would have slayed her. Lena understood. It was an asshole move on Luke's part. If she were honest, it didn't make her a great person either. Still, it made her desire for Luke more intense. After they dropped Tabatha off Lena moved to the front seat. Luke drove to the corner of Tabatha's street and parked. "My home or Justin's?"

Luke already knew the answer, so Lena decided to be coy. "I thought Justin said he needed me home. Isn't what all this is about?"

"He did say he was nervous about being alone. That wasn't a lie, but I think you know what this was really about."

He ran his fingers up her leg before leaning in to nibble her ear. "So, what will it be Sweetness?"

Lena was having a hard time controlling her breathing as he was making her body tingle in all the right places. Still, she had to make him work for it. "If I say Justin's?"

Lena gasped as Luke had made it up to her inner thigh and was applying pressure on her wall. "Then I'll be disappointed, but that's where you will go. He isn't expecting you home so you might frighten him."

With his other hand he caressed her cheek. Her body was on fire. Panting Lena answered, "I think you know where I want to go."

"Say it Sweetness," he said as his fingers hit her sensitive area.

She couldn't take any more of the game. "Your place. I want to go to your place."

Luke took his hands away, "Good answer." He drove back to his apartment in record speed, afraid she might change her mind. Fortunately, traffic for New York City was light as they sped through the streets. This time Luke wouldn't let anything get in his way of making her his. At least for the night. As he ushered her out of his car she pulled him into a passionate kiss. His hand went up her short dress to caress her naked bottom while she ran her fingers through his hair. He needed to get her into the apartment before they didn't make it there. They waited so long for this moment. Still entwined in an embrace Luke lifted her to take her to the elevator in the parking garage and pushed the button. Lucky for them there was no one else in the garage, however if there had been they were so involved in one another they might not have noticed. Luke put her down long enough to punch in his code to his apartment. He was vaguely aware that they might be giving the security people quite a show, but when she jumped up on him and wrapped her legs around his waist he no longer cared. Finally, the elevator arrived at his apartment. Luke bypassed everything on his way to his bedroom. In the bedroom Lena ripped open his shirt and threw both his shirt and jacket on the floor. As much as Luke wanted this Lena did too. So many nights she dreamt about having his hard naked chest pressed against her body. His chest was magnificent, and she had to touch it. To be close to him. Never had she recalled wanting another man more than at that moment and she bent down to suck on one of his nipples. Luke could sense her eagerness and was aroused that her want matched his own and threw her on his bed. There was no stopping they had gone too far and no matter what reservation either of them had, their desire surpassed any rational thought. On the bed Lena quickly removed her dress as Luke stopped to take in the view of her lying on his bed in only a black lace thong. She was a vision unmatched by anything he had seen before. As he removed each one of her shoes, he massaged each leg before putting the shoe down all the while keeping his eyes glued to her. When he did, she moaned with pleasure, and he knew it was a sound he wanted to hear forever. Luke wanted to savor every minute of this, but Lena was ready. In her mind they had waited long enough, and she pulled him down to her. Her mouth tasted like the alcohol from the club and Luke needed to know that this was happening out of passion and not because she was drunk. He broke the kiss and looked at her beautiful blue eyes searching for the answer. In her eyes he saw it. She was present, but the question had to be asked. "Tell me you want this. Not because you drank too much but because you have been fantasizing about this as much as I have." Luke wasn't a praying man, but at that moment he was praying for the answer he really wanted.

The question caught her off guard. She had a couple of drinks but knew that was not what this was. She responded as she dropped her panties to the ground. "I thought you knew this was a foregone conclusion. Don't worry just lose those pants and fuck the shit out of me but put a condom on first."

Oddly he cringed at the idea this was fucking but was not something he was going to battle at that moment. Instead, he obliged. He really hated condoms, but he would have hated not having her more and reached for one he had put in the drawer that afternoon after dropping his pants and underwear. She knew he would be glorious, and he was. Part of her worried that he was larger than she was used to, but then quietly considered she didn't really remember everyone. After the condom was secure, he crawled on top of her and placed his fingers on her special spot. He could feel how wet she was and any doubt he had about whether she was drunk or wanted this dissipated. Slowly he massaged her area while she moaned with pleasure. He wanted to taste her and moved his hand to make room for his tongue. When he did, she screamed "I won't last. Fuck me. Put it in now." He couldn't help, but smile. Instead of obliging, he continued his until he felt her body relax and she was screaming his name. That really was the most beautiful sound, and he could wait no longer. Before she could calm down, he was inside moving at a feverous rate. He wanted to be gentle, especially after what he knew she had been through and tried to slow down. When she said she wanted to fuck she meant it while he slowed down, she quickened. Skin on skin. Need on want. The wait was over, and they were engrossed in each other's passion. It was not long before they each found release and fell into each other's arms completely sated. Luke laid on top of her for minutes starring at her beauty as she glowed from the sweat he knew he was responsible for.

When he unwillingly broke contact, he noticed a different look on her face. He threw the condom and missed the trash but didn't care. He could get that later and took her in his arms and kissed her forehead. "Are you okay Sweetness?"

"Sure." Something about her tone wasn't convincing and he had to know what was going through her head. "What are you thinking about?"

"Honestly."

"When are you not brutally honest?"

Even though he was right about her candor, she wasn't sure she wanted to hear the answer. Usually, she would be okay with leaving after sex, but that night she didn't want to, and she knew he wasn't in this for a relationship. Staying could mean this was more than what it was, and she didn't want to overstay her welcome. If this was one and done, she wanted to know before she went too far down a hole. "I was just wondering if I should go back to Justin's now."

Luke removed his arm from her and sat up to look at her. He didn't understand where this was coming from. "Is that what you want?"

> **Comment:** the answer

His eyes penetrated hers. She didn't want to leave, but all of this was so new to her. "I asked you first. Is it what you want?"

Luke was racing through his action wondering if he had done something to cause this question. Afterall it was out of the ordinary for him to want to have a woman stay the night. As hard as he tried, he couldn't come up with anything that might have indicated she should leave. "I'm confused. What about tonight made you think that I would want you to leave now?"

Lena tried to look away from him a little embarrassed. Gently he moved her head back to where he could see her eyes. "I may be assuming, but this is usually the part of the night where I am aching to leave, and I would bet money you are the same way. I just figured it was done, and it was great, but now."

Luke cut her off. He hated the idea that she had been with other men, but he was certainly no virgin so he couldn't really focus on that. What he needed to do is focus on the here and now and assure her that he had no intention of not having this happen again and again and not in the way he sees Tabatha. She was special. This was special and he had to find a way of letting her know that without scaring her. "What exactly do you think happened tonight?"

Lena didn't understand the question. "Uh we had sex. You were there. Do you remember?"

It was sex but coming from her mouth he didn't like hearing the word. "Sex. Is that what you call it?"

She was trying to be nonchalant, "What would you call it? Good sex. No, I would even go as far as to say great sex, but a spade is a spade it was sex."

Even though he knew where she was coming from, the words still stung a little. "And what if I said I don't think it was just sex?"

Lena couldn't believe her ears. That night she thought if she had sex with him, she could get it out of her system. Even if deep down she may have wanted more, she never allowed the idea to really surface. If she was honest with herself, she wasn't even sure she wanted more with him. Although he had a tender side, he didn't show it often and she wasn't sure if she liked him. One thing she did know was in the bedroom they were compatible. "I don't know what I would say. I know that we have this attraction, but I feel like you don't like me half the time and I know I don't like you. I mean the way you manipulated the situation tonight"

Luke cut her off before she could finish, "Wait a minute. I manipulated you?"

"Really. We both know you followed me to the comedy club with every intention of bringing me back here tonight."

As much as he wanted to deny it, he knew that they both knew that would be a lie and he was trying to be different with her. "Maybe I did do that, but you can't tell me that you didn't want this as much as I did. You could have walked away and said no."

Lena sat up. "And you would have been fine with me leaving with Trey?"

Luke laughed. "Well, we both know that wasn't going to happen, but I could have taken you back to Justin's."

"That's exactly what I mean. You commanded me to come with you."

"Let me get this straight so you had sex with me because I commanded you. If that would have worked, I would have done that days ago." Luke smirked. In Luke's mind this was a ridiculous conversation. If there is one thing he knew about her, she had free will. He experienced it firsthand.

Lena sensed that she was about to lose and pouted. "Don't make fun of me. You know I wanted to be here even if everything in my head was telling me otherwise. My body had a mind of its own. That leads me back to my original question now that you have had me is challenge over? Do you still want me here?"

This was a pivotal moment and Luke had to make sure he answered clearly and seriously. She was looking for reassurance and he knew that. He looked her in the eye and said, "You're not going anywhere tonight. I want you here. This is all new to me."

Lena cracked a smile, relieved. "What is?"

"I understand what you are saying. Full disclosure, normally I would be looking for an excuse to get you to leave, but I like having you here. Honestly, I have never wanted a woman to stay more or at all even."

"Luke, you were married."

"I told you that was a marriage of convenience, so it never felt right. This does. If I am honest part of me did think that once we had sex, I might be able to get you out of my system. That didn't work. Now that I have had you, I'm greedy."

He leaned in to kiss Lena's lips. It was a kiss that was filled with so much promise. Lena climbed on top of him to straddle him. They were both still naked, so before they could go any further Luke awkwardly looked for the box of condoms. He really hated them. Since it was the only way he could have Lena, it was worth the price. "Do you think we could lose these one day?"

Lena again ripped the condom open and put it on, feeling his firmness with anticipation. "Do you really want to talk about this now or?"

It wasn't the time to talk about it. Luke pulled her into a kiss, answering the question without words. Since the night with the paint, it had been Luke's fantasy to have her from behind and he turned her around cupping her breasts with his hands and fondling her nipples determined to have her doggy style. The reality was so much better than the fantasy and they found release together. At that moment she knew she was his and hoped he felt the same way. He did. Together they slept with their bodies wrapped around each other satisfied and exhausted and in unfamiliar territory, but happy.

****

That same night Justin had trouble sleeping. The penthouse without Lena seemed so empty. Many times, he went to check on Anne, fearing that there was a problem even though he knew he would hear the monitors if something were to happen. It was so much more comforting having Lena there. Anne's night nurse was pleasant enough, but she wasn't Lena. Justin wondered if this was what his life was destined to be. Soon Lena would return to her normal life, while Justin would be left with his own thoughts and memories of happier times. With Faith growing stronger it was only a matter of time before she would be home. Maybe she would help fill some of the void, but there would still be a major hole in his life that was left by losing Anne. Although he couldn't wait to have Faith home, it also terrified him. Justin knew next to nothing about babies let alone the needs of a premature baby. The nurses in the hospital told him that premature babies must be monitored closely for the first year because problems can occur. Even though Martha offered to come when Faith came home, Justin wondered if he could persuade Lena to stay to help with the baby at night. It was true that Anne's nurse would be there in case, yet there was no one on staff that he trusted as much as Lena. He did consider if asking her to stay was selfish because again she would be putting her life on hold to help him, while he could offer her nothing more than friendship. Briefly he thought about how Lena looked when she left the house and wondered if there could ever be more. Justin's feelings for Lena were growing, even though he was still committed to Anne. He had vowed a lifetime with Anne. As long as she was alive, he would honor that vow even if it meant never having anyone else in her place. The doctors all agreed that Anne could go on like this indefinitely. There will come a time when her body just shuts down, but that could be years from now. In the early hours of the morning Justin finally gave up on trying to sleep and went to work in the home office. There was still so much to prepare before the case went to trial in a couple of weeks. As he worked, he thought about his father, hoping he would never become like him. Faith deserved better and he needed Lena to ensure she got it. It was then that he resolved to ask Lena to stay.

****

When Lena woke up the next morning, Luke was still asleep. His beautiful muscular body was wrapped tightly around her making her bask in the serenity of the morning. Often when she woke up with a man, she was filled with regret. This time was different. No matter what happened between them next, she had no regrets. Quietly she got out of bed removing his arm from her body to use the powder room. On her way to the bathroom, she picked up her clothes and noticed the closet door. She knew what was in there and wondered if the way she and Luke had expressed their desire was enough for him. After everything she had been through in her life, there was no way she would want to partake in those activities. It wasn't that she was prude or against experimenting, but the roughness of it all could never be part of her sexual encounters. If she and Luke were to continue with whatever this was, she would have to find a way to express that to him. Suddenly she began to feel frightened, thinking of a future with Luke. Even though he expressed that she meant something to him, she still questioned if their night was a one-time thing. They were so different. It was too much to think about. Instead of assuming anything, she decided to shower and dress. In her backpack purse which she dropped in the foyer was a change of clothes she had packed, since she had been prepared to sleep at Trey's. After retrieving her bag, she went to the shower to get ready to return to Justin's. It was still early morning. She promised Justin that she would be back early. That was the perfect excuse to leave and allow her to collect her thoughts and reflect on how she felt. While Lena was showering Luke awoke, disappointed to see that she wasn't in bed or anywhere in sight. He recalled how she left the last time she spent the night and was greatly relieved to hear the water in the bathroom. At first, he considered joining her. With great restraint, he decided to go to the kitchen to make coffee since this was all still new. For the first time in a long time, he was happy. Lena wasn't anyone he would have pictured himself with. She was better and he couldn't imagine ever being with anyone else. By the time Luke came back to the bedroom carrying two mugs filled with coffee, Lena was dressed in her white sundress. With the morning light upon her, Luke realized that Justin was correct. She did look like an angel. Luke handed her the coffee mug and kissed her soft lips. "Good morning, Sweetness. You're up early."

She smiled. "I promised Justin I'd be back early so I need to get back."

With Luke's free hand he caressed Lena's face. "It's still early. Can I convince you to stay just a bit?"

Lena leaned into to his touch knowing full well what he meant. The offer was tempting, but she really did need to get back. "Sorry, I really do have to go."

Even though Luke was disappointed he understood. "If you're sure I can't persuade you, give me a minute to dress and I'll drive you."

"That's okay. I'll can get an Uber." Lena walked towards Luke to give him a peck on the cheek, "I'll see you later."

It was obvious to Luke that leaving wasn't completely about Justin. There was more to the story. "Are you okay?"

"Of course, I just really need to get back."

Something about the way she was answering was off and he needed to find out what. "I'll drive you."

She shook her head. "I'd rather Justin not know I was with you last night."

There it was. She was embarrassed. The thought angered Luke although he did have his own worry about telling Justin what had happened. After all Justin warned Luke to keep his distance. He just didn't like what her reasoning for Justin not knowing could be. It was obvious there was more to the feelings Justin and Lena had for one another. Even if Lena could help Justin move on, Luke was not prepared to give Lena up. There had to be someone else that could help Justin. A little more harshly than what was intended Luke replied. "Are you ashamed of what happened between us?"

Lena thought to herself, this was exactly why she wasn't sure she wanted this to go further because of him not Justin. "What? No."

"Then why. You're a grown woman."

This argument would get them nowhere. She really needed to think and thought rather than fight it was easier to agree to have Luke drive her. The condition was that he drop her off. It was fair compromise, and Luke went to shower while she drank her coffee. Shortly after Luke went to shower, Trey called to make sure she made it home okay. She felt terrible about leaving him the way she did and apologized again while omitting the fact she was still with Luke. Trey wasn't happy with how Luke had treated her. "Your boss' brother can be a real ass. What's his deal anyway?"

Lena really didn't want to elaborate on any of the details from the prior night but could understand why Trey felt that way. Many times, she thought he was an ass too. The only explanation she could offer was that Luke worries about Justin. Sometimes he goes about things the wrong way. It wasn't totally a lie. Luke did worry about Justin. The problem was his worry for Justin wasn't why he acted the way he did. She felt guilty for it omitting facts, but she wasn't prepared for any questions or Trey's potential disapproval. It was too soon, and she was still processing how she felt about things. After discussing Luke, Trey asked if she wanted to meet for lunch. Ordinarily she would love to have lunch with him, but they agreed to meet the following day because she was too tired. As she hung up, she realized Luke was staring at her with eyes like ice. He had been listening to her conversation and was not at all happy that she was making plans with a man she had sex with.

"How long have you been standing there?" Lena questioned.

"Long enough. I hope that wasn't the one-night stand." He knew it was even before her face said it was. "You're not having lunch with him."

His comment pissed Lena off. She couldn't understand why he always went back to that. "His name is Trey and what's your problem?"

"My problem is that you are talking to that guy in my house."

"That guy is my friend and after you were such an ass last night, he called to check on me."

Luke couldn't contain his jealousy. "That guy who you call your friend wants to fuck what's mine. I have a right to be pissed."

He took things too far. She finally had a real friend and wasn't prepared to give that up for anyone. "What's yours? I'm sorry when did I give you my ownership papers?"

"You know what I meant."

"Do I? Let me make something perfectly clear to you. You don't own me. No one does. As for Trey. He is my friend. Not my booty call nor am I his. Can you say the same about Tabatha?"

In the midst of the argument, Luke kept telling himself to let it go. She went home with him and that was what mattered. The problem was he couldn't stop himself, even if she did have a point about Tabatha. The difference was he had been honest with

Tabatha about his intentions. He knew Trey was saying that he was fine with friends but secretly hoping for more. "Tabatha knows where she stands."

Lena had to wonder if he was lying or just clueless because the woman hanging all over Luke the prior night absolutely wanted more. "Don't kid yourself Luke. That might be what she told you, but she's not on the same page as you." Luke knew she was right. He had sensed a shift in Tabatha's feelings. That wasn't the point. They were talking about Trey. Before Luke could say another word Lena calmly said, "I think this conversation needs to end while we can still be friends. This needs to be a one and done thing because we are just very different people."

Her words surprisingly cut Luke. This was not how the morning after was supposed to go. He really didn't know what he wanted from Lena, but he knew it wasn't a one-time thing. Luke moved closer to her to try and take her in his arms. When he did, Lena moved away. Out of hurt Luke went into defensive mode and lashed out, "So are you in the habit of becoming friends with your one-night stands?"

Instantly Luke regretted his words, especially after he saw Lena's face. Lena hadn't expected that type of cruelty from him. Maybe she should have. It just seemed so out of character from the

Luke she knew. He was arrogant, but this was a side of him she hadn't seen and knew she didn't like. Before going for the door to leave, Lena looked him the eye and told him to go to hell. As he reached to stop her from leaving, she moved quickly from the bedroom, down the steps and out the door. Even though he was insisting on driving her there was no way to stop her. By the time he grabbed a shirt, keys and wallet she quickly took the elevator to the lobby, hailed a cab and was gone.

As upset as Luke was about her leaving and how the morning went, he secretly loved the way she challenged him. In his apartment Luke thought about how the morning was so different than he had planned. Their night together was wonderful, and he thought they were turning over a new leaf. How was it that in the light of a new day they were fighting again? He knew he had taken things in the wrong direction. The problem was he was his father's son and couldn't help himself. Luke tried to call her to apologize. As expected, she didn't answer. Before he could leave a message, he received another call. It was from a restricted number, so he answered, hoping it was Lena. Tabatha was on the other end and told him that she was on her way to his apartment with breakfast. Disappointed that it wasn't Lena and not interested in seeing Tabatha, Luke quickly picked up his keys to go to Justin's, while explaining he wasn't home. Tabatha was clearly upset as she asked when she could see him again. Luke thought to himself that he wasn't having a good day with women. The one woman he wanted to stay, he chased off. While the one he didn't want kept trying to see him.

****

The cab ride back to Justin's did nothing to calm Lena's anger down. When she entered the penthouse just after ten in the morning, she mumbled to herself that no one was going to tell her whom she could and cannot see. As Lena rambled, she looked over to see Justin sitting on the sofa drinking coffee and reading the paper. He was dressed in his workout shorts and tight T-shirt.

"You're right Angelina. No one owns you." He smiled. "Rough night?"

No matter what was going on in her life, she was always happy to see Justin and her anger dissipated. "The night was great. It was the morning that was rough. How's Anne?"

"The nurses say no change, so that's good, I guess." He wished he could say there was a change for the better, but even he was starting to believe that wouldn't happen. "Do you want to talk about your rough morning?"

Lena did want to talk to Justin but knew that she couldn't share because it was about Luke. As she tried to think of a way to get out of talking to him, she told him that she would be back after she checked on Anne. Once she left the room, Justin called out to her. "I guess that's a no then."

His response put a smile on her face and softened her mood. Justin was always genuine whereas with Luke everything was so complicated. There was a hidden meaning to everything. Lena checked on Anne and whispered to her, "I don't blame you for hanging on. He's a special guy." Unbeknownst to Lena, Justin had followed her and overheard. "We think you're pretty special too."

Lena had no idea he was there and was embarrassed. "Thank you." She really wanted to change the subject. "I'm starving. Do you want breakfast? I know Mrs. Warner is off and I'd be happy to cook."

It was obvious she was upset, and he really did want to help so he continued to follow her, hoping she would talk to him. "Breakfast would be great." It was such a relief for Justin to have her home again. Without her, the house was so empty. As they entered the kitchen Justin tried again. "Now do you want to tell me what had you so angry?"

He wasn't going to drop it, and she couldn't tell him who caused her anger. It wasn't that she was embarrassed about having sex with Luke. She just worried it could change their dynamic and she didn't want that. Since she also didn't want to lie, she told him as much as she could. "It was nothing. I had an argument with the friend I stayed with last night. I just didn't get much sleep last night. I think I am cranky."

Justin seemed to accept her explanation. "Me either."

Lena was worried. "Did something happen?"

"No."

"Then why?"

"Just trying to figure some things out."

Lena was curious about what he was trying to figure out, however since he didn't press her about her mood, she decided to offer him the same curtesy.

Within twenty minutes breakfast was ready. The two sat at the table to eat. For breakfast Lena prepared bacon, eggs and toast. While they were eating Lena tried to tell some of Will's jokes. Justin laughed harder when she couldn't deliver the punch line than when she could tell it right. As they were having breakfast, Lena's mood completely lightened. She was enjoying herself in his company and the feeling was mutual.

Justin needed to express how much he missed her, "Last night was lonely. I like having you around." His honesty caught Lena off guard. She always enjoyed being with Justin too. It was the other stuff that was a problem. Justin continued. "I know that I have no right to ask you this, but when you go back to work would you consider being my roommate?"

"You need the rent money?" Lena joked, making Justin laugh.

"No, I just need this. Right now, you're the only person who can get me to laugh this hard. I don't want to intrude on your life, but please just think about it."

As he reached over to squeeze her hand, Luke walked in witnessing their tender moment. His mood was made worse by the cozy scene he just walked in on. After the prior night it should be him having breakfast with Lena. Lena was filled with anger but decided to act nonchalant. "Want breakfast Luke? There's plenty left."

"Yeah, Luke get a plate. She's a great cook."

Lena thought to herself that it was just eggs and bacon. It didn't take much to make Justin happy. Luke on the other hand was a different story. He was having a hard time playing casual because there was still too much that needed to be said. Part of him was still angry, but the other part of him wanted to make it right with her. As he joined them, he eyed Lena suspiciously to try to figure out her mood. "So, what were you two talking about?"

"Angelina was telling me about the comedy show she went to last night. She's bad at it though." Justin teased, as he felt a chill coming from his brother directed at Lena. Lena was exhausted and had no desire to be around Luke, so she got up to clear the plates.

Justin couldn't understand her change in mood. They were just having a nice time and everything changed. He questioned if the reason was Luke. "Don't worry about the dishes. You cooked. I'll clean up."

"If you're sure. Listen, I'm beat and am going to take a nap. Excuse me."

When Lena was gone Justin turned to Luke. "What the hell was that about?"

It wasn't Justin Luke wanted to talk to. "What?"

"The icy chill in the air between you too."

"I have no idea what you mean. We're fine. She's just tired. You heard her."

It was more Luke's reaction to Lena that had Justin worried. Since it was clear Luke wasn't going to share, he decided to tell Luke about the idea he had for the case. The two brothers went to his home office to work.

While they were working, Lena pondered Justin's offer, wondering if she should stay with him or not. Even after her night with Luke she still had to consider her feelings for Justin. They were more than friendship or at least she thought they could be. Her feelings aside she also had to consider that she had always been a private person. With that understanding, she was surprised by how much she enjoyed living with Justin. It was nice to have a friend to share things with at home and not be alone in an empty apartment. Even when she lived with Gus, she often came home to an empty apartment because of his work schedule. The downside to her staying was the fear that the longer she lived with Justin the more of an emotional connection she might have with him. After her night with Luke, she thought he might be the one. The morning only reiterated that they were too different. As much as she didn't want to she had to acknowledge that she also did also have real feelings for Luke, even if it was Justin she believed she could fall in love with. "A relationship should be with someone who puts you at ease. Not someone who constantly pisses you off." She thought to herself. Luke was too complicated and confusing for her. The tender man was someone that Lena knew she could grow to love. It was his other side that she could not deal with. Whoever she chooses, she feared she would be the one who was hurt.

It was after four when the brothers emerged from the office. Justin decided to go to the hospital to see Faith. The plan was that Luke would continue working, and on his way back from the hospital Justin would bring back Chinese food for everyone. With Justin gone, it would give Luke the opportunity to talk to Lena. As soon as Justin closed the door Luke went to see Lena. While he knocked softly on the door, Lena debated if she should tell him to enter. Nothing had changed between them. She was still undecided about her feelings. If she didn't answer, he might think she was still sleeping and leave. Through the door Luke called out. "Lena, I can hear the television. We need to talk before Justin gets back. Please let me in."

Lena was surprised to hear that Justin had left. With him gone she was alone in the penthouse with Luke. Alone if one did not consider Anne or the nurse. She was too weak to resist him and with no barrier to shield her she wasn't about to open the door.

"Luke, I think we said what we needed to this morning. I just don't have the energy to go another round with you. If we don't stop now, we won't even end up friends."

He wasn't interested in being friends. "I don't want to fight. Will you please let me in?"

Lena heard the pleading in Luke's voice and couldn't resist him. "Fine. Come in."

Luke opened the door to find that Lena had changed from her sundress to a black camisole and tiny white cotton shorts. Her hair was pulled into a ponytail. It was the first time that Luke realized how young she really looked. After everything Lena had been through in her twenty-five years, she always seemed so much older than her chronological age. By the time Luke was twenty-five he was a successful lawyer and engaged to be married while all his law school friends were still out late womanizing. The fact that they were both forced to grow up before their time was something they had in common. All day he wondered what he was mad about. Was it the fact she had a male friend or was he worried because she made him feel? With her, he felt things he never thought he was capable of, and it scared him. He had to make her understand. As soon as he saw her all he wanted to do was take her in his arms. Slowly, he moved towards her. She on the other hand was still extremely angry and moved back. "Why do you fight me? Why do you fight the feeling?"

Lena shrugged, "Not giving into temptation when something is wrong only makes us stronger."

Her comment stung, but he was working hard to control his tone because if he didn't, they wouldn't be able to work this out. "Is it wrong? Did it feel wrong last night?"

If he had been his arrogant self, she knew she would be able to keep away, he was showing the other side, the one she liked which made it harder. "God. I don't know if it's wrong or not. Last night felt right, but today I'm more confused than ever. Our sexual chemistry is unpalpable, but as I said earlier, I'm not even sure we like each other. You have two extreme sides; one I like and the other I want nothing to do with. It is so hard to think straight when you are around."

She turned to escape the intensity in Luke's emerald eyes. When she did, he went over to her and wrapped his muscular arms around her waist. As much as she wanted to fight him, being in his arms did feel right. Instinctually, she leaned her head back into his chest as he whispered in her ear. "You have turned me upside down too, but you need this. We need this."

Every bone in her body was telling her that he was right. Whatever else was going on between them she couldn't deny how she felt in his arms. Luke could tell from her body relaxing that he was getting to her and started nibbling on her ear lobe before moving his way down to her neck. As hard as she tried to keep her anger, she knew it was a losing battle. Luke knew it too and was quietly relieved. He was trained to fight for his clients but this time he was fighting for happiness. He turned her around to look into to her eyes. "Do you want this?"

Lena sighed, defeated. She was no match for his sexual paralysis. Now that they had become lovers, she could no longer deny him. "You know I do."

Luke pulled her into a passionate embrace. Their tongues entwined with need. Lena led him into her room further, while he closed the door with his foot before he kicked his shoes off. Within seconds she was standing in front of him dressed in only her thong panties. Luke laid her gently down on the bed and removed his grey T-shirt before laying back down on her. She rolled him over so that she could have control this time while he mumbled in between kisses that she needed to go in his pocket. There she found a condom. As she knelt before him to remove his jeans, she teased. "Am I that predictable?" she asked, holding the condom.

Luke rolled her to her side and sat up. He kissed her gently. "Predictable is not a word I would use to describe you. Stopping last time almost killed me. These will be with me whenever I think I could see you." He wanted to taste the essence of her being and placed her on her back. Before she could put the condom on, he lifted her back on the bed. Slowly he removed her panties, touching her inner body. Lena moaned with pleasure as Luke kissed her pierced navel, moving his way south to her inner thigh before spreading her thighs and circling her clitoris with his warm tongue. He showed her no mercy. Not that she wanted it. It was no time before she found her release screaming to God and calling out Luke's name. Lena lost herself in pure orgasmic pleasure. As she was coming down, Luke swiftly threw his boxers to the ground and put the condom over his long, hard member. He couldn't wait any longer and began kissing while climbing on top. She could taste herself as their tongues savored each other. With their mouths intertwined and still wanting control, she rolled him over to his back as she placed his member inside of her. Luke moaned as she moved at a slow torturous pace, pulling him in and out of her. It was killing him not to be able to control with the pace. He tried to roll her over, but she wanted the power and he was prepared to give it to her. As her need for him intensified, she quickened the pace. Lena found her release first then Luke. Even though everything about them felt so wrong, this felt so right. She dropped her naked body on top of him exhausted and content. He rolled her over and took her in his arms as she drifted to sleep.

****

It was seven when Luke woke her with gentle kisses, telling her Justin would be back soon. Lena could tell Luke's hair was wet, indicating that he had just showered. Before Justin arrived, Luke had to go back the Justin's home office to work. First, he needed to tell her that there was no way they were just a one-time thing. More confused than ever Lena opened her mouth to respond, however before she could say anything he kissed her and left her room. Naked Lena sat on the bed with head in her hands. She couldn't understand the power Luke had over her. It was too intense. Even still she believed there was no way their relationship could go anywhere. She needed a sign to tell her what to do and asked for her father's help, but none came.

Justin arrived home with Chinese food just as Lena was finishing showering. She came out dressed in a tank top and short running shorts as the brothers were seated at the table drinking wine. Over dinner Luke and Justin talked about work while Lena found herself silently wishing that she could combine the two men into one perfect man. "If only Luke had Justin's soul," Lena thought. Even in a state of turmoil Justin always knew exactly what

Lena needed, showing her how much he cared. That was not always the case with Luke. The problem with Luke was she couldn't deny that he ignited things in her she didn't even know existed. In addition, at times he really did have a sweet side. As she played with her food deep in thought, she noticed both men had stopped talking and they were staring at her trying to decipher what she was thinking. It made Lena uncomfortable, so she needed a change in direction. "How's Faith?" That question always worked to distract Justin. Not that she wasn't interested in the answer.

"She's wonderful. I can't wait for her to come home and put her in Anne's arms."

Luke and Lena looked at one another. For once they seemed to agree as they were both concerned that Justin was hoping for something that couldn't happen. Unfazed Justin continued. "I know it won't make a difference with Anne's condition. Don't look so worried, but I believe that they'll know each other is there. Faith was inside Anne for months, so they must have a connection."

Lena reached over to take Justin's hand. "I believe that too." She hoped it was true even if she wasn't completely convinced.

After all, if anyone tried to tell her that her father wasn't sending her signs she would be upset.

Justin smiled at Lena, believing she understood. Her support was appreciated more than anyone could know. It was written on Luke's face that he didn't believe any of what Justin had said. Even though he did have to admit the thought seemed to give Justin solace. That is why he opted not to comment. A part of Luke wished he understood the way Lena did. He wanted to comfort Justin; he just had no idea how. Conflicted, he also wasn't entirely happy that Justin and Lena had such a strong connection. When dinner was over the brothers went back to work in the home office while Lena went to her room.

It had been a long confusing weekend, and she was exhausted. As soon as she fell into bed she drifted to sleep. That night she dreamed of two men each at separate corners. One man had a halo and the other had horns. Although she couldn't see their faces, she recognized them as Justin and Luke. There was a voice in her dream telling her to choose her path and make sure it was a wise choice. Lena woke, startled before she could make her decision. It was evident what the dream meant. If she continued with Luke, she would be taking the dark path while Justin would lead her to light. "Oh, Daddy was this the sign that I asked for?" she asked. The thought of Luke leading her down a dark path really frightened her. Even though spending time with him was enjoyable, she wasn't willing to let him lead her down a dark path. The last time she was there she almost killed herself. Remembering how tender he could be, Lena wasn't entirely convinced choosing Luke was the dark path. When they had sex, he acted as though she was the only woman in the world. Still, she had seen what was in the closet and had to consider what his preferences might be. The fact was he had never made any mention of trying that or had he pressured her in any way to partake in something she couldn't handle. Even without that the real problem was that outside of the bedroom, Luke had real control issues. It was hard to really know whether she would get the tender man or the bossy ass. That didn't mean that Justin was right for her though. Yes, he was a good man, but he was still so in love with his wife, and she believed he should be. It was way too soon for him to move on. The problem was she lived with someone who hadn't been able to get her heart back and knew how painful waiting for that person to see the light could be. She wasn't sure she could live that again. The more she thought about her dream the more she believed her father was trying to send her a sign. He was trying to warn her. Maybe Luke was the dark side after all. "Okay, Daddy I understand, I'll try and stay away from him," she whispered not really convinced that she would be able to "but you have to help me be strong."

****

Justin and Luke felt that they had come up with the perfect strategy for their case. It was a strategy that even their father would have to support. They were finally ready to present the details to him the next day. After they had finished everything, Luke decided he would talk to Justin about Lena. He hated lying to his brother especially since he could tell how dependent Justin had become on her. "You like having Lena here, don't you?"

Justin was surprised by the question that had come out of nowhere. He paused for a minute before answering. It was an answer he had thought about many times but never voiced it out loud until that moment. "I do. She gives me hope. Not that Anne will recover, but that everything will one day be normal. It's very reassuring having her here. Why?"

Luke knew his response needed to be well crafted because he was happy that something or someone made his brother happy even if it was his someone. "I'm glad she can do that for you, but you do realize that she'll return to her normal life soon?" It was not that Luke wanted to hurt his brother. He dealt with facts and that was a fact.

Justin was fully aware that his agreement with Lena was ending. That's why he spoke with her in the morning about staying. Since Luke seemed worried, he decided to make him aware of his intentions. "I've asked her to stay. Even after she returns to work."

Luke was surprised. It never occurred to him that Justin would ask that of her. "You did? What did she say?"

Justin shrugged. "She didn't answer. Honestly, I'm not sure what she'll do, but I hope she considers it."

Luke wasn't sure if he wanted her to stay there or not. Lena made Justin happy, and he hated the idea of her living in her neighborhood, but he also didn't want her to get closer to Justin when their relationship was so up and down. Cautiously, he proceeded, "If she stays, what are you going to do when she wants to start dating? I mean she's a very attractive woman. How long do you think she'll want to be single?"

"I know she has that friend whom she stayed with last night. I can't stop her from having a life. Selfishly I wish that she would stay here forever, but I know one day she'll move on. I just hope it's with someone who's worthy of such an angel."

Luke felt guilty that he was lying to his brother. It wasn't really a lie, just an omission. If things continued as he hoped, he would eventually have to tell Justin. First, they needed to figure out what was happening between them so as not to hurt Justin. For the time being he was comfortable keeping their affair secret. If things between them didn't work out, Justin would never have to know, however if Luke got his wish they would have to tell Justin soon.

Chapter Fifteen

After a restless night's sleep, Lena woke early and decided to go running. She quickly put on her blue running shorts and grey tank top before leaving her room. As she was leaving, Justin offered to go with her. He was also dressed in workout shorts with a black T-shirt. His offer took Lena by surprise. She liked to run alone, but when he joked that she needed an escort to make sure her ankle was healed, Lena laughingly agreed. Quietly she wondered if Luke had made the same joke if she had had the same reaction. Remembering her dream, she decided it didn't matter because their relationship couldn't continue. The outside air was muggy. Since it had rained the previous night dew fell from the trees on them as they ran through Central Park. Even though it was early in the morning, the temperature was already over ninety-five degrees and the warm droplets felt refreshing. At first, they were able to keep an even pace with one another until their competitive nature took over and they decided to race each other back to the penthouse. Lena ran as fast as she could but lost to Justin by a hair. She teased that he only won because he had longer legs. Justin played along to not bruise her ego even though he knew he had gone easy on her. When they returned laughing, Luke was in the penthouse waiting. Again, the sight of the two of them so at ease made him jealous. He hated feeling anything negative toward

Justin, but he wished that Lena was that comfortable with him. Upon seeing Luke, Justin was flustered since he hadn't realized the time and knew he was late. Before hurrying off to shower, he told Luke he would be ready in twenty minutes. Justin wasn't the only one flustered by Luke's presence. Lena wasn't happy to see him, although he had done nothing wrong. It was after her dream she wasn't yet ready to face him and had planned on doing her best to avoid him. With Justin out of the room, she went to the kitchen to get a bottle of water instead of acknowledging him. Luke followed unaware of her awkwardness. He was too lost in his own thoughts. "He's becoming too dependent on you."

His declaration caught Lena off-guard. "What?" She shook her head to not engage. "I have no intention of doing this with you this morning. It's just too exhausting."

Luke didn't want to fight either. All he really wanted to do was pull her in his arms and kiss her so that she wouldn't think of another. Even knowing that, Luke was unable to stop himself from continuing the banter. "Is that your plan? Make him so dependent on you that he never wants you to leave? He's never going to love another the way he loves Anne."

Lena was hurt, Luke thought so little of her, but more than hurt, she was pissed. The best thing she could do was end the conversation before it went further. "What exactly makes this any of your business?" She started walking out of the room while saying, "Now if you'll excuse me, I need a shower."

Luke thought about what Lena said and her question. Deep down Luke recognized that Lena was doing nothing wrong. His problem was that Luke knew nothing was happening between Justin and her because of Justin's love for Anne. Not because she wasn't interested. That was the part that was making Luke crazy. He could see how much she cared for Justin even after their sexual encounters. It should make him happy that Justin had someone to lean on, yet he couldn't help but be jealous. Luke wasn't ready to end the conversation and continued to follow her as she went to her room. "I don't want my brother hurt any more than he is now."

"Neither do I. It's good for him to find a normal routine and have some fun. If I can help with that, I'm happy."

In the middle of their argument, Justin came out asking what was going on. The fact that they were having a heated discussion was apparent. What he didn't know is what it was about. There was something amiss and he wondered what he was missing. "What's going on?"

Lena turned to him. In unison she and Luke both responded, "Nothing." Lena realized how that looked and knew Justin was smart enough to figure something was going on. "I think I'll let Luke explain. By the way Justin, I'm going to meet a friend for lunch, so I'll be leaving here for a couple of hours this afternoon. I'll make sure Anne is covered but wanted you to know." She knew that would drive Luke crazy and took satisfaction as she felt the daggers Luke's eyes were throwing at her. When Justin nodded in agreement, she left them to shower. There was no way Luke could follow her without raising suspicion and she felt she had won that round.

With Lena gone, Justin still wanted to know what he had walked in on. "Do you want to tell me what the hell was going on?"

Luke certainly couldn't tell him what the argument was about. "I think I just rub her the wrong way sometimes. Come on we need to get to the office."

It was believable as she wasn't the first woman Luke irritated. At that point he had bigger problems than Justin's questions. After Lena mentioned having lunch with a friend, his concern moved from Justin to Trey. Luke wasn't at all happy, she didn't do as he requested and cancel her plans with Trey. Justin wasn't the threat that Trey was. Anne was a barrier to a relationship with Justin, but Trey didn't have any barriers. Plus, Lena had already had sex with Trey. It made no difference to him that it only happened once. The idea made him crazy. Especially since he knew he had no way of stopping her from meeting him. He wondered why she didn't have any female friends. All her friends were male and that made him uncomfortable. As soon as he got into the office and was alone, he texted Lena.

"It was decided no lunch with him. CANCEL NOW!" Within seconds Lena texted back, "You said no lunch. I said, go to hell. My answer is still the same." She wasn't going to make this easy. Luke saw red. He responded, "Don't test me. CANCEL THE LUNCH!" Within seconds Lena wrote back, "The true Luke. No dark side for me. I'm out."

What did she mean she the dark side and was out? Luke pondered the words as he reread them. Before he could respond, he was called into a meeting with his father. As Justin presented the strategy to John and their client, Luke couldn't stop thinking about Lena's text. John could tell Luke's thoughts were elsewhere and called a break so that he could pull Luke aside to tell him to focus. John had no idea where Luke's thoughts were and didn't care because this case was too important. Luke knew he was right, even if he couldn't stop himself from thinking about Lena. This woman was driving him crazy. When the break was over it was Luke's turn to present, which took his mind off Lena. That didn't last long because as soon as lunch was delivered, he went back to thinking about Lena being with Trey. Even though he knew it wasn't true, he tortured himself by imaging she was letting Trey touch her in that special way. What was worse was the feeling of being powerless. If there had been any way for him to leave the meeting he would have, but there wasn't. He would have to deal with Lena later.

****

As always Lena was enjoying her time with Trey. She had gone back to Brooklyn to lunch at a burrito place that was one of her favorites. The restaurant was crazy busy, but they were able to find a table standing up to eat. Being with Trey was even more comfortable than being with Justin. With Trey there were no lingering sexual desires. She could completely be herself. In the short time she knew him he had become an important part of her life. Many times, she wished she had the same feelings for Trey as she did for Justin or even Luke and didn't understand why she didn't. After all Trey was great in bed. She just didn't have chemistry with him. It would make her life so much easier if Trey were the one she wanted. Over lunch the conversation was light. They mainly talked about the comedy show. Trey also invited her to attend a club opening on Saturday night, which she was happy to accept. After she accepted, he mentioned that he hoped Luke didn't show. He also wasn't believing Luke showed up at the comedy club by coincidence. Lena knew at some point the conversation would turn to Luke and his bad behavior. As Trey spoke negatively about Luke, Lena believed he had every right to feel the way he did because Luke was rude the night of the comedy show. Even though she agreed, there was a big part of her that wanted to defend Luke. When Trey left the table to go to the bathroom Lena's thoughts drifted to the intimacy that she and Luke shared. Just thinking about it made her feel warm. She wondered how she could indeed give up on something that felt that good. Lena was so lost in thought that she didn't realize Trey had returned to the table. It wasn't until he waved his fingers at her face that she realized he was back. He was curious about where her mind went. "Hey, where did you go?"

Lena didn't want to lie, but she wasn't prepared to tell him about her and Luke yet. "I was just thinking. You know how I have been helping my friend with his wife."

"Yes."

"His baby was born premature, and he asked if I would continue living with him after she came home. He is a little nervous about being a new dad."

Trey couldn't blame him. Lena had told Trey about Anne, so he could understand why Justin asked Lena to stay. As much as he empathized with Justin, he wasn't sure that was what was best for Lena. "Would you quit your job? I thought you loved nursing. At least that's what you said the night we met."

Lena blushed at the mention of the night they met. "No, I would be like his platonic roommate. It would save me a bundle in rent."

Trey was suspicious. He had met Luke and if Justin was anything like him, Trey was wary. "And what would he get out of the deal?"

"Company. Someone to help him with the baby in case she has any medical needs."

"That's really nice, but what about having a private life? Friends? It sounds like this guy is becoming too dependent on you."

There was that word again. Luke used it earlier and she brushed it off, but somehow when Trey said it, she silently considered it. "Was Justin growing too dependent on her? If he was, is that a bad thing?" Before they could finish their conversation Trey told her he had to get back to work as he only had an hour for lunch. If she wanted, she could call him later to continue the conversation. Even after he left, she stayed and reflected on what both Luke and Trey had said.

On the subway ride back, she decided to put her earbuds in and focused on going dancing Saturday night because she was tired of thinking. It had been a long time since she had been dancing, and she was really looking forward to going. By the time she arrived at Justin's she was in a great mood until she saw Dr. Castillo standing in front of the penthouse building. The fact that he was there shocked her because how could he have known she was staying with Justin. Since they had left things so awful, she initially thought about turning around and hiding out until he left. She couldn't do that because she was going back to work soon. There was no way she could avoid him forever. After taking a minute to get her courage she approached him nonchalantly. "Dr. Castillo, what are you doing here?" Her tone was harsh to cover up the fact that she was terrified. His behavior the last several times they interacted was so odd. It was almost as if he was unhinged. That's what scared her the most, but she didn't want to give him the satisfaction of knowing he intimidated her.

"I learned from the nurses at the hospital you were staying here." That wasn't possible because Lena knew she had told no one at the hospital. He was lying. Instead of calling him on the lie, she decided to play along. He continued. "We need to talk before you go back to work. We were friends once; can we please try and find a way to be friendly with one another?"

Even though she wasn't sure they were ever really friends, he was right about settling things before she went back to work. That was why she didn't hide, and he really did seem genuine. After knowing what she did about him, being the doctor that treated her that awful night and keeping quiet there was no way she could ever trust him again. That didn't mean they didn't need to have a professional relationship. She really didn't want to talk to him and offered the only olive branch she was willing to consider. "I think if we just keep things professional, we can work together again."

Dr. Castillo wasn't accepting the branch and urged her to talk more. "Please let's just go somewhere private to talk. There's a coffee shop uptown. No one will hear us there. Come on I'll drive."

It was busy on the street and Lena noticed the doorman watching them. What they needed to say should be said in private. She didn't want anyone in the building overhearing, so she apprehensively agreed. His black Audi was parked in front of the building. She wasn't sure it was a good idea to get into the car with him, even though she did. As a precaution while Dr. Castillo was getting into the other side of the car, Lena texted that she was with Dr. Castillo. She thought she was texting Trey, but in her haste, she accidentally texted the information to Luke. Dr. Castillo got in the car and locked the doors before speeding away from the curve. Luke felt his phone buzz in the middle of the meeting. This time he wasn't jealous. He knew her being with Dr. Castillo wasn't a good idea and responded that she needed to get away from him. Traffic in the City was heavy, but Dr. Castillo was weaving the car in and out of the traffic sporadically. When Lena's phone buzzed, she realized it was Luke who she had texted. Before she had time to regret her mistake or respond, Dr. Castillo threw her phone in the back seat. "You won't be needing that."

Instantly Lena knew she had made a mistake in going with him even though she didn't want to give him the upper hand by sounding as terrified as she was. Calmly she asked, "Why? Where are we going?"

"You'll find out in time."

"Why don't we start talking now? What is it you wanted to say to me?"

"You kept me waiting for months. Now it's my turn. We can talk when we get to where we're going."

They were driving out of Manhattan and were on their way to Brooklyn. At that point Lena was frightened. She no longer cared about settling things with him; she just wanted to get away. Firmly she said, "Pull over and let me out. I don't think this is a good idea."

"What wasn't a good idea was setting me up. Now we're going to talk on my terms and you're going to give me everything I want."

When Lena tried to unlock the door to jump out, he grabbed her arm and began to drive faster. If she jumped out of the car she would be injured. In silence she sat trying to figure out her next move. She needed to get to her phone, but he had thrown it too far back. By the time they arrived at Lena's apartment, Dr. Castillo had shown her how unhinged he had become. Lena started to think about the self-defense classes Gus made her take. She was taught when in danger don't leave the scene. It was too late for that. She needed to come up with a plan before he got her alone in her apartment. He was bigger and stronger than her, but she still had her feminine charm and his ego. She batted her eyes at him and suggested they go to the corner bar for a drink so that they could talk. This time he wasn't about to fall for her flirtatious behavior. He grabbed her arm to pull her out of the car. His grip was tight as he was dragging her up the stairs into the building and up to her apartment. She tried to wiggle him loose, expressing he was hurting her. He didn't care if he hurt her and that was evident. When that didn't work, she tried to think of some of her self-defense moves. The instructor had shown them how much damage a key could do, and she planned to try. At her apartment door, she took her time fishing for her keys from her midsize purse. She needed the extra time to calm her nerves and hopefully to have him become more anxious and distracted so that she could quickly jab him. Once she found them, she continued to pretend to look for them until he became completely frustrated. When he moved to grab her purse, he released his hold. Quickly she jabbed, missing her intended target. Instead of his eye she slashed his face. The cut wasn't enough to distract him. All it did was anger him further. He slammed her against the wall. "You little Bitch. This is my time. Now get inside."

He grabbed the keys from her hand and unlocked the door before forcing a kicking and screaming Lena inside. No one came to her rescue. She was in the apartment with the door locked almost instantaneously. Once inside Lena looked for another way to escape knowing the only way out was the door. The words "keep him talking" entered her head as she looked for something that she could hit him with. "What do you want?"

"Don't play dumb. You know what I want."

"The video and recordings?"

"That's right, but you need to learn what happens to teases."

Her heart was racing so fast she thought he could hear it. The way he looked at her was terrifying. He had already proven that he had no problem hurting her and she needed to think quickly if she was going to save herself. In her head she kept reassuring herself that she would make it out of this, but the truth was she wasn't sure she could until she noticed a knife on the counter in the kitchen. She needed to get it without drawing attention to what she was planning and gradually was backing up. Fortunately, her apartment was small so there wasn't much space to manipulate. "Were you always this insane?"

"I think we both know who's unstable and I have the proof. You came on to me for months. When I expected the payout, you started fucking the husband of my patient. I think you still need professional help. Now where are the tapes." He shouted as he hit the wall.

With the punch she realized that making him angry wasn't the right strategy. She decided to try another approach to allow herself enough time to get into the kitchen. Slowly she moved. "You have it wrong. I'm helping Justin. We aren't together." She hoped that it would appease him for a minute.

It didn't, "if you aren't fucking him then the asshole brother."

She couldn't deny that. She was surprised he knew where to find her, so she had no idea what he really knew and again changed her strategy. "The copies are in Justin's office. If you want, I can call him and ask him to bring it here."

He snapped. "Nice try but how stupid do you think I am?"

As sweet as she could, Lena responded, "I don't think you're stupid. In fact, I know how brilliant you are." Lena thought to herself that he was brilliant, but crazy. "You went through my apartment. You have everything here. The only other copy is with Justin."

It was true and she hoped he would believe her. Even if he didn't, she was moving forward with her escape plan. Dr. Castillo did believe her. He had taken apart her apartment. As she moved towards the kitchen, Dr. Castillo realized she was eyeing the knife and lunged at her. His grip was tight, so she leaned down to bite him. Instantly, she felt his hand hitting her hard against her face above her jaw. The hit was so hard that she fell to the floor. In anger, he picked her up by her hair and threw her on the bed. At that moment she lost her fight and complete panic set in. Visions of her past came into her head as he began to unbuckle his belt. Before he laid on top of her, he opened his shirt and lifted her short, denim skirt. She kicked her legs screaming at the top of her lungs. Suddenly there was a loud bang. Out of nowhere, Luke kicked the door in and was moving at lightning speed towards Dr. Castillo who had just got off Lena when he heard someone come in. After Lena didn't respond to any of his texts, he left his meeting using the GPS on her phone to track her. It was obvious what he had walked in on. Luke's fury took over as he punched Dr. Castillo in the stomach. Dr. Castillo lunged at Luke, but Luke was too fast and moved out of his way. Luke punched his jaw, forcing him down. As Luke continued his assault, he yelled at Lena to call the police. Lena had never been so happy to see anyone in her life. It took her a minute to realize she was safe. Once she got her faculties back, she begged Luke to stop punching Dr. Castillo. She was afraid Luke would kill him and tugged at Luke to get him to stop. Raged filled every part of Luke's being. So much so that it was hard for him to register Lena's pleas and stop to look down at a bleeding Dr. Castillo. Even as Luke's knuckles were swollen and bruised, he still wanted to teach the doctor respect. However, Lena was tugging on his arm, so he needed to get composure. In Luke's mind this wasn't over though, and he reached for his phone to call the police before getting off Dr. Castillo. When he did Lena begged him not to call. She just wanted to go home. As she said the word home, she thought to herself that she was home and questioned when the place she had lived for several years no longer felt that way. The idea made her sad, but she had bigger worries. This couldn't be the way Gus finds out about what happened. Plus, she couldn't go through it again. This wasn't the first time she had been in this situation. The last time she went through this even as the daughter of a police officer the District Attorney put her on trial. Even though Alan disappeared before the case went to trial, prior to that her every action was put into question. The experience was awful and at that moment one she had no intention of reliving. She knew that the fact that she willingly got in the car with him would be a factor. The doorman could testify that she went without duress. A fact she now knew was stupid. As she pleaded for him to put away the phone, Luke could hear the desperation in her voice. At this point Dr. Castillo sat up, smugly watching this unfold. He knew Lena wouldn't press charges and was just waiting for Luke to cave, which he did because he didn't want to make things worse for her. As much as he wanted to do more Lena was what was important. He put away his phone, lifted Dr. Castillo up and threw him out the door. Before he slammed the door Luke threatened him to never come near Lena again or he would finish the job with pleasure whether Lena wanted him to or not. It sounded like a threat, but it was more of a promise. When Dr. Castillo was gone and her adrenaline normalized, Lena ran straight into Luke's arms. This had been the most terrified she had been since Alan and in his arms she was shaking. At first, he was grateful that he got her there on time and was able to be there for her, but the more she trembled the angrier he became. No one had the right to treat another human being that way, especially someone as special as Lena. Luke held her petite body still raging with anger. "Why did you make me let the bastard go? I could kill him."

Lena didn't want to talk about why. She could feel the tension that filled his body and see from his facial features how angry he was and knew he was serious about his intentions. She wanted to calm him down because there was no way he would understand why and changed the subject to what she wanted to know the answer to in hopes of distracting him. "How did you find me?"

Luke was confused at the question. The point was he did find her, and she was in a compromising position, so they should act.

As he was calming down, he responded, "When you didn't answer any of my texts, I had your phone traced."

His answer was a little surprising, but when you have the money that Luke has Lena thought anything was possible. For a minute she thought about the invasion of privacy aspect, but she was so grateful he arrived on time she didn't care. "Thank you. Thank you for coming. I don't know what would have happened if you hadn't."

Luke didn't even want to think about what would have happened if he hadn't arrived when he did. The idea of it made him hold her tighter. "Don't worry Sweetness. I'd never let anything bad happen to you."

As he held her Luke tried his best to reassure her that she was safe. Even though he still wanted her to press charges, he thought it best not to push her too hard, especially since he knew what she had already been through. She was the only thing that mattered, and she was with him. Until that moment he hadn't realized that he was more than angry. He was terrified. Not just for her, but also for him because he didn't know what he would do if something happened to her. He released her long enough to look at her face. There was a large red mark from where Dr. Castillo hit her. What was worse than the obvious bruises on her face and arms, was the terrified look in her beautiful blue eyes that were clearly stained from crying. If Dr. Castillo had still been there, he would have killed him and believed no jury would convict him when they heard what a monster that man was. Lena noticed she wasn't the only one who was bruised. From the fight Luke's jaw was swelling and the knuckles of his right hand were bleeding and swollen. It hurt Lena to see, as she felt it was her fault. She should have known better than to get in his car, but she honestly hadn't realized how unhinged he was. Silently, she wondered how she missed that fact. Lena lifted Luke's hand to gently kiss the bruise and offered that she hoped it didn't hurt too much. The fact that she was concerned with his pain even though it was her who was the victim was astonishing to Luke. The thought that Justin was right, she was an angel came to him. Lena released him and went into the kitchen to fill a couple of bags of ice. They both needed it. She gently placed the bag on his hand while looking to see if it was broken. "You might need to have this X-rayed" she said holding his hand.

With Luke's left hand he took the other bag of ice and held it to her cheek. His touch was so gentle Lena wondered how she could have ever thought poorly of him. "I will go to the hospital if you do." Luke said, knowing exactly what her answer would be.

Lena gave him a half smile, "If you hadn't come."

The idea of could have happened was too painful for Luke to think about. He caressed her face, "Shush. Don't think about that. I did come and you're safe.".

"I'm sorry."

Luke smiled. Softly he asked, "For what?"

"I should never have gotten in the car with him."

"Look at me Sweetness." Her eyes met his. "None of this was your fault. You need to believe me." Before she could respond Luke stood up. "Come on. Let's get you home."

For the second time that day the word home seemed to have a different meaning. "This is my home. At least it used to be." Lena looked around her apartment sadly. She still hadn't straightened up from the break-in. Now with this she wondered if she would ever be able to think of her apartment as home without feeling violated. Luke saw the sadness in her face and wanted to make it better but was at a loss.

Before he could say anything, Lena offered, "I just want to go to Justin's please. I need to get out of here."

Luke agreed and held her close as they walked down the steps to his car. He could feel her body still trembling. At that moment he knew he could never let her go. All he wanted to do was take her in his arms and take away all the pain of the day. If he could. He wanted to take away all the pain of her childhood too. She meant that much to him. On the entire way back to Justin's she was silent, and Luke was lost in finding the right words to comfort her.

As soon as they got inside the penthouse Justin saw her face. Instantly, he was worried. "Angelina. What happened? Are you okay?" He opened his arms as she went running to him. It was Luke who saved her. Lena knew that, but it was Justin who would make her feel safe. Justin asked Luke what had happened as he held a trembling Lena. He knew something had to have happened for Luke to have left the meeting so abruptly. When the doorman told him that he saw Lena go off with a strange man he realized whatever it was that made Luke leave had to do with Lena. Obviously, he was right to be concerned. Luke told Justin the details as he knew them while looking at Lena. This time he had to admit to himself that he was jealous she was seeking comfort from another man. He wanted to be the one to offer that to her.

Justin led Lena to the sofa. Gently, he asked her what had happened. Lena told him everything as he held her at his side.

Justin couldn't understand why Dr. Castillo wasn't in prison. "You have to call the police."

How could she explain to make the brothers understand? She knew Luke didn't understand it either. Since she couldn't find the words all she said was, "I can't."

Since Justin didn't have the background information about her past, he wasn't as easily swayed as Luke. "What if he does this to someone else? You don't want that, do you?"

He had a point. "Of course not." It would kill her to know that he did this to another woman, and she could have stopped it, but she wasn't prepared to face the police. The obvious answer was to call Gus who she feared would be more vengeful than Luke.

Everyone was content with calling Gus. Justin knew Gus was the reason Lena was with Anne the day she was shot and although he didn't know the extent of the nature of their relationship, he knew that he was important to Lena. The problem was that Lena's phone was still in Dr. Castillo's car, and she didn't know his number by heart. Instead, she had to call the police station directly. At first Gus thought it was odd she didn't call him directly but understood when she explained that she had lost her phone. The pain in Lena's voice was evident as she asked him to come see her.

Gus tried to get her to tell him on the phone, but all she could say was just please come.

Gus knew Lena never asked for help unless she really needed him and dropped everything. His initial thought was that it was one of the Armstrong brothers who had caused her difficulty. He ran out of the station prepared to do battle and arrived at Justin's within ten minutes. By the time Gus was in the penthouse, he was in full protective mode especially after he saw the bruise on Lena's face. She didn't seem to be uncomfortable with either brother, yet he still wasn't convinced one of them didn't do that to her and gave them a stare that would cut ice. Gus was no match for John. Even with Gus' gun neither brother was intimidated and Justin welcomed him in. Immediately he went to Lena and demanded answers from Justin and Luke. The case on Anne was still ongoing and he continued to investigate that she may have been the target. His fear was that Lena got caught up in that too. The one person Lena always counted on was Gus because he was with her through the worst times in her life. He would get her through this too. Luke already knew who Gus was to Lena, but Justin still didn't. Gus held her tight on the sofa as Lena explained what had happened from the beginning. With a whisper, so low that neither Luke or Justin could hear, Lena said, "Gus, this doctor was Dr. Castillo. The one you know who treated me that night."

All eyes were on Lena, but she was not prepared to let everyone else know about what had happened and paused. Although Luke also knew about her past, he wasn't prepared to tell her he did and feigned his reactions. Gus knew what she was talking about and didn't require any explanation. In a recent conversation he remembered her asking about Dr. Castillo but could see her apprehension in continuing. "This might be easier if you two left the room." Gus stated.

Luke wasn't going anywhere and let that be known. Lena felt she owed him and Justin both an explanation and continued. "He knew things and threatened to tell the hospital about it if I didn't have sex with him."

"Bastard," Luke snapped. That reaction was real, and he wished he had killed him.

They all looked at him feeling the same way. Lena finished telling him about what she had done to Dr. Castillo, the break-in, the notes they each left and ended with the most recent events. Gus was devastated she had gone through all that alone. He was furious and told her that he was going to file the report. They needed evidence so that it wasn't his word against hers. Luke interjected that he was a witness. Gus turned to him and stated as a lawyer he should know that what he saw would help, but it wasn't enough.

Dr. Castillo could claim that they were playing rough when Luke entered. Or since she cut his face, he could say that she attacked him first. They needed more evidence. Justin and Luke both knew if they were Dr. Castillo's attorney they would argue the same thing. As Gus picked up the phone to order for forensics to go to her apartment, Lena stopped him. There were enough people at the hospital who could attest to witnessing their flirtation. What was worse is all the details of her life could come out. Even though she knew it was wrong, Lena told Gus she couldn't go down that path again. He begged her to reconsider but had witnessed first-hand her devastation the last time. There was no way he could insist if she wasn't ready. Luke and Justin also tried to get Lena to change her mind, but Lena knew too well what all of this would do to her and for what. He would probably plead guilty to assault since she willingly got into the car. All he would get was a slap on the wrist while she was left to pick up the pieces of her shattered life. Luke was furious at Lena's refusal. "So, he just walks. That's not possible. What about Lena?"

"I'll have every officer in the state make the bastard's life a living hell. That I promise. Lena, I think its best you come home with me tonight."

She appreciated the suggestion but wanted to stay where she was. "Gus, I'll be fine with Justin and Luke."

In his most stern fatherly voice Gus said, "I'll be dammed if I'm leaving you with strangers tonight. Come on do as you're told."

This time Justin interjected, "With all due respect we're not strangers. We care very deeply for Lena. Anything she needs we will help her, and he won't dare come into my home. She is safe."

Gus could see that Justin was genuine and softened. "Look, I appreciate everything you both did for her today, but this is a family matter now and she belongs home with me."

Lena hugged Gus hard. It meant the world to her that he wanted to take care of her, but the last time she was a kid. Now she was an adult who needed to figure things out for herself. "Gus please. I really want to stay here tonight. Please try not to worry about me. I'll be fine. Thank you for coming, but right now I want a hot shower and to go to bed."

Gus could see how exhausted she was and didn't want to fight her. As much as he wanted to make this better, he knew she had to decide what was best for her. "Fine. But you call if you need me."

"You know I will. I love you."

"Back at you kid." Gus stood up. "Now I'm going to scare the lights out of the bastard doctor."

Even though she knew it was futile she begged Gus to just leave it alone. He hugged her tightly and looked at Justin before leaving. "Take care of my girl."

"Don't worry I will."

"What Justin means is we will."

Luke was not going to be left out of this. Gus was starting to soften up towards Justin, who seemed okay, but he knew all about Luke and didn't trust him at all. Gus looked at him and said, "Stay away from her. I'm leaving her here with your brother. Not you."

Before Luke could respond, Lena defended him saying that he was the one who saved her. That didn't make Gus feel better. This was not the time for that argument, and he left before he said something he wouldn't regret but would upset Lena.

When Gus was gone, Lena went to thank Luke again and left to take a shower. Luke nodded and smiled. There was no way he was going to let anyone hurt her. She meant too much to him.

After she left the room Justin was curious why Lena was compelled to call him. Luke wanted to tell Justin they were together. He just couldn't without Lena's permission even though he knew it would have to be done soon. Instead, he responded that it was a question he would have to ask Lena. The truth was he wasn't sure why she texted him because they weren't on good terms. He was just grateful she did and that he got there on time.

Mrs. Warner had left early that day due to her daughter being sick and needing help with her baby. There was no time to prepare dinner before she left. During one of the conversations Lena had with Justin she mentioned that her mother used to prepare the most wonderful Mexican dishes. The thought made her wistful. In an effort to make her feel better Justin thought that Mexican food might be comfort food for her, and decided that he would go get some. There was a special place not too far from the penthouse that prepared authentic dishes. The problem was they didn't deliver. Since Justin didn't want to leave Lena alone, he asked Luke if he minded staying to watch over Lena while he went. Luke thought that was a stupid question because he had no intention of leaving Lena in her state. To Justin though he responded that he would be happy to stay. As soon as Justin left, Luke went to Lena's room. She was sitting on her king-sized bed in the fetal position staring at the wall with tears in her eyes. As much as she wanted a shower, she hadn't yet been able to get the energy to go into the bathroom. Luke approached her with concern. "Are you okay?"

She looked up at him with her big, blue eyes. "I will be, but right now I'm just exhausted."

Luke held out his hand and asked her to go with him as he led her into the bathroom. In the bathroom, Luke turned on the shower. He could see how fragile she was, and his heart ached. "Let me take care of you tonight?"

She had no idea what he meant, but was too tired to fight, so she agreed. Slowly, Luke removed her sandals one at a time. Next, he asked for permission to take her tank top, and her denim skirt off. The last thing he wanted was to scare her more than she was already. She nodded to give him permission. Lena shivered as he went for her bra. Luke backed off immediately. He motioned for her to get in the shower that was large enough for two, but didn't touch the remainder of her clothing. Lena wanted to cleanse herself of Dr. Castillo's hands and removed the remainder of her clothing. As she entered the shower, she reached for the shampoo. All of this was too much for Lena and she fell to the floor of the shower sobbing uncontrollably wondering how she could be so wrong about a person. As Luke saw her pain, he removed all his clothing except his boxers and joined her in the shower. Gently, he lifted her off the floor and held her tight as she again to cried into his bare chest. He rubbed her back trying to soothe her as he reached for the shampoo. Softly, he began rubbing the shampoo through her hair, massaging her scalp and rinsing it clean. Afraid to touch her body in any way that she could misunderstand, he poured the soap into the loofa and handed it to her. She took it and started scrubbing so vehemently that her skin turned bright red. All she wanted to do was get the feel of Dr. Castillo's hands off her. It was a heart-wrenching scene for Luke to watch, even though he understood what she was trying to do. To calm her before she ripped her skin, Luke took her hand to slow the motion. With his hand on top of hers they cleaned her entire body. There were bruises on her arms from where Dr. Castillo grabbed her. She also had a giant bruise on her back from where he slammed her against the wall. Anger ran through Luke's veins as he examined the proof of the day's events. He still wanted her to press charges and believed they should take pictures. From the look on Lena's face, so scared and hurt, he felt that he couldn't approach the subject at that moment. The best way to help her was to follow her lead. He had known that she had survived much worse than this attack and he was going to make sure she got through this too. When she was rinsed off, Luke shut off the shower water. As he wrapped her in a fresh, fluffy, white towel, she had never felt so cherished. The way he took care of her was exactly what she needed. Luke walked her over to her bed and kissed her forehead. She smiled a slight smile before he went to her drawers. Inside her drawers he found panties, an old pair of boxers and a pale pink T-shirt that he pulled out. When he handed her the clothes, he noticed that she was sitting on the bed still in shock over what happened to her. Again, she wondered how she could have completely misread the doctor. After Alan, her guard was always up and never in a million years did she think he would do this to her. Certainly, if she had known he was there that awful night she never would have started a flirtation with him. All this gave Lena a headache and she put her hands over her face in disbelief. It was killing Luke to see her in such pain. He kneeled in front of her, but she didn't look up at him even as he reached for her hands. As sweet as he was being she needed time alone to process and asked him for that. Luke didn't want to leave her side but understood. Before leaving he kissed her cheek and told her he would be in the other room when she was ready. She smiled, but it wasn't the one that lit up her beautiful blues. This seemed forced as her eyes looked vacant. Luke wondered how long it would take to see the smile that brightened his mood again.

Soon Justin came home with the Mexican food, and they called Lena for dinner. Instead of the clothes Luke had selected she had on a large sweatshirt that engulfed her petite frame and shorts. He eyed her and she expressed that she was cold. The chill she felt was really an inner chill that even the sweatshirt couldn't help. When she saw what Justin had picked for dinner, she knew it was because of the conversation she had had with him about her mother. For the first time in a long time, she had people who cared about her other than Gus, and it did make her feel a little better. Just not well enough to eat. As sweet as the gesture was and as much as she appreciated it, food wasn't going to make her feel better. What she needed was sleep, however she didn't want to be rude and silently played with her food while Justin and Luke looked at each other for ideas as to how to help her. Neither one had an answer and the dinner was awkward. At one point, to break the silence Justin started talking about Faith. He knew Lena was always interested in her progress and hoped the conversation would take her mind off things for a bit. It did until they he ran out of things to say. During the awkwardness Justin noticed the way his brother looked at Lena and wondered if something had happened that he wasn't aware of. After thirty minutes, Lena excused herself. She knew after a goodnight's sleep she would feel better. Even though both Justin and Luke were concerned, they understood. Quietly Luke wished he was going to bed with her; however, he understood that couldn't happen and considered sleeping at Justin's as a just in case she needed him scenario. When she was gone Luke suggested it would be best for him to stay the night. The idea made Justin even more suspicious that there was something more happening. "What's really going on?"

Luke didn't want to lie and with the way he was feeling about Lena knew Justin was going to find out soon anyway. "Honestly, I'm not sure. She has been all I think about and now seeing her like this. I just want take care of her."

Justin couldn't believe what he was hearing. He knew Luke well and loved him, but he also knew how Luke treated the women in his life. "Luke, she needs care."

Offended Luke responded, "You think I don't understand that? I get how delicate she is. Especially now. I was the one who found her remember? You didn't see how scared she was of that bastard. It took all my will power not to kill him."

Their conversation was interrupted by loud screams coming from Lena's room. In record time they both ran to her room. She looked up at them not really seeing them. "He knows where I am. He'll come after me."

Justin sat on her bed and held her as she cried hysterically. "No one is going to get you here. You're safe. I promise."

She heard the words but didn't understand them and started to get out of bed. "I need to leave. He can't find me."

That was all Luke needed to hear. The most important thing was for her to feel safe. Clearly, she wasn't at Justin's for the moment. He took a bag from her closet and started packing Lena's things. Justin was confused. "What are you doing?"

"She doesn't feel safe here. We can't bring her to her apartment, so she's coming home with me." Luke went into the bathroom to get additional items.

"I don't think that's a good idea Luke. She's safe here."

"She doesn't feel that way now. He got to her here. This is what's best for her. Ask her."

Justin looked at Lena. She was clearly terrified and he began to wonder if Luke was right. Even though he knew she was safe, Dr. Castillo had approached her outside his complex. The most important thing was Lena. "Do you want to go with Luke? Would that make you feel safer?"

Lena held Justin tighter, "I just want to sleep and wake up from this nightmare."

Luke was standing there with her bag packed. Looking at Luke and wishing he could help more Justin agreed it might be the answer for the night. They could figure out another solution in the morning. It didn't matter to Luke if Justin agreed or not. He wanted her with him and that was it. The fact that Justin agreed did make things easier. Luke offered Lena his hand. After everything that happened that day, she knew she was safe with him. He was not the dark path.

They drove to his place in silence. Lena felt like she couldn't breathe and rolled down the window. Even through the humidity, the warm air on her face gave her comfort. Luckily traffic was unusually light, and they made it to his place in 20 minutes. As soon as they arrived in the apartment parking garage Luke grabbed Lena's bag and offered her his hand. Again, she accepted. In his presence she was starting to feel better.

Once inside the apartment Luke walked her straight to his room placing the bag he packed down. "Do you need anything?"

Lena nodded that she didn't and began to crawl into his bed under the covers. Luke's satin sheets were smooth, but it was the comforter that gave her warmth. The air conditioner in Luke's home was just the right temperature, yet she was trying to lose the inner chill. Immediately she closed her eyes while Luke changed into his pajama pants and T-shirt before asking for permission to get into bed with her. It was his bed, but somehow asking permission seemed the right thing to do. If she said no, he would sleep in James' room next door.

Sleepily Lena responded, "I don't want to be alone tonight."

That was the answer Luke wanted, and he curled up next to her. She put her head on his chest while he wrapped his arms around her. "You're safe Sweetness. Rest now." He kissed her head.

The words she never thought she would say came out of Lena's mouth, "I feel safe with you today." And she meant them.

Even though Luke never wanted this to happen to her, he was grateful to hear her say that and kissed her head again. In her mind Lena marveled at how hands off he had been all day. It made her wonder if he did really care. Afterall she could feel his warmth and concern. It made her feel special.

Luke pulled her closer, "Rest now. Tomorrow will be a new day. A better day."

All she wanted to do was sleep, but she knew her nightmares would return. This incident already had triggered them. The thought scared her. "I'm exhausted, but I'm afraid to sleep. In my dreams, I will see him." It wasn't Dr. Castillo, she worried about seeing. She hated it when Alan was in her dreams. Now as a grown woman now in charge of her own sexuality. Alan was a predator who took something very special from her. Not her virginity which he did take, but her innocence. That was something she could never get back.

"I'm here Sweetness. Trust me. No one will ever hurt you again."

"I do trust you." As soon as she said the words, she knew they were true. Gone was the feeling that Luke would hurt her or that he would be a dark path.

"If you trust me, will you do something for me?"

Lena looked up at him. At that moment she would do almost anything for him. "Yes."

This was a subject Luke had to tread carefully on. Gently he said, "I know you don't want to press charges now" She started to interrupt but he held a finger to her lips, "Just hear me out." She nodded in agreement, and he continued. "Please let me take pictures in case you change your mind." The idea that Dr. Castillo was going to get away with this was weighing on his mind. He hadn't wanted to push, but he still felt they needed some proof in case.

It's not that she didn't agree that Dr. Castillo should pay and considered sending her proof of his cheating to his wife out of spite. Deep down she knew Luke was right and agreed even though she didn't think she could do it at that moment. One day she may hear of someone else he mistreated, and they could bond together.

As soon as she agreed, Luke picked up his iPhone before she could change her mind. Mentally Lena was preparing herself. The first picture of the bruise on her face wasn't too bad. It was when he lifted her sweatshirt and took pictures of the bruises on her back and arms that brought up painful memories. The police took pictures of her bruises when she was younger and in the hospital. That was hard, somehow this was even harder. With Gus by her side the last time she believed she would get justice. Justice never came though since Alan skipped town. This time she wasn't naïve enough to believe justice always came. Maybe if they found Alan, she would have got it. Often, she wondered how he was able to disappear without a trace and questioned if he had passed away. Lena was lost in her own thoughts when she heard Luke say the pictures were sent to the Cloud in case they needed them. After he put his phone down, Luke pulled her close to him. It was over. Another chapter in her life she would lock up and eventually get over. She couldn't let Dr. Castillo have her power and needed to feel whole again. By shutting down he would win, and she wasn't about to let that happen. Lena lifted her head up to position herself at an angle where she could reach Luke's lips and kissed him with everything she had. At first, he was not sure how much he should respond, but the kiss she offered was filled with passion.

Luke tried to pause, "Lena we don't have to do this." She could sense his apprehension even before he said the words. He was all she needed to forget, and she climbed on top of him. Straddling him she removed her sweatshirt and tank while whispering, "You may not, but I do. I need to feel you inside of me."

She could feel his member harden underneath her at the site of her naked breasts. There was never a time when he didn't want her, but she was in a delicate condition. If he made the wrong move, he could lose her. Before he did anything that could potentially hurt her, he needed to know that this was what she really wanted. He gently held her face so that he could look her in the eye. "Are you sure you want to do this?"

Lena realized after experiencing what she had that day some women would never have wanted to be touched. She was different though. The feeling of intimacy was what she craved. It was her way of healing. His eyes were searching for her answer. It was a plea, "Yes. I really need this. I need us. Please help me forget." There was so much sincerity in her eyes.

"If you want to stop at any time, just say so. We'll stop."

"Don't worry." Lena kissed him again. Luke rolled her over so that her back was pressed against the blue satin sheets. When she winced from the bruise on her back, he stopped again. She knew it was going to be her to take charge and she pulled him into a kiss. Her need was evident. Before he made another move he whispered, "Don't worry Sweetness, I'll take care of you." She knew that was true. He had already taken great care of her. Gently he kissed her soft wet lips. Her body was covered with bruises, and he tenderly kissed each one starting with the one on her face. As he kissed the large bruise on her back, he took his tongue and went up her spine sending shivers throughout her body. She needed him then and begged for him to enter her. He opened the drawer to pull out the condom. Even she was disappointed when she saw them. She wanted to feel the real Luke inside her. For a moment she thought about telling him to forget them. Since she wasn't on the pill common sense prevailed and she decided against it. As soon as the condom was on, he began to play with her clitoris and entered. With him inside her, Lena could feel her need for him. Not just for pleasure, but she actually needed him as she needed no other. Something changed between them that day, and it went into every tender touch and kiss. That night Luke was gentler than he had ever been with a woman even Jessica. So many emotions and feelings were silently expressed as they slowly made love. They were able to find their release together. Exhausted Lena laid her head on Luke's bare chest. Panting Lena expressed, "Oh my God. That was amazing."

Luke kissed her head and caressed her naked back, "You're amazing."

"Do you know what would make it better though?"

Luke eyed her suspiciously. He thought it was perfect. At least it was for him anyway. Luke asked, "What?"

Lena smiled at his reaction. "First answer this question. What are we to each other? Am I wrong to think things changed?"

"You aren't wrong. I really care about you."

"If we are going to do this, I want to feel the real you. No condoms. We could get tested, and I could go on the pill. That's if you want." As Lena said the words, she wasn't able to look at him. It had crossed her mind that he might not want to be exclusive.

If he wasn't, since she was growing to care too much for him., that would have ended things for sure.

"Let me make sure I understand this. If we get tested that would mean that we couldn't be with anyone else afterwards?"

Maybe she was too presumptuous. If it had been any other night, he would have made her sweat out an answer, but not after what she had been through. He had to take the nervous look off her face. "Don't worry Sweetness. I think from the moment I met you; I didn't want any other women. You drive me crazy in so many ways, yet you are the only one I want in my bed."

Lena peered in the direction of his closet, "Is this enough for you? I mean those things I just don't think. Well, know that isn't me."

Luke wasn't sure it was him anymore either. With the other women he needed to keep from getting bored. He knew he could never tire of Lena. "The answer to your other question is yes, you are more than enough for me."

Lena placed her hand on his member. With her fingers she circled the rim as Luke responded by hardening and asking, "Again? I thought you were tired?"

Lena laughed as she kissed him, "Again and again and again."

"Good thing I love a good challenge," Luke teased as he pulled her on top of him. He could get used to this, he thought.

They made love until the early morning hours. Around four in the morning they fell asleep naked with only Luke's boxers between them. In an unexpected turn of events Lena didn't have any nightmares that night. She believed it was because Luke held her tight. It was nicer being in strong loving arms than alone in an apartment. With Luke at her side, she knew she would come out of this stronger and felt she already had.

****

Back at the penthouse, Justin again couldn't sleep. He saw something had changed between Luke and Lena and was worried about that as well as Lena's mental state. Justin tried to assure himself that Luke was just being a good friend. Deep down he knew Luke didn't friend women. It was hard for him to see his angel so fragile. If Luke were to hurt her worse, Justin wasn't sure how he would handle it. After tossing and turning for a while, he went to see Anne. He hoped that even in her current state she would be a sounding board for him. Lena had become very important to him in a short amount of time. As he discussed Lena with Anne, Justin realized he might be a little jealous of Luke. There was no way he was ready to move on from Anne. If he were ever ready, Lena would be his choice. It wasn't fair to expect her to wait for what might be one day and he knew that. He hoped Anne wouldn't be able to sense his feelings for Lena and assured her she would always be his number one.

The look in Lena's eyes when she came home and after her nightmare was haunting him. He decided that he needed to make sure Dr. Castillo could never hurt her again and came up with a plan. His law firm represented the hospital. They also represented several of the board members' private interests. He contacted two that he believed would be most inclined to side with Lena. Without Lena's permission he couldn't tell them what happened. However, he thought that he would e-mail them to let them know that Dr. Castillo was a liability. He knew from his search when Dr. Castillo was Anne's doctor that he was one of the top cardiologists in the country. The board members wouldn't want to let a man of his esteem go easily which is why Justin had to prepare a convincing case. In the e-mail Justin told them that he had a woman contact him about suing Dr. Castillo and the hospital for sexual harassment. With her permission as a means of protecting their interests and to avoid conflicts of interest, he thought he would notify them before any legal action was taken. He also wrote that if Dr. Castillo were removed from his position, she wouldn't pursue her case against the hospital. Even in the late hour one of the board members e-mailed him back almost instantaneously. In response she wrote that off the record this was not the first complaint that the hospital had faced because of Dr. Castillo. That fact didn't surprise Justin. The doctor was a piranha . Briefly he wondered why he nor Luke were aware of these complaints until he read further that John had advised them to warn him if another complaint was lodged, he would be facing termination. Even with new evidence they couldn't act until they gave Dr. Castillo the opportunity to explain his actions and asked who the woman was. Justin responded that he wasn't at liberty to provide that information at that point, however, there was a video and voice recording as evidence. The best solution for the hospital would be for the board to recommend he seek employment elsewhere before his reputation was destroyed. She couldn't agree with that without having another cardiologist with his skills to replace him. It was important for Justin to get this taken care of for Lena and he suggested that he would speak with a friend of his who had also become a top-rated cardiologist. When Anne was in trouble, he contacted him to seek his opinion. To Justin's dismay he agreed with Dr. Castillo. During their conversation, he mentioned that he might be interested in a position on the East coast since he was in Seattle and his family was still in New York. Justin would personally call him in the morning. The response was that she would wait for the information to discuss it with the other board members. Justin thanked her, saying that he would contact her as soon as possible. Their conversation made Justin feel better. Soon Dr. Castillo may no longer be a problem and Justin went to bed. He didn't sleep well because he was still worried about Lena with Luke.

Chapter Sixteen

Even though he didn't have much sleep Luke woke up around seven the next morning. The sun was shining through the window, but since he knew Lena needed her rest, he gently removed himself from her entwined body so that he could close the blinds to the window. As he was about to climb back into bed his phone vibrated. He knew that leaving the meeting the way he did his father would be furious. He also knew that his father had been blowing up his phone all night. Not that he cared. Since he didn't want to wake Lena, he walked out into the hallway to answer the phone. A very irate John was on the other line.

"What the hell was that yesterday? Do you have any idea how much this case means to the firm? To your career? Where are your priorities?"

Luke wasn't about to share what happened with his father and knew his priorities were exactly where they needed to be for the first time. "Calm down Dad. I knew Justin had everything under control and I had an emergency?"

"Justin isn't the lead counsel on this case. What could possibly have been as important as that meeting?"

"That's personal. How did the meeting end?"

"You're lucky that Moore loved the strategy. Now get your butt into the office."

Luke wasn't about to leave Lena until he made sure she was okay with everything. He also wasn't about to wake her. "Actually, I have some things that need taking care of here, so I'll be working home this morning."

John was even angrier, "Luke."

Luke cut him off, "Goodbye Dad."

After he hung up, he checked his voice mail and deleted his father's messages without listening to them. He already knew what they would say so there was no point. Justin had called around six to see how Lena was. That was one he needed to handle, but he had no idea how. They had made some decisions about their relationship, and it was time he told Justin what was happening with them. It was a conversation that needed to be done face to face. Since he knew Justin was worried, he called him back.

Immediately without saying hello Justin asked. "How is she?"

Luke understood his concern and knew Lena was also important to Justin. "She's still sleeping, but better I think."

"I'm glad. I came up with a plan to get rid of Dr. Castillo."

Luke was all ears as Justin told him what he did to ensure Lena's safety. All that needed to be done was wait for the response from Justin's friend. His idea impressed Luke. He was grateful that Justin had made the arrangements. Even though he knew their relationship had changed, he still worried she would see Justin as her hero. It shouldn't matter who got rid of Dr. Castillo. What was important was that he was gone, yet somehow it did matter as her connection to Justin was undeniable. Luke's lack of enthusiasm made Justin wonder what was wrong and asked about it.

"It's just Dad. He's a little pissed that I left the meeting yesterday." It was not completely a lie.

"A little pissed is an understatement. He called me this morning demanding to know what was going on with you."

"What did you tell him?"

"To ask you. He doesn't need to know Lena's business."

"No, he doesn't, and he really wasn't happy that I said I wouldn't be in to the office until later this afternoon either."

"You're going to stay with Lena?"

"I just want to make sure she is okay before I head in."

Justin wasn't happy they were getting so close. "What's going on with the two of you?"

What could he say that wasn't a total lie? Fortunately, his father called at the right time. "I must go there's someone on the other line. I'll talk to you when I get in." He didn't have to say that it was his father, and he had no intention of answering.

"Okay, but have her call me when she wakes up."

"Will do."

After he hung up quietly, he went back into his room to dress for the day. The one thing John was right about was that he needed to put his focus on this case. With Lena safe in his bed, he could. When he went downstairs, he was greeted by Grace who he asked for breakfast and coffee for two. The "for two part" surprised Grace but she said nothing. The only company he ever had stay over was James and he was too young for coffee. When breakfast was ready, he asked her to bring it up to his room where he sat in the blue LaZboy chair with his laptop, working. He really didn't want to be too far from her in case she needed him. A couple of times Lena stirred, but didn't wake up. Even after Grace brought up breakfast, she stayed asleep. Around eleven thirty Lena finally opened her eyes. The first thing she saw was Luke working in the chair. Surprised to see him she asked, "You stayed?"

Luke put down his laptop and climbed back in bed. "Where else would I be?"

Lena nuzzled into his white button-down shirt. "Uh, work. I mean you are dressed and ready to go."

He kissed her head. "Now why would I go there when I could wake up with you? How are you today?"

Lena felt bad. She knew she took him away from the client yesterday and now he was working from home. "So, you stayed to check on me?"

"No, I stayed because I wanted to."

"You don't need to hover, but I am glad you are still here."

"I have something for you."

Luke reached over to the end table and handed Lena a bag with an iPhone in it. He had ordered her a new one as soon as he got up. Luckily the law firm had extras, so he just needed it couriered to him.

"What's this?"

"A phone."

"I know it's a phone, but why?"

Taking it out of the box Luke handed it to her. "You needed a new one. I took the liberty of programming mine and Justin's number already."

She did feel lost without her phone and wasn't about to ask the doctor to give it back. "Thank you. How much do I owe you?"

Luke laughed. "How about a thank you Luke?"

She wanted to argue, but he was caressing her naked back, and she was having trouble thinking. When he touched her, she couldn't think of anything but how her body felt. In her mind she thought this conversation could wait and lifted her head up to kiss him. "I have a better way to say thank you."

As hard as it was, he broke this kiss. "You have no idea how much I wish we could right now, but you have to eat your cold breakfast, call Justin and get dressed. We have a visitor coming in less than an hour."

"A visitor. Who?"

"Don't get upset, but the phone wasn't the only thing I arranged for this morning. A doctor is coming by to give us our test and to discuss birth control with you."

The mood was broken instantly. Lena sat up upset. "You what?"

Luke shrugged, "I really hate condoms."

Lena had to smile at his response. At least it was for that not because of her bruises, which is what she initially thought. As much as she didn't like him trying to take charge of her life, she realized this was more about him. The fact was she was as eager as he was. She had never been in a relationship where she even considered no condoms and was looking forward to the feeling. Still naked Lena got out of bed giving him a full-frontal view of her voluptuous body.

"Okay. Your loss. Give me fifteen minutes to shower and dress."

"What about breakfast?"

"I'll eat after."

That response didn't make Luke happy. She didn't eat dinner and now she wasn't eating breakfast, and he urged her to reconsider. Before she grabbed her bag he had packed and went in the bathroom she told him to be careful because she still knew what was best for her and he was overstepping. What Luke thought was caring could be construed as overbearing. That wasn't his intent, but he also had never felt this way and agreed to back off a little. That was good enough for her. In the bathroom she looked in the mirror she could still see the bruises that were marked on her body. She couldn't believe he made a doctor's appointment with her looking the way she did. As an ER nurse she knew what the doctor would think when he/she saw the bruises. Her face was mostly healed and could be covered with makeup. It was the other bruises that were a problem because they were still visible. If she was going to be examined by a doctor he/she would surely see them and question him. To prevent that she wondered if she could cover them with clothes, and she looked in the bag to see that Luke had packed short sleeved T-shirts. They were appropriate for the summer, but did nothing to hide the marks. After the shower Lena came out in her short denim skirt and pink bra. Luke was back at his computer. "Luke, do you mind if I borrow one of your shirts?"

At first Luke didn't understand the question until he saw the dark, purple marks on her arms. He went over to her and wrapped his arms around her waist. She saw where his eyes were looking and said, "any doctor would ask questions."

Luke hadn't even considered that, but more importantly he wanted to know how she was, "Are you really okay?"

Lena shrugged. "They are just bruises. They will heal. The important thing is to not give him any more power. I know that. It may take time, but I'm off to a good start."

Luke marveled at her strength. She wasn't going to give in to the pain, even though he knew she was hiding some of it maybe from even herself. The bruises would heal, but what he did to her emotions that would take time. Time he was willing to give. "Do you want me to cancel with the doctor?"

Lena turned to face him. Her blue eyes met his green. "Nope. I just need a shirt."

"Anything that I have is yours." He meant it too. He would do anything for her and walked into his closet to pick out a light blue collared shirt. It was way too big for Lena's petite frame, so she tied the bottom in a knot. Luke couldn't believe how much he liked the idea of her in his shirt. He was about to tell her that the doctor could wait when her new phone rang. Justin was still worried about her and had heard back from his doctor friend. Dr. Castillo would be finding employment at another hospital. He was excited to tell her the news. She picked it up as soon as she saw Justin calling. Once she assured him that all was right with her, he told her the news. Instantly, she felt like a huge weight had been lifted off her shoulders. She could go back to work without Dr. Castillo looming over her. "Thank you so much."

"I was glad to do it. That bastard belongs in jail, but this was the next best thing."

Now was as good of a time to ask Justin about living with him. After everything as much as it pained her, she couldn't envision ever living in her apartment again. "I wanted to ask you if the offer to be your roommate was still good? I would really like to help with Faith."

Justin was thrilled. He hated being in the large penthouse without her. "You know it is."

"Good." Lena saw Luke's face wasn't happy and didn't understand. "Justin, I have to go. I'll talk to you later." After she hung up, she turned to Luke. "What's with the face?"

Luke couldn't believe how disappointed he was that she was planning on returning to Justin's. It made sense that she wouldn't want to go back to her apartment, yet he hated the idea of her living with his brother and not him. "So, you're going to stay with Justin?"

Lena went and wrapped her arms around his shoulders. "Justin has been good to me, and we can help each other. If there is one thing, I have learned from all this is it's important to lean on those who care for you when you need them."

What she said made sense. Justin did need her, and it was too soon in their relationship to even consider moving in together. He threw her on the bed and lifted her skirt. She could feel his hard member rubbing against her panties. "As long as my needs get met too."

"That won't be a problem. How much time did you say we had?"

"Enough."

Luke swiftly unbuckled his pants and pushed them to the ground before removing her panties. He reached for the condom which she took from him and placed it over his hard member. In no time he was inside her, pumping at a fast pace as their mouths met. This was not about making love. It was about him taking possession. She needed to know that she was his and Lena understood what he was doing. If he needed this to reassure him, Lena would give it to him. Besides it was a pleasurable way to make a point. With each pump, he hit her spot until she found release in the most pleasurable way. As he came, he yelled out, "I can't let you go." That was understood. Lena's only response was, "Then don't."

****

It took the doctor no time to administer the AIDS tests and examine Lena. If she saw the bruises she didn't comment. As a nurse Lena needed very little information about birth control and decided to get the shot. By the time their results were back, the shot would take effect, and they would be ready to lose the condoms as Luke put it. Since Lena missed breakfast, Grace had prepared turkey sandwiches for lunch. It was the first time since her lunch with Trey that Lena had even thought about food, and she was starving. Over lunch they discussed Luke telling Justin about them. Lena hadn't realized until Luke told her that Justin had warned him off her. There was something sweet about that, although normally Lena hated people making decisions for her. Luke was worried about what Justin would think. Lena tried to reassure him, but he still knew it would be a hard conversation to have. When lunch was over, Luke needed to get to the office. He went upstairs to get his tie and jacket with Lena following behind. As he stood in front of the mirror tying his tie, Lena asked if it would be okay if she stayed another night. She wasn't ready to leave her sanctuary and would make him dinner. The way Luke felt at that moment it would be okay if she never left. He told her to phone if she needed anything and promised to let her know what time he would be coming back. As he kissed her goodbye, he couldn't believe how welcome the idea of coming back home to her was. He would try not to be late.

After Luke left the room, Lena began talking to her father. "If you were here daddy, my life would've been so different. Since you're not, I need you to know this feels right. I'll not go into the dark and hope being with Luke will show us both to the light. Please show me that you understand."

In her heart she knew her father was supporting her. There was a reason she accidentally texted Luke and not Trey as she intended. That was something she was glad he hadn't asked and hoped he never would. She believed the mistake was because Luke had the means to find her. Trey would have been worried, but he didn't have Luke's means. Whether it was or not she was taking that as her sign.

Alone in the bedroom she decided to take another look in the closet. They had already discussed this, yet it still weighed on Lena's mind. This was her first real relationship, and the idea of experimenting intrigued her. There was no way that she could let him tie her up, however maybe there were some things she would be willing to try. Not just for him, but for her too. There was little that she understood about that world and decided if Luke wanted, she might be willing to let him take the lead as long as he understood the boundaries. Right now, neither had any complaints, which was good enough for her and closed the closet door. She didn't want him to know she was snooping.

****

Lena wanted their night together to be perfect. Luke had packed her nothing special to wear, so she decided to go shopping. While she was walking along the busy Manhattan streets, Gus called to see how she was feeling. She assured him that Luke and Justin had taken very good care of her. Even though she insisted she was back to her old self, he begged her to get back into survivor's therapy. To make him feel better, but with no intention of doing so, she agreed to think about it. Several of the rape survivors had trouble being touched by a man afterwards. That was never a problem Lena had. She craved physical attachment. It wasn't that anyone in the group ever told her she was wrong for her feelings. In fact, they were always supportive, but Lena was never totally comfortable there. After getting off the phone Lena, who had walked into Macy's, found the perfect dress. It was a red strapless dress that accented her curves in just the right way. She also purchased a pair of high heel black sandals with no straps. Since the dress and shoes were on sale, she found another dress to going dancing with Trey Saturday night. Trey had become very important to her. If Luke didn't like it, he was still going to have to accept it. There was no way she was going to give up her first true friend for anyone.

****

Luke made it into the office a little after two. As he put his things on his dark wooden desk, he stopped to look out the window. With Lena in his life everything seemed so different. He was actually happy. The only other time he had felt this happy was when James was born. Justin had asked Luke's secretary to call him as soon as Luke arrived because he wanted to know how Lena was handling everything. When he spoke with Lena, she seemed fine, but there was something off when he spoke with Luke. He wanted to know what that was and entered Luke's office as he was staring out the window." Look who finally decided to come in." Justin teased.

Luke turned to see Justin there. "You sound just like Dad."

"Oh God. Don't say that. I don't ever want to sound like him. How's she really?"

"Bruised emotionally and physically, but she will be okay."

"She asked me to tell you that she wants to stay another night at my place but will be home in the morning."

Justin could no longer deny there was something going on with them. Why else would Luke have brought her back to his place and why would she want to stay there? Luke wasn't going to avoid the subject this time. "Alright. What the hell is going on with you? First you are at each other's throats. Now she can't leave you."

Luke shrugged his shoulders because the explanation was simple, "I told you. I care about her, Justin."

The words Justin had been dreading came out of Luke's mouth. "Please tell me you didn't do what I think you did after I asked you to stay away from her. I mean what kind of a person takes advantage of someone in her state?"

Luke lifted his hand to let him speak his peace which did stop Justin from ranting. He wasn't sure if he should tell Justin it was not the first time, they had been together or not, but he also didn't want his brother to think he took advantage of her in a vulnerable state. The fact that Justin believed he could do that hurt him. Luke was a scoundrel when it came to women. There was no denying that, but Lena was almost raped. Even he wouldn't take advantage of someone in that situation. "What kind of an asshole do you think I am? I can't believe you think I could take advantage of someone in her state. The arguments, the secret looks you have seen has all been foreplay. I knew how you felt about it and didn't want to tell you until I knew where this was heading."

"So, where's this heading? I know when it comes to women, well you are who you are. It never bothered me before because it was none of my business, but I care about Lena and don't want to see her hurt."

In his most sincere voice Luke offered, "It's different this time. I really care about this woman. When have you ever heard me say that?"

Maybe Luke had mentioned caring about someone in the third grade, but Justin knew he had never said that in his adult life. Even about Jessica. At least not in the way he was speaking about Lena. Luke could tell by Justin's face that he was softening and continued. "You're my brother and I love you. You have to know I would never have broken a promise to you if she wasn't important to me."

That Justin knew that to be true. Luke had been there Justin's entire life. He wouldn't intentionally do anything that might hurt Justin in the long run. There was really nothing Justin could do except wait to see how everything worked out. Luke seemed sincere. "I'm going to tell you this and then we will drop the subject. If you hurt her any more than she has already been hurt, you will have to deal with me."

"If I hurt her, you can do your best. I'll deserve it."

That was the last they spoke of it that afternoon. There was too much work to be done. They needed to focus on the upcoming trial.

It was about six when Luke texted her that he would be back around nine. That gave Lena plenty of time to cook dinner and get ready. She had decided to make arroz con pollo which was one of her favorite dishes her mother used to prepare. Hers was nowhere as good as her mother's, but it still tasted delicious. As many times as she tried to make it, there was an ingredient that Lena couldn't figure out missing. Luke's kitchen was a dream to cook in. It was equipped with the latest appliances and was so large that she had plenty of room to spread out. Cooking in his kitchen was very different than cooking in the one in her apartment. Not that she did much of that there because there was no point in preparing large meals just for her. Occasionally Gus would come over for dinner and she would experiment with her mother's recipes. Outside of that her menu consisted of cereal and frozen dinners. While dinner was cooking, Lena went to get dressed in her new dress. It was odd, but she was actually nervous. It wasn't as if she hadn't spent plenty of time with Luke, but this was different. This was their first real date. If she were to think back at her love life, it may be her first date ever. For this reason, she wanted everything to be perfect. When she was certain she looked her best, she went downstairs to set the table. Before Joyce went home, she had asked her where to find a tablecloth, china and wine glasses. Joyce had offered to set the table for her, but she wanted to do everything herself. As she was setting the table, Luke entered just before nine. The dress had the reaction Lena hoped for as Luke couldn't take his eyes off of her. He loosened his tie and walked over to her with lust in his eyes. Even after working all day, Luke still looked handsome, dressed in his black suit and white collared shirt. Instantly he went to her, taking her mouth to his in a passionate embrace that left Lena breathless. No other man had ever had that effect on her. Luke ran his hands down the in curve of her back down to her behind before lifting her on to the granite countertop. Her dress rode up and she could feel the coolness of the granite across her thong clad backside. Cool surface to her steaming body ignited her further and she wrapped her legs around him still not breaking away from his kiss. Before they could go any further one of her shoes fell off making a loud noise on the white tile floor. Lena laughed, telling him it was a sign that they should eat first. Disappointed Luke helped her down from the counter. He picked up her shoe to slide it back on caressing her naked leg as he did. It was a simple gesture but made Lena's already stimulated body quiver with desire. Lena insisted that he sit while she went to get the food. She had put a bottle of white wine on the table which Luke opened and poured. "Smells delicious. What is it?"

"Arroz con pollo. It's my mother's recipe and was one of my dad's favorites." She placed the food down on the table and served him.

Luke took a bite as Lena awaited his reaction. She could tell by the way he reacted that he did enjoy it and was satisfied enough to start eating herself. As she tasted it, she said to herself that it was good, but still missing that special ingredient. Since she believed she would never see her mother again, she was sad that she would never know what that ingredient was. Luke's voice broke her melancholy mood. "This really good, but not as delicious as you."

Lena laughed. "What kind of cheesy comment was that? Seriously down boy. First, we eat. Trust me when I say you'll need fuel for later."

Slyly Luke looked at her, "What happens later?"

Lena's eyes burned, "You'll just have to wait and see."

Luke started eating quickly while Lena laughed. "Anticipation is good for the soul and conversation is for getting to know each other. How was your day?"

"Busy. The best part was coming home to you."

His answer made her smile. "Did you talk to Justin?"

Luke took a sip of wine. "Yes. He knows how I feel about you now."

"And how is that?" Luke put down his wine glass and took Lena's hand. "Desperate to have you back in my bed."

"I think that's a forgone conclusion, but right now I want to know what Justin said."

Luke really didn't want to talk about Justin. He did understand that is was important to her to know and continued, "Let's just say he didn't throw a party, but he didn't throw a punch either."

Lena knew she needed to also have the dreaded conversation with him. She had no idea why she was so nervous. They had become really close and the thought of upsetting him made her feel troubled. "I'll talk to him tomorrow."

"And say what? That you can't keep your hands off me or that I'm the best you ever had."

"Is that all you think about? Sex?"

"Right now, with you in that dress, looking at me with those beautiful blue eyes. Yes, all I can think about is bringing you upstairs and having my way with you."

His honesty caught her off guard. She wanted him too from the moment he walked in the door. Lena stood up, put her napkin on the table and held out her hand. "I think dinner is now over."

Quickly Luke got up and lifted her into his arms. "Thank God. I thought I was going to bust."

Lena looked at the mess in the kitchen. She didn't feel right leaving them for Grace. "What about the dishes?

"Fuck the dishes."

"Luke, I don't want to leave the mess."

She was infuriating. "If I promise to clean up before Grace comes in tomorrow, can we go upstairs?" As soon as Lena nodded yes, he scooped her up and carried her up the stairs as fast as he could, placing her on the bed. "Can we try something?"

Uneasy, Lena asked, "Something?"

"Just trust me okay." She nodded that she would. He went into his dresser drawer and instructed her to take off all her clothing. The length of his member was bulging through his pants as he removed his shirt. Since the time he was in her apartment and saw her vibrator, he had long fantasized about watching Lena masturbate. From his drawer he pulled out a vibrator that looked similar to Lena's. Shocked Lena responded, "You've got to be kidding me. I thought you said if I had a real man, I would never need that thing."

"You won't. At least not alone. Trust me this will be pleasurable for both of us."

She felt embarrassed but agreed since this was something he really seemed to want. He laid next to her taking her hand across her body. When he removed his hand, he asked her to continue touching herself as she did when she was alone. She closed her eyes so that she wouldn't see him looking at her and did as he asked. Initially she started playing with her nipples. Moving her one hand across her abdomen down to her special area where she lingered. Seeing her like this Luke wondered if he would be able to control himself long enough to see his plan through. Luke was finding it almost impossible not to touch her. Instead, he kissed her passionately before handing her the vibrator. She took it from his hand. She was turned on even if she was embarrassed. By this time Luke was only in his boxers. He was holding his member watching with pure desire. This time she wanted to see his reaction and watched his face as she placed the vibrator on her special area. It was a two prong vibrator with rabbit ears that worked magic on her clitoris. This was extremely erotic, and Lena moaned loudly. Her free hand was still fondling the nipple of her breast. First one than the other. Luke licked his lips slowly thinking about how nice they tasted in his mouth. That small gesture set her off screaming as her orgasm overtook her body leaving it quivering from gratification. Luke took the vibrator from her hands, inserting it in her again. Gently he pulled it in and out. With his hand, he was playing with her clitoris. Lena moaned. "Please."

"Please what Sweetness? What do you need?"

Lena could feel herself building again as she screamed. "You. I need you. Please you take me not the toy."

Luke kept with the motion and used her words from dinner. "Anticipation is good for the soul."

If Lena hadn't been in the needy state she was in, she would have laughed. Instead, his words were her undoing. Again, she found her release. Before her body came down Luke was already getting ready to put the condom on. Lena took hold of his hand, asking him to let her. Luke handed it to her. Before putting it on, Lena bent down to kiss his member. She wrapped her lips around the shaft and ran her tongue up and down the length as he moaned in appreciation. Slowly, she pulled the condom up. He no longer could wait and rolled on top of her. "I want you so badly," he whispered before kissing her mouth. With her back on the bed, she lifted her body to meet his as he entered at a punishing pace. Lena was surprised and yelped. He paused for a moment to make sure she was okay. She lifted her body, indicating that she wanted him to move. Luke complied, moving in and out at a fast pace. Her body was keeping with his intensity and pace. As her body began building for the third time, Luke told her she was beautiful. That was her undoing. Lena called out his name while she climaxed. Luke found his release shortly thereafter. As he fell on top of her, he asked what she thought of that. Exhausted, Lena told him that she could get used to this. The intensity between them was undeniable. Luke had taken her to places she had never been to before. Breaking contact Luke kissed the top of her head telling her that he could get used to it too. As they sleepily held each other basking in the afterglow, Luke thanked Lena for dinner. No woman that wasn't on his payroll had ever done that for him. Lena giggled that it was her pleasure, and it was. Soon they drifted into a deep sleep holding each other.

Chapter Seventeen

A little after seven in the morning Lena reached out to an empty bed. She had felt the sunrise on her face and was disappointed to find she was alone in the large king-size bed. When she looked around and didn't see Luke, she went into the shower to get dressed. It had been two days since she was at Justin's, and she needed to get back. In the shower she thought about what she would say to him, knowing that he wasn't happy with her relationship with Luke. Somehow, she would make him understand how happy Luke made her. After she was out of the shower, Lena dressed in denim cut off shorts and one of Luke's shirts tied. If she was going to convince Justin, she didn't want him to be looking at her bruises that were still visible. With her bag packed, she headed down the stairs where she heard Luke on the phone in his office. She could tell from his tone that he wasn't happy with whom he was speaking with. The door to the office was open and Lena stood for a minute wondering if she should interrupt him to say goodbye. Luke was dressed in his grey suit pants and light blue collared shirts. Before she could decide if she should enter Luke looked up and saw her. Instantly his demeanor changed as he smiled at her and motioned for her to come in. He loved seeing her dressed in one of his shirts. There was something about it that made him feel that she was his. As she entered, he ended his call.

"Sorry I didn't want interrupt you. I just wanted to say goodbye."

"Goodbye?"

"I need to get back to Justin's and you need to get to work."

Luke leaned in to kiss her as he tasted her freshly brushed teeth. "Umm. Give me a minute and I'll drive you."

"That's okay. I think I should face Justin alone."

"I can drop you off."

"I like the subway."

There was something about the way she challenged him that always turned Luke on. She was so different from any other woman he knew. Most of the women he dated came from money and didn't know what it took to make an honest living. Lena worked hard for everything she had. Plus, she was not only beautiful and smart, but she was genuinely caring. "I'd feel better if."

Lena cut him off, "If I let you drive me. I know, but really, I want to go alone. Call me later okay."

She reached up and kissed his lips before turning to leave. He wanted more of her and pulled her to the brown leather sofa in his office. He was clearing the files from the sofa when she noticed one with her name on it. Lena lifted the blue file. "What's this? Why does it have my name on it?" Luke was at a crossroads. He didn't want to lie to her, but he also didn't want to tell her he had done a background check either. They had gone too far in the relationship for him to tell her. Since he remained silent Lena opened the file to find the investigator's full report on her. "Oh my God. You ran a background check on me."

Luke's persuasive ability was at a loss and all he could think to say was, "It's not what you think."

"It's not what I think. My name, address, age, parents. It's all here." Lena turned to the second page where she found the information about Alan. In shock she felt as betrayed as she did when she found out Dr. Castillo knew about that night and whispered, "You knew. This whole time you knew what happened to me and never said anything."

Luke pleaded, "Let me explain."

"How can you explain invading my privacy?"

When Luke tried to put his arms around her, she pushed him off her. She was either too hurt or too angry. It was hard to tell.

"You were getting close to Justin and Dr. Castillo alluded to some things. I had to find out. I had to protect my brother."

"From me? The crazy girl who tried to kill herself. Oh my God. Does Justin know?"

"I think he suspects, but he learned nothing from me."

"Well, I guess I should be grateful that the only one lying to me was you."

"I never lied. It's a simple background check. We run them on all the employees at the firm."

"With their consent, I'm sure."

She had him there and he could feel her slipping away. Desperately he tried to turn the table. "Yes, but don't tell me you didn't look for information on us too."

"Sure, public information on the internet. I didn't hire someone to do it for me. I have to go. I can't be here right now because I can't even wrap my arms around this." Lena walked towards the door.

"You can't leave. We need to settle this."

Before she left, she turned to Luke still holding the file. With tears that she was willing not to come in front of him in her eyes she said, "I think we already have settled this. You betrayed me."

Her words stung even more because she left after she said them. Luke thought about following her, but decided instead he would give her some time. With time he hoped that she would calm down and understand why he did it. At least he hoped she would.

****

By the time Lena arrived at Justin's she was more furious than she was when she left Luke's. She called out for Justin who had already left for work. Since she was in no mood to talk about Luke, she was grateful for that. After putting her bag and file in her room, she went to talk to Anne's nurse. There was no change in Anne's condition. She sat down on the bed to begin to work out Anne's leg muscles and started to talk to her. Even though she knew Anne wouldn't answer her, she wanted to use her as a sounding board. After all the time she spent with Anne, she felt as if they were friends. She couldn't believe Luke had betrayed her in that way and bet Justin never had Anne investigated when they started dating. What was worse was that he didn't even feel he had done anything wrong. How could he have known the whole story and never say a word? How long had he known? Mrs. Warner interrupted their conversation. There was someone at the door to see Lena. When she asked who it was, Mrs. Warner told her it was a delivery man. He was instructed to only make the delivery to her personally. Lena went to the door to find a man with a large bouquet of red roses with a card that read "Please we need to talk. Luke." Luke had obviously made the order when his calls went to her voicemail. Lena was acutely aware that he had tried many times to call and text her, but she didn't answer. She couldn't talk to him until she had sorted through her feelings. The flowers did nothing to lighten her mood. Maybe if they had been irises, she would have seen it as a sign, but roses were just a gesture. Mrs. Warner interrupted her thoughts. "Beautiful flowers dear."

They were, but at that moment Lena didn't want them. She kept the card and handed the flowers to Mrs. Warner. "I think you'll appreciate them more."

Mrs. Warner had warmed to her when she realized how much of a source for comfort she was to Justin. "Are you okay Miss?"

That was a great question. In the last two days she had almost been raped, decided to give up the apartment she loved and felt betrayed by the man she actually saw a future with. She didn't think Mrs. Warmer would understand and only offered, "It's just been a rough couple of days."

Mrs. Warner could see her pain and walk over to her and put her hand on her shoulder, "Can I get you anything?"

There was really nothing she could do, "No. Thank you. I think I just need to rest."

Lena stopped in the kitchen to eat yogurt before going to her room. The file on her bed was staring at her. At Luke's she didn't fully read what was in it, so she opened to see exactly what he knew. Everything was there in black and white. The sexual abuse charges, attempted suicide, Gus taking custody of her and Alan's disappearance. All the details of her life that she never shared were all summarized in a neat report. She threw the file across the room and collapsed to her bed crying until she finally was so exhausted that she fell asleep.

When she awoke at four, she checked her phone to see ten texts from Luke. There was no way she could read them just yet. The wound was still too fresh. Instead, she decided to go for a run to clear her head. It was summer and extremely humid, but she didn't care. At that moment it was the only thing she could do to help her collect her thoughts. By the time she returned to the penthouse she was soaking wet with sweat. Her curly hair was frizzy, and her eyes looked like a raccoon from her eyeliner and mascara. It wasn't until she realized that Justin was home that she remotely cared what she looked like. He had just come home from work and was still dressed in his navy-blue suit, red tie and white collared shirt. As she entered, he greeted her, genuinely happy she was home. "Hi Angelina."

She was surprised to see him because she thought he would be working late. "Hi. You're home early?"

Justin looked as if he was gaging her mood. "How are you?"

Right now, Dr. Castillo was the furthest thing from her mind. She was focused on something in her mind as violating, "If you are asking about how I am after what happened. I'll heal."

"Glad to hear that. Look you may not want to talk to me, but Luke told me about the file."

"He told you?"

"Not what was in it, but he said he had you investigated. I'm sorry. Luke can be a little overprotective. To be fair the firm does run them on all new employees."

Lena could tell Justin was trying to make excuses for his brother and wasn't in the mood to hear them, especially since it was the same one Luke had used. Her voice was a little more raised than she meant it to be. "Employees who grant permission I get, but I thought we were friends." Her voice faded lower, "I thought he and I were more."

Even though she lowered her voice, Justin still heard her. They were friends and he would never have done that to her, but Luke had trust issues. "We are friends. Look Luke is far from perfect."

"He told me you warned him off me."

Justin couldn't deny that he had, but he also saw how upset Luke was when he told him about the file. "My brother is a great guy. He had always been there for me, and I love him, but when it comes to women and relationships well it's not his thing. I just didn't want to see you hurt. With that said I have never seen him with another woman the way he is with you. He was frantic today worrying that you wouldn't forgive him. I truly believe he cares."

"He cares so much that he had me investigated. Look I really don't want to talk about this anymore. Can we please change the subject?"

Justin tried to no avail to plead Luke's case. Since it was getting him nowhere, he tried something else. "Go shower and change. The trial will begin soon, and I feel like blowing off some steam. Would you care to join me? We can go anywhere you recommend."

That was music to Lena's ears and exactly what she thought she needed that night. Lena excitedly responded, "Sure. I know just the place. Give thirty minutes to get ready."

"Great."

While Justin changed into jeans and a black T-shirt, she put on her white sundress. Since he had said anywhere, she wanted to go, she took him to her neighborhood bar to play some pool, have some beers and talk about anything other than Luke. As always, being with Justin was easy. They steered the conversation off

Luke. Justin wasn't sure how he felt about their relationship and neither did Lena at that moment. Instead, Justin told Lena about teaching Anne to play pool. The two laughed as Justin told her that Anne had actually hit a ball so hard it landed in someone's drink. Talking about Anne and the fun they used to have relaxed Justin. He was happy to have someone who really seemed interested. Lena never offered him pity; she only listened and laughed. During their evening Luke texted Lena several times asking where she was. Eventually when Justin went to the bathroom, Lena decided to respond, letting him know that she was out with Justin and would talk to him later. Lena's phone buzzed back immediately, but she decided to ignore it as she and Justin were having too much fun. After beating Lena at pool for the second time, Justin ordered some bar food. Lena hadn't eaten anything other than the yogurt and greedily grabbed a hot wing. She had some ranch dressing on her lip which Justin gently wiped away. After eating, Lena challenged Justin to a game of darts. Justin had never played before and was very bad. Lena decided to help him by holding his arm from behind. She could feel the muscles in his arm bulging as she directed his shot. When Justin made a bull's-eye, he hugged her proudly. His arms felt right around her. At one point she thought she was growing deep feelings for Luke, but this investigation was the worst form of betrayal and to keep it a secret was even worse. They more than connected in the bedroom, but outside the bedroom they had real issues. There was none of that with Justin. Of course, there was none of the sex either. Everything was so easy, and they connected on the emotional level she couldn't seem to get to with Luke. They both were feeling the effects from the beers, so when someone played an old Journey song over the speakers, Justin asked Lena to dance. It was an offer she quickly accepted. Having Justin's arms around her felt amazing as he moved her gracefully. Lena loved to dance, and Justin had a huge grin on his face. The two closed the bar, before calling the car service to take them back to his penthouse, a little buzzed and in a much better mood. When they arrived, Justin thanked Lena for a great time, kissed her cheek before going to sit with Anne.

As soon as Lena went to her room, she decided she needed to finally respond to Luke and picked up her phone to call him. They had left things unsettled. If she wanted to have a grown-up relationship, she couldn't ignore him forever. Even if she wanted to, the fact that she lived with Justin made it impossible to do so. Luke picked up on the first ring. "Lena. Where the hell have you been?"

Lena was in no mood for his attitude. She was a little drunk and wasn't about to put up with it. "Why don't you ask your investigator? I'm sure he can tell you where I was."

Luke was angry that he hadn't heard from her all day and was in a foul mood. "Don't give me that shit. We need to talk."

It was clear from the attitude Luke was giving her that he really didn't think he did anything wrong. Maybe in his world that was okay, but in hers, it was a violation. Instantly, she regretted calling him and knew what she had to do even if it hurt her. "I'm not sure there is anything left to say."

"I think you're overreacting. You were terrified and I needed to understand what was going on. Let me ask you this. Would you have ever told me?"

She couldn't answer that. It was personal and never anything she talked about with anyone but maybe Gus. Even they never really used the words. They just referred to it, knowing what the other was saying. "If I did or didn't it wasn't up to you to make that decision."

His temperament went from anger to desperation. "You were hurting. I needed to know how to help you." His words weakened her fury. He cared. Maybe he went about showing it the wrong way. They both admitted they were new to relationships. As painful as it was if they were going to have a relationship it was better that he knew. At least this way she didn't have to say the words. All that might be true, but he still should have told her that he knew. Instead, he kept lying, pretending he didn't know. "I just don't know. On one hand I feel violated, but on the other hand I kind of understand why you did it. All this is just so hard."

"Have dinner with me tomorrow. We can talk this through."

The call ended after Lena and Luke made plans for dinner. Lena's head hurt and she went to bed feeling a little more secure about things, even though nothing had truly been resolved.

Chapter Eighteen

When Lena woke up the next morning, Justin was already seated at the table eating his breakfast. His face lit up as he saw her. Justin had good news. He received confirmation late in the night that Dr. Castillo was moving to Montana. His reputation was hit when the board asked for his resignation. Lena felt as if a huge weight had been lifted off her and hugged Justin tightly to thank him. She had no idea what she would have done without him arranging this. Justin still wished that Dr. Castillo was in jail, but aside from that this was the best possible solution. Mrs. Warner offered Lena her normal yogurt breakfast and she sat with Justin pouring herself a cup of coffee from the silver pot on the table. While seated Lena mentioned she would be going back to work soon. With the trial starting Justin would feel better having her there with Faith. If she was interested, he would make sure that the NICU understood that she had full visitation rights. The fact that he trusted her so much made Lena feel special. Faith was the most important thing in Justin's life, and he was entrusting her with Lena. She promised to visit regularly. That was a huge relief to Justin as he knew the trial was going to take up all his free time. He didn't want Faith to feel abandoned. Before mentioning she was having dinner with Luke that night, she assured him that Faith would never feel abandoned. Without her saying a word Justin sensed she was still apprehensive about the relationship. Since he still wasn't entirely comfortable with Luke and Lena dating, he had made the decision to only offer opinions if asked and to just listen if needed. Their conversation was so easy. Again, Lena thought about how much they acted like a married couple. Minus the sex of course. While Lena was thinking how nice it would be to have this daily, she briefly allowed her thoughts to travel to what it might be like to be married to Luke. "Everything would be so much easier if I could combine the brothers," she thought again. Justin interrupted her thoughts by letting her know that he needed to get ready for work. This brought Lena back to reality and she wished him a good day before she went to check on Anne.

After getting dressed, Lena went to the hospital to finalize her return. The hospital's gossip was about Dr. Castillo's departure. Lena was relieved by the confirmation even though Justin had told her earlier. She pretended to be surprised by the news as one of her co-workers told her about the departure. Some of them had seen her flirtation with him and questioned if she knew anything more. Even though she did, she wasn't going to say anything. What happened was none of their business and she never was one for gossip anyway. They seemed disappointed when she denied knowing anything and some of the rumors were so ridiculous that Lena smiled. Being back at the hospital felt right and she was excited that her first day back would be Tuesday.

After all her paperwork was completed, she started to head to the subway, but felt her phone vibrate. A message from Luke appeared letting her know he would pick her up at seven. No matter how apprehensive she was about the relationship she was always excited at the prospect of seeing Luke and responded that she would see him then.

****

All day Luke could think of nothing but Lena. They were supposed to be finalizing their strategy for the big trial, but Luke's thoughts were elsewhere. There was so much Luke wanted to tell Lena. He hoped that he would be able to get his feelings out without fighting with her. More importantly he had to make her understand that running the background check was never meant to be a violation of her privacy. After much thought he finally understood how she could see it that way. She meant a lot to him, and he was worried that she didn't know that. Expressing emotions for Luke was foreign. Every time he tried with Lena the wrong thing came out. This was rare for Luke who prided himself on normally being a smooth talker. Idly he wondered if this was what falling in love felt like. She was all he thought of since the day he met her. For the first time he could see himself being with one woman for the rest of his life. As Luke was getting ready to leave, John entered his office insisting that they had important business to discuss. Luke tried to explain he had plans. They could talk in the morning, but John wasn't to be pushed aside. Frustrated, Luke hoped that their conversation would be short.

****

As Lena was getting ready for her date with Luke, she went through her closet many times to pick the perfect dress before finally deciding on a purple halter dress. She made her eyes smoky and put light pink lipstick on. After fixing her hair in an updo she was ready. Even as she dressed to impress, she was apprehensive of how the night would go. The hurt she felt couldn't easily be undone and he didn't seem to understand that he had done wrong. After everything he did to help her, she owed it to him to hear him out. Trust was a hard thing for Lena, and she really wasn't sure he could convince her to try. If he couldn't she wanted him to see what he was missing. On the other side no man had ever made her feel so desired. That was a feeling she didn't want to end, so she hoped he could sway her. At seven thirty she still had not heard from Luke. Justin came home at seven forty-five to find Lena on the sofa waiting for Luke. The look of desire on Justin's face secretly made Lena happy. Even though she was with Luke, and he was devoted to Anne, she still liked the idea that Justin found her attractive. Justin sensed that there was something wrong with Lena. "Is everything okay Angelina?"

"Not really. I'm waiting for Luke who is almost an hour late for our date."

"He hasn't called you?"

"No."

Justin rolled his eyes. He hated that Luke could be so inconsiderate to Lena even if he understood the reason why Luke was detained. "Luke was in with my father when I left the office. It looked important."

Determined not to shed any more tears over Luke, Lena smiled and shrugged. "I guess it was more important than our date." Luke made his choice, and she needed to move on. "It's fine Justin. You were right he isn't capable of a real relationship, and I was a fool to think he could be."

"Angelina, I really doubt that. Believe me when I tell you when Dad wants to speak with you…." Before Justin could finish Lena interrupted. "Please don't make excuses for him. He could have called, texted, whatever. I'm just done."

Justin really had no idea what he could say to make this better for Luke, so he needed to make her feel better. "You look too pretty to stay home and wait. Let me take you out."

That did sound like a great idea. They had so much fun the previous evening that she agreed. He asked for a few minutes to check on Anne before they left. While he was with Anne, he tried to call Luke, but he didn't answer. Justin kissed Anne and said he really didn't understand Luke. Lena could be Luke's Anne, and he was too dumb to see it. Within fifteen minutes Justin was back. Since neither had heard from Luke, Justin took Lena's hand and said, "I'll be honored to escort you out tonight."

"Honored." Lena laughed while Justin smiled.

"That's right honored."

"When you put it like that, how can I refuse?"

Justin took her to the nicest restaurant Lena had ever eaten in. There was romantic music playing by a band. Couples were dancing to the music as the Maître d' led them to a center table overlooking the dance floor. The restaurant lights were dim. Each table had a candle on the table. Through the candlelight Justin admired Lena's beautiful blue eyes, but didn't say a word as he knew it was Luke she preferred to be with. Over white wine they spoke about the case which Justin felt was going to be a challenge even though he believed they had come up with a solid strategy. Since Lena had spent hours working on the case, she was grateful for the update. Even if he was just talking to keep her mind off Luke standing her up. By the time their lobster dinner arrived, it had worked. She was excitedly discussing her return to work. As discussed, Justin had made the arrangements for her to spend time with Faith. The hospital administrator wasn't happy with his request at first since she wasn't family, however, she was persuaded after some calls from the hospital board were made. Halfway through dinner Lena received a text from Luke. She couldn't help herself and wanted to read it. To not be rude and read it in front of Justin, she excused herself to the ladies room.

"Sorry. Had meeting with Dad. Please wait for me." At that point he was over two hours late. She couldn't believe that he expected her to wait for him without hearing one word from him. That wasn't the type of relationship she wanted. She needed to feel important. If he had called or texted, she would have understood, but not this. Her eyes filled up as she texted him back. "Too late. Out with Justin." Proud of herself she fixed her makeup and received another text from Luke.

"Still need to talk tonight. What time will you be back?"

There really was nothing left to say except this wouldn't work. She already felt betrayed and now like her feelings weren't a priority. "I think you said it all tonight."

Before she returned to the table, Luke texted back. "Let me explain please."

Even though she read the message she didn't respond. Instead, she joined Justin who had ordered chocolate mousse for dessert. Although Lena was upset over the fact it was really over with Luke, she was determined not to let it ruin her time with Justin. Upon her return to the table, it was obvious that there was something wrong. "Are you okay, Angelina?"

She really didn't want to put him in the middle any more than she already had, but thought he had a right to know. "I'm fine, but you don't have to worry about me and Luke. It's over." As she said the words out loud she felt the tears in her eyes, but again fought them off.

Although Justin was relieved, he could see the decision caused her pain and said he was sorry. She knew that he wasn't supportive of their relationship and appreciated that he was trying to be a friend. There was no way she would keep her composure if they continued discussing Luke and she didn't want to ruin their night, so she changed the subject. As the two ate their dessert they talked about the police search for who shot Anne. It wasn't a comfortable conversation for Justin to have as the police still had no leads. Lena assured him with Gus on the case it wouldn't remain unsolved. For that Justin was grateful. He hated the idea that no one would be punished for virtually ending Anne's life and he really hoped that he would be able to understand why this all happened. The way it was, he was left with so many unanswered questions. He was trying to focus all his energy on Anne and Faith. It was just hard to think that he might not get justice for them. That was something Lena could relate to but warned him that finding the responsible party may not bring him the closure he was seeking. He hoped that wasn't the case but understood she could be right as well. The case wasn't something they spoke of often and it took Lena's mind off her problems. Justin had real problems. She hadn't even been in a weeklong relationship with Luke. It didn't change the fact that she was hurt though.

By the time dinner was over and they returned home Lena finally allowed her feelings about ending her relationship with Luke to come out. Alone in her room she cried. As hard as it was going to be it was for the best that it ended early before she got in too deep. The problem was that she did have deep feelings for him. She needed her father now and prayed to him crying before she got into bed, "Daddy give me strength to do this."

****

Luke was up pacing, knowing he had made a big mistake. His first instinct was to go to Justin's to force Lena to hear him out. That might make things worse, so he decided to let her cool off first. If only he had been more insistent with his father Lena might be with him. Luke couldn't let this be over. He decided to text her again. "I understand you are upset. You have a right to be. Let me make it up to you."

Still there was no response. The rest of the night Luke had trouble sleeping. All he could think about was trying to salvage his relationship with Lena. She had to forgive him. In the middle of the night, he decided to go to Justin's early in the morning and ask her to breakfast. With Justin there she was less likely to cause a scene, and it was easier now that Justin knew they were together.

Chapter Nineteen

When he arrived in the morning Justin was the only one home. After seeing Lena hurt the prior night, Justin was angry with Luke and told him to just leave Lena alone. Luke wasn't about to do that and explained just that. It was clear to Justin that Luke cared for Lena. Reluctantly he offered support. Honestly, he didn't want them to be together, yet he also didn't want to see either one of them upset. Although Justin hadn't heard her leave, he knew she ran most mornings and offered to let Luke wait for her return while he went to the hospital and then the office. After an hour when she hadn't returned Luke knew he had to get to the office and left Lena a note on her pillow before going.

****

Lena had figured Luke would show up at the penthouse and decided to call Gus for an early morning breakfast. It was her way of avoiding him although she always loved seeing Gus. This also gave him an opportunity to make sure she was alright after the Dr. Castillo incident. He knew Lena well enough to know that something was wrong, but she insisted that she was fine and told him what Justin had done for her. The news that Dr. Castillo wouldn't be a threat to her made Gus grateful to Justin, although he also had a conversation with the doctor. His chat was more of a threat to have him arrested if he so much as looked at Lena the wrong way. Even if he pretended, he wasn't, Dr. Castillo was rattled by Gus' presence especially since he talked to him with three other officers who had been Ryan's friends. Gus didn't dare tell Lena about that though because he knew she would be worried about him. A move like that could hurt Gus' career. When it came to Lena he didn't care about the consequences. All the station officers who knew Ryan and watched Lena grow up felt a sense of protectiveness towards her. They knew she had been through a lot, and they always stuck by family. Even the younger officers knew Lena and how much Gus cared for her. They would all have his back too. There was nothing for her to worry about, but he knew she would anyway. Gus again brought up the idea of the support group even after she assured him, she was fine. It was what she couldn't tell him that was causing her pain. After breakfast, Gus asked her to go to the station to visit "the guys." Actually, they weren't all men, but Gus always referred to his fellow officers as "the guys." As much as Lena enjoyed seeing her father's friends, she wanted to go to church and light candles. Gus knew that she would do that when she was hurting and said nothing more. He could tell that she was dealing with things in her own way and that made him feel better. As breakfast ended, he hugged her tightly and told her he wanted to see her more often. She liked that and walked towards the church to light candles for her father, Anne and

Faith. In the church she prayed for strength to leave Luke alone. She also prayed for Faith, Anne and Justin.

After seeing Gus and spending an hour in the church she returned to Justin's feeling better until she saw Luke's note. As she had predicted, she knew from the note that he had been there. For a moment she thought about throwing it away but couldn't do that without reading the contents. "Sweetness. I can't tell you how sorry I am. Please call me. Luke"

Lena wasn't yet strong enough in her decision to see or speak to him. Instead, she decided to text him. "Saw the note. Thank you, but there really is no point in talking. Hope we can be friends one day. I will always be grateful for your help."

Convinced there was something he could do, Luke read the text over and over. Many times, he tried to call and text her but received no response. That put him in a foul mood all day. He was at a loss but was determined. Luke decided once again to send her flowers. When she received them, she knew they must be from Luke. Hesitantly she opened the card. "I never beg but will grovel if you give me a chance."

The only response he got was a text, "Please stop."

As the day went on it was getting harder to stay strong, so she called Trey to see if he wanted to go to the movies. She needed to keep busy and hoped being with Trey would provide her with a distraction. Trey gladly accepted the invitation. Lena texted Justin to let him know her plans and asked if he wanted to join. The movie seemed like a good idea and he too accepted. Shortly after Lena's text, Luke came into Justin's office to see if he wanted to have dinner. It had become clear that Lena had no intention of working things out and he didn't want to be alone. When Luke asked Justin, he told him he planned on going to the movies with Lena and her friend. Justin could see that Luke needed him and offered to cancel. Luke knew exactly who Lena's friend was. It was Trey and there was nothing he could do about it. Luke didn't want Lena to be alone with Trey, vulnerable, so he insisted that Justin keep his plans. There was work that Luke needed to get done anyway.

"Are you sure? I can call her now and cancel."

"No don't. I really need to get Dad off my back by working. Have fun."

"Luke."

"I'm fine. Really. Go."

****

At the movies the three of them enjoyed an action thriller. It wasn't a movie Lena would have normally picked, but she certainly couldn't sit through a romantic comedy. Even if she were in the mood, Trey and Justin would probably not enjoy a "chick flick." For a brief moment she thought to herself that she needed a girlfriend. She just didn't know who could fill that role. During the movie Lena sat between the two men sharing popcorn. It didn't matter what they saw, Lena's mind wasn't on the movie. Many times, she wished Luke was with them but stopped herself before going too far down that path. To keep herself further distracted after the movie she suggested they all go out for beers. They found a bar close by the movie theater. The bar was not too crowded, and they were able to find a table in the corner where they ordered beer and ate hot wings. Initially Trey was disappointed that Justin joined them, but Justin and Trey liked each other. The three acted as if they had known each other for years and told stories of their misguided youths. Their upbringings were very different; however, their stories were very much the same. When Justin told the story about sneaking out of the house and borrowing his father's car without permission to impress a girl, they laughed. Especially after he mentioned that he totaled his father's Mercedes. Lena realized for the first time that before Anne Justin must have had a wild streak. Often, he would say that Anne saved him from himself. She never understood until after hearing some of Justin's wild partying stories. Lena only wished she had an Anne. Gus was always there for her, but his work schedule had her being home alone a lot. She too would go to parties and got herself into trouble. Trey was from an all-American family. His stories were not as crazy as theirs. The night was just what Lena needed as they laughed most of the evening. By the time they left each other Justin and Trey had become good friends. While they were leaving the bar Lena noticed a final text message from Luke telling her he understood that it was over.

Even though it was what Lena said she wanted, the idea of it really ended made her sad. Justin realized that she was upset. Figuring it had something to do with Luke, he put his arm around her trying to offer reassurance. She knew as long as she kept herself busy, she would be okay until it really was. It still hurt. At home, once more, she cried herself to sleep.

****

After working late, Luke came to the realization that Lena wasn't going to give him another chance. It wasn't like him to give up on anything. Especially something that was as important to him as Lena had become, but he feared hurting her more. After several scotches Luke thought he would lose himself in Tabatha, who was more than willing to oblige. She hadn't heard from Luke since the night of the comedy club or the morning after and was excited when he called. Her first thought after hanging up the phone was that she knew he would come back to her. The young girl was just a fling. They were meant to be together. Being with Tabatha didn't help him forget. He wished she was Lena and wasn't even able to pretend otherwise. After he had been with the real Lena no amount of role play could be a substitute. From the moment Tabatha arrived he wished he hadn't called her. Still, he needed to try to forget and the two went to his bedroom. Sex with Tabatha was always a distraction, however this time he felt as if he had cheated on Lena. He couldn't understand his feelings because it was she who had ended the relationship. Yet the guilt was overwhelming and a foreign feeling to him. Even when he cheated on Jessica, he never felt that way. Luke pretended to check his phone and told Tabatha he needed to go to James who had become ill to get her to quickly leave. It was a lie, but he couldn't bear to continue the evening with her. Before she left, she told him not to let so much time pass for the next time. Alone with his own thoughts Luke poured himself another scotch and wished he hadn't been stupid enough to lose Lena. If she did give him another chance would the fact, he had sex with Tabatha kill it? He regretted so many things and sex with Tabatha was at the top of the list. The most important thing was to win her back.

See what happens next in Hopes Springs Eternal.

www.ingramcontent.com/pod-product-compliance
Lightning Source LLC
LaVergne TN
LVHW011941060526
838201LV00061B/4169